ON
WINGS OF
DEVOTION

Books by Roseanna M. White

LADIES OF THE MANOR

The Lost Heiress
The Reluctant Duchess
A Lady Unrivaled

SHADOWS OVER ENGLAND

A Name Unknown
A Song Unheard
An Hour Unspent

THE CODEBREAKERS

The Number of Love
On Wings of Devotion

Dover Public Library
Dover, Delaware 19901
302-736-7030

THE CODEBREAKERS • 2

ON
WINGS OF
DEVOTION

ROSEANNA M. WHITE

BETHANYHOUSE
a division of Baker Publishing Group
Minneapolis, Minnesota

© 2020 by Roseanna M. White

Published by Bethany House Publishers
11400 Hampshire Avenue South
Bloomington, Minnesota 55438
www.bethanyhouse.com

Bethany House Publishers is a division of
Baker Publishing Group, Grand Rapids, Michigan

Printed in the United States of America

All rights reserved. No part of this publication may be reproduced, stored in a
retrieval system, or transmitted in any form or by any means—for example,
electronic, photocopy, recording—without the prior written permission of the
publisher. The only exception is brief quotations in printed reviews.

Library of Congress Cataloging-in-Publication Control Number:
2019949601

ISBN 978-0-7642-3182-7 (paper)
ISBN 978-0-7642-3546-7 (cloth)

Scripture quotations are from the King James Version of the Bible.

This is a work of historical reconstruction; the appearances of certain historical figures are therefore inevitable. All other characters, however, are
products of the author's imagination, and any resemblance to actual persons,
living or dead, is coincidental.

Cover design by LOOK Design Studio
Cover Photography by Mike Habermann Photography, LLC

Author is represented by The Steve Laube Agency.

20 21 22 23 24 25 26   7 6 5 4 3 2 1

To Kim,
for all your enthusiasm
and encouragement over the years.
I'm so blessed to count you as a friend.

❖ ❖ ❖

Be merciful unto me, O God, be merciful unto me: for my soul trusteth in thee: yea, in the shadow of thy wings will I make my refuge, until these calamities be overpast.

Psalm 57:1

1

A stranger stalking down the street shouldn't make her hands tremble in anticipation. Arabelle Denler forced her breathing to calm, forced an easy smile to her lips for the soldier whose bandage she'd just changed, and stood with the old bandage balled up in her bowl. "Is there anything else you need, Captain?"

The thrashing of his head from side to side may have been the answer to her question. Or it may have been simple agony. Poor chap. He'd just arrived in Charing Cross Hospital yesterday after ordnance had stolen his entire left leg.

"Ara!" The stage whisper came from the hallway, where Eliza, one of the volunteer nurses, motioned her frantically.

He'd be stomping down the street any moment. Brooding and aloof and mysterious and so handsome that just looking at him could make one's heart crack a bit.

She resisted the urge to dart out. Black Heart, as the papers had dubbed him, was of no concern to her. She had a fiancé. And more, she had a purpose. Right here, right now. Resting a hand

7

on the captain's shoulder, she closed her eyes and whispered a quiet prayer. Only after her *amen* did she move away, her pace no faster than it ever was. The fact that she didn't stop at any other cots in the ward had nothing to do with the view out the window and everything to do with the fact that her shift was over and she needed to deliver these bloodied bandages to the laundry on her way out.

If the window facing Agar Street happened to be on the way to said laundry, that was pure coincidence.

And if she went into the little room where the nurses and volunteers took their brief breaks rather than directly to her destination, she could blame it on Eliza, who seized her by the arm and tugged her into the cupboard of a room with a giggle. "Hurry."

Arabelle rolled her eyes, even as she knew it was more to cover the thumping of her own pulse than because she found their daily ritual silly. She slid the bowl of sullied bandages onto a table and quickly washed her hands before golden-haired Eliza pulled her over to the window.

"There!" Susan, a pretty girl of perhaps eighteen who had been volunteering here for only a half year, leaned into the windowsill until her cheek was pressed to the pane.

Arabelle tugged her back an inch. Gracious, but sometimes these girls made her feel ancient. She was only twenty-five, but she couldn't recall ever acting so giddy simply because a man was walking down the street. "A bit of propriety, if you please, Sue. He could look up again, and you don't want him to catch you staring."

The girls had about fainted dead away last week when he'd glanced directly up at their window and sent them all a devil-may-care grin. As if he knew exactly what they were doing and the effect he had.

"What *are* you three doing?"

Arabelle turned to smile at another volunteer—who was usually gone long before this hour of the day. "Lily! What are you still doing here?"

8

Lilian Blackwell, her red-gold brows lifted, sauntered into the room. "I had to swap my hours today so I could help my mother with something this morning." She drew even with them and peered out the window. "What's going on out there?"

Eliza bumped Susan companionably on the shoulder. "She has no idea what she misses every day. *He* walks by, Lil. The fellow the papers have dubbed Black Heart. I declare, he must be the handsomest man in all England."

Something odd flashed in Lily's eyes. Recognition, perhaps. Ara tilted her head. "Do you know him? He's working at White-hall now it seems. With your father?"

Lily's smile was vague. She backed away from the window. "I couldn't say. Daddy works with so many chaps, you know. Though I can certainly assure you he isn't one my mother has invited over to dine with us."

Eliza and Susan's laughter turned to playful shoving as they each jockeyed for prime position at the window.

"Need I separate you two?" Arabelle made a show of putting a hand on each of their arms and pushing them a few inches apart, positioning herself between them as a barrier.

Not so *she* had a better view out the window.

Oh, fiddlesticks. Who did she think she was fooling?

Lily had retreated to the door. "Well, I'd best hurry along. This odd schedule today has me all sorts of discombobulated. I'll see you in the morning, Ara. Eliza, Sue, it was nice to actually work beside you today."

A chime of farewells soon turned into excited exclamations of "There he is! He's coming!"

Arabelle drew in a deep breath even as her eyes sought the familiar stride of Black Heart. He was stomping at a faster clip than usual down the street. No teasing grin would be shot up at them today—that was clear from the angry set of his jaw and the hands clenched into fists at his side.

His nickname was no great mystery. One had only to watch him for a few moments to see the resentment—some would call it hatred—that held him in its teeth. Arabelle's fingers settled on the windowsill. She'd never met the man. But she knew him. Knew how the bitterness could eat at one, gnawing away until there was nothing left but sinew and bone, no heart to speak of.

Just looking at him took her back to those dark days. The days before Aunt Hettie, before the Braxtons, before the Lord had shown her how He'd always been by her side. When it was just her and a dead mother and a missing father and a village rector who hadn't a clue what to do with a seething ten-year-old girl.

Father God, he wears his pain like a uniform. She watched Black Heart pound the pavement ever nearer to their window. *But you can reach him, as you reached me. Touch his heart, Lord. Break it, if you must. Show him that you're there, right there beside him.*

She'd prayed nearly the same prayer every day for months. Every day he stalked by Charing Cross on his way home from the Old Admiralty Building, where he'd somehow ended up instead of in front of a firing squad. To hear the papers tell it, he'd killed his entire squadron—willfully. Five flying aces taken out in their prime by his jealousy and hateful nature, all because of an argument with one of the pilots.

He chose that moment to glance up. No smile upon his lips, not today. And who knew what he could really see behind the glass. But it felt as though he looked directly at her, straight into her eyes. As if with that glance he was challenging her daily prayer for him. *God isn't here*, that look said. *No one is.*

But He was. And He would show him. She knew He would.

"I could bring a smile back to those lips," Eliza said to the glass, a wistful look in her eyes.

"You? No, he needs someone young and fresh and hopeful to change him." Susan grinned down at him, though he didn't look up again.

Arabelle took a step backward. "I wouldn't put any hope in changing a man, Sue. None of us can change anyone else—not unless they want to do it themselves." But the Lord could. And from the first moment she'd spotted that angry pilot, she had the strangest feeling that He was chasing him.

"I meant *inspire* him to change." Susan patted her hair, pinned just so under her white kerchief, as if Black Heart would be able to see it from the street.

"Are you girls wasting time at the window again?" The ward matron brought them all around with a start, her nearly permanent scowl etched into place between her brows. She leveled a finger at the lot of them. "Back to your posts, or I'll have you all reassigned, and you'll never be on this side of the building again."

Arabelle lifted her brows. Her shift had been officially over for twenty minutes, but she'd wanted to take care of the unfortunate captain before she left. The cantankerous Nurse Wilcox had no right to badger her, though Susan and Eliza were only halfway through their own shifts. Which was, perhaps, why they scurried out with mumbled apologies. Well, that and the fact they were in the Voluntary Aid Detachment and Arabelle was a trained nurse, which gave her a bit more authority. She planted her hands on her hips. "I'm on my way out, Nurse Wilcox."

Wilcox sniffed and turned from the room. "Be on your way, then. I'll not tolerate you idling about when you're not working, setting a poor example for the other impressionable young ladies."

Arabelle reclaimed the bowl of soiled bandages and pasted a smile into place. "Of course. We wouldn't want them to pick up any bad habits." *Like scowling at and judging absolutely everyone.*

The matron sent that narrowed gaze over her shoulder. "Are you being disrespectful, Miss Denler?"

"Wouldn't dream of it." Aloud, anyway. She didn't need the position, not in terms of the pittance it paid. But she certainly needed the occupation. Best not to make her superior *too* angry with her. Though why the hospital matron, Nurse Jameson, tolerated Wilcox's attitude Arabelle didn't dare to guess.

By the time Arabelle reached the doorway, Wilcox had bustled

11

off to terrorize someone else, leaving her free to turn toward the laundry.

Another friend slid into place beside her—a friend who routinely exasperated the matron, very much on purpose. "Did she catch you staring out the window at a certain grounded pilot again?"

Arabelle shot a warm smile at their most famous volunteer. "I was not *staring*, Your Grace. I was praying for him."

"Mm-hmm." Brook Wildon, the Duchess of Stafford, looped her arm with Arabelle's and leaned close. "You and your father are still coming to dinner tomorrow, aren't you?"

"Yes. It's been ages since I've seen Ella and Rowena and—"

"He'll be there." Brook punctuated her statement—and Arabelle's stumble—with a grin. "Thought that might silence you."

Silence her? It baffled her. She couldn't imagine that man sitting down to a swanky-as-the-war-allowed dinner party in a duke's home. "But—"

"You know my husband served with him at Northolt. Not in the same squadron, of course, but he knows him well." Brook tucked a bobbed curl behind her ear and steered them toward the back stairs. Which was a good thing, because Arabelle had forgotten where she was supposed to be going. "He's been wanting Camden to come to dinner for months, and he's finally accepted."

Now? To the same dinner party Arabelle was attending?

As if reading her thoughts, Brook offered another maddeningly cheeky smile. "Fortuitous indeed, since we needed him for an even number. Otherwise you would have been without a partner."

Arabelle gripped her bowl and prayed the look she sent her friend was withering. "Don't smile at me like that, Brook. You know perfectly well I'm engaged."

"What I know is that Edmund Braxton is nothing to you but duty, and you deserve more from life." She paused at the top of the stairs. "You deserve someone to make you genuinely happy. Someone to *love* you."

The tightness of her throat didn't lessen any with a swallow. "Such talk has no place in this world. Not anymore."

"Oh, don't be a ninny. Love always has a place," said the woman who'd had the good fortune of falling in love with her best friend.

Arabelle lifted her chin a notch. "Let's not be foolish, Brook. Our generation of men has been reduced to a minimum, and I'm fortunate to have a fiancé at all. I cannot hope for one who came to me for reasons of love."

Brook's green eyes sparked. "Of course you can."

"No. There are exactly one million two hundred thousand reasons a man would choose me for his wife, and none of them are love or attraction."

Brook folded wool-clad arms over her chest. She was dressed to leave for the day, too, but would go from the front, as that's where her driver would be waiting. "You are more than your aunt's fortune."

Absolutely. She was also her father's heir, if he didn't manage to spend what remained of *his* half of the Denler fortune after the war was over. Not that she'd put any stock in *that*. Adventure still waited in the world, after all, and Lawrence Denler wasn't one to sit back and let other men find it in his stead.

Arabelle held tightly to her bowl and moved on to the stairs. "Say hello to the boys for me."

"Ara."

"I'd better hurry. I'm running late again—don't want Father to worry." She didn't pause to await another chastisement from her friend. Though Brook was more than capable of chasing after her, if chastise she truly wanted to do. But she must have decided that the next round of their eternal "to marry for love or convenience" debate could wait for another day.

Only when Arabelle had reached the bottom of the stairs, and the heat and smells from the laundry wafted out to greet her, did she pause. Drag in a breath. Let her nostrils flare. Maybe she didn't love Brax, not like Brook did her Justin. But Arabelle had made her choice with eyes wide open. Because she *did* love his family. His home. And without her—or more correctly, her inheritance—he stood to lose it. His aging mother would be reduced to a pittance to live on. And dear Sarah, who had helped Arabelle through that dark patch of her own life, would be sacked as housekeeper.

She couldn't do that to them. Not when it was within her power to help. It was why she'd said an eager "Yes" the moment Brax came to her after her aunt's death and proposed. He'd been clear, honest, forthright. He respected her, *liked* her enough to be up front about his reasons. She'd just inherited a sizable fortune. He needed it to keep Middlegrove running. They could have an amiable, friendly marriage, built on a solid foundation. After the war, he'd give her the family she craved. She'd keep his ancestral home from ruin.

They'd both win.

Four years ago, it had sounded noble and good. Four years was a lifetime ago.

Well. Nothing would be accomplished by dillydallying outside the laundry. She bustled in, deposited the stained bandages, and then hurried back up to collect her hat and coat. A few minutes later, she'd said her farewells to Eliza, Susan, and her other friends and stepped into the bite of a London winter wind.

She joined the other silent pedestrians on the street, bustling along to escape the bluster of February. She'd been fortunate to find a position here, a mere twenty-minute walk from her home in Westminster. Father would be waiting. Probably. Maybe. Unless he'd gone to the Explorers Club again to compare stories with the other adventurers stuck at home while U-boats prowled the seas.

Paper crackled in her pocket when her satchel brushed against it. She'd had a letter from Brax yesterday but had waited until lunch today to read it. His missives came regularly, once every two weeks. No lines of poetry or waxing on about their postponed dreams. Just facts. But that was all she required, and all she sent in return.

This one read more like a newspaper article on the advances

in the field of naval diving than a letter from a man to his sweetheart. Which, granted, made her smile. He'd always been fascinated with all things maritime. As a child, he'd been obsessed with the revelation that Arabelle's father owned a yacht and had sailed it across the Atlantic to Central America. He'd not been put off in the slightest by Ara's snappish answers to his questions. Thoughts of her father, who was at the time missing in the wilds of that distant continent, hadn't exactly been what she'd wanted to dwell on.

Arabelle turned right onto the Strand, holding her coat closed a little more tightly. She nearly ran the last stretch of her daily trek, until the familiar views of Buckingham Palace filled her vision. She turned toward the row of townhouses directly across from the palace. Naturally, the one Aunt Hettie had purchased had a floor more than the ones adjoining. Because, she'd said, if she was going to abandon her villa in Italy, she'd do it in the height of English style.

A waste of money, to be sure. But it was home.

Ara bustled up the steps to the door, which opened before she even reached it.

Parks gave her a warm grin as she came inside. "Another cold one, Miss Denler?"

"Unfortunately." She returned the young butler's smile. After dear old Harcourt passed away last year, it had been nearly impossible to find a replacement for him, as so many men were caught up in the war effort. Parks had already been to the front and sent home again with an injury that made him unfit for duty, though it didn't hinder his abilities in the house. "Is Father at home?"

Shutting the door behind her, Parks motioned upward. "In his study."

Parks's sister, Ruth, stepped forward with a hand out. "May I take your coat, miss?"

These siblings were, at present, the sum total of their live-in staff. They had a cook, but she lived elsewhere. "Thank you, Ruth."

After handing over her outerwear, she jogged up the eternal flights of stairs.

Gaslights—blocked from the street by the dark curtains that regulations demanded—shone from Father's study as she neared its doors. She tapped on the doorframe.

He didn't look up. She hadn't expected him to, not when she saw he had a map tacked to the wall and was, inexplicably, dangling upside down from the edge of his desk, looking at it.

"Father. What in the world—"

"My question exactly, sweetling. What in the world was I thinking when I drew this map? I have it wrong, all wrong. The ridge of that mountain didn't continue northward in this stretch. I can see it in my mind's eye. I viewed it from the peak of the next mountain over, you know. Only at a different angle."

She leaned her shoulder into the doorpost. "If you slip off your desk again—"

"You'll patch me up as you did last time. Handy thing, having a nurse for a daughter. I told the boys at the club as much just last week." He put down a weathered hand to the floor, though. "You really ought to come with me on my next expedition. You'd be invaluable."

"Mm." She folded her arms over her chest, pressing her lips against a laugh as her father tried to lever himself back up. He wasn't exactly a young man anymore, but according to him, Lawrence Denler was still fitter and sprier than any explorer the world over. "I'll be married by the time you set sail again, and Brax may have something to say about his bride heading off into the wild blue yonder."

"Bah." Apparently giving up on pushing himself back upright, he placed both palms on the floor and instead pushed off the desk with his feet, turning half a cartwheel and nailing the landing as Arabelle straightened and gasped her protest of the move.

His face bobbed back upright with a grin better suited for a boy of five than a man of fifty. "There we are. And I say no one has really lived until they've tasted a bit of adventure. Come with me, Ara. We'll find Atlantis together. Write a few history books."

Leave everything—and everyone who mattered—behind, he meant. Chase after what was always elusive instead of holding tight to what was right before one's nose. She dug her fingers into her palms. Bit back the angry answer that still, after all these years, wanted so desperately to come out.

She wouldn't. She *wouldn't* speak it. She shook her head. "Don't forget that we're dining with the Staffords tomorrow. I don't want to have to hunt you down at the club again."

His smile was impish, bright, crooked, and pierced by the same single dimple in his left cheek that she knew occupied her own. "The duchess would go with *her* father into the wilds, I daresay."

A truth that made her laugh, chasing away that old pain. "I daresay she would. How unfortunate for you that you had me for a daughter instead of her."

"Nonsense." With the same gusto he'd used to vault off his desk, he came to her side and planted a loud kiss on her forehead. Not many men could achieve that feat, but she'd inherited her unusual height from him, after all. "I'll get you out of England yet. You'll see, sweetest. You'll see the allure of it once you've had a taste."

For some reason she couldn't decipher, his claim made a pair of stormy eyes and an angry posture fill her mind's eye. She shook it away. It wasn't that she didn't understand the wanderlust. It was that she knew its cost.

He tipped up her chin until her gaze met his. "I've always come home, Ara."

Eventually. Thus far. Her smile felt small and bare upon her lips. "And I'm sure you always will. Until the time you don't."

She'd never subject her own family to that question. All she wanted was a steady home, a husband who returned to it each night, and children who could trust she would *be there*. She may not be beautiful or clever or alluring, but she could offer Brax that much.

And he'd go off diving into the depths of the sea every chance he got, until the time *he* didn't come home.

With a sigh, she turned away from her father. Perhaps she should have promised her fortune to a landlocked gentleman whose estates were on the rocks instead.

2

She'd gone too far. Phillip Camden barged into his building, letting the door crash shut behind him. The woman had written to him at work this time. She had some nerve, addressing her latest venom-filled letter so that his own blighted superior handed it to him.

You'll pay, she'd written. Again. *If it's the last thing I do, I'll see you pay for his death.*

As if he didn't pay every blighted day he woke up and realized the nightmare still had a hold of him.

He took the stairs two at a time. Up the first flight of stairs, the second. His flat was there, right next to the landing, but he was sorely tempted to keep going, to keep his feet hammering in time with the headache. Maybe he would have, had the figure outside his door not halted him by her mere presence.

Camden came to a halt so suddenly he nearly tipped backward. "Mum?"

His mother held out a hand, gripped his arm, steadied him before his disrupted balance could topple him back down the stairs. Amusement glinted briefly in her eyes at the name he hadn't used for her since he was a lad. "Hello, Phillip."

Shock always had a way of bringing out the boy in him. He cleared his throat and leaned over to give her cheek its obligatory kiss. "What are you doing here, Mother?" She hated London with the same passion with which he'd hated seeing that all-too-familiar script on the letter in Commander James's hand.

If Amelia Camden was here, there was a blamed good reason for it. Or, more likely, a bad one.

Because that was all that seemed to be left in the world. Though he'd hoped to insulate his mother from such truths.

She patted his cheek as she'd always done, as if to say, *It's my job to protect you, not the other way round.* "I needed to talk to you. And I couldn't trust it to party lines or a telegram, nor wait for the post to reach you."

A rock settled in his abdomen where his stomach should have been. He shoved a hand into his pocket, past the offensive letter, past the ever-present wing pin he kept in there to remind himself of who he'd once been, and came up with the key to his flat. "What have I done this time?"

His mother chuckled behind him as he fit the key into the lock. "For once, my dear Philly, it has nothing to do with you and your pranks."

Pranks. Oh for the day when the consequences of skipping classes or putting pepper in the headmaster's tea were all he had to worry with. No threats of court-martial. Or firing squads.

He made the expected show of wincing at the old nickname. "What, then? Don't tell me Jeremy's found some trouble. I won't believe it of him." With their older brother fallen at Gallipoli, only the youngest of the Camden boys was left to get himself into a pinch. Something completely foreign to Chaplain Camden, aside from when Phillip and Gilbert had dragged him into it as children.

"It isn't your brother." Mother's voice was tense as she followed him into the dim expanse of his flat.

He turned the knob to raise the lights, trying to ignore *her* exaggerated wince as she saw his living arrangements. "Welcome to the Camden Manor of the future."

"Not amusing." She wrinkled her nose at the stack of dishes

he hadn't bothered to clean up yesterday. Or the day before. Or, frankly, the day before that. He'd get around to it when he ran out of clean ones in the cupboard. "Haven't you a housekeeper in this building? Perhaps you ought to take your lodgings at—"

"Mum." He used the familiar name again solely for effect as he latched the door behind them. "If it's not me or Jer, that only leaves Cass." His fingers curled into his palm. Cassandra was just a baby—or had been the last time he'd been at home on a daily basis. Granted, he knew she was nineteen now, fully grown, but . . .

His mother's lips thinned. "She's got herself in quite a spot of trouble."

"It's a bloke, isn't it?" All of a sudden he saw her as she'd looked at Christmas, rather than how he usually imagined her—in short dresses and braids. Her hair had been swept up, her dress fashionable and accentuating her trim figure, and her eyes, now that he thought about it, had been far too sparkling. "Who is it? I'll hunt him down. I'll knock him flat. I'll—"

"That would do very little good, given that it would change none of the consequences that bring me here." Mother stepped closer and gripped the hand he'd fisted, covering his eager knuckles with her fingers. "I need you to keep your head, Phillip. And help me find the best course of action. Your sister's with child, and though the young man responsible claims he loves her, he also claims he's not at liberty to wed her."

Camden bit back the words that wanted to sear his tongue solely because he knew his mother would box his ears for them, despite her having to reach up half a foot to do so. She'd made the stretch before.

Keep your head. That had never been his forte. He forced air in through his nose, out through his teeth, and stomped over to the window, yanking the blackout curtains away a few inches so he could look down into the dismal winter street.

Calm. Calm. After a few more seconds, he turned slowly back to face his mother. "Is he married?" Why else wouldn't he be at liberty to save Cass from ruin, when it was *his* fault she'd landed there?

Camden's fingers tightened on the curtains. He'd been no saint in his own life, to be sure—but he'd also never dallied with a girl from a good family, one who had principles and expectations.

Of course, Jeremy never failed to point out that avoiding girls who recognized the sin didn't alleviate the sin itself.

Mother cleared her throat. "Not yet. But he's betrothed."

"What of it?" Camden jerked the curtain back into place, largely just to have something to tug. "Tell him to break the engagement and—"

"You think I haven't tried that already?" Her voice shook. Her hand, as she lifted it to brush away a stray tendril of dark hair, shook too. And worse, she didn't even check the cleanliness of the sofa before she sat down, wilting onto a faded cushion. A sure sign that she wasn't herself. "He refused. Said it was complicated. That if he did that, he'd soon be forced to sell his estate, wouldn't be able to support his own family, and Cassandra would be in dire straits anyway."

Camden snorted. "Obviously not a very innovative chap if the only solution he can find is a fiancée. One with money, I presume?"

Mother nodded. "Rebecca," she said of her closest friend, "recalled reading of the betrothal in the papers just before the war. The woman inherited a staggering sum from a spinster aunt. Keeps company with the nobility, though her own family is several generations removed from a title." A shrug lifted her shoulders and then let them sink down into a despairing slump. "I cannot quite believe I'm asking this of you, Phillip, but . . ."

She focused on the model airplane he'd splintered to bits in the throes of a particularly dark night a few weeks ago, then swung her gaze slowly up to where he stood. Her fingers spread flat against her legs. Bracing herself. "I think we need your particular brand of convincing to move this fellow to do the right thing."

Despite it all, a grin tugged at the corners of his mouth. "Well now. Never thought *this* day would come."

And there, there was the matching grin on his mother's face. She did a bully job of hiding it most of the time, but he'd come by his mischief-making honestly. "He had the gall to cite you as one of the reasons he couldn't wed Cass." She lifted her chin, pure maternal protectiveness in her eyes. "It would serve him right if the very reputation he obviously fears convinced him of the wisdom of doing the right thing, wouldn't it?"

She stood, all trembling gone, and glided over to him. Her fingers were warm and strong as they wove through his. "Strike a little terror into his heart, Phillip. It would do him good."

Who would have thought he'd find reason to laugh in this situation? He nodded toward the tiny kitchenette. "If you can find the kettle, why don't you put it on? I'll clear the table. We'll have a plan by nightfall."

A shade of relief colored her smile now. "I knew I could count on you."

"When it means playing the bully? Absolutely." He leaned over to kiss her forehead. He couldn't tell her not to worry—he couldn't assure her that he'd manage what she wanted. But he'd try. She'd known he would. He gave her a gentle push toward the disaster of a kitchen. "What do we know about this bloke?"

His mother scurried away, though she recoiled just enough upon entering the kitchen to show him that her spirits were on the rise. "He's a good man, overall. I've met him several times and have always been struck by that. From a good family with an estate in Gloucestershire. Despite being the eldest son, he joined the navy directly before war broke out, just after his engagement. He's a diver now."

Interesting. Or it would be, if the clod hadn't taken advantage of his sister. "Stationed at Portsmouth, I assume?"

Mother nodded and made a face as she reached with two fingers toward a handle protruding from behind a stack of plates. "Are you human or swine, Phillip Camden?"

"You're my mother. You tell me."

A dish towel came sailing his way and smacked him directly in the face. She always *had* had perfect aim. And the towel reeked. He tossed it to the floor and swore himself to a trip to the laundress first thing tomorrow. "How did Cass even meet him?"

"In town. We've mutual friends." A long sigh joined the sound of water rushing from the tap into the kettle. "But she must have sneaked out at some point. Or lied to me about some of her outings. I am not so irresponsible a mother that I would knowingly let my daughter be alone with a man. Despite all evidence to the contrary."

Camden stacked the old dishes on the table and tried not to wince on her behalf. With her eldest gone, her second son deemed a villain by the press, and her daughter in a precarious position, Jeremy was the only one left to really prove her truly excellent mothering. "What's his name? Do I know him?"

"I suppose it's possible your paths have crossed somewhere or another. Edmund Braxton. His grandfather was a viscount."

Camden gathered a fistful of dirty cutlery and let the name roll about in his head. "I don't believe I know him, though the name sounds a bit familiar. We likely have some shared acquaintances. What of the fiancée?"

"Miss Arabelle Denler."

That struck a louder bell. He waited for its peals to fade into something sensical, letting his brows draw into a frown. "That sounds more familiar. Do you know anything about her?"

The tap water was still running. Apparently Mother wasn't above sullying her hands with dish soap when the circumstances demanded it. "I made it my business to learn what I could. She lives here in London, in Westminster. Her father is Lawrence Denler—the explorer. He's discovered a few ruins in Mexico that earned him a place in the Explorers Club. He claims to be hot on the trail of Atlantis."

"Interesting." He'd always wanted to do a bit of exploring. To fly over the few remaining wilds and see what there was to be seen.

The stack of plates and bowls wobbled a bit in his hands, and the letter in his pocket scalded him through the fabric of his uniform. If Mrs. Lewis prevailed, he wouldn't be free to dream of such things much longer.

He couldn't quite meet his mother's eye as he deposited the dishes in the sink full of suds. Losing Gilbert in Gallipoli had torn her to bits. What would it do to her if she lost *him* to a firing squad? No medals of heroism to soften the blow. No sure knowledge that he'd died trying to save others.

He could still see his big brother's eyes—snapping and superior as he bossed him around. He could still see the combined exasperation and amusement on Gilbert's face as he declared no fewer than a dozen times, *"You'll either be a hero or a villain, Phil. Try to pick the right one, will you?"*

Camden opened a few cupboards until he came up with a reasonably clean dish towel. "Do we know anything else about this Miss Denler?"

"She works at a hospital somewhere in London."

Hospital. That was it. He picked up one of the dishes his mother had just washed and gave it a swipe with the towel. "Charing Cross. With Brook Stafford." A breath of laughter seeped out. "That's why her name sounds familiar—those noble friends of hers are mine too. The Staffords. We're attending a dinner party together tomorrow."

"God be praised. He must have had His hand in that." Mother clasped dripping hands to her chest, her eyes wide. "You can speak with her, tell her what's happened. Convince her to end the relationship."

"Maybe. Though that's hardly dinner conversation—or so my mother would say."

"Odd, my son has never let such propriety bother him before." She beamed at him. "At the least, it can be a way to forge an acquaintance so that you can approach her another day without causing her alarm."

"But I'm so *good* at causing upstanding young ladies alarm."

He had only to grin at them through a window to send the gawkers scurrying back like schoolgirls caught out by their teacher. Well, most of them. The one figure in the window the other day, the tall, dark-haired one, hadn't scurried or seemed the giggling type. He hadn't been able to make out her face, but her posture had remained erect and unapologetic. Challenging, even.

His mother ignored him. "Jeremy will be home soon on leave. Cass would like it if he could marry them."

"She's sure it'll happen?" She'd always been too optimistic for her own good. It had probably never once occurred to her as she let the reprobate talk her into a compromising situation that it wouldn't be all sunshine and daisies if she gave in.

"She wasn't. Until I said I'd have you help convince him. You know she thinks you capable of anything."

Sweet little Cass. He dried another plate and stacked it atop another in the cupboard. "Tell her not to worry. I have a feeling I'll be an ace at ruining an engagement."

And he couldn't help but chuckle at the flicker of uncertainty in his mother's eyes. "Don't be an ogre, Phillip. Miss Denler is an innocent in all this."

"It's this Braxton bloke who made himself an ogre." And frankly, he wasn't sure what he thought of such a man becoming his brother-in-law. "Don't worry, Mum. I won't do her any lasting harm. Just free her of the man who didn't play her true anyway."

The kettle whistled, drawing his mother away from the sink with a shake of her head. She had more strands of silver in her hair than when last he'd paused to notice. His fault, no doubt.

Well, and Cassandra's. Some of the blame surely went to his sister this time.

"Don't do anything you'll regret, Philly."

He grabbed the tin of tea from the shelf. "I don't believe in regrets."

Or at least he hadn't room in his life for any more of them. Heaven knew the ones that plagued him each and every day were enough for any man.

Admiral Hall didn't just stare at a person. He *blinked* at them in a way that made the nervous tic look like the ticking clock of judgment. Because it made him want to squirm, Camden instead stood stock-still, hands clasped behind his back, chin raised.

Military discipline had never been what drew him to the Royal Flying Corps—that had been the airplanes, pure and simple—but a bit of it *had* been drilled into him.

The Director of the Intelligence Division, fondly called DID by everyone under his command, just kept on staring and blinking from behind his desk. "I never thought I'd see the day, Major, when you came to me asking a favor."

And it galled him to do so now. He swallowed. "Dire circumstances, sir."

"More dire than your own execution, apparently, because you still seem a bit irritated on occasion at my interference with *that*." Hall's lips twitched up.

Because if his old friend Drake Elton hadn't insisted Hall recruit him to the intelligence hub of Room 40, it would all be over now. All the guilt, all the pain, all the hatred. He raised his chin another notch for good measure. "Far more dire, sir. My mother has asked me to make a trip home when I have a few days' leave."

"Ah well. One mustn't argue with one's mother." The admiral grinned and leaned forward. "You haven't had more than a single day off in a week since you joined us, Camden. By all means, take a few days' leave to attend to family matters. I can approve up to a week."

A week with no work to occupy him. No puzzles to distract him from his own mind. He nearly cringed. But then, maybe Cass's troubles would provide distraction enough. He may well know tonight what he was really up against when he met Miss Denler. "Thank you, sir."

"You are quite welcome. Now, if there's nothing else . . ."

Camden saluted and took the hint, leaving DID's office and

stalking down the busy corridor until he could slip into the room to which he'd been assigned last autumn. After they let him out of the storage closet where they'd originally jammed a desk for him. To spare the others his company, they'd said.

He jerked his chair out from his desk and slumped into it.

His nearest neighbor shot him an arch look. "Problem, Camden?" De Wilde had a column of figures scratched onto her paper, a new intercept before her. She'd have it cracked in minutes.

He shoved a hand through his hair. "Had to ask Hall for a favor. Asking for favors puts me in a foul temper."

"*Everything* puts you in a foul temper."

"That is blatantly untrue." He opened the container he'd fetched from the pneumatic tubes before spotting Hall walk by and drew out his own telegram to turn from encoded German message into plain script. He flashed De Wilde a smile. "Pretty girls put me in a lovely frame of mind."

She *was* pretty, this sole female cryptographer of the intelligence hive. But he only pointed it out to irritate her. In part because she was involved with that old friend, Elton. And in part because she was just so much fun to irritate.

Her scowl was predictable. "Number twelve, Camden."

She'd long ago educated him on her list of ways to discourage flirtation. Number twelve, if he recalled aright, involved itching powder and a man's underthings. He made a show of wincing. "You're a cruel creature, De Wilde." He pulled a copy of a codebook forward.

It wasn't flying airplanes, this work. No wind whipping about him, no blue horizon, no gun's trigger under his hands, ready to shoot through his prop and take down an enemy craft. The rush of adrenaline, the quick reflexes, the victory that sang through him every time he got to add another tally mark to his downed-enemy count . . . all those things were missing from his life now.

But it was still better than what he deserved. Better than anything he'd hoped for after his entire squadron went into the sea in a fireball. All but him. He squeezed his eyes shut for a moment to rid them of the horror, though it did no good. That image would remain burned onto the back of his eyelids for all eternity. He forced them open again and got to work.

Nonsense words. Numbers. Moving it all around in whatever way the codebook told him to do, putting it together again. The hard part had already been done today, as soon as the new day's codes began coming in at midnight, by whoever was on the night shift. They were the ones who had the hard task of finding the new variance. All the day shift had to do was use it.

He'd miss his own night shift this week if he was in Portsmouth instead of the Old Admiralty Building. What a shame.

The squeak of the mail cart's wheels drew his attention when he had only a few words left to go. His stomach knotted. He had no reason to get any post here at the office. None. But that hadn't stopped the letter from coming to him yesterday.

And it didn't stop Commander James from walking in again a few minutes later with another rectangle of white held out to him, and with censure in his eyes.

As if Camden wouldn't have been happy to toss the letter to the stove's hungry flames. He snatched it from his superior's hands with a near growl that was the closest he could come to a *thanks* and ripped it open.

He knew the handwriting by now. Mrs. Lewis. Widow of one of his pilots whose bones now rested at the bottom of the Channel. He'd looked upon this script nearly every day for months. Today's variation on the theme was short.

You're one day closer to your end.

He balled it up and tossed it into the wastebasket with the other rubbish. For once, Mrs. Lewis had it wrong. His end had come the same day as her husband's. He was drifting ever farther away from it, into the expanse of nothingness.

"Everything all right?"

He ignored the concern in De Wilde's tone and stood. He knew she considered herself his friend. But eventually she'd figure out that it wasn't just that he didn't *want* any friends right now—he *needed* not to have them. Because his friends had a bad habit of ending up dead. "Just ducky."

He tossed his decrypt into a basket for the secretaries to type up and grabbed another intercept. One more, and his half day would be over. He'd go home, dress for dinner at the duke's, and try to be pleasant for a few hours—for Cass's sake.

His end may have come the day his squadron died. But his sister wouldn't be meeting hers any time soon. Not if he had anything to say about it.

3

Zürich, Switzerland

Diellza Mettler drew in a shaking breath as the curtain closed, holding her pose until the last sweep of the stage lights turned to shadow. Then she scrambled off the stage to make room for the next cabaret act. One of the other girls stood in the wings, holding a warm robe into which Diellza gratefully shoved her arms after she'd set down the ostrich-feather fans she'd hidden behind in her dance. Her sheer costume didn't just leave little to the imagination of the men in the audience—it also provided precious little warmth on a cold February night.

Aurora smiled and nodded toward the stage. "Quite a reception."

Diellza didn't turn back. Frankly, she scarcely heard the cheering and catcalls still filtering through the heavy velvet curtains. Any pleasure with her performance tonight had paled when she spotted that one particular face in the audience.

She managed a smile for Aurora, though, and tied the belt snugly around her waist. "Are you finished for the night?"

"Thankfully." Aurora led the way out of the wings, into the hallway that connected the stage to the dressing rooms. She had already changed back into her dress and coat, a sure sign that she'd be leaving within minutes. "Did you want to grab a bite to eat? I'm famished."

Diellza saw the face again. Honey-blond hair. Brows that were twin lines above eyes of ice blue. The scar that slashed across his forehead, from his hair's part to his ear, adding interest to a face that might otherwise be too pretty for a man.

Alwin Weber.

She kept her smile casual and tried to look tired rather than a-sizzle. "I think I'll just go home tonight. Maybe next time."

The pretty brunette didn't seem to find anything strange in the refusal. She buttoned her coat and grinned back. "I'll ask Annemarie, then."

Diellza waved her on her way and wove through the press of laughter and shouts from the other girls. The hall would be open for another two hours, but she didn't go on again tonight. She could elbow her way to her dressing table and sit, examine the face that looked back at her the way Alwin would.

Her hair, long and blond, tumbled free in waves. Pulling her hairpins close with one hand, she gathered the locks with the other and coiled them. It wouldn't do to go out on the street with loose hair hanging down her back. She'd wipe the rouge from her lips, too, though the kohl she used to ring her eyes was difficult to remove.

Alwin would be waiting outside, so she hurried. Hair up, paint off, then she slithered out of her costume and into her regular clothes. Heavy coat upon her shoulders, she snatched her handbag from her locker and hurried out into the winter wind.

Alwin slouched in the alley right where she'd expected him to be, the red glow of a lit cigarette catching her gaze even before the streetlights revealed his profile. Her stomach twisted into a braid of anticipation. He always did this to her. Tied her up into equal parts expectancy and dread.

Because he'd be here only a day or two or three. Then off he'd go again. But during that day or two or three . . .

He straightened as she neared, a smile blooming across his

lips. "Diellza, my *Liebling*. How is it you've grown more beautiful in my absence?"

Try as she might for a cool, detached approach, her feet betrayed her and practically skipped the last few meters until she was in his arms. "Alwin! It's been too long."

His answer was a hum of agreement as he kissed her, long and slow, pulling her flush against him. She was only vaguely aware of his cigarette tumbling to the ground and smoldering there.

A long but too-quick minute later, he pulled away enough to smile at her. "How have you been?"

Her fingers dug into his overcoat. One of these days, she hoped to see him in uniform—he must cut a fine figure in it. A far happier thing to think about than the life she'd carved out for herself here since she returned three months ago. "Well enough. How long?"

Grinning in that way that put a crease too long to be called a dimple in either cheek, he kicked his cigarette into the gutter— where a dancer would likely see and rescue it—and turned her toward the street, an arm snug around her waist. "I leave on Sunday. But until then, I've a room at the Central Plaza Hotel. You'll join me?"

He phrased it as a question, but they both knew it wasn't. They both knew she'd take every moment with him that she could get. "I work tomorrow."

"I believe you feel feverish. Don't you think? You had better send a note round in the morning letting them know you're ill." Alwin stopped at the entrance of the alley to press another kiss to her lips. Then he motioned with his head to a car parked nearby. "Our lift."

She was already composing the note in her mind. By the time she'd settled beside him on the seat of the automobile and his driver had cranked the machine to life again, she had it written, but for paper and ink.

"I was concerned for you." Even through her coat and his gloves, the hand he brushed down her arm left a trail of warmth. "When they told me you'd been tossed out of England. I trust my people saw to your safety?"

His people? A snort of disbelief escaped her lips before she could stop it. "I've seen or spoken to no one since your last visit, Alwin. I came here because I knew I could get my spot back at the dance hall." All on her own, as she'd been since the first time Alwin had taken her in his arms when she was seventeen. When her father had caught them. When he'd said in that booming voice, *"If you would dally with him, you're no daughter of mine."*

Though Alwin's brows drew together and he made a *tsk*ing noise, she wasn't so stupid that she thought anyone under his command had actually disobeyed him by not looking after her. She'd known since she was seventeen that she was only a diversion for him. Nothing more. Nothing to be bothered over when she wasn't right there before him.

But if she could just *stay* right there before him . . . When they were together, the rest of the world faded away. After this dratted war was over, it would all be different. He could take her to Germany, set her up in a little cottage somewhere near his home in Hamburg.

"My apologies, Liebling. I will chastise my men who were supposed to assure your safety. Although you landed on your feet, I see. As you always do." The look he gave her combined pride with something far more electric as it swept over her face.

The heat of it burned away the response that leapt to her tongue. *"As if I've ever had a choice."* Instead of speaking it, she smiled and nestled into his side. "It was no great hardship to be asked to leave England. I never much liked it there."

"Well, I am sorry to hear that." Something in his voice . . .

She jerked back upright, the heady feeling his presence always gave her lessening a few degrees. Suddenly she was aware again of the familiar Zürich streets sweeping by, of the driver who sat behind the wheel. Her nostrils flared. "No. I am not going back. I *cannot* go back, they have me on a list now—"

"Liebling—"

"Don't *darling* me." She pressed fingers to her lips. Never in her life had she imagined saying those words to him. Even now she nearly corrected herself, begging him to keep on calling her his Liebling forever. But no. On this she must stand firm. "If I step foot on English soil again, I'll be arrested. I'll not go the way of Mata Hari, Alwin. Not even for you."

It wasn't exactly true. But he needed to think it was. He needed to decide, for once, to protect her.

Instead, he reached a hand into his pocket and pulled something out. In the sporadic flashes of streetlights through the car's windows, she could make out only that they were identification papers, a passport. Her heart sank down into her stomach, where it knotted up with that tangle he'd already made of her.

"I realize, my love, that Diellza Mettler cannot step foot back in England. But they hardly search every arriving face and compare it to your photograph. With all due affection, you are not *that* wanted. Not by the British government."

His inflection, combined with the inches closer he leaned, were meant to convince her that to *him*, she *was* so wanted.

She knew better. And yet her heart pounded with the possibility, the delusion, the ever-gnawing hope that it was true. She swallowed and lifted her chin. "So you've made false papers for me?"

"It proved unnecessary after your sister's death last week." He handed over the passport as if it were a shopping list. As if his words hadn't just turned her blood to solid ice.

She couldn't reach out. Couldn't move, but for an excruciating blink. "My sister's what?"

He froze, too, eyes flashing. "I thought you knew."

How could she have, when she'd been cut off from Friede as completely as their father? "You know well I've not spoken to her in five years."

"Yes, but . . . her obituary was in the paper." His face shifted. "Forgive me. I forgot you don't read the newspaper."

Friede. Diellza's eyes slid shut, blocking out Alwin's handsome face, the cloaking shadows, the back of the driver's head. Letting images of her sweet little sister fill her vision instead. *Friede*. They'd been only eleven months apart in age. Growing up, they'd always tried to pass themselves off as twins, and through much of their lives it had worked. Sweet Friede, with her innocent dark eyes. Her quick smile.

"How?" The word came out a croak. "How did she die?"

"Giving birth to her second child." Alwin, at least, spoke softly. Reverently.

Diellza dragged in a long breath. She'd not been invited to the wedding four and a half years ago. But she'd gotten wind of it, and she'd gone anyway. She'd snuck up into the balcony of the church so she could peek out and see her sister in bridal white, beaming with pure happiness at Max Boschert. And Max had looked down on her with adoration, his expression never once hinting that Friede wasn't the sister their father had meant his young business partner to marry.

Before Diellza had "ruined" herself with the visiting German sitting beside her now.

"Here." The papers pressed their way into her fingers. "She has no use of these anymore."

By instinct, her knuckles bent, her fingers curled around the passport. But she didn't want to open it. Didn't want to look and see *Friede Boschert* in stark black print, her sister's face in the photograph. Something strangely dark and gnashing bubbled up in her throat. "Did you steal it from her desk during her funeral?"

"Not personally. But yes." No apology softened his tone. Or maybe it did, and her ears were too full of pain to hear it. "I am sorry, Liebling. I did not mean to injure you with unwelcome news. Come. Come here."

His arm came around her shoulder and drew her against him again. Warmth emanated from him, along with scents of cigarettes and beer and the same cologne he'd been wearing since she first met him. She let it work its comfort, because filling the widening gap inside her with *him* seemed preferable to letting it yawn open until it swallowed her whole.

"There now." His lips pressed against her head, and his hand rubbed a circle on her back. "There is nothing you could have done."

She could have obeyed her father. Married Max. Then Friede wouldn't have been having his baby, so it couldn't have killed her. Or she could have kept in touch with her, despite *Vater*'s iron-fisted pronouncement against it, and then she could have been with her. She could have said good-bye.

Now Friede's identity scalded Diellza's fingers. "You want me to get into England as my sister."

"It is not a *want*, Liebling. It is a need. This may be our last chance to really strike at the heart of the British command."

When she blinked, she could feel her lashes sticking together with kohl and tears, no doubt ready to make a mess of his jacket. She pulled away a few inches and jammed a hand into her coat pocket, trying to remember where she'd stashed her handkerchief.

His appeared under her nose. "Here."

She took the folded white square without a word and used it to mop the mess beneath her eyes. "I don't know what you would expect me to learn for you in England. The information I was able to discover last time—"

"Was quite valuable. More, you managed to set the stage in ways we hadn't dared to hope. So that this time . . ." He touched a gloved finger to her chin and tilted her face up. In the street-lights, she caught a flash of his beautiful blue eyes, of the faith that shone out from them. "This time you can do far more for us. Put your skills to use."

Her fingers tightened around her sister's passport. "What do you mean by *skills*?" She had few, and most of them were the sort that got one disowned by one's father.

"Not that. Not this time." Though he smiled at the mere suggestion and leaned in to caress her lips with his. "No, Liebling. I mean the skills you learned from your father."

Had her blood not already been a frozen floe in her veins, it likely would have run cold. And not for the first time, she wished she had the strength to tell this man she loved *no*. "You can't mean . . . I'll be killed if I . . . Is that what you want? To be rid of me?"

"No, no, no. You misunderstand." He stroked his fingers down her cheek and smiled straight into her eyes. Straight into her heart. "We have a plan, my love. I will explain it all to you. It may require a bit of time for you to reestablish communication with the key player, but as soon as you've accomplished your mission, we have an extraction plan ready to go. You will be well. Out of England again within hours of success."

Her nostrils flared. She had no love of the British—her sentiments had rested with the German people and their shared heritage long before Alwin had sealed her loyalty with his kisses. But did she hate them enough to risk her life again?

His fingers wove their way into her hair, no doubt threatening the hastily jabbed pins of her chignon. His forehead rested on hers. "And then, Liebling . . . and then it will be over for you. I swear it. I'll never ask another thing of you, but that you come to Germany with me."

Her pulse kicked up. "Will you? Ask that?"

"As soon as the war is over." His nose trailed down her temple. "I've a house already set up. A pretty little cottage like you said you wanted. You can tend the flowers and take your coffee on the back lawn and we can be together."

She sagged against him, the kohl-smudged handkerchief in one hand and her sister's identity in the other. One assignment, and all the uncertainty could be finished. No more dancing. No more leering men she had to decide whether to accept or reject. No more turning down familiar streets and pretending she'd not once walked them as the daughter of Luca Mettler.

She could just be *his*.

With a sigh, she nodded. As no doubt he'd known she would.

4

The air in the room shifted, though Arabelle couldn't quite pinpoint how. The conversation didn't alter. The gazes of Ella and Rowena didn't shift to the door. No lights flickered, no glasses shook.

But Ara knew it the moment he entered the room, and her spine went straighter a full three seconds before she heard Stafford call out, "Camden! There you are. We were beginning to think you'd changed your mind."

Her fingers tightened around the glass of lemonade she held. Everyone else turned to the door, so she had no reason not to follow suit. Except that no one else seemed to feel as though electricity were coursing through the room.

Major Phillip Camden, Black Heart himself, headed straight for the duke with an arrogant half smile and an outstretched hand. "Come now, Stafford. You know I never change my mind."

"Allow me to make introductions." Stafford motioned to her father, who stood at his side with a snifter of cognac in hand. "Mr. Lawrence Denler, explorer of Mexico and Central America. Den, my friend from the RFC, Major Phillip Camden. One of our best pilots."

Her father reached out with eyes agleam. He *would*. The skies, he'd said no fewer than a half dozen times in her hearing, were the next great frontier. "Excellent, how do you do? I never tire of speaking with pilots. Is it true you were one of the first to test the synchronization gear for our side?"

Even with his back to her, Camden's thoughts were clear in his posture. A bit of pride in the tilt of his head. A bit of bitterness in the hunch of his shoulders. She'd grown all too familiar with the look of a man in pain at the hospital. And though this one may have no amputation or disfigurement, he was clearly hurting.

Did he realize it?

Before Brook could smirk at her from where she stood with her husband's aunt—Father's dinner partner this evening—Arabelle turned back to her friends. Their conversation hadn't been interrupted by the new arrival. They were still discussing the sweet letters to the soldiers that their children had helped write.

"I've a box of scarves to send along with them too," Rowena said, her inflection still hinting at her Highland burr.

"I've a few to add to it. I've been teaching Addie." Ella grinned, flashing her matching dimples. "She may finish one before the war is over, if she uses bulky enough yarn. And if her little brother stops pestering her for a few minutes at a time."

Arabelle smiled and told her heart to stop aching with longing at every mention of children. She would have her own soon enough. The war would end, she and Brax would marry, and she could begin filling Middlegrove with little ones again.

"Ara."

At her father's call, she turned her head to find him waving her over. And he looked far too excited. Making it a point to keep her gaze from straying to Major Camden, she whispered an "Excuse me" to Rowena and Ella and slipped toward the men. She couldn't quite resist a sardonic lift of her brow as she approached. "I know that look. What trouble have you found this time, Father?"

"Adventure, sweetling. Not trouble." He clapped a hand to Major Camden's shoulder as if they were already fast friends.

Knowing her father, they were. It took him all of two minutes, if his stories could be trusted, to make friends with head-hunting cannibals. Why would a grounded pilot take any longer?

"This young man was just answering my questions about how much space one would need to land a Sopwith. It may be just the thing to take back to Mexico with me when I go, if I can get one on the yacht. Do you recall the cargo space on the *Daphne*?"

She finally glanced at Camden when he tried to choke back a laugh at her father's question. It seemed he couldn't fathom that she'd know such a detail.

Which made her a bit annoyed that she didn't. Blast it all. Ignoring both sparks and shadows in his sky-blue eyes, she focused again on her father. "I've never studied the numbers, I'm afraid. But you took an automobile, a printing press, and two pallets of cognac with you last time—"

"For gifts," Father was quick to put in. "I assure you, I make no attempt to put away such impressive volumes myself."

"Of course." Camden tipped his head forward, still grinning.

"My point being that the cargo room is quite impressive," she continued. "I had the opportunity to see a Sopwith last month when I visited Northolt with Brook, and I think it would fit."

"I still haven't forgiven you for going without me." Her father's eyes sparkled with teasing through his scowl.

"Well, had you been at home when you said you would be rather than at the Explorers Club, you wouldn't have missed your chance."

Father chuckled and chucked her under the chin as he'd been doing since she was five. Or quite possibly longer, though she had no memory of him before then. He'd been off on an expedition hunting for the City of Gold in her smaller years.

"Forgive me, Camden. I didn't introduce you. My daughter, Arabelle Denler. Ara, Major Phillip Camden."

She shifted her lemonade to her left hand so she could extend her right. "How do you do, Major?"

No one ought to be allowed to smile like that. Nor to have a gaze so very piercing. The warmth of his fingers seeped through her satin gloves as he bowed over her hand, never taking his eyes from hers. "I'm afraid the duchess has forbidden me from answering that question with any honesty, upon pains of torture. But please, call me Camden. I feel a bit of an imposter using my rank when my service has disavowed me."

Well, no beating around the bush for this fellow. She could respect that. She smiled and reclaimed her fingers. "Camden it is."

Father continued his prattle, but Ara's attention flagged a minute later when she realized Camden was still looking at her. No, *studying* her. Which men never did—unless they knew of her inheritance and were trying to determine how best to wheedle some of it out of her.

She braced herself for the questions. Was she interested in making an investment? Had she heard of this cause? Or perhaps considered donating to that other thing?

Camden blinked and turned back to her father. "Have you a pilot in Mexico already? If not, I seem to be available, assuming I'm not shot at dawn by then."

Father laughed as if it were a great joke. "Careful, lad. I never forget an offer once made. And as my daughter all too often reminds me, I never shy away from stealing fellows away from normal life and taking them on my adventures with me."

"And rarely does he bother to bring our butlers and drivers back."

"Can I help it if they develop a thirst for adventure?"

An argument she'd never win, so she just laughed, a bit relieved when the Stafford butler announced dinner.

At least, until Camden offered his arm to her. "I believe we've been paired for the evening, yes?"

"Mm." She settled her gloved hand on the black sleeve of his dinner jacket. She ought to find a way to bring up Brax before he thought plain Miss Denler would be angling for more than a dinner partner. "Brook is forever bemoaning that my fiancé isn't stationed nearby to give us an even number."

"And where is he stationed?" Camden asked the question in

a smooth, polite tone that said he wasn't actually interested in the answer.

"Portsmouth. He's a diver in the navy."

"Really?" He led her into the exodus, falling in behind Rowena and Nottingham. "How small a world—my family's home is just outside Portsmouth."

"Perhaps we ought to plan a trip," Father said from behind them, the duke's aunt safely on his arm. "You can visit your family, Ara can see Brax, and you can advise me along the way on how to get my hands on a Sopwith."

Heaven help her. She couldn't quite imagine spending two hours trapped in a train carriage with this man. Or worse, in the wind-whipped cabin of their Model S. Were it someone else who'd made the suggestion, she'd take comfort in the fact that the trip would never materialize.

But her father had a strange habit of making things happen in exactly the way he flippantly declared they would.

Camden craned his head over his shoulder. "What are you doing tomorrow?"

Father laughed. Arabelle huffed. It was absurd how often this happened. "Don't even think about it, Father. You've already committed to tea with Mr. Forrester tomorrow, if you recall. And after church I'm driving out to visit Sarah while she's at her sister's."

Her father's sigh would have sounded perfectly natural coming from one of Brook's sons after having been denied an extra biscuit before bed. "Very well, not tomorrow. How does your schedule look next week, Camden?"

She made a show of leaning closer to her escort so that she could stage-whisper, "It *is* possible to deny him. I promise you. I've done it at least twice. Perhaps three times."

"Ha! She denies me every single time I ask her to join me on an expedition." Father leaned closer to his own partner. "Seems to think she'll have to stay at home with her husband or some such rot."

Lady Abingdon obligingly laughed. "How silly of her."

Camden chuckled as he led her into the dining room. And while he helped her into her chair, Arabelle said a silent prayer that the laughter would banish a few of those shadows in his eyes for good.

She wasn't pretty. Camden speared a raisin from his bread pudding and listened with half an ear to Denler's tale of the storm that had nearly wrecked the *Daphne* on his way home last time, but he kept his gaze on the man's daughter. She wasn't pretty, but she did a fair job of hiding it. Her dark hair was well arranged, her dress as fashionable as wartime allowed, and she carried herself with all the confidence of a girl who had spent most of her life at one boarding school or another.

Cass was prettier—happy as he would have been had no man ever noticed such a thing. And this Arabelle didn't have the same lightness about her that his sister did. If the match between her and Braxton had been for money rather than love, then he could see why a chap might be drawn away.

"Perhaps all those airships will be put to more pleasant use after the war," the duchess said from her place adjacent to Stafford at the head of the table. "Then you could simply *float* across the ocean next time, Denny."

Denler laughed, and so did his daughter. Camden freed another bite. She had a dimple—one. In her left cheek. It was the most interesting thing about her face.

She was a nice girl, though, that was clear enough. He had no desire to cause her pain. But the fact remained that she stood squarely between his sister and happiness.

She had to be moved.

Her father turned toward the duchess, but Camden pasted on a smile and directed it toward The Obstacle. "So, Miss Denler." He kept his voice low enough that it wouldn't interrupt any of the other conversations going on around the table, but loud enough to bring her gaze over to his. "This Sarah you're visiting tomorrow. A school chum?"

Arabelle lifted her brows. "All that studying you've been doing, and that's the most interesting question you can devise?"

A corner of his mouth tugged up. Cheekier than he'd expected, he'd give her that. "Apparently."

She tilted her head to the side. "Not a school chum, no. That was Victoria Braxton, through whom I met Sarah. Sarah was the daughter of the steward of their estate, Middlegrove—and is now housekeeper there."

Camden lifted his wine glass, though he did no more than sip at it. It would be too easy, at this point in his life, to let alcohol blur the edges for him. And he knew himself well enough to know that he might never emerge from that. "And you're visiting her to . . . discuss changes you intend to make to the estate as its mistress?"

Her chin came up in a way that looked oddly familiar. "I am visiting her because she's my dearest friend."

Didn't mind rubbing elbows with the domestics? Interesting. But not quite as interesting as the piece of the puzzle that clicked into place. His lips twitched. "Were you by chance standing at the window of the fourth floor at Charing Cross Hospital on Wednesday last?"

She worked there—she well could have been. He could swear he recognized the challenging tilt of her jaw. And how many nurses of her height could the hospital really have?

She didn't flush at the question, and if she'd been one of the tittering females watching him walk by every blasted day, one would have thought she'd have the grace to blush over it.

Instead, she merely blinked. "You're going to have to be more specific, sir. I pass by windows rather frequently."

He compared her shape with the silhouette from the window. It was her. It had to be. He sent her the same smirk he'd sent to her giggling friends. "You know exactly what time I mean."

"I have no idea." But the quirking of her mouth gave her away, and she chuckled at her own failure. "They think they can save you with their youth and determination and undying love."

A snort of laughter slipped out as he set his glass back on the table. If only they could. "You're too sensible for such notions, I suppose."

He'd meant it as a jest, perhaps a bit of absent-minded flirting, but her returning smile was sad and far too serious.

"Someone can save you, Camden. But I am certainly not He."

Blast. He felt his brows pulling into a scowl and could do nothing to stop them. "Now you sound like my little brother."

"Do I?"

"He's a vicar—a chaplain now." He tacked on his usual sneer for the topic. "Never cared for vicars."

Arabelle didn't look too compassionate. If anything, amused. "No doubt he became one just to spite you, then."

"Probably." *He'd* certainly done plenty to spite Gilbert. Jeremy . . . not so much. He'd always been too blasted *good* to spite anybody.

"Is he your only sibling? The Reverend Mr. Camden?"

Her question jarred him back to the table. "No. There were four of us. Three now, as our eldest brother fell in Gallipoli in '15. Me, Jeremy the Vicar, and Cassandra."

How could her smile be pure joy, especially when aimed at a stranger, and following on the heels of news of death?

"What a magical childhood you must have had. I always wished for a big family."

His gaze darted to Denler. In the hour they'd been acquainted, Camden had easily pieced together that the man had been gone for most of his daughter's life, until the war stranded him in England. That would, he supposed, make it a bit difficult to add to the family. "I generally described it as annoying rather than magical." But she had a point. He couldn't think of a single childhood memory that didn't involve his brothers, usually with Cass tagging along behind.

Something about the gleam in her eyes made it clear she heard the unspoken memories, not just the spoken snarl. Which was odd. Few could see through his bluster.

But he couldn't focus on that right now. He had to focus instead on the mission. It was too bad he hadn't been able to get her and her father on a train to Portsmouth tomorrow—that would have been an easy solution. But perhaps he could instead use her visit to this Sarah the housekeeper to his advantage. "Sounds as though you filled yours with friends instead. Victoria Braxton and Sarah—and presumably Victoria's brother. Your fiancé, correct?"

Shadows deepened her hazel eyes as she said, "Yes."

Blast. *That* wouldn't get him any more information on where Sarah lived. And blast again—the duchess was even now standing, signaling an end to dinner proper. She'd lead the ladies away, and it would be half an hour or more before the men joined them again. He'd spent too much time trying to put his finger on the type of person she was and not enough on drawing information from her. Now he'd have to try to corner her later, before they all went their separate ways for the night.

Or . . . He stood with the other men as the ladies took their leave. And then settled his gaze on her father. Or he could take a different tack. As the men all shifted seats closer to Stafford, Camden made it a point to take the one beside Denler.

He let the conversation pick up again, just watching. Stafford teasing his father-in-law, Whitby deftly turning it back on him, Cayton jumping in to prod a bit at his cousin the duke, too, before Nottingham—Cayton's brother-in-law—sprang to Stafford's defense with such exaggeration it sent them all into peals of laughter.

The sort of group he'd once belonged to himself. Brothers, through the years of shared life if not by blood. For a moment, he saw them all—his squadron. Half of them from backgrounds that never would have landed them in shared company were it not for the war, but brothers forged through years of fire. He'd pulled those working-class blokes along into the high life with him, showed them how to have a good time. Ignore consequences. Do whatever in blazes they wanted, because who knew if tomorrow they'd still be alive to enjoy it?

And now they weren't.

He wouldn't let it hurt. Not now. He had another task to focus on, so he leaned close to Denler, who was chuckling along with the other gents. It was time to forgo subtlety, before the evening ended altogether. "May I ask you a question, sir?"

Denler's merry gaze shifted to him. "Absolutely."

"What think you of Braxton?" Might as well get a father's take on the bloke, if he was to be married to Cass before the week was out. With their own father gone for a decade and Gil lost, too, it would fall to Camden now to play that role.

Denler waved a dismissive hand. "Fine enough fellow, I think. To be honest, I don't know him well. He's been in Portsmouth since I've been home, and we've only met a few times." Then his eyes went shrewd as he obviously considered the reasons a chap might have for such a question. "Why?"

Cam pitched his voice low but kept his tone easy. "Because I'm afraid I can't allow him to marry your daughter."

Denler lifted his nearly empty wine goblet. "And why is that?"

"Because he's going to marry my sister instead." He met the older man's gaze and held it firmly. "It's . . . necessary."

Denler's lips went tight. Tight as the fingers around the stem of his glass. "Are you telling me he played my daughter false?"

Camden dipped his head. "And now is hiding behind the betrothal as a reason he can't make an honest woman of my little sister."

With one motion, Denler drained the last sip of wine. With the next, he set the crystal down with a determined *thunk* and leaned close. "What have you in mind?"

The situation was nothing to smile over. But he had to appreciate a man who saw so quickly what was at stake. "Just a little . . . adventure. To convince him to do the right thing."

He'd hooked him with that magic word, he knew. Still, Denler tapped a finger on the table. "Ara won't forgive it if you steal her chance at a family."

"With all due respect, sir, your daughter's forgiveness isn't my priority."

"I suppose not. Though it must remain mine." He heaved a sigh and set his gaze on the middle distance, no doubt willing a happy resolution to materialize there.

As if happy resolutions even existed in this world any longer. Another sigh joined its mate. "Well. I know there will be consequences for her heart—but she would be the first to say that where there is no fidelity, there is no relationship anyway. Tell me your plan."

He did, in whispers that the other gents didn't seem to notice. And with Denler's stamp of approval, Camden stood with a bit of the weight off his shoulders as Stafford declared it time to rejoin the ladies.

"Not I, I'm afraid." Making sure his usual smirk was in place, he moved to his host with a hand outstretched. "Thank you for having me, Your Grace. It wasn't an entirely wretched evening."

Stafford laughed and clasped his hand. "The highest of compliments from the likes of you. But why are you off so early?"

"Things to do." He had to find someone with an auto to lend him tomorrow. And petrol enough to drive it out of London, where he could intercept Arabelle Denler on her way to visiting her friend. And determine a way to get said borrowed vehicle back to whomever he ended up borrowing it from.

He could just show up at the Denler residence and lay his case before her. But if he was going to disrupt someone's entire life, he might as well give her a story to tell about it. And who else could claim to have been kidnapped by the infamous Black Heart? With her father's permission, but no one needed to know that part.

"Stay out of trouble, Camden." Perhaps with some, it would have been a teasing farewell. But the duke was serious.

Cam grinned. "What fun would that be?" He backed up a step, two, and raised a hand in farewell to the collection at large. "Good evening, gentlemen. Give the ladies my regards."

A few minutes later, he had coat and hat and was back out in the frigid night, whistling his way to the nearest tube station.

It was going to work. It was. He had some details to sort out yet, true, but they'd fall into place. Or be wrestled there. His mind flipped through the puzzle of it during the ride home. There were a few chaps at the office with automobiles. He hated to owe any of them a favor, but . . . well, desperate times and all that.

He hurried to his flat, let himself inside—it was much tidier after Mother's visit—and stopped dead in his tracks. Someone was here. The lights were on, the scent of tea drifted over him, and a hum came from the sofa that he'd recognize anywhere. He let a curse slip out, largely because he knew it would put an end to the humming. "What the devil are *you* doing here?"

The intruder rose from the couch with a smile. "Trying to chase the devil out of *you*, Phillip."

He snorted and moved to give his kid brother a crushing hug. "Good luck with that one." He grinned as he pulled away. "Actually . . . your timing couldn't be better. You're going to help me kidnap a girl tomorrow, Jer."

His brother didn't wince. Didn't flinch. Didn't moan. He just sighed and rubbed a hand over his face. "Heaven help me. What have you got us into this time?"

5

How dreary the nearly barren road out of London looked in the February afternoon. Even the sun seemed tired and weak, barely trying to cut through the clouds overhead. Arabelle gripped the wheel of her Standard and willed spring to come earlier than usual. They needed it, all of them. A bit of brightness to remind them that even a war that spread its ragged wings the world over couldn't bring an end to the cycle of life.

She rounded a bend and squinted at the object up ahead on the road. Another car, from the shape and size, but she was catching it up quickly enough that her foot came off the accelerator by instinct, even before she spotted the figure that stepped into the road and waved his arms in a clear signal of distress.

Probably ran out of petrol. It wouldn't be the first time she'd had to lend some to a stranded motorist whose goal had exceeded his ration. She braked, easing her Model S to a halt behind the parked Vauxhall.

The man was in a navy uniform, dark hair visible beneath his cap and a smile upon his face that looked almost, nearly familiar, though she couldn't place why. It was possible she'd met him before, she supposed. Her job put her in contact with soldiers and sailors by the thousands.

He jogged over as she opened her door and stepped out. "Thank you for stopping, miss. I'm in a bit of trouble."

"So I see." She smiled back at him, trying again to place him. Dark hair, eyes caught between blue and green, a sweet smile. As he turned to motion toward his silent car, his profile made her draw in a breath. He almost put her in mind of . . .

"That'll do, Jer. I promised you you'd not have to lie." A second man emerged from the car, this one decidedly familiar and grinning exactly as he had the night before when he called her out for watching him from the hospital's windows.

Arabelle sucked in a breath and planted her hands on her hips. "Major Camden. Why do I get the sudden feeling trouble is afoot?"

It must not be too nefarious a plot, though. *Jer* must be his brother Jeremy, the vicar and chaplain—which did in fact match the white collar to his uniform, which she hadn't noted at first. Surely a man of the cloth wouldn't be party to something untoward.

Though, come to mention it, the reverend did look a bit sheepish as he glanced back at her. "Don't worry, Miss Denler. It's all for the best." With that, the younger brother started back for the supposedly stranded car while the pilot landed himself behind the steering wheel of hers.

"What are you doing?" She dashed round to the other door before he could decide to drive off in it. She couldn't exactly fathom *why* he'd try to steal her car and abandon her outside London, but suddenly all the stories she'd heard whispered about England's favorite villain came to mind.

Still, he grinned at her in that maddening way of his. "Taking you for a drive, darling. Don't worry, I've already obtained your father's permission."

Her breath hissed out from between her teeth. Father *had* seemed a bit too jolly upon their return from church, when he wished her a happy journey and bade her, "Have a grand adventure." It was his usual farewell. But he'd said it this time with a particularly bright twinkle in his eye, hadn't he? A *knowing* twinkle.

She closed her door. "A drive to *where*?"

"Portsmouth."

For a moment she could only stare at his profile while he checked the road for nonexistent traffic and pulled out, pointing the Standard's nose in the direction opposite Sarah's. "Why?"

He paused for a moment, watching as his brother pulled out onto the road again as well. Only then did he ease her Model S forward. "You're due for a reunion with your fiancé."

Her stomach went tight. Was Brax somehow behind this? Were he and Camden old school chums? Had he . . . No. Or perhaps he . . . Definitely not. She could think of no reason Edmund Braxton would ever enlist the aid of a man like Phillip Camden in any plot. For that matter, she couldn't imagine Brax ever thinking about her enough to plot anything at all.

She kept herself against the passenger door and angled to face him. "Was this my father's idea?" He wasn't one to really care overmuch about her romance. Or lack thereof. But he *was* the sort to want her to experience a bit of spontaneity.

Camden tilted his head, that smile still playing at the corners of his mouth. "No. But he approved it."

"Brook's, then."

His brows rose. "Most decidedly *not*."

Then what in the world would possess him to waylay her on the road and drive off with her? "Explain. Now."

Rather than another grin, he shot her a dark look. His posture was the picture of ease, except for the fingers of his left hand, which gripped the wheel far more tightly than the smooth road demanded. "It's very simple, Miss Denler. I'm going to deliver you to my home outside of Portsmouth. Shortly thereafter, a panicked Edmund Braxton is going to show up, drawn by the note my mother will have had delivered to him. At which point you, darling, are going to put a neat and tidy end to your engagement."

A scoffing laugh puffed its way through her lips. "Oh, am I? And why, pray tell, would I do that?"

"Because he's got my sister with child, that's why."

The words fell like ordnance upon her ears. Upon her heart. Upon her soul. Denials sprang to her tongue—he wouldn't, he couldn't have, he'd *promised* her—and then Camden's fingers tightened even more on the wheel, and the truth strangled her.

Even if this man's heart were as black as the papers said, he didn't wreak havoc with everyone he happened across at a dinner party just for the enjoyment of it. There was absolutely no reason he'd lie to her about something like this. Unless he were intending to hold her for ransom, he had no reason to target her at all.

For one wild second, she scrabbled to believe *that* instead. This was about her money, not about Brax. Black Heart was trying to wheedle some of her fortune out of her father.

But the ticking of the muscle in his jaw convinced her otherwise. He was angry. The dark, determined kind of anger that led men charging into alleys with fists raised and blades at the ready. And it was aimed ahead of them, on the road.

At Brax.

On her exhale, out went all the denials, all the disbelief, all the delusions. In the second her respiration paused, that all-too-obvious truth smacked her in the face.

This wasn't about her at all. *Nothing* was ever about her at all.

And then on the inhale, pure fury unlike any she'd known since her mother's senseless death set every nerve alight. "That snake!" Her hands landed on the only thing nearby—her handbag—and flung it to the floorboards. "That odious *worm*! I asked him—I asked him when he proposed if I could trust him to remain faithful to me, knowing he didn't love me, and what did he do? He swore on bended knee that he'd be true—*swore* it! The prig. The ratsbane. The artless lewdster!"

"Been reading Shakespeare, have you?"

His amusement only stoked the flames. "And you—you couldn't

tell me this in a considerate way? Had to make a show of it, did you?"

His mouth was still twitching. "Brax, darling. Your anger belongs to Brax."

"I've more than enough of it to go round! Why do you insufferable men always think you have to plot and control everything? Take me for a drive, force me to do the right thing, is that it? As if I haven't the *sense* to end a farce of an engagement of my own volition? You couldn't have just told me what he's done like a reasonable human being, in the privacy of my home?"

"Well, I—"

"No, of course not." Wishing for something else to throw, she yanked off her gloves and slapped one to the seat, then the other. "You and my idiotic father have to hatch this ridiculous plan. And your brother! A man of the cloth!"

"Leave him out of this. He agreed only to what your father had already consented and not to anything more."

The sound that came from her throat might have been a laugh if it weren't so hideously broken. She gripped the mockery of a ring on her left hand and tried to jerk it off her fourth finger. It stuck on her knuckle, turning her broken laugh to a growl, but she forced it off. Pulled back her arm. Aimed at the open space beside her.

"Whoa, whoa, whoa." Camden's hand gripped her wrist just as she was moving into the swing. "It isn't the ring's fault."

It wasn't a ring. It was a broken promise. It was a symbol of everything she'd never have now, and it bounced onto the seat like her mother's book had bounced onto the floor as her last labored breath left her.

Camden snatched it up. "Why don't I just hold this for you?"

"Give it to your sister, you mean?" She couldn't look at him. She turned instead to put her face into the wicked winter wind blasting in. Maybe it would blow away the hurt.

Her father had known. Camden must have told him last night. He'd known, and he'd said nothing to her then, or this morning, or on the way home from church. He'd just blithely put their extra petrol into the boot. *"In case you run into someone in need,"* he'd said. And he'd kissed her cheek and sent her off here to be intercepted by this known rogue.

Her fingers curled into her palms until her nails dug shallow crescents into her flesh. "Why do you need me for this? Why not just waylay *Brax*?"

"Apparently he is hiding behind the engagement. Refusing to end it and do the right thing."

"Of course he is." Not because of any affection. Oh no. Not because he really felt bound by that promise he'd made her. "He'll lose Middlegrove without my money."

"So my mother told me." He paused, and though she didn't turn to see it, she could feel him looking at her. "And then there was me. For some bizarre reason, he didn't fancy making Black Heart his brother."

The pain resonated, like a bell ringing after it was struck. Now she turned her head. Away from the wind and into the echo of *his* pain.

He knew. He knew what it meant to be judged always, not for who you were but for your circumstances. To be seen as nothing more than the label society had applied. *Heiress. Villain.*

"So you send him a note saying that the Black Heart he so despises has . . . what? Kidnapped his fiancée?"

His smile didn't eclipse the pain. Just joined it as he glanced over at her. "Now you're getting the picture. According to the papers, I'm a danger to every girl with whom I have a conversation. What do you think he'll believe I've done to you? Knowing what *he's* done to my sister?"

She sighed. Or laughed. Or cried. She wasn't sure which name best fit the sound. "Wonderful. In addition to losing my fiancé, I'll also lose my reputation."

"You really think he's going to tell anyone?" Camden's laugh mocked the idea. "Your reputation will be as safe as you choose to keep it. Although if you want to entertain your tittering friends at the hospital . . ."

Maybe by Tuesday, when she was due back in, that thought would be more alluring. At the moment, she couldn't think beyond facing down Brax. At the Camden home. Where this other young woman would be.

She'd be beautiful. Arabelle knew that just by looking at her two brothers, handsome both. Did Brax love her? She hoped so, hoped he wouldn't have compromised a girl otherwise. And yet she didn't want to see it.

She squeezed her eyes shut. She couldn't think about it. It would turn anger to agony, and tears would come, and she would *not* fall to pieces crammed into her car with Phillip Camden. *Think about something else, Ara. Anything else.*

"Where was your brother going?"

"Hmm? Oh. To return the car he'd borrowed from his bishop." The amusement wasn't scoffing in his tone now. It added a lilt to it. "Not that he told him, I'm sure, why he borrowed it. He'll catch the afternoon train and meet us at Foxwood."

"Where?"

"My family home." He shot her a look, though it was too brief for her to parse it fully. "Not exactly as grand as a house in Westminster, nor as expansive and ancient as Middlegrove, but it's home."

Home. She hadn't really had one since her mother died. And it seemed she wouldn't get to change that after all, when the war finally ended. *If* the war ever ended. "And you're certain Brax will come?"

"Oh, he'll come. My mother can be very persuasive."

She turned to face him, her every muscle tight. The ache—it pulsed. Writhed. Pierced. "I'll play along with your little charade. On one condition."

Black Heart lifted a black brow. "What's that?"

"I get a shot at him first."

"You're bringing her here? How could you? How do you expect me to look her in the eye knowing what I've done?"

Arabelle paused in the corridor as the panicked voice filtered from the drawing room Camden had been leading her toward. Cassandra Camden was apparently no keener to meet Arabelle than she was her. She shot a look at the girl's brother and kept her feet planted where they were.

The drive had been a blur of cold wind and angry silence. She never would have chosen her windowless car as a means to travel from London to Portsmouth in the dead of winter, but Camden and her father hadn't given any thought to that.

Her focus had snapped back into place, banishing all the swirling should-have-beens as Camden had pulled up on a tree-lined drive a few minutes ago.

No, his home wasn't a house in Westminster. And it was perhaps an eighth the size of Middlegrove. But what it lacked in size it made up for in charm. Ivy sneaking its way up the walls, gardens that would no doubt be a riot of color in spring . . . It reminded her of the little place Mama had let when Ara was a girl, while Father was away. Even walking through the door and being embraced by the scent of cinnamon brought back memories of happy days.

But even in a place like this, the heavy clouds outside could find their way in. The daughter of *this* house was clearly not full of only good thoughts.

"Cassandra, that's enough of your histrionics. Your brother is doing his best to help you. And if you are too ashamed to face the woman whose fiancé you've stolen, then perhaps you ought to have considered that *before* you put yourself in this situation."

Camden directed a crooked smile toward the door and nodded. "That would be my mother."

"So I assumed." But she didn't want to go in there. She didn't want to face his sister. Couldn't she wait somewhere else to face down Brax? Outside, perhaps? She was already frozen solid; another hour or two of icy wind couldn't possibly make a difference.

Cassandra must have had the same idea. Running footsteps from within soon turned to a girl bursting out the door and running smack into Camden. "Oh!" She looked up into his face, darted a glance over at Arabelle, and dissolved into tears.

Oh, fiddlesticks. She was pretty, yes. Startling blue eyes beneath her warm brown brows, delicate features. Petite, slender, everything a man would want to protect and cherish. And she was *young*. Young like Susan and Eliza, and still bright with it.

She buried her face in her brother's uniform jacket and clung on for dear life.

Blast it all. Ara couldn't dislike her, much as she wanted to. When Phillip Camden's arms came around his sister and held her tight as her shoulder's shook, that became crystal clear. This wasn't some heartless vixen. Just a young lady who'd made a mistake and now didn't know what to do about it.

Another wounded soul. Arabelle could see the pain in the curl of her fingers in Camden's jacket, sense it bleeding from her heart. It could fester, if things didn't work out. It could break her.

Please, God. She didn't know what to pray. Hadn't imagined praying for this girl at all. But helping those who were hurting was what the Lord had called her to years ago. *If you want to be healed*, He'd whispered into her heart when she was around Cassandra's age, *then heal others.*

He hadn't warned her how *hard* it would be sometimes.

Arabelle's hand reached out and rested on the girl's shaking shoulders. "I'm sorry."

That brought her head up, away from the sheltering crook of her brother's arms. Those too-blue eyes were wide as they gaped at her. "*You're* sorry?"

Arabelle nodded. Swallowed. "Yes. Sorry you're going through this. And sorry I'm what's made it worse for you."

Cassandra shook her head, wildly enough to send a few curls slipping from an already precarious chignon. "You are the only innocent one in this fiasco! I never should have—I didn't know. I didn't know he was engaged, but even so. I never should have . . ."

Her fingers released her brother's jacket, and she turned to face Arabelle.

Ara dug up her nursing smile. The one she wore when she knew the soldier on the cot before her needed it most, when it was hardest to give. When wounds were festering and gangrene was setting in and bleeding wouldn't stop. The smile that tried so desperately to offer hope in the midst of hopelessness. She held out her hands, and the younger woman gripped them. "We all do foolish things for love."

New tears flooded the girl's eyes, and she sniffed. "It's no excuse. I know it isn't. I didn't mean to put myself in such a situation, and when he confessed he was already betrothed—oh, Miss Denler, I'm a wretch."

Speak truth. That's what the Lord had taught her to do, if she wanted to bring healing to another heart. Not the hard and ugly side of truth—that the leg would have to come off or the infection couldn't be stopped or that yes, this young woman had done something wrong—but the eternal Truth. "You're no more a wretch than any of us, Cassandra. You're a sweet young woman who made a mistake."

Small, elegant fingers tightened around hers. "I've ruined my life!"

"No, you haven't. You've a family who loves you and will see you're taken care of, no matter what. And Brax must love you too. He'll do the right thing." Her voice cracked, but she prayed the girl didn't notice. Prayed she wouldn't feel it, that splintering of her own heart, as she drew her in with an arm around her shoulders.

A sob ripped through Cassandra as she leaned into Arabelle. "Even if he does love me now, he won't for long. He'll lose his home, and he'll blame me for it. Even if he doesn't mean to do so, he will. He'll come to hate me. To resent our child."

Arabelle's breath was crushed from her lungs by that truth. He wouldn't mean to let it affect him, Cassandra was right. But it would. It would spread through him like an infection unless he cut it off at the source, unless he let Someone properly cleanse him of it. But Brax had never had much use for talk of faith.

Words flashed before her eyes, so clearly that she knew it was more than a passing thought. The report she'd just read three days ago, the happy sentence that had concluded it. *Our investments have been wise. The sum we agreed upon has, as I projected, done quite well for you during these unfortunate years of war. It will be sufficient to secure Middlegrove without compromising the core of the legacy your aunt left in my trust for you.*

Which just made those splinters of her heart ache all the more. Would He ask this of her too? Was this, in fact, why her trustee had been so determined to keep her from dumping the bulk of her inheritance into Middlegrove—at the Lord's prompting? Inspired him to work so diligently to ensure that she would have plenty for other good works?

It wasn't fair. She was supposed to get a family from the bargain. A home. A life surrounded by people she loved.

Maybe she was meant to be always the nurse, moving from one cot to the next, helping for a time and then fading out of the lives she worked to touch.

It sounded so bleak just now.

Renewing her smile, she rubbed a hand over Cassandra's arm. "Let's not borrow worries, Miss Camden. Our God can work wonders on a man's heart, especially when he is the warm recipient of a family's love. For now, focus on the happy things. We'll set Brax straight, and he'll marry you. You'll have a beautiful little one. Your life is only beginning."

Cassandra sniffled and dashed at her eyes. "You're too good. Comforting me, when I've wronged you."

"*Brax* wronged me. You didn't know I existed." She gave the girl a wink. "Trust me, I don't intend to be so kind to him when I see him. Which I daresay will be soon, so you had better go and tidy up, I think."

Cassandra touched a hand to her swollen eyes, then to her

fallen hair. "I suppose you're right." Then she leaned over and gave Arabelle a quick, fierce embrace. "I will repay your kindness, Miss Denler. Somehow, someday."

Easy words. But Arabelle had a feeling she meant them. She smiled and hugged her back. "I look forward to it."

6

Arabelle Denler was either a saint or a madwoman. Perhaps a bit of both. Camden shook his head and looked away from Miss Denler and Cass, toward his mother, who stood gaping at them in the drawing room doorway. She met his gaze, his own thoughts reflected in her eyes. This wasn't at all what they'd expected. But his mother wasn't one to let a little thing like complete stupefaction compromise her manners.

As Cass bustled off, she bustled in. "What a reception we've given you! And you fresh from the road. You must be an icicle. Come, Miss Denler, warm yourself by the fire. Phillip, your brother's train ought to have arrived. Hadn't you better fetch him from town?"

"I'm an icicle, too, you know. And Jer has two legs, doesn't he?" He'd go in a moment, as his mother knew he would. But first he watched her usher their unwitting guest into the room.

Her back was straight as a biplane's wing, and she moved forward with the image of perfect confidence, even though inside she had to be quaking. Didn't she?

Mother would like her. They were obviously cut from the same cloth—the kind robust enough to survive a gale.

With a shake of his head, he turned away. He hadn't really paused to consider how Miss Denler might react to Cass, but had someone asked, he probably would have wagered on a catfight. Especially after her tantrum in the car—which was warranted, he granted.

His fingers were only now starting to thaw a bit, and he figured that if Jer had gotten to Portsmouth, he could start for home on his own. A few minutes in the cold would do him no harm. Camden took the stairs two by two, not even glancing at the familiar portraits and landscapes on the walls, the end tables with the same candlesticks and doilies that had been there as long as he could remember.

He rapped upon his sister's closed door. "Cass? You all right?"

The door opened, and Cassandra's sheepish face soon filled the space. She'd taken her hair down, the pins prickling out of her mouth evidence that she was in the process of putting it back up. She motioned him in with her head and took the pins from between her lips. "I was a complete ninny down there, wasn't I?"

Her room was still every bit as young and girlish as it had been when she first moved into it from the nursery at the age of twelve. Pink this and white that and a bunch of ridiculous frou-frou that had, so far as he could discern, no purpose but to clutter up the place. How was this any better than stacks of dishes? He crossed his arms. "If ever you had an excuse to act a ninny, I daresay that was it."

"I didn't expect her to be so . . . *kind*." With a sigh, she sat upon her dressing table's stool. "Go ahead. Lecture me on my irresponsibility and stupidity and complete lack of principles and—"

"Who do I look like—Jeremy?" Camden shook his head and eased to a seat at the foot of her bed. Gingerly, lest some of the pink get stuck to him somehow. "You were stupid. You know it. But we'll get it all sorted, and in a few years this will be nothing but a faded memory. Something to laugh over." Assuming the ladies would ever deign to speak of such matters, which he highly doubted.

She twisted her hair into a coil and began slipping pins into it. "I suppose. But the look in Mum's eyes when I told her . . ." She wilted. Shoulder slumping, hands falling to her sides. "How in the world did you get used to seeing that look on her face? The one that says you've disappointed her?"

Camden laughed. He'd gotten the look plenty of times over the years, to be sure. Enough that he'd learned to see beneath it. "It's only the look she's practiced to keep us in line, Cass. To cover the fact that she's found plenty of mischief of her own through the years and finds more amusement in it than she thinks she should let on."

She spun to face him. "Perhaps in your pranks. But in *this*?"

He lifted a brow. "You think this is any worse than when she came to see me in prison?"

Cassandra winced. "I suppose not."

"But do you know what she did then?" He'd tried not to think of it much. It seemed wrong to focus on the light of hope she'd been, when the fact remained that his men were dead and he was responsible. "She reached between the bars, gripped my chin in her fingers in that way she does, and told me she knew me, she loved me, and that this was not my end."

He stood, took the two steps to reach his sister, and gripped her chin in his fingers. "We know you. We love you. And this is not your end, Cass. Miss Denler was right about that—it's just your beginning."

The tears in her eyes this time weren't so sad, he hoped. "Just like it wasn't your end."

His fingers fell away. He was still here, so his mother had technically been right. But every day was borrowed time for him. He knew it. Sooner or later, Mrs. Lewis's and the press's constant pestering of the justice system would overwhelm any reluctance the brass had about prosecuting an officer. Maybe new evidence would surface. Something would happen. He knew it would. Something to end his miserable excuse for a life.

It wouldn't be so for his sister. "Is this what you want, Cass? To marry him? Not because you feel you *have* to—do you want to? Because if you don't, I'll find another way. We can set you up somewhere they don't know you, say you're a war widow—"

"Phillip." She caught the hand that had retreated to his side and gave his fingers a squeeze. Not the quick, fleeting kind most people would give. No, she held it in the way she always had—clinging, holding on, and not letting go. "I want it more than anything. I promise you. I love him."

He nodded and squeezed back. "You know I'll see he pays for it if he hurts you." He'd move the very earth if necessary. Or the seas, in this case, and drag the diver up by his air hose.

"I know. Phillip . . ." The confidence on her face melted into concern. "You'll be all right, won't you? All this nonsense about you sabotaging your squadron's planes—"

"Poppycock. That part was tacked on just a month ago in an attempt to fan the flames, that's all."

"—and killing those men on purpose. Has it gone away? The papers . . ."

He could still see their faces. Miller and Greyson and De Were. Montagu and Lewis. Their smiles, the day before. The glances they'd exchanged that morning.

The panic upon them in the air that afternoon. Well. On *most* of them.

He plunged a hand into his pocket, his fingers flicking aside the ring Arabelle had tried to throw out the window and finding the bronze-copper wings with *RFC* at their junction. They'd only had the pins for a few months at the start of the war. Stupid things had caught on everything, ripping their uniforms, so woven ones had been sewn on instead. Most of the chaps had tossed their pins. Camden had instead tossed his into a box. Hadn't found it or even thought of it until after The Incident. After the men at the base had locked him in his barracks, before the Military Police arrived. He'd sat down to look through the snapshots of happier days, the few mementos from home he'd stashed away, and found it. He'd slid it into his pocket that day, and it had lived there ever since.

His thumb ran along the bumped lower edge of the wings, traced the letters. "Don't worry for me, Cass." He gave her the mischievous smile she'd expect from him and pulled his hand from hers. "You know I'm not one to stay down for long."

His sister clearly didn't believe the confidence. "Phillip."

"I need to go and fetch Jer from town before your fellow arrives." He leaned over, dropped a kiss onto her forehead, and spun away. "Be back directly."

He jogged down the stairs, along the front hall, smiling just a bit at the friendly female voices within the drawing room, and tried not to think of the heat that would be blazing from the hearth. Though when he stepped outside, the shiver he had prepared faded away. Warmer air had moved in—no doubt with the dark clouds boiling over the harbor. He needn't save his brother from cold so much as rain, he suspected.

And it looked like he needn't save him at all. Even as he turned toward the carriage house, the puttering of an engine on the drive broke into his hearing. He paused and turned, waiting for whomever it was to come into view. If it was Braxton instead of Jeremy, he'd sock the bloke in the nose before he went after his brother.

But no, it was Neville's little runabout, and that meant his brother would be in the passenger's seat. Jeremy's childhood friend had been rejected for service because of his being nearly deaf, which meant he still lived in the city, right beside the train station. Ought to have assumed Jer would knock on his door the moment his train got in.

Camden strode back toward the front of the house as the car squeaked to a halt—Nev really should check on those brakes. But then, Nev wouldn't be able to hear the ghastly sound they were making. Cam lifted a hand in greeting to Jer as his brother climbed out but ducked his head down to meet Neville's eye. He didn't know all the signs for automobile parts, but a bit of pantomiming got his point across.

Comically, it seemed. Neville laughed at him. "My brakes?"

His speech had always been a bit garbled but understandable. Camden nodded. Neville gave him a lazy salute. "I'll check them. Thanks."

The runabout pulled off again, leaving Cam to drift closer to his brother.

Jeremy let his bag fall to the steps and cast a glance at the house. "How did it go?"

"Shockingly well. She was furious—at Braxton—but is Cass's new best friend."

The lift of Jer's brows was impressive. "Really? I'm looking forward to meeting her properly. She must be quite a girl if she didn't faint dead away at having Black Heart kidnap her."

Camden gave his brother a playful—mostly—punch in the shoulder. "I inspire batting lashes more than fainting. I hear they all think they can save me with their undying love."

Jeremy's eyes flashed. "There's only One who can save you, Phil. And—"

"Stow it." He ought to have known better than to say the word *save* around his brother. "I already got that particular lecture from Miss Denler. Who, let it be noted, isn't one for batting lashes either."

"Now I *really* need to meet her."

Camden rolled his eyes and leaned down to heft Jeremy's bag. Though he paused before picking it up, his ears straining again. The putter of the runabout had faded, but another engine's clatter sounded now, turning in at their drive. "I think our next guest has arrived."

"Father God, give us your wisdom and peace and guidance, that all this may work out to your glory."

Camden shot Jeremy a scowl. Much as he would love to blame Jer's training, the annoying fact was that the youngest Camden brother had *always* burst spontaneously into prayer. "I don't think God has much to do with this particular situation."

Jeremy wasn't fazed. He just turned to watch for whatever auto might appear through the bare-limbed trees lining their drive. "Your ignorance is showing, brother. God has much to do with everything."

"Simpleton." Camden gave Jeremy a shove.

Jeremy shoved him right back. "Heathen."

The clouds spat out a few stray drops, more bluff than rain. Camden swiped a bead of moisture from his cheek and turned to watch the car barreling toward them. In contrast to the slow amble of Neville's runabout, this one was bouncing along at a clip fast enough to loosen the bloke's teeth. It came to a dust-swirling halt a few yards from where they stood, and Camden straightened, awaiting his first glimpse of this Braxton fellow.

He wasn't that tall—that was his first impression. Not short exactly, but Miss Denler probably topped him by two or three inches. He must have run off without his cap, because his hair blew about in the wind, curly and damp-looking. His jaw was square, ticking, and his hands were in fists at his side as he stormed their way.

"Where is she?" the bloke demanded.

Camden folded his arms across his chest and opened his mouth to answer.

Jeremy beat him to it. "Cass? She's inside. She—"

"Not Cass. Ara. What have you done to her?" Braxton's gaze—part angry, part panicked—barely even glanced off Jer. No, it was too busy shooting harpoons straight through Camden.

He couldn't quite decide if it was to the man's credit or not that he was so concerned for his fiancée's well-being. He ought to be, on the one hand. But on the other, if he were, he oughtn't to have dallied with another woman. Camden lifted a brow. "Concerned for her *now*, are you? It's a bit late for that, don't you think?"

"Phillip." Jeremy's censuring voice was, at least, low. "What exactly was in that note you and Mother sent to him?"

Before he could answer, had he wanted to, Braxton was upon them and made the mistake of giving Cam a shove. "You cur! Dragging an innocent into this! Only a villain would involve her!"

The shove had started it. Had gotten his blood simmering, had made his muscles snap by rote into a posture as familiar to him as breathing. Knees bent, legs coiled and ready to spring, arms loose, limber, with his fingers half curled toward his palms. Never in his life had he turned away from a fight, which meant plenty sought him out.

Still, he didn't mean to let instinct have its way. Not until the word *villain* slapped at him. Then he couldn't help but answer the strike with one of his own.

His fist was in the chap's nose before he could convince it to exercise a bit of patience.

Perhaps Braxton would have ignored the quick surge of blood and come after him, had a feminine shriek not interrupted them. It took Camden's ears a moment to process *which* female had shouted, until he saw the tall form running their way from the front door.

And Miss Denler looked fit to skewer him. "Camden! You promised!"

Braxton shifted. Subtly, but purposefully. He faced his fiancée, presenting his profile to Camden, and reached into his pocket for a handkerchief, which he pressed to his nose. "You honestly expected this monster to honor a promise not to strike me?"

"Don't be an idiot, Edmund. I didn't make him promise not to strike you." She'd reached them now, and that look of fury she'd directed at Camden five seconds earlier transferred to Braxton— and multiplied. Before the bloke's eyes could even go wide, she'd pulled back a fist of her own—with perfect form, let it be noted— and sent it into his already gushing nose. "I made him promise to let me have the first shot."

Braxton's knees buckled. Jeremy shifted, and for half a second Camden thought he meant to catch the blighter. But no, he slid to Camden's side as their guest crumpled to the ground. Gaze on Miss Denler, his brother leaned close and whispered, "I like her."

Arabelle tilted Brax's face into the light of the drawing room's lamp and probed his nose far less gently than she normally would have.

"Ow! Easy, Ara!"

"Stop blubbering." Her knuckles still stung from where they'd connected with his face, but she deemed it an acceptable price to pay.

When he tried to pull away, she stopped him with a tug on his hair. He'd probably end up with two black eyes by tomorrow. Served him right.

He scowled at her, though there wasn't much force to it. "If this is the way you nurse all the chaps—"

"Didn't I already ask you not to be an idiot?" She hadn't really met his gaze yet. It had been easier to focus on mopping the blood from his face. But she met it now, looking long and hard into the eyes that should be familiar . . . and yet weren't. She'd scarcely seen him in the last four years. And before that, he'd been nothing but Victoria's brother. Sarah's employer.

He sighed and looked away. "Did he hurt you?"

She kept on looking at his averted eyes. Not studying the bruises beginning to form. Not noting the deep, bright blue she'd memorized when he proposed so that she could try to convince herself she could get lost in them easily enough. No, all she could see was the way they darted to the door.

She knew well whom he was looking for. And it wasn't the *he* of whom he'd spoken. She straightened her spine and lifted her chin. "Why would he? I was just a pawn to get you here, Edmund, surely you know that. Surely you know I'd have socked *him* in the nose had he tried anything more."

At least he looked back at her, a hint of a smile on his lips. "You always were a scrapper when backed into a corner."

Her lips curved a bit too. She'd made quite an impression on her first visit to Middlegrove, she supposed. It had unfortunately spanned the first anniversary of her mother's death, and she'd been in a foul temper. *A powder keg*, Mrs. Braxton had called her later that day. After a spark had set her off.

The smile faded. This was more than a spark. This was her whole life's plans going up in flames. "I apologized for taking out my anger on you when I was eleven. I must confess I don't feel so inclined today."

Another shift of his eyes, but this time they simply dropped to the bloodied handkerchief still in his hands. "What did he tell you?"

"What his mother told him. That his sister is with child, and the babe is yours. Will you deny it?" She leaned back in her chair, wanting to see his body language as well as his face.

His shoulders sagged. All the answer she needed.

Her own nose ached, as if she were the one who'd just taken two fists to it. Blasted tears, threatening her again. She drew in a long breath to tame them. Something she'd practiced for the last fifteen years and perfected in the last four. No crying in the wards—that was the hospital matron's first rule, and one with which Ara heartily agreed. "I only ever asked you for three things, Edmund. Honesty, fidelity, and a family someday."

"I know." Torment clawed at his voice. Should that soothe her? Should she be glad he was clearly distressed by his own choices? He raked the curls off his forehead and forced his gaze up again. "I didn't mean for this to happen, Ara. Please know that. I never wanted to hurt you, never wanted to betray you. I didn't set out to do so. I wasn't just seeking my own pleasure, like some of the chaps do. I just . . . you've met her?"

His face changed even with that roundabout mention of her. A light in his eyes, a brightening.

Arabelle wanted to curl into a ball to ward it off. She nodded. "She's a sweet young lady."

"She's friends with the wife of one of the other officers. We met about a year ago, I suppose, but we didn't . . . I mean, I never tried . . ." He blew out a breath and lifted a hand to rub at his nose in the way he always did, only to wince away from his own fingers at the first brush. "This is blighted awkward."

She dug her fingers into her legs. "Don't think you have to spare my delicate sensibilities, Brax. I'm a nurse to an ever-rotating ward full of injured servicemen. My sensibilities have long since been numbed. Obviously you were attracted to her."

His cheeks actually flushed. "It's not the sordid details I'm trying to avoid discussing. It's that . . ."

Her heart twisted. "You fell in love with her."

He stretched forward and caught up one of her hands. "I didn't mean to do so—didn't *want* to do so. I denied it for so long, determined to be true. I suppose that's why, when it got the better of me, I forgot myself so fully."

She stared at his fingers on hers. He'd held her fingers like that when he'd proposed, when he'd slipped his grandmother's ring onto one of them. But other than that, he'd never really touched her. Never even a hand to her back to guide her into a room.

"You have a choice to make." She'd already thought out each of the words she had to say to him. Already devised the test that would determine what she did tomorrow when she got back to London. She didn't tug her fingers free, though she wanted to. Just concentrated on keeping her back straight, her chin at that strong angle, and her eyes locked on his. "You can marry me—a friend who perhaps someday you may come to love—and save Middlegrove. Or you can marry Cassandra—the woman you love, whose future you've put in jeopardy, who is having your child—and risk your home. The decision is yours."

Obviously a question he'd been mulling over since Cassandra told him the news, given his initial responses to the Camden family. But perhaps it had been shock and fear that had made him refuse their pleas then.

Because now he scarcely even blinked. Just squeezed her hand and gave her that sad, let-her-down-easy smile. "I'm sorry, Ara. I am. But I won't be any more unfair to you than I've already been. You deserve more than a husband who's given his heart to another. More than one only after your inheritance."

Her smile was no doubt every ounce as sad as his. And a few pounds more sardonic. "It isn't about me." It never was. "It's about her. As it should be at this point." She jerked her head toward the door. "Go. Tell her you mean to make her your wife. She's in the library."

First he leaned over and kissed her cheek. "I know I can't make this up to you. But if ever you need anything, don't hesitate to ask. Please."

What she needed was a family of her own. The one thing he couldn't give now. She put on her practiced smile and nodded. "I know you're a friend when I need one."

He squeezed her fingers again. And then was gone. Out the door as swiftly as the wind, in search of the girl he loved.

She gusted out a long breath.

"What exactly was *that*? I thought you said the engagement was over whether he agreed or not."

She jumped at the voice, blaming her overly loud exhale for her lack of attention. Though it could well have been her mental distraction that kept her from hearing the step of Phillip Camden as he'd entered the room and come to scowl at her.

Shouldn't he be thanking her? Perhaps such words weren't in Black Heart's vocabulary. All of a sudden the day seemed to have stretched on forever and weighed heavy on her limbs. She just wanted a quiet place. Some darkness. The leisure to cry. "We value more dearly what we choose freely, Major." She nodded toward the empty door. "I simply gave him the opportunity to *choose* Cassandra."

Camden grunted and sat in the chair his mother had occupied earlier, beside the hearth. She'd never have thought he could look so at home in a room like this. It was all soft colors and feminine touches and well-loved, well-lived-in comfort. Whereas he was all sharp angles and male arrogance and hard edges.

Yet he looked perfectly at home in his mother's chair. So comfortable that he had no qualms about narrowing his eyes at her. "And if he'd made the wrong choice?"

Her fingers wanted to dig into her legs again, but she resisted. Brax hadn't noticed such a thing, but she had a feeling Camden would. "Then he'd have found his selfishness netted him nothing."

But he'd made the right choice. It hurt *her*, but it was still the right choice. Which meant he'd netted everything.

She stood, holding herself upright by sheer will. "Excuse me. Your mother said she had a room where I could tidy up." And fall apart in peace.

7

London had seemed lovely six months ago. Of course, six months ago it had been August, the height of summer. Diellza tugged her coat tighter and pulled her hat a little lower. The snows of Switzerland had changed to a decidedly English rain during her trip, but somehow it didn't feel any warmer here than it had in Zürich.

A man jostled her from behind, but she didn't react other than to catch her balance. The last thing she wanted to do was draw any attention to herself in this particular line. Not the official's attention, and not the attention of any of the other passengers who had just disembarked with her and now stood waiting to be given entrance into the country.

Or sent away.

She told herself she had no reason to be nervous. They wouldn't find the secret compartments of her three trunks; they wouldn't realize she had anything suspicious with her.

"Next."

The couple in front of her moved onward, and the official motioned her forward. Diellza pasted on a smile and offered her passport.

He took it with the air of a man who did this exact task thousands of times a week and flipped it open. Looked at the photo. Looked at her.

Don't hold your breath. You have no reason to be nervous. She and Friede had always looked nearly identical. She'd taken care to style her hair the way her sister had done for the grainy little photograph. She'd used her kohl to paint a mole into the place where Friede had one, just above her left eyebrow. This low-grade civil servant surely wouldn't question her.

His eyes moved to the words, and he made a note in the ledger open before him. Even without really looking, her mind interpreted each line and curve that he wrote. *Friede Boschert.* He made a few more notes, but she looked away with careful disinterest.

"Purpose of your visit, Mrs. Boschert?"

She glanced back to the man again and put on a smile, at half its usual brightness. "I have come to stay awhile with my cousin in Essex. She needs help with her little ones."

"Cousin's name?"

"Marie Miller." She had no idea to whom the name really belonged, but it had been the one on the sheet of paper Alwin had told her to memorize. *A Swiss native who had married an Englishman just before the war*, the words had said. Presumably if they looked into it, they would find truth enough to appease them.

He made another note. "Length of stay?"

"A month. Just until after the new babe is settled." She offered another smile, as if the thought of squalling infants and fussy toddlers made her knees turn to pudding.

Friede has a fussy toddler and a squalling infant who now will never know their Mutter.

She blinked the thought away.

The official stamped Friede's otherwise empty passport and handed it back with a bored smile. "Have a pleasant visit, ma'am."

"Thank you." She tucked the booklet back into her handbag and stepped through even as the man called out, "Next!"

Phew. Her hands had the slightest tremor in them, but that was easy enough to hide as she clipped her way through the

crowd to where the train's baggage compartment was being un-
loaded. Her trunks were already on the platform, one of them
open as a uniformed man poked through them.

There were other men doing the same to other trunks. No
cause for alarm. Still, she would have liked to snap at him to
get his paws off her things. Instead she waited calmly until he
closed the trunk's lid and refastened it. He'd not found any of
the hidden compartments, given that he casually moved on to
the next group of luggage.

Diellza caught the eye of a scrawny-looking stevedore who
couldn't be more than fourteen and motioned him toward her
trunks.

The adolescent loped over with a hopeful-puppy smile. "Can
I help you, miss?"

"Yes, please." She handed him the slip of paper she'd already
prepared. "Could you deliver my trunks to this direction?"

"Aye."

She didn't stick around to supervise. According to the information Alwin had provided, her new boardinghouse would close its
doors for the night within the hour, and she didn't fancy being
locked out.

She knew which tube line she needed to get there and the stop
at which she should get off. Still, by the time she stepped back
into the chilly rain, darkness had crept over the city. The neigh-
borhood wasn't exactly dismal, but it wasn't exactly not. She put
up her umbrella and hurried along as fast as her pumps allowed,
searching each building she passed for the glint of tin numbers.

Finally, there it was. She hurried up the doorstep and rang
the bell, willing the landlady to answer promptly. Her shaking
now had nothing to do with nerves and everything to do with
the wet and the cold.

After an eternity—or perhaps half a minute—the door opened.
Diellza blinked at the onslaught of light and tried to make out
features rather than silhouette.

"Yes? Come in, please." The woman stepped to the side and

motioned her in. "Oh, you poor dear. You're all wet. Are you by chance Mrs. Boschert?"

Diellza shook the rain off her brolly as she lowered it and then stepped inside. Good thing she'd once practiced answering to that surname when she thought it was she who would marry Max someday. She smiled and nodded. "Mrs. Humbird?"

The woman closed the door behind her. "That's right. The telegram from your brother said I ought to expect you this evening. Are you hungry? I saved supper for you."

Diellza sagged a bit in her soggy shoes. The woman looked to be only in her forties, her hair a vibrant blond and her face scarcely lined. She was beautiful, if a bit faded. Tired-looking and thin, but not sour-faced. "Supper would be lovely."

"Your belongings?"

"I hired a stevedore to deliver them."

"Very good." Mrs. Humbird held out a hand. "Let me hang up your coat, and then I'll show you to your room. Do you mind eating in the kitchen? It's warmer there, and the dining room has been set for breakfast already."

"That will do just fine." She'd acclimated her ears again to English on the train, but it still felt a bit odd on her tongue. She knew she had a slight accent—and a German accent in England was a dangerous thing right now. But generally any discomfort was alleviated when she let it be known she was Swiss. "It was a long journey from Zürich."

"A journey I know well." The lady nodded toward the wall.

Diellza looked over and blinked at the framed photograph. The Grossmünster—one of the city's most recognized cathedrals—with a beaming Mrs. Humbird in front of it, on the arm of a handsome man who looked about her age. The mister of the Humbirds, were she to guess. Who looked decidedly British. But seeing the woman on that backdrop . . . "Are you Swiss as well?"

Mrs. Humbird laughed and hung Diellza's dripping jacket on the coat-tree. "That is how your brother found me—we've a few mutual friends, it seems. Did he not mention it?"

Her "brother" mentioned only what he thought she absolutely needed to know, apparently. But then, she hadn't been any more interested in extraneous conversation during their few hours together than he had been. Diellza shook her head. "If he did, I missed it. I do tend to ignore half of what he says."

Her hostess kept on chuckling. "A sister's prerogative. This way, dear. Only up one flight."

The woman chatted a bit about her last boarder—Penny, who had just married her sweetheart while he was home on leave and was now to live with his mum and help with the smaller children—but she didn't seem to expect any responses. Which was good, because exhaustion was setting in, and English was always harder to speak when she was tired. Though she could probably use German with her landlady if she was also from Switzerland.

More a warning than a welcome. It meant her every mumble would be understood.

"Here we are." Mrs. Humbird fitted a key into a door, swung it open, and held out the key. "I'll go over the house rules after you've eaten. Nothing one wouldn't expect. I think you'll like the other girls—you'll meet them at breakfast, I imagine."

Diellza stepped into the room. It was dark, but she turned the lights up and looked about. It reminded her a bit of the bedroom she'd once shared with Friede. A quilt on the bed that had probably been stitched by somebody's mother or grandmother, cheerful little sprigs of violets on the walls, a few shelves, a deep armoire, a wash basin and pitcher on a stand in the corner.

"Lavatory and bath are just down the hall here—you'll share with two other girls."

That was no worse than her flat in Zürich. And though no doubt one of the rules would forbid male visitors, she wouldn't have to resort to entertaining on this trip anyway, so it hardly mattered. "It is perfect. Thank you."

Mrs. Humbird gave her directions to the kitchen and then left her to tidy up. She could only do so much without her trunks, but she felt a bit better when she made her way to the cozy kitchen and quite revived after the bowl of hot soup. The stevedore arrived at the garden door while she was eating, so after her meal she could settle in in earnest.

Not having seen any of the other girls yet nor determined where, exactly, Mr. Humbird might be—away at war? Was he even alive?—she set about unpacking.

Perhaps someday, when Alwin had taken her to Germany, she'd have a maid again to do such tasks for her. That was a happy thought. Someone else could hang and fold and roll, and she could curl up before the fire with a fashion magazine while Alwin read a book. She let the image float her away for a moment before her fingers brushed against the false bottom of the trunk.

Her gaze darted to the armoire. There was nowhere in there she could hide her secrets. But she could claim she wanted to keep the biggest of the steamer trunks out of the attic to use as a table. It would fit there, against the wall.

She emptied the smaller trunks and opened *their* false walls. Took out the two metal tubes—one short, one long—from the one, the two corresponding wooden pieces from the other. Opened the bottom of the largest trunk and slid the sets into place beside the action.

For a moment she just stared at the cold metal. Her father's handiwork. His design, made especially for her. He'd made this piece himself back in her competition days, laboring with love over each scroll of metal, each coat of varnish, going over the mechanism again and again to make sure it was smooth and perfect. That with a few clicks, she could change out the barrels, the stocks, for whichever purpose she pleased.

This was the closest she'd been to him in years. She knew the lines of metal so much better than she knew the ones in his face these days.

She reached back into the hidden compartments and gathered the accessories too. The stripper clip that would feed the weapon from the top. The cleaning kit. The tools Vater had taught her to use to fix any problems she might have. Then she ran a hand over the polished wood of the rifle stock. "My old friend," she whispered in German. The one thing she'd taken with her when she left home. The one thing she couldn't bear to part with.

The one thing that her father had ever labored over for her.

She shut it into the shadows, put a few items that wouldn't fit into the armoire into the trunk itself, and scooted the trunk against the wall.

Vater might be able to disown her. But he couldn't make her unlearn all he'd taught her. No matter what he said, she was still the daughter of Switzerland's premier gun manufacturer.

And with that gun in her hands, she was still one of the best shots in Europe.

8

Whatever his failings—and Camden felt sure the man had plenty beyond the obvious—he had to admit that this Braxton blighter was positively moon-eyed over Cass. He'd watched them closely for the last two hours, while a wedding was planned in what must be record time. Jeremy promised to procure the necessary special license first thing in the morning, and they'd be married by luncheon.

"I can't believe you punched him," his mother muttered at him. "How are they to take any wedding-day photographs now?"

Cam grinned. "By my estimation, only one of the black eyes is my fault—I only hit him once. Credit for the other goes to Miss Denler."

Mother sighed. But the amusement was there, hidden under it. He could hear it. "I ought to have cautioned you both to aim for the stomach."

He darted a gaze across the room to the empty chair that had held their guest a minute ago. "Did she abandon us?"

"Hmm?" Mother followed his gaze to where Miss Denler wasn't. "Oh, I didn't see her leave. Perhaps she only stepped away for a moment. I imagine if she was retiring, she would have said something."

Perhaps. Or perhaps she'd just been ready to make her escape.

No doubt what his sister deemed festivities over dinner had grated on her every last nerve.

"Mum, what do you think?" Cass motioned their mother back to her side, though what other detail she could possibly want to confer about was beyond him.

Camden rolled his eyes and kept to his corner. A few more minutes and he'd make his own escape—he could handle only so much chatter.

"She went outside."

"What?" He turned to frown at Jeremy, who'd come up beside him. He still wore his uniform, his solid white collar the only difference between his and any other naval officer's.

"Miss Denler. I just saw her slip out into the garden." Jer jerked a head toward the corridor.

"Has it stopped raining?"

"I don't believe so."

"Are there any brollies by that door?"

"Who's to say? I didn't check the stand." Jeremy held up a hand before Camden could fire off his next question. "I didn't investigate, Phil. I just saw the door closing on her. One can hardly blame her for wanting to get away from this particular conversation though."

"My thoughts exactly."

"I had a few minutes to speak with her before dinner." Jeremy leaned a shoulder into the wall, though he kept his gaze on their sister and the man soon to be her husband. Could he rightly be called a fiancé when the engagement was but hours long? "Lovely girl. I like her. I'd half a mind to assure her that if it's a husband she wants and isn't picky about who it is, I'd take on the job."

Camden rolled his eyes. "I do realize you think you need a Mrs. Vicar when you get home for good, but perhaps you ought to know a girl more than five minutes before you propose."

"It was at least half an hour by that point." Jeremy chuckled. "Besides, any girl who's willing to talk to the infamous Black Heart about the Lord would no doubt make a perfect vicar's wife."

She probably would, at that. Though he certainly wouldn't encourage his addlebrained brother by saying so. "I daresay she's in no great hurry to jump again into a betrothal."

"Oh, I don't know. She confessed that she wants a family above all."

Camden sent him a sharp look, though Jeremy never seemed to be pierced by them. "In the two seconds you could have spoken to her, she said that?" The pup *did* always have an uncanny knack for drawing people out.

Jeremy shrugged. "We took that from her, you know. Took her future away. What she'd been planning all these years. We took her security and her dreams."

An uncomfortable wiggle came to life in Camden's chest. The one he knew far too well. The one that led him into every bit as much trouble as the spark of mischief-making he'd inherited from his mother. "Don't." It was a command for that sprout of guilt as much as for his brother. "If she's so determined to have a husband and family, I'm sure she'll find one."

Jeremy looked at him like he was stupid. "Are you aware by how many times women outnumber men just now?"

Keenly. And as long as he was considering how many women that allotted him and not the number of brothers and friends he'd lost, it was a fine proportion. He waved it away. "I'm also aware of how much her net worth exceeds that of most young ladies. She'll find another poor soul like Braxton whose estates are on the verge of bankruptcy after the war and make him a very happy man."

Blast, but his brother had a way of drilling holes through him with those soulful eyes. He ought to have grown out of the puppy-dog looks by now. Or Cam ought to have grown immune to them. "And that's what you'd wish for her? To be taken advantage of by some money-hungry gentleman who doesn't give two figs for *her*?"

Camden pushed away from the wall. "I didn't say I *wished* it."

"And I find it difficult to believe, based on what you've told me, that her father will really serve as a gatekeeper. He did, after all, consent to letting you kidnap her."

Camden winced. Perhaps that didn't speak so very highly of the man's fatherly sense. It did seem decidedly outweighed by his sense of adventure. "Miss Denler has proven herself quite capable of looking after herself."

"She's also proven herself willing to promise her future to someone who has absolutely no appreciation for her." Jer shot a glance at the moon-eyed Braxton.

Camden bit out a low curse and spun for the room's exit, making it a point to knock his shoulder into Jeremy's. "I don't much like you, you know that?"

His brother chuckled as he followed him out. "What have I done this time?"

Funny. As if he didn't know perfectly well. As if it hadn't been his whole point. "I daresay every newspaper reporter in the country would lambast you for the foolishness of saddling *me* with any responsibility for another living thing."

"Whoever said I was saddling *you* with the responsibility? I said *I* would take it on."

Camden shot his brother a look. And intercepted, just as he'd known he would, the smug little grin Jeremy didn't wipe off his face fast enough. "While you're out at sea preaching to a bunch of sailors?"

"Well." As if the thought had just occurred to him, Jeremy pursed his lips. "I suppose I might need a bit of help with it until the war is over."

Camden grunted and strode down the hallway, toward the garden door. There *was* a brolly in the umbrella stand. That meant Miss Denler hadn't taken one, as there was never more than that single one here. He snatched it out.

"Where are you going?"

"Exactly where you want me to go." He made an exaggerated bow. "Out into the miserable wet to make sure Miss Denler is well."

Jeremy clearly tried to tamp down the grin. He utterly failed, but he clearly tried. "Try not to be a complete ogre."

Hissing out another curse, Camden reached for the door.

"Phil?"

He paused, turned.

Jeremy's smile had lost the smugness. It was puppy-dog soft. "You're a good man."

A fallacy so blatant he could do nothing but snort out a scoffing laugh in reply. He gripped the handle again.

"I mean it. Don't let them win. Don't let them kill you for what you didn't do."

His fingers tightened around the cool metal until it warmed. His eyes squeezed shut. "Who says I didn't do it?"

"*I* say. I know you, Phillip. I know you'd sooner die for your men than—"

"But I didn't, did I?" He yanked the door open, welcoming the slap of wet wind in his face. "They're all dead and here I stand. The evidence speaks for itself."

Before his brother could smack him with any more undeserved encouragement, Camden stepped outside and cut him off with the slam of the door.

The silence was instant, complete, and filled with the drumming of rain. He stood there for a moment, surrounded by uninterrupted night, and wondered how a sound like rain could somehow make the silence more complete instead of less.

He raised the umbrella and cast a glance in either direction, trying to determine which way Miss Denler would have gone.

He ought to have grabbed a torch. With the windows all covered, no light spilled out from inside. And with the rain clouds blocking the moon, there was no light from the sky. But his eyes soon adjusted to the night, and he knew these garden paths better than he knew his siblings' ticklish spots. He had no trouble finding his way.

Even so, he almost didn't spot her. She sat still as statuary on the low stone wall at the garden's edge, her face turned up to receive the cold rain.

He shivered just looking at her. The rain had brought warmer air, yes, but not *warm* by any stretch of the imagination. And there she sat with only her overcoat for protection, no doubt soaked through from sitting on the sopping stones.

He ought to say something. Something about catching one's death of cold or not having sense enough to come in out of the rain or . . . or something normal. Something his mother would say. Something to draw her back inside.

But as his eyes picked out where she stopped and the night began, he knew too well the curve of her spine. The slump of her shoulders. The defeat that had her turning her face up into the icy water coming down.

He knew it from every reflection he'd seen of himself in the last three months.

His fingers went tight on the umbrella's handle. "I believe you forgot something." He stretched out the covering.

She didn't move, but for her lips. "No thank you."

Well then. He closed the brolly, leaned it against the wall, and settled himself beside her with only one wince when the cold water soaked through his trousers and accosted his flesh.

Now she turned her head, though he felt it more than he saw it. He focused his gaze on the sky, where a lighter patch of dark rested to the south. The clouds must be thinning there. Perhaps the moon would make an appearance and the rain would stop.

"You needn't leave your family for my sake."

Camden breathed a laugh. "No, but I need to for my own sanity."

She didn't question that. Maybe she even smiled a bit—hard to say in the dark, but he could well imagine that lonely dimple winking out. For a long minute she didn't say anything. Just let the rain patter on the stone between them, carrying on its own conversation.

His eyes slid closed, damp lashes sticking together. He used to dream he was a bird—a tiny bird, zipping in and out between the water that fell like bullets. Zigging and zagging and shooting at the droplets with his miniature guns until each one splashed into steam.

He used to watch the skies, waiting for the rain to clear so he could hop into his Sopwith, so he could zig and zag and shoot at the German planes and know he was saving someone on the ground—his fellow soldiers when he was still in France, civilians when he was stationed back in England as part of London's defense.

Now here he was. Probably never to take to the skies again.

"What will you do, do you think?" Her voice whispered through the raindrops, quiet and easy. "After the war?"

He blinked the water away and opened his eyes to the shadowed world. He ought to have an easy answer, he supposed. Some plan.

But how could he have a plan for that someday, when he knew it would never come? He shrugged. "Find an airplane that someone will let me fly, I suppose. Go with your father, perhaps, if he was serious."

"Father is *always* serious about his adventures. But you don't think you'll do that." She turned to face him, though he could only guess at what she could see in the night. "Why? Because you'll have to return here? I imagine this place is yours now."

He shifted on the unforgiving stone. "Technically, perhaps." But it should have been Gil's. Gil had loved it. Loved every aspect of keeping the old place up, making it flourish. When Cam was gone, it would go to Jeremy—it could be good for a vicar to have a place of his own, right? Or perhaps he'd let Cass and Braxton have it, since it seemed the fellow could lose his own estate now. He could imagine Jer making that sort of gift to them.

Another beat of silence. Another soft question. "If not here and not adventuring . . . what, then?"

He braced his hands against the smooth wet stones. Maybe it was the dark. Or the understanding in her tone. Or the sheer enormity of it all. Whatever the reason, the truth seeped out. "I imagine I'll be walking into a courtroom. And from there, I imagine it'll be a quick walk back out of it to stand in front of a brick wall."

He dreamed it more often than he didn't. Feeling the cold bricks against his back. Darkness over his eyes. A brisk voice barking out something he couldn't hear clearly through the hood. He heard his own voice, asking for the hood to be removed, insisting that he'd look his fate in the face.

Then light. Too much light. A moment of blindness, and then he could see them—the men of the firing squad. All with their rifles at the ready. All looking on him with pure hatred, fingers itching to pull the trigger at the command.

Only in his dream these weren't men randomly selected and assigned. They were *his* men. Miller and Greyson and De Were. Montagu and Lewis. The men dead because of him, ready to take their revenge.

Something warmer than the rain brushed his fingers and drew him back to now. Her fingers, making contact with his and then retreating. Perhaps the touch was accidental.

He didn't think so. Nurse Denler simply knew a hurting man when she saw one and was accustomed to giving comfort. Well, he was no invalid. He sat up straighter and drew in a breath. "How about you? Will you keep nursing after the war?"

"I hadn't planned to do so. Not before."

Of course not—she'd have planned on getting married, having babies, running an estate. *Idiot.* Why did he even ask?

But her sigh didn't exactly sound sad. Just . . . resigned. "I could, though. Or perhaps . . ." And now a brightening in her tone, like the moon trying to break through the clouds. "Perhaps *I'll* go with my father on his next expedition. Like he's been begging me to do. Why not? I have nothing holding me here now."

"He'd be pleased if you did. The two of you seem close."

A soft breath slipped out. "Now, perhaps. Honestly, I scarcely knew him until the war kept him home. He was never here more than a month at a time, once every two or three years. And his letters were lost as often as they were delivered."

Not so unlike many families now, when their fathers were off fighting. So many missing. So many dead. Except the war would end—Denler's adventures didn't seem to. And he could hear the lingering pain of that in her voice. "Who did you have, then? To look after you? Your mother?"

He felt her look at him again, no doubt wondering why he cared. He nearly snapped out that he didn't, that it was merely curiosity.

But she'd been slapped at enough for one day. He wouldn't add to it.

She wiped some of the rain from her face. "My mother, yes. Until I was ten, when she died quite suddenly. A bad case of the flu. She was perfectly well on Monday and dead on Friday."

He winced in sympathy. "And your father wasn't here?"

Her laugh carried an edge of bitterness. "We hadn't heard from him in six months at that point. And I didn't hear from him for another eighteen. I thought I'd lost him too. Lost him to the jungles while he was off searching for El Dorado or Atlantis or whatever ridiculous legend had him by the throat at the time."

Mother dead, Father missing . . . He frowned into the night. "What did you do then? There was an aunt, wasn't there?" The one who had left her all the wealth.

"Aunt Hettie, yes. Father's sister." Her chuckle was a bit lighter this time. "She wasn't so easily located either. A telegram was sent to her villa in Italy, along with letter after letter. Eventually one of her staff there thought to forward them to the abbey where she'd been staying on what she called a spiritual retreat."

Sounded like a bunch of rot to him, but that was hardly the point. He couldn't imagine being utterly without family at the age of ten. "What did you do then?"

"Threw a royal tantrum." A genuine laugh now, at her own expense. "I was sent to a boarding school, and I was none too happy about it. But until my aunt and father were located, I went home with one of my new friends from school on holiday and lashed out at the world every chance I got."

"Sounds perfectly reasonable to me."

"I thought so. Though to be honest, it got a bit tiresome, being so angry all the time. But perhaps you disagree. Perhaps you find comfort in it still." She pushed off from the wall and stood. "I think it may be time for a cup of tea and a change of—well, fiddlesticks. I didn't think this through. I *haven't* a change of clothes."

Camden's fingers had curled into fists at her casual accusation. The one cloaked in understanding and delivered so softly, so matter-of-factly. But he forced his hands to relax again and stood as well. "Your father said he would stow a bag for you in the boot of the car. It ought to be waiting in your room."

"Ah, I ought to have known. He does always say that sound planning is the backbone of spontaneity."

He turned with her, back onto the path, back toward the hulking shadow a shade darker than the surrounding night. Her story wasn't the same as his—losing her mother, lost to her father. . . . It wasn't the same as being responsible for the deaths of those entrusted to one's care.

And yet, to one's heart, it wouldn't feel so different. Empty was empty. Angry was angry.

There was comfort in it. In clinging to the only thing one could trust—one's own raging bitterness. The one thing in the world guaranteed not to leave without warning, whose promises to hold one close could be counted on.

He picked up the abandoned umbrella and let his fingers clamp down too tightly around it. "Your circumstances obviously changed." It came out as an accusation, though he hadn't meant it to. "Your aunt was found. And your father." His men, though, would never come back.

"Eventually. Though I saw neither of them until I was fourteen, and four years is an eternity to a child. I'd grown exhausted with the weight of my anger long before then." She took a few steps, though they seemed a bit uncertain on the dark path.

He found her arm, lifted her hand, and tucked it around his elbow.

Her fingers pressed, eased up again. A silent thanks. "Do you know what I came to realize?"

"Let me guess. That God is kind, despite all evidence to the contrary. That He loves us, though He has a lousy way of showing it. That—"

"No," she said on a laugh. "Or rather, yes, but before I was willing to hear that, I had to come to a more basic realization."

"My brother would say there's nothing more basic than believing in God's love."

"While he has a point, that's a bit like telling a starving child there's nothing more basic than bread, isn't it? Such knowledge does him very little good when he cannot feel its effects in his own stomach."

He didn't dare to agree. All too well he knew that agreeing on any point would make way for the next one. And he'd had this conversation too many times already. It had been drilled into him all his life. It had never mattered to him when he was a lad. It was just something to try to push guilt upon him—that's what he'd thought until The Incident.

And now . . . no one knew. No one knew how heavy that weight of guilt was. How crippling. They could say all they wanted that God was love. Camden wasn't even sure that kind of love existed.

Not that her type, his brother's type, ever needed encouragement to go on. "What I came to realize, Major Camden, is that we cannot defeat circumstances with circumstances. When an unforeseen event has crushed us, another cannot make it better. Finding my father would not solve my problem. It wouldn't bring my mother back. It wouldn't heal me of the pain of losing her. *Nothing* would."

No. Nothing did.

"But that didn't mean pain needed to rule me. I could decide to be better *despite* my circumstances. Now, the *how* . . . I did need God for that. So I won't bore you with the details, as you clearly don't want to hear them yet."

He sighed. "My brother's right. You *would* make a fine vicar's wife. He has an opening by his side, if you want to apply for the position. He's amenable."

Her laughter now carried none of the shadows her voice had before. Though to his ear, it wasn't a laugh of delight—just of amusement. "Oh heavens. He's a sweet lad, isn't he? But he seems so very *young*. How can a chaplain active in the navy in a time of war still be so very young?"

A question he'd asked himself endlessly. "A special talent of his, I suppose. Though I imagine the two of you are the same age, give or take."

"Well. I won't be insisting upon a double wedding tomorrow, even so. But it's sweet of him to say such things."

Good to know she had sense enough not to jump into a new relationship just because another was taken from her.

Even so, Jer was right. She would be the prey of every money-hungry gentleman left in England, and her father didn't seem the type to fend them off on her behalf.

Heaven knew *he*, though, could scare any upstanding chap by his mere presence these days. And it would be simple enough to keep a watch over her. Within a few seconds, he had what he deemed a sound plan. A few questions to Brook Stafford would fill in what blanks remained, and Denler had issued him an open invitation to drop by their house in Westminster anyway.

This guilt, at least, he could assuage.

9

The man's flesh was covered, nearly every inch of it, in ghastly blisters. It was one of the worst cases Arabelle had seen since mustard gas was introduced last summer, and she'd shooed Sue and Eliza away when they offered to help. There was precious little they could do for . . . Private French, she saw when she checked the paper clipped to the end of his bed. Aside from administer drugs and ointment to dull the pain until his poisoned skin could heal.

Up until now he'd been unconscious, first from the pain and then from the opiates. But he was coming to now, and with thrashing limbs and screams. Ara slid into the chair at his side and grabbed one of his hands. "Hush now, Private. It's all right. You're in hospital, in London, and we'll have you patched up and well again in no time."

Eight weeks, at the least. Perhaps more, as his case was so acute. But she smiled down into his fevered eyes when he opened them on her.

"Gassed," he panted. "I was gassed."

"I know. But it won't kill you. Your mask did its job." He hadn't breathed it in—if he had, he'd have suffocated on the battlefield as the toxins bound with the water in his lungs and drowned him.

Still, mustard gas had another trick up its sleeve. Even when the box respirators protected one's lungs, it saturated the soldiers' clothing and burned their flesh, trapped there by the wool until they could discard their infected uniform.

Poor Private French had been knocked unconscious by a grenade during the gassing and had been passed over as dead. By the time he'd come to and crawled back to safety, he'd been left too long in his saturated uniform—his very clothing now an enemy.

She squeezed his hand—one of the few unblistered places on his body, along with his feet and face—and reached for the pot of salve she'd brought over. "I'm going to spread some of this on your blisters, all right? It should soothe you a bit. Are you hungry?"

"Gassed." His eyes were hazy. From the fever, perhaps, as his body tried to fight against the poison invading his skin. Or perhaps from the horror. The panic it induced was, so far as Arabelle had seen, even more dangerous than the toxins themselves.

She forced a smile that he wouldn't see. But perhaps he'd hear it, if it could penetrate the fog. "I know. And I know right now the pain is nearly unbearable. But you lived, soldier, and you'll keep on living."

His head lolled her way, and he blinked at her, his eyes clearing for a second before hazing again. "Sarah?"

She kept the smile in place, her thoughts winging to her own Sarah, with whom she hadn't got to visit. When would she get another chance? Her friend had so little free time. And Ara didn't exactly fancy a visit to Middlegrove now. "My name is Nurse Denler. But if you'd like to write to your Sarah, we can transcribe a letter for you."

His eyes slid shut, pure misery digging lines into his face.

Arabelle held his hand in both of hers and closed her own eyes. She murmured a prayer for him, just loud enough that he'd be able to hear it.

After her amen she got to work with the salve, spreading it as gently as she could over every inch of the damaged skin on his front. They would have to let it dry, turn him over, and give the same treatment to his back.

"Nurse. Water?"

She closed the jar of ointment, whispered a farewell to the blistered soldier, and turned to another of the cots against the wall opposite. The poor chap propped up against his pillow had fresh bandages where his arms used to be. He'd been here several weeks already. The physical pain was becoming less . . . but she knew that only meant the emotional would come to the fore. How was a man who'd worked in a factory from the time he was ten to make a living without either of his arms?

Her job just now, however, was not to wonder. Her job was to smile, pour him a glass of water, and lift it to his lips in a way that made it clear it was a joy to assist him. "There we are, Sergeant. May I get you anything else?"

His head fell back again. "I'm ready to write a letter home. Will you take it down for me?"

It was a task she usually handed to one of the volunteers who hadn't been extensively trained. But she didn't see any of them about, and her shift was over anyway, so she might as well spend her time doing one last kind deed for someone, rather than hurrying into the nurses' little break room and looking out the window.

No, she wouldn't be doing that anymore. Not because she would find the brooding figure of Black Heart any less compelling now that she'd spent two days in his company.

No. Because now she knew he wasn't just handsome, wasn't just in pain. He was a man who adored his family. A man who sat with a girl in the rain, putting aside his umbrella to share the cold with her.

Dangerous, that's what he was. And not because of whatever had killed his squadron.

The sergeant's letter was, unfortunately, short and to the point. A few factual sentences informing his wife that he'd lost both arms, was recuperating in London, and that she was to prepare the children for the disfigurement because he expected to be released in the next several weeks.

No words of warmth. Of hope or fear. He couldn't let that loose just yet, she suspected. It was a tenor carefully held, vibrating, in his voice, and if he were to unleash it . . . Emotion could be a geyser. She'd seen it so often.

And oh how well she knew it.

She folded the bare facts of the sergeant's future into an envelope and took down the direction he dictated to her. "I'll get this into the post for you."

A nod was his thanks, and his eyes slammed shut.

Arabelle couldn't hold back a sigh as she slipped from the ward. This war was destroying her entire generation. Those it hadn't wiped out entirely it was trying to take apart piece by piece. And what could she do? Try to stitch the physical gashes back together, but that was only a stopgap.

Father, show me. Day by day, week by week, and in the years to come. Show me how to help each one.

"Ara! What's taking you so long? You're going to miss him!"

Arabelle slid the sergeant's letter into a stack of other soldiers' mail and barely spared a glance for Susan. She wasn't about to say what she happened to know—that Phillip Camden wouldn't be walking home from Whitehall today anyway, because he'd not gone in on this Tuesday morning. Rather, he'd be on the night shift tonight. *"Well, I suppose I won't miss my night shift after all,"* he'd said on their way back to London yesterday.

She'd asked him why in the world he had a night shift at the Admiralty, but he hadn't answered her.

None of her business. None of her concern. And certainly not something she wanted to bring up with her friends here. She opted for what she hoped looked like a harried smile. "I need to hurry out, Sue. I have—"

"Oh, bah. You already spent the entirety of your lunch break holed up with your solicitor in Nurse Wilcox's office." Susan wrinkled her nose at the very mention of the matron. "You need a *bit* of fun in your day."

"And to tell us about the duchess's dinner party." Eliza bustled toward them with bright eyes. "Smashing, I assume. What does it look like? Their house, I mean. Nothing compared to their country estate—I've seen photographs of Ralin Castle. But from what I hear, the house in Grosvenor Square is—"

"It was lovely." Ara gave the two girls the same smile she gave the men in the wards. Bright but practiced.

Eliza let out a dreamy breath. "Were there any handsome men there? Officers, perhaps?"

"As if she'd have paid attention." Susan laughed. "Even if there were, she probably would have made a point of flashing her ring at them to make it clear she's—Ara? Where's your ring?"

Fiddlesticks. Couldn't she have held it close for at least a day? If it wouldn't have been utterly pointless, she would have tucked the bare-fingered hand into her apron pocket. She sighed and tried not to recall the look on Brax's face when Camden had fished the mockery out of his pocket over that dreadful dinner and slid it across to him. Edmund had at least had the grace not to slide it immediately onto Cassandra's finger.

But he would. The jewel would join the plain gold band he'd provided for the ceremony. Probably rested there now.

Her throat felt tight and dry. "Well, I . . . I went to Portsmouth on Sunday. Brax and I have decided to call it off."

"No!" Eliza's eyes went wide with horror. "But *why*? He's so handsome!"

"That is hardly reason enough to marry someone." It came out a bit more peevish-sounding than she intended. And perhaps a bit snappish. Ara squeezed her eyes shut, sucked in a calming breath, and muttered, "My apologies. But if you'll excuse me, I'm still a bit unsettled by it all, and I'd like to go home."

"Oh, poor Ara." Susan slid an arm around her shoulders.

She ought to have kept her eyes shut a moment more. Then she wouldn't have seen the look of pity that Susan and Eliza exchanged. *Poor Ara* indeed. No doubt they were thinking that now the plain, gangly, not-getting-any-younger Arabelle would never find a man.

No doubt they were right. And she wouldn't blubber about it.

Life could be meaningful and fulfilling without a husband, after all. She could travel. Be with her father. Fill her empty, aching arms with orphans, perhaps.

"Girls!" Another pretty young volunteer came flying down the corridor. Ara couldn't readily remember her name—she was new, fresh-faced, and already fast friends with Susan and Eliza, given the way she darted toward them. "He's coming in. *In!* As in, in *here*. I just saw him turn in at the door!"

"What?" Eliza's voice emerged as a squeak.

Arabelle's stomach went tight. She didn't have to ask who *he* was. "Perhaps he's visiting a friend."

It must have sounded reasonable to the others. They visibly calmed, took a few deep breaths, fluttered their hands only a little. But somehow, Arabelle couldn't believe herself so easily. He hadn't mentioned having any friends in hospital, and there had been plenty of time to do so during the ice-cold drive back to London yesterday.

But why else would he be coming in here?

She was tempted to ask the upstairs volunteer which door he'd come in, so she could hurry toward the other. A mere twenty-four hours since they parted company wasn't quite enough for her to feel entirely steady again.

But she'd been trained to face worse than a bit of weakness in the knees. She lifted her brows at the trio of girls. "Well, don't just stand there like a flock of hens, ladies. Back to work. Impress him with your industry and caring natures, if impress him you mean to do."

Her smile went genuinely amused when they scattered like the very hens she'd called them. She half expected to see feathers fluttering in their wake. For her own part, she hurried to grab her cape, gloves, and handbag so she could make her getaway.

She wasn't fast enough. The moment she exited the coatroom, he entered the corridor from the stairs, and his gaze latched onto her.

Fiddlesticks. Any thought that he couldn't possibly be here to see her flew out the window as he stalked directly to her.

Well. If she wanted her friends to forget about her newly broken engagement and all thoughts of *Poor Ara*, he was certainly helping. She caught a few squeaks of surprise from the ward door he swept past.

Arabelle went right on tugging her gloves into place and met him with a lifted brow. "Major Camden. This is a surprise."

"What in blazes have you done?"

Not the greeting she'd expected. Especially since he didn't say *in blazes*. She kept her brows hiked. "Let the matron hear you talking so in here, and she'll give you injury enough to require you to become a patient."

He stopped a scant foot away from her and glowered down the two inches he had on her. "I just got the most interesting telegram from my sister. Seems a miraculous gift was anonymously delivered to her new husband."

Already? For being altogether against her plan, Mr. Weatherby, her trustee and solicitor, certainly hadn't wasted any time in carrying it out. She pinned her hat into place. "Oh? Whatever has that to do with me?"

He folded his arms over his chest. "No one else even knows they've married yet. Much less has the means to make such a gift."

Well, she hadn't considered his first point. She ought to have cautioned Mr. Weatherby to wait until the announcement had appeared in a newspaper. "It seems someone does."

"Ara."

He might as well have touched her with a live wire. She started, her glance flying past him to the faces peeking at them. And the ears no doubt hearing every word they said. "When did I give you permission to use my first name, much less a nickname?"

He smirked at her. And gracious, but it was far too handsome a smirk. "You can call me Phillip, if you like. Turnabout."

"I'll turn about, all right." She pivoted in proof, making it a whole two steps before he was at her side, taking her hand and looping it around his elbow to rest on his arm. Sunday night, in the dark of the rain-soaked garden, it had simply been polite, to keep her from stumbling. Now it was absolutely infuriating, especially when he held her fingers there. Keeping her voice low, she hissed, "What are you doing?"

"Giving your friends something to talk about. Ought to distract them from a broken engagement, don't you think?"

As if anyone would believe she was actually involved with him. Or rather, that *he* had any interest in being involved with *her*.

She angled her own smirk up at him. "If you're going to call me Ara, then a simple Phillip won't do, will it? What was it your mother called you?" As if she could have forgotten, as unfitting as it had seemed. "Oh, I know. Philly."

That wiped the grin from his face. And lit a spark of challenge in his eyes. "Try it, darling, and I'll give you a big sloppy kiss here and now to really set tongues to wagging."

Pity or punishment? Either way. "My, you do know how to set a girl's heart aflutter."

"I certainly do. Though you don't strike me as the type who cares for fluttering."

As if it mattered. "Not particularly, no. I'm more the type for nobility and faith."

His face screwed up. "Do you ever have *any* fun?"

"Loads of it. Just not the sort that lands me in trouble."

They'd reached the stairwell, and he led her down with an amusingly exaggerated blink. "We seem to have differing definitions of *fun*."

A laugh filled her throat. She couldn't help it. "And whose has worked better in the long run?"

Rather than granting her point, he let silence fall until they reached the first landing and then leveled that accusing look on her again. "Back to my initial question, if you please. Why the devil did you give them your money?"

Again, her every muscle twitched. Never in her life had anyone simply *talked* about such matters so openly, outside of a solicitor's office. It wasn't done, not among polite society. And, despite all evidence to the contrary, he *had* been born to polite society, though she might not have believed it had she not met his mother and seen his home. "This is really none of your concern."

"It's Cass."

And that was all the rebuttal he needed for that one. She sighed. "Your devotion to your sister is admirable—"

"I don't care about admiration."

"Clearly." Which made it all the more admirable. "But what I choose to do with my legacy is up to me and me alone."

The arm under her fingers went taut. "He betrayed you, and you rewarded him."

"No. He made the right decision, and I obeyed the prompting of the Lord." If only she could have said it without that hint of a tremor in her voice. He wouldn't miss it. She knew he wouldn't.

And he didn't, as evidenced by his snort. "Your God asks you to give your legacy to a faithless prig? Then I think I've been right all this time to avoid Him."

He couldn't really think Brax was faithless—if he did, he never would have let him marry Cass. But that was hardly the point. She sighed. "Avoid Him as you may, I daresay even you have heard the story in the Gospels of the rich young ruler and how difficult it is for a rich man to enter the kingdom of God."

"Always found it absurd. If everyone goes about giving away all they have—"

"He does not ask everyone to give all they have. But if He does, are we willing? Truly willing?" She shook her head. "Whatever He asks of us, whether it be a fortune or a pittance or our time or our devotion, we can be sure it will be painful. Cutting out what stands between us and God always is. But we can also trust that in the giving, we'll gain something far more precious."

Only their footsteps on the cold block of the stairs whispered against the silence. "So this is just about you not wanting to be a camel trying to squeeze through the eye of a needle?" Clearly he *did* know the story. No doubt he knew all of them, as surely as his brother did.

They reached the next landing, and she dragged in a breath that tasted of sorrow. "The money was not the difficult thing, Major Camden. I don't hold it so tightly that losing some causes me any pain."

He didn't glance down at her. But his movements were stiff. "You must resent me, then. It's your dream of a family you didn't want to relinquish, and I forced the issue. Ought I to beg your forgiveness?"

"Would you?" She narrowed her eyes, let a smile play at her lips. "I'm trying to picture it. I'd expect you to fall to your knees. Hands clasped in penance before you. Perhaps a tear or two glistening in the corners of your eyes to really convince me of your—"

His laugh cut her off, and the look he sent her . . . It was knowing. Amused. Granted the absurdity of the picture she painted and applauded her for the painting. It was the look of a friend.

But his words resonated, despite her jest. It *was* her dream that the Lord had asked for. The thing it had hurt to hand over. She felt as though she stood bare now before Him, bereft. A woman in mourning.

There would be no home. No husband. No children. There would be no friend ready to share a cup of tea. No sister whose letters would warm her on cool winter days. Every single vision she'd clung to in these awful years, stripped away.

The blast of cold, damp air jerked her back to bleak reality as he led her outside. She drew up short. "Thank you for your very thoughtful tending of my reputation, Major. But I imagine this is where we part ways."

He merely turned, her hand still on his arm, toward the Strand.

She tried to pull against him, but he was holding her hand in place again. "Haven't you a night shift at Whitehall?"

"Not until eight."

Oh. It was likely, then, that reaching his own flat required a trip on the tube—perhaps he meant to walk this way to the nearest station. After all, this was the direction in which they usually saw him walking. "Ah. In what section of the city do you live?"

He shot her a glance. "Why? Planning to pay me a visit?" The glance turned to a wink and the impish grin that made her friends swoon. "That would certainly affect your reputation, darling, but I'm not certain you'd like the results."

She willed herself not to blush. And thanked the Lord that after four years of nursing men in every possible state, she'd learned to control it. "You know very well I was merely trying to determine if we're heading in the same direction."

"We are."

If he was going to poke fun at her with this taciturn response to her every action, she might as well poke back a bit. "You do realize, I hope, that *your* reputation is going to suffer rather terribly if the press sees you with the likes of me. A plain, boring nurse rather than an actress or musician or—"

"Blast." He came to a sudden halt, gaze locked on nothing as thoughts whirred all but visibly through his eyes. "The reporters. I hadn't thought of that."

She stiffened. She couldn't help it. She'd thought she was merely joking, deprecating herself along with him. She'd thought him not that superficial. Maybe she'd been wrong. "Are you serious? You actually care whether people think your skills as a charmer are suffering because you're out with a girl who isn't beautiful?" Her spine snapped straight, and she pulled her hand from his arm. "Well, rest assured, Major—I'm certain they'll only think you're suffering my company because of my money." She strode onward, jaw set.

"Don't be an idiot, Ara. It's beneath you." Unfazed by her temper, he matched his stride to hers. "It's what they'll say about *you* that concerns me. Do you really want to be branded as Black Heart's next victim?"

"I hardly care." But she sidled away when he reached for her arm. And made a show of looking over her shoulder. "Besides, I don't see any flash-lamps."

He pursed his lips.

She furrowed her brows. Clearly, the threat of lurking reporters worried him. But clearly it wouldn't if this short promenade were the extent of their interaction. "Camden? What are you up to now?"

He didn't answer. Just shoved his hands into his pockets and kept pace beside her.

"Camden."

"I don't think you really have cause to worry." The way his gaze drilled through the other pedestrians made it clear his mind was turning.

"Why would I be worried about sharing one five-minute walk?"

He sliced a look over at her as though she were a complete idiot.

A shake of her head did nothing to clear it of the only reason that presented itself, outlandish as it seemed. "You don't mean— why would you make a habit of walking with me?"

His mouth tightened, and his gaze drilled ahead of them again.

Quite a gaze it was too. Oncoming passersby went out of their way to steer clear of him, a few going so far as to step off the curb into a puddle to give him ample room. It would have been comical had it not been confounding.

"Well, I'm no slouch when it comes to brains." Making a point of brightening her own countenance to counteract the storm on his, she tucked her gloved hands in her pockets for a bit more warmth. "I can solve this puzzle. Why would Phillip Camden decide he has to walk frequently with someone he only just met a few days before? Well, that's fairly obvious. My sparkling personality has convinced you that I'm just the sort of person you need for a friend and—"

"I'm not interested in making friends." He didn't just say it—

he *shot* it. Like each word was a bullet spewing from the barrel of his mouth.

A blanket statement, then, not one aimed at her.

Of course he would feel that way. She'd learned enough about men in combat to know that those in one's squadron were one's friends, brothers, world. And his were all gone. It would still be too fresh for him to see that that was when one needed friends *most*.

"All right. You're not seeking a friendship. And you certainly didn't fall in love with my breathtaking face during our travels, so that leaves . . ." His words from the stairwell echoed between her ears. *"You must resent me. . . . Ought I to beg your forgiveness?"* She sighed. "Guilt."

Camden rolled his shoulders. "I don't believe in guilt."

"Funny. You sound awfully heavy with it." She rolled her eyes at his grunt. The tube station was just ahead, its sign promising freedom from this conversation, surely. He would go his way, into the station. She would continue her walk home. "You know, if you feel a pang of conscience for being an agent in the end of my dreams, we can settle this quickly. Say you're sorry if it will help. I'll give you my official forgiveness, and onward we go."

"I don't apologize."

Now *that* she believed.

"And I'm not interested in forgiveness."

When a gust of wind tossed spikes of cold mist into her face, she turned her face downward. "You seem to define yourself quite a lot by what you are *not*."

"And you're far too quick to let people define you by what you *have*. You've made a target of yourself."

"I beg your pardon?" Her feet planted themselves firmly by a bus stop where buses hadn't stopped for two years. "How exactly have I done that?"

He spun to face her, blue eyes shooting shards of ice. "Letting yourself be branded nothing but an heiress, defined by nothing but your inheritance."

Nothing but? She would have argued, if she could get out anything beyond a furious sputter. All her years of training, of nursing, and he dared to call her *nothing but an heiress*?

"Now you don't have the protection of an engagement, so every ravenous wolf of a gentleman in need of a cash influx is going to be knocking at your door, ready to offer his hand to the desperate spinster who was just rejected."

She stepped back, knocked breathless for one moment. Blasted by the cold, by the ugliness of the words, by the fear of them and the untruth of them and the hideous *truth* of them and not sure where one stopped and the other began. She made to step around him.

He took her by the arm as she moved past and somehow swung her around in such a way that they ended up in the mouth of an alley, out of the way of the crowds of people still streaming past. "Perhaps it wouldn't be so bad if you hadn't already entered into one engagement for purely monetary reasons."

"My reasons were *not*—"

"But *his* were, and everybody knows it. Which means they all think you're willing to make such an arrangement."

Her nostrils flared. "Well, they'd be in for a surprise."

He tilted his head. "So they take a different tack and instead pretend to fall in love with you, woo you. Trust me, Ara, there are scores of men willing to do so. I know them."

Pretend. They would *pretend* to fall in love with her. All anyone could possibly do.

Her eyes burned. And as she'd done on Sunday, she opted for the safer outlet. Anger. "And what if they do? It's no business of yours."

He straightened. "I'm making it my business. You did right by my sister, so I'm doing right by you. I'll not see you throw your life and your fortune away on some money-grubbing scoundrel. I may not be good for much these days, but I can at least scare off the rabble."

Unbelievable. "The papers have something right, anyway—

you are a madman. A raving lunatic." She moved to step past him, back onto the street.

He blocked her. "You'll not dissuade me, Arabelle. I've made up my mind, so just resign yourself to an escort."

"I don't need a . . . a *guard dog*!" She moved to sidestep him in the other direction and, as soon as he shifted to compensate, darted around him on the first.

He was at her side within a step. "Woof."

It was anger simmering. It had to be. She couldn't let it be amusement, couldn't let it be gratitude, and *certainly* couldn't let it be hope. "Go home, Camden."

"No."

"I don't want your company."

"Too bad."

"I'll have my father—"

"I've already spoken to your father. He thinks it capital of me to want to champion you. And has issued a standing invitation for me to come by in the evenings and chat about aviation and the possible applications of the field to his own."

He *would*. She gritted her teeth, picked up her pace, and angled her face up at Camden, ready to lambast him with the only truth that might get him to call off this ridiculous plan.

You'll do me more harm than good.

The words died before she gave them breath. Because when she looked up, he was looking down, and those too-blue eyes of his weren't just cold. They weren't just patronizing. They weren't just determined.

They were the very thing he'd called her—desperate.

"I may not be good for much these days. . . ." He'd been stripped of his squadron, his brothers-in-arms, his purpose. He'd been told he was a villain.

He needed to help. Someone, somehow. He needed to prove, if only in some small way, that he was worthwhile.

But couldn't Cass be his proof, or Jeremy, or his mother, or some other person he actually knew? Why did it fall to *her*?

He needs to help. This time it wasn't just a thought. It was an echo in that place in her heart where the Lord whispered.

She faced forward again. *Lord God . . . this is a bad idea.* She wasn't weak, not like Camden had said she was.

But she wasn't strong either. Not when it came to him.

10

This was a bad idea—and next time he saw his manipulator of a brother, he was going to tell him so. Hunched against the drizzle of the evening, Camden hurried across the parade grounds, trying to rid his mind of the many expressions he'd witnessed—and evoked—on Arabelle Denler's face that afternoon.

The anger he understood. That was a basic defense, one of which he'd grown particularly fond over the last three months. Anger was simple. Anger was easy. He could deflect hers without any fear of real damage to either of them.

It was her blighted *goodness* that baffled him. How the deuce could anyone really be so selfless and generous as to hand over what must have been a goodly chunk of her inheritance to a perfect stranger and a man who betrayed her?

That sort of generosity had no place in a world set on stripping one of all that mattered.

The Admiralty's Old Building loomed, a welcoming shadow in the night. Camden picked up his pace, the promise of warmth making the wet wind bite down all the harder. Arabelle Denler was . . . all sorts of impossible things. Too generous. Too good. Too innocent. The sort capable of grinning away her flaws or shortcomings, joking about her lack, and hurtling onward down whatever path she deemed right without any thought to how it might hurt *her*.

A particularly nasty gust of wind tore down the street, inspiring him to mutter a curse and run the last few yards to the door. Jeremy was probably way off. Camden wasn't the one to guard her, to protect her. The press hadn't really been hounding him all that much in recent weeks, so if he could just keep his head down, they probably wouldn't bother her. But even if her reputation survived a brief link to him, all that goodness, that innocence, that light . . . Black Heart ought to stay far away from it.

But he'd made a promise, and he meant to keep it.

No, it was worse than that. He pushed through the OB's doors, past the security guards who nodded a greeting to his familiar face, and into the hushed, sleepy interior. Despite all good sense and all claims to the contrary, he *liked* Miss Denler. She had spunk. Grit.

And a strange brightness to her spirit that contrasted so sharply with his. Being in her company this afternoon had been a bit like walking into warm, lit halls after a night out in the rain. She made him infinitely aware of all he lacked. And more than a little aware of how all that he *was* gnawed at him.

He jogged up the steps, determined to shake off thoughts of his new charge. Never mind that she was sure to cause him all manner of trouble. Never mind that she'd likely have him breaking his rule of *no more friends* within the week if she kept up her absurd combination of fiery spirit and ridiculous goodness. Never mind that the thought of England's money-hungry gents trying to take advantage of her already gave him a headache.

He had to shift his mind to the task at hand: work.

The first time he'd served a night shift, he'd hated it—too quiet, too strange, too *wrong* for a building that was usually bustling. But he'd grown accustomed to it over the past three months. Accustomed to being the only one in olive green amid a sea of naval blue. Accustomed to sinking down every day into a hard wooden chair behind a scarred wooden desk when he ought to have been buckling into the pilot's seat of his Sopwith, ready to defend London against Gothas and Giants and zeppelins and whatever other airborne monsters the huns might send their way.

He'd grown accustomed to it. But he didn't *belong* here. He plunged a hand into his pocket, tracing the outline of the brass wings.

The mist must have turned to genuine rain—it tapped at the window he hurried past. It meant there weren't likely to be any raids tonight anyway. And made him glad to be inside, dry and still warm from the coffee he'd recently been sipping in the posh library of the Denler townhome. *"From Colombia,"* Denler had said as he handed over a steaming cup. *"Best in the world, you know. I had the locals teach me how to roast the beans myself."*

He'd never been a coffee man before, but as Denler rambled happily on about the difference between freshly roasted quality beans and the burnt and molding rubbish that was often imported by the shipload, he had to admit the black liquid in his cup could make a believer out of him.

Better still, it had chased away the dregs of fatigue. He pushed into the familiar confines of Room 40 and nodded a greeting to the other cryptographers already there. De Wilde, Culbreth. He'd beaten de Grey in.

Culbreth frowned at him. "I thought DID gave you the week off." No doubt he wished he'd taken it too. It was no secret that Camden wasn't well liked here. No doubt because he'd made every attempt to keep it that way. He'd already been transferred from another night shift team to this one, as De Wilde was the only one in the intelligence hub who actually seemed to *like* him. No doubt solely because of her relationship with Drake Elton, who'd been a friend too long to turn on him now.

"What can I say? I missed you." He sent an exaggerated bat of his lashes to the blond man, who rewarded him with a roll of the eye. But he offered no other explanation for his presence.

Culbreth didn't ask for any clarification either. Though no

older than Camden, he was a serious man. Rarely smiling, always seeming deep in his own thoughts. Based on the way the others cajoled him and exchanged glances when he failed to laugh, though, he hadn't *always* been that way.

Camden never asked for any explanations. He enjoyed taunting Jeremy by saying he didn't believe in heaven or hell. But he did. Especially hell. Its name was War, and it existed right here on earth. And when the demons of hell roamed freely, even men who never saw direct action, like the codebreakers he now served with, experienced their horrors in one way or another.

He scraped the legs of his chair against the floor as he pulled it out, unbuttoning his overcoat even as he sat. He ought to hang it up so it could dry, but his eyes had already gone to the stack of papers on his desk. He settled for shrugging out of the thick wool and letting it drape over the back of his chair.

The admiral had known he'd be in tonight—Camden had sent a note round first thing this morning—otherwise the stack no doubt would have been left on someone *else's* desk. But Cam was glad he'd left it for him. He recognized the opening code, telling the admiral what and from whom it was, from a packet he'd decrypted from the same agent last week.

Mason, in Mexico. The author-turned-marine-turned-intelligence agent had been tasked with locating and destroying a new radio technology that the Germans had installed across the pond. No one had explained to Cam what it was, exactly, but he knew enough to realize that keeping the huns from getting it operational was crucial. If they got these Audion valves working, then they would no longer have to use the system that allowed England to intercept their every message. Which meant these cryptographers would no longer deliver decrypts to the Admiralty, and they'd no longer have the edge in the intelligence game.

No, the valves, whatever they were, had to be destroyed. And not just because Camden would again be out of a job if they failed. It could turn the tide of the war, and the tide was only just beginning to favor them.

He drew out a pencil, paper, and codebook, and flipped over the cover sheet to reveal the first page of code.

"How was your trip to Portsmouth?"

Camden paused with his pencil raised and arched a brow at De Wilde. Since when did she, of all people, care for small talk?

Since she wanted him to know she'd discovered his whereabouts, apparently. She wore a bit of a smirk in the corners of her mouth to set off the red sweater she was scarcely ever without.

She never could stand a puzzle to be unsolved.

Camden wasn't about to let it get to him. "Successful."

"Visiting family, weren't you? That's what DID said." Culbreth didn't bother glancing over as he spoke, just kept scratching away at his own decrypts. "I hope they're all well."

So polite, that one. "Just ducky."

"Did you . . ." De Wilde's words trailed off into a sniff. Then another. She stood, took a step closer to him, and sniffed again. "Coffee. I smell coffee on you. Where have you been? Where did you get it?"

He'd never seen that particular light in her eyes. "Easy, De Wilde. Were you anyone else I'd offer to kiss you to give you a taste, but Elton might shoot me for that kindness. I didn't even realize you liked coffee."

"It smells like home." Her eyes slid shut, and she drew in a deep, lingering breath now. "There was a little café down the street from our house in Louvain." Her eyes opened again and narrowed into a frown. "Where did you find it? Lukas would love a pound of coffee for his birthday."

"Supplying your brother's birthday wishes is hardly my priority." He made a point of turning back to his desk.

He could ask Denler, though, if he knew where Cam could find a pound. Not imply it must come from his own stash, of course. But he might know someone else who had some available for purchase. The price was likely to be astronomical, but no need to worry with cost until he knew if it was even possible.

Footsteps sounded in the corridor, and a moment later de Grey bustled in, whipping off his wet coat. "The skies let loose as I was coming in. Frightful night." He paused. Glowered. "Oh. *You're* back."

His tone wasn't quite as hostile as it used to be. Camden would have to debate whether that was a good or bad thing at some point. "Only to torment you, de Grey." He pulled the stack of papers into a better position.

"Rain means a quiet night, so I for one am grateful for it," Culbreth muttered. He glanced at the clock on the wall. "We've still a few hours before the new codes come in. We had better clear out the day's backlog beforehand."

Fine by him. Camden got to it, moving his eyes from codebook to message and back again, scratching the decrypt onto the fresh paper as he went. He wasn't as fast as the others yet—came of having been at it only three months rather than three years—but he did a fair enough job. Otherwise Hall would have sent him back to prison. He'd said as much the day he brought him here.

"Do the job well, and you'll serve out the war here. Fail, and I'll hand you back to the army and the firing squad awaiting you."

Cam had snarled something like "Why wait for me to fail? Send me back now" in response. But that was when he could still see the fireball every time he closed his eyes. When he could still hear the screams of his men over the whine of his engine, over the stalling coughs of theirs. When he wanted nothing more than to join them.

He gripped his pencil and focused on the words he was scrawling onto the page.

Back in Mexico City and following leads for purchase of remaining Audion valves in country through intermediaries. Seeking trustworthy Mexican men to infiltrate Iztapalapa facility, which is guarded round the clock. Proving a challenge. They are distrustful of what they term a "gringo." My hired translator is dependable, I believe, but he is unknown to them, too, being of a more educated class.

Camden's lips tugged up a bit as he continued his decrypt.

Were Drake Elton not already being put to use in Spain, he'd recommend Hall send him to Mexico to assist Mason. He was one of the only Englishmen—or half-English men, as the case may be—who Cam knew was fluent in Spanish. Though the sort spoken in Spain differed from the dialect of Mexico, didn't it? So perhaps he wouldn't be all that useful.

Not that solving the problem was Camden's job. Just turning a coded word into its decoded counterpart. That was all. No actual problem solving, no flying out to meet the enemy, no action at all.

The tip of his pencil snapped with the pressure he was putting on it. He muttered an expletive and pulled his drawer open, fishing around until he came up with the small metal sharpener. He twisted the pencil inside it, amazed as always at how the action made him feel thirteen again, trapped in a classroom when all he wanted was to be outside, perched in the high branch of the ancient oak in the academy's southwest corner, gazing up at the clouds and dreaming of flying among them.

When he dropped the sharpener back into the drawer, his fingers brushed against paper. Since he never kept paper in there, it inspired him to yank the drawer out a few more inches and actually look down into the shallow space. Another curse found his lips when he saw one of those wretched envelopes etched with that familiar script.

Mrs. Lewis. She wouldn't take a break just because he'd left London for a few days. No doubt this was delivered yesterday or today and Commander James had stowed it for him.

He shoved the drawer closed again. Codes. Decrypts. Mexico. Audion valves. That was all he had time to think about right now. Maybe coffee, when he was taking a break. And the Denlers.

But Mrs. Lewis and her words of hate could wait.

The room was cold. Diellza huddled as near to the radiator as she could without draping herself over it. Pulling a blanket over her shoulders, she indulged in one shiver and then drew the stack of newspapers into her lap. They'd been delivered today, just as Alwin had promised they would be.

"To give you all the information I have," he'd said in their last hour together, as he'd slid his arms back into his jacket. "Without wasting our time together now."

She'd felt the thrill course through her, even as he'd turned away, toward the mirror.

"You caused quite a stir, Liebling. That squadron you were getting information from—they're all dead now."

"What?" She'd paused with one stocking rolled up her leg, their names and faces flashing before her. Miller, Greyson, De Were, Montagu, Lewis, Camden. Despite being Alwin's enemies, and hence hers, they'd been a likable band of gents. She'd not wished them any particular harm. She'd certainly not wished them *dead*.

But Alwin had chuckled and straightened his tie. "Well, all but one. Fingers point his way for being responsible, but he has not been executed for it." His reflected gaze had sought her. "Camden? You mentioned him in your reports."

He'd been the squadron leader, the one she'd tried first to get information from. He'd been as tight-lipped about anything of import as he'd been charming. Hadn't taken her long to realize she'd have to slip her arms around someone else's neck if she wanted anything to pass along to Alwin.

She rolled her stocking up and lifted her brows. "I cannot believe that. Camden and his men were like brothers."

"And brothers have been killing each other since the first pair of them." He'd shrugged, faced her again. "I don't care if he really *is* responsible, Liebling. The important thing is that we use the question to our advantage. And he has put himself in the perfect position for us to do just that."

Now, as Diellza smoothed out the stack of newsprint that all bore photographs and headlines of Phillip Camden, she knew that Alwin had, as usual, been quite right. This stack of papers represented *only* the ones that had mentioned the major and his squadron. And it was entirely daunting to think of reading through each and every article.

She settled in with the laborious English words and the stingy radiator and the patter of winter rain on her window, sucking in a breath as she worked her way to the end of the first article, all about the terrible accident during a routine patrol along the coast that had resulted in the deaths of five pilots.

Accidents among the pilots were far from rare, with deaths in their ranks so common they were all but assumed. That was no doubt partly why they lived fast and loose, as reckless on the ground—with women, booze, and gambling—as they were in the skies. Because they never knew what night would be their last, they wanted to live while the living was good.

But these weren't men taking enemy fire over France. They were merely running a patrol along the coast. There'd been no German aircraft. And this was no green crew—they were patched together in 1917 from survivors from the front, men who had earned a calmer but no less important assignment. Men who would *not* let their craft stall in a routine maneuver, who certainly wouldn't take out their entire formation without some outside catalyst.

This first article made no accusations. It just said that the only surviving squadron member had been taken in for questioning.

She turned to the next article in the next paper, this time with a photograph of Camden in handcuffs front and center. A tiny twinge brushed against her heart at that. Seeing him arrested and executed had never been a particular aim. Not before, anyway.

Now, though, it would have to be. Alwin felt sure that he was the key to their plan.

And from the look on his face in this photograph, he'd play perfectly into her hands. He was a troublemaker, always ready for a fight. Reckless, like most of the pilots.

According to this reporter, he'd forgotten who the true enemy was that day in November. No fewer than four mechanics reported seeing him tussling with another member of his squadron that afternoon. Half the aerodrome had heard him shout, "Not if I kill you first!"

But no one on the ground had seen what had happened. Just a blazing fireball as two of the machines collided midair. Several onlookers had rushed outside in time to see the planes plummeting into the Channel.

Five of them. Five of the six in No. 5's less-than-half-strength squadron. Only one still circled, and when that one had landed again at Northolt and Phillip Camden had emerged from it stone-faced and silent, it hadn't taken long, the reporter said, for those on the ground to piece together what had happened.

The black-hearted major had made good on his threat.

It wasn't until the fifth paper in the stack that the headline hinted at what had snagged Alwin's attention. BLACK HEART RELEASED: VICTIMS' FAMILIES OUTRAGED.

Her eyes devoured the words as fast as her brain could translate, her breath balling up in her chest. The journalist had no explanation to offer the reading public, just the facts. For some unknown reason, Major Camden was seen with a navy escort, exiting the prison where he'd been held awaiting trial and execution, en route to one of the Admiralty's office buildings. Rather than being returned later to his cell after divulging whatever information they sought, he was shown to a flat. He was seen reporting the next morning to the same Admiralty office building.

It made no sense, and subsequent articles were quick to point it out. Why would an army pilot be working for the navy? What had happened to the charges? Were they dropped?

Each paper seemed to have its own explanation, all of which painted Camden in a dark light. Some said he was being shown special favors because he was not just an officer but a gentleman. That the officers in charge of military justice were always quicker to hand down punishment to the common man, the common soldier, than to one of their own.

Others made the more reasonable claim that a lack of evidence had led to his release, at least until more could be found.

Still others came right out and accused Camden of making a deal with the devil to attain his freedom . . . though they never said if they meant the actual beast or some politician or high-ranking brass, and the question was put so wittily that even Diellza's rusty English had to appreciate it.

She leaned back with a sigh as she finished the last of the articles, which had been focused not on Camden himself but on the widows of his fallen comrades, who were crying out for justice against him.

She knew her next step. Find Camden. Discover whatever she could about what really happened—or at least, what she could best use against him.

Her throat went dry at the thought. Alwin hadn't seemed to consider one very real possibility—that whatever had gone wrong in No. 5 could be because of her. If Camden had found out about her real reasons for cozying up to him and his men, he could have decided to take matters into his own hands. If that were the case, he'd be as likely to snap her neck as smile at her if she showed her face to him again.

She drew her lip between her teeth, stared at one of the papers with his face on the front, and considered. They'd been a tight-knit lot. Camden always at the head, the heart, leading them onward from his place in the middle of them.

How odd their little band had seemed to her before she realized they were more archetype than exception in the RFC. A leader who was obviously of the gentle class—his confident mien gave him away as surely as did his educated speech—rubbing elbows and downing gin alongside the non-commissioned officer who came from a mining family, a mechanic from a long line of mechanics, and even a Canadian farmer.

"Our need for good pilots," Camden had said as he lounged back in his booth at the pub and surveyed his laughing men, *"outweighs our need to keep the so-called riffraff in their places. If they have the skill, they can earn the wings. Full stop."*

The article claiming it was only his social status that had led to his release speculated that perhaps his fair-mindedness had run out. He was tired of the "riffraff" he was forced to serve beside.

Or perhaps he'd realized not all his men were as tight-lipped as he was.

She huddled into her blanket, and her fingers found the blue agate of the pendant Alwin had fastened around her neck on their last morning together. "For luck," he'd whispered, tracing its line along her throat and then kissing her.

His gifts over the years had been few. Fewer than those from the other men she'd had to entertain to put food on her table. But that made them all the more valuable.

Her eyes slid shut. She'd have to take the risk, but she could at least control how she did it. Find him first in public, where he'd be highly unlikely to kill her then and there. And his first reaction to seeing her would tell her all she needed to know.

She was an expert at reading men.

She ran the pad of her thumb over the marcasite flowers mounted on the stone and pressed until they left their outline in her skin.

Spring would come. Germany and its allies would make a final push, rally, win this blighted war. And she would spend the summer—the autumn, the winter, every season—at the little cottage in Germany he'd promised her. Alwin at her side.

One bullet, rightly placed. That was all the ticket the dream required.

One. Little. Bullet.

11

They had the globe out—the ridiculously enormous one—and maps spread across nearly every inch of the floor. Arabelle's monkey of a father hung precariously from a wingback chair to point at something on a map without stepping on it. And Phillip Camden had planted himself in front of the globe and was tracing a finger along some line or another, invisible to her where she stood.

She'd been standing here in the doorway for a full two minutes, just surveying the mess they'd made with utter bafflement. How could two grown men have created such havoc in the twenty minutes since she'd left to answer a letter from Sarah?

Camden tapped a finger against the globe. "Here, I should say. Looks like a fairly central location for a base of operations. Do you know if there are any fields or meadows nearby that we could turn into a landing strip?"

Father stretched a little farther, squinting at one of the maps. "Well now, I think—ah!" His chair wobbled.

"Father!" Arabelle rushed forward, her feet for some reason trying to avoid the patchwork of overlapping maps even as her hands reached forward, willing themselves to grow long enough to steady the wingback.

No good. Even had she darted directly to him, she'd have been too late. He toppled to the ground, the chair landing on top of him.

But he was laughing, so she abandoned panic in favor of a huff of aggravation. "Fool man," she muttered loudly enough to be heard over his laughter. She heaved the chair off him.

"Didn't trod on my maps, did you, Ara?" Father propped himself up on an elbow.

"Right through the middle of them all, and I made sure to muddy my shoes beforehand too." Chair back on its feet, she offered a hand to her father, her eyes sweeping over him for any injury. "Are you hurt?"

"I'm of stouter constitution than *that*, sweetling." His eyes danced with merriment as he put his callused palm in hers and let her help him up. Only, no doubt, so that he could get back to his feet without putting them in an actually useful position. Oh no, he kept them all but under the chair to avoid his papers, which required her to grunt and strain to actually get him upright with so very little help from *him*.

The globe snorted a laugh. Or perhaps the man obscured by it.

Arabelle shot him a scowl. "Lovely of you to offer your assistance, Camden."

"Far more entertaining to watch you manage it." Blue eyes laughed at her from over the horizon of Africa. "All right, Den?"

"Right as rain." Rather than simply stand like a normal human being, Father, still gripping her hand, twisted about on his overbalanced toes and perched on the arm of the chair. Naturally, it protested by tipping again, though he still had his toes on the ground so he didn't go for another spill this time. "Ara? Do you mind?"

She blustered out a sigh. And perched on the opposite arm. "Is this what you mean to have me doing when you get me to Mexico? Be your counterweight?"

"Don't be ridiculous, sweetling—you don't weigh enough to make a useful counterweight in the field." He sent a wink over his shoulder at her. "I need you for charming the locals with that lovely smile of yours and stitching us up when charm fails and we find ourselves dodging Amazonian spears."

She blinked at him. *Spears?* "The Amazon isn't in Mexico."

Father chuckled and turned back to his maps. "Good to know your geography is up to snuff. But Cam and I have been going over the clues I've amassed, and we may have to venture farther south in our quest. Brazil, specifically—which is a shame, as I've scarcely any good contacts there and scads of them in Mexico. But the artifact given to me there was not *from* there, you see."

He motioned to his desk, where a lump of something that faintly resembled a bowl presided over the mess. He'd already shown it to her, pointing to this design and that method of engraving as if she had a clue what they signified.

Her mind was still caught on that *our quest.* It hadn't sounded to her ears as though he'd meant *our* as in him and her. It sounded like *our* as in him and Camden. She looked over at what she could see of their semi-permanent guest, the top of his head just visible over the North Pole. In Portsmouth, she'd been sure his offhanded mention of joining her father wasn't earnest.

Now, though, he'd spent hours with her father, caught up in his plans. Had Father managed to convince him?

It was good that he was looking to the future, planning something. And her father deserved credit for managing to engage him so fully in the week since he'd begun seeing her home.

Still. She couldn't quite wrap her mind around the idea of traveling across the Atlantic with *him* too. Living for months or years in a camp, likely the only female, surrounded by these two and whomever else they hired or lured into the expedition. On the one hand, it *did* sound like the sort of adventure worthy of a novel—jungles and close scrapes and tracking down mysterious ruins.

Ten-year-old Arabelle would have been thrilled beyond measure had her father come home and informed her she'd be completing her education in the field.

But he never had. And twenty-five-year-old Arabelle was

keenly aware of how ill-suited her life thus far had been to living in the wilds. And even more keenly aware of the way her pulse kicked up just a bit too much every time Phillip Camden grinned at her.

It wouldn't do. Not in general, and certainly not if they both ended up on Father's next expedition.

But the effect would wear off, wouldn't it? It only stood to reason. She'd never grown particularly weak-kneed over Brax, after all, and he was plenty handsome. Her blindness to it must have been a result of how long she'd known him. Extended exposure dulled the senses. Much like how nurses' stomachs eventually stopped turning at the sight of blood.

By that logic, these evenings in his company were ultimately good for her.

From far below, the faint sound of the doorbell reached its fingers upward. Arabelle frowned and glanced out the window. It was seven o'clock—fully dark. They rarely got visitors after dark these days, unless it was by invitation. The streets were too difficult to navigate with the lamps either painted over or lit by gas rather than electric.

"What do you think, Ara?"

"Hmm?" She jerked her head back around, still not quite used to hearing *Ara* trip so easily from Camden's lips. And he'd been using it almost exclusively these seven days, every one of which had found him here in her father's study.

Maybe her senses *weren't* so quick to dull.

He knocked a knuckle against the globe, sending a hollow *tock* into the room. "The tribe your father thinks the Atlantean bowl came from is at least a hundred miles up the Amazon. We're trying to determine how big an expeditionary force we would require and how many people to carry all the gear. What medical supplies will you need?"

She couldn't stop the frown. "Why are we going so far inland if the goal is Atlantis? Would it not be underwater?"

"The lost city itself, yes." Father nudged a map with his toe, presumably to better align it with its neighbor. "But we're still hunting for more knowledge of it. That is what I'll be seeking first."

She cast another dubious glance at the bowl. "I'm still not convinced that artifact has anything to do with Atlantis."

Both men shot her a look that combined incredulity with injury. "Of course it does!" Father exclaimed.

"Have you looked at the thing?" Camden hopped to a seat on the desk—one of the only remaining safe surfaces—and held the bowl aloft. "Greek-style patterns. Keys and waves. And a trident—which everyone knows is the symbol of Poseidon, who was the purported god of Atlantis."

She shook her head. "It is not a Greek key. It's an Aztec one."

"Poppycock!" Eyes alight, Father grinned at her. "The Aztec designs use triangles rather than perpendiculars."

"So perhaps it is an early version, or a variation. And you certainly can't deny that Aztec icons often include waves."

"But not tridents." Camden pointed a finger at her, as if catching her out on the clincher.

He looked . . . happy. Normal. Like any other gentleman caught up in a debate on something utterly useless.

She crossed her arms over her chest. "That is *not* a trident."

"Traitor!" Father spun to face her, eyes ablaze but a smile hiding in the corners of his mouth. "Absolutely it is."

"It is *not*. It's simply where a larger design has been worn away." She gestured toward the lump of clay. "And your so-called trident shaft is just a scratch."

He snorted. "I suppose you believe the story put out by that charlatan Schliemann—that the Azores are the tips of the sunken Atlantean mountains."

She blinked at him. "I have no idea. But that would certainly make more sense than it being in the new world. At least the Azores are near the Mediterranean—the part of the world with which Plato was familiar, to have brought us this myth to begin with."

"*Myth*, she says." Camden's lips wore half a grin. The challenging half. "How is this story any less believable than, say, a flood that covered the whole earth?"

"It could have been the Great Flood that sank Atlantis, you know," Father tacked on, as if that settled it.

She kept her narrowed gaze pinned to Camden. "Nearly every culture the world over has a flood story in its mythology, which tells me that they've preserved a kernel of truth that has been wrapped in mystery. Whereas the only mention of Atlantis is in one of Plato's dialogues. If it were so great a civilization, it would appear in other texts. I'm sorry, gentlemen, but I believe you're chasing a chimera."

"No, no, sweetling, the chimera was slain in Lycia. Not Atlantis." Father somehow managed the delivery with a straight face.

"Oh, for—"

A knock on the doorframe interrupted her, along with the all-too-amused clearing of Parks's throat. "Excuse me, sirs. Miss. There's a Lord Penshaw below." He held up his silver salver, on which a card rested. He wasn't fool enough to try to walk the maze of maps to hand it over.

"Penshaw?" Father frowned. "Penshaw. Penshaw . . . Ara, do we know Lord Penshaw?"

She searched her mind, eventually coming up with a blurry image of a face. "Perhaps. I believe we met him at one of the Staffords' dinner parties some years ago. At the start of the war."

That didn't wipe the confusion from his brows. "Why the deuce is he calling?"

"Shall I ask him?" Parks lifted his elegant brows, his posture not bending so much as an inch.

"No, no. Just show him up. We'll discover his reasons soon enough, shan't we, Cam?"

"Mm." Camden was still turning about the not-Atlantean bowl in his hands. "I have a pretty good guess already."

Parks, rather than turning to do as bidden, looked pointedly at the floor. "And where, Mr. Denler, shall I have him sit when I show him up?"

"Hmm? Oh." Father blinked at the paper rugs he'd set out. "I suppose we don't need Antarctica out just now. If we remove that, he can make his way to the leather chair."

"Very good, then, sir." Parks turned and vanished from the doorway.

Father hopped and skipped his way across the floor to fold up Antarctica. Arabelle tried to ignore the gaze Camden drilled into her. She settled rather defiantly onto the cushion of the chair whose arm she'd been holding down and drilled her own gaze right back.

She didn't need to ask him why he was glaring. She knew—or assumed, as a few more vague memories of Penshaw floated through her mind and settled into place. A widower, if she recalled aright. With an estate somewhere in the West Midlands. An estate that Camden was obviously assuming had some debt stacked against it. Because why else would a landed nobleman they barely knew be coming to call?

He was probably here to see her father—he'd no doubt heard bits and pieces of one of his expeditions and wanted a fuller story. Perhaps he meant to invest in a future adventure, after the war. That's why most gentlemen came to call, as Camden would no doubt soon discover.

A few minutes later, twin footfalls warned of the arrival of Parks and Penshaw. Arabelle rose, prepared to greet him, though the carpet of maps convinced her that she needn't try to get to the door to offer her hand.

Her theory looked good as Parks announced the man—an earl—and Lord Penshaw entered with a bow of greeting. He looked to be about Father's age or a bit older. Sixty, perhaps. Grey hair, a waxed moustache that curled at the ends, a suit of fine wool that bespoke a tailor. No doubt exactly the sort who fancied himself a patron of archaeology and wanted to fund an expedition.

"Mr. Denler, how good to see you again." His lordship held out a hand to her father and strode to where he still stood beside the leather chair, folded maps in hand.

Father shook. "Capital, just capital. It's been . . . how many years?"

"Nearly four, old boy. Since the opening days of the war, I believe." Penshaw turned to her. "And your lovely daughter. How do you do, Miss Denler?"

He moved toward her, not even pausing at the first crinkle of paper under his heels.

"I say! Mind your step!" The welcome in Father's voice disappeared under a wave of outrage.

Lord Penshaw paused halfway across Australia and looked down at his feet. "What the devil?"

"How do you do, my lord?" Arabelle gave him a smile. And put a bit of warning in it. "You may find it wise to backtrack across the Southern Ocean there and find safety in the chair beside my father. Antarctica is the only safe haven for visitors just now, I'm afraid."

"Oh. Well, I . . ." He spun, presumably searching for a safe trail back to the chair.

She could tell the very millisecond he spotted Camden. He froze. Then stiffened. Then jutted out his chin, as if the twin curls of his moustache were fists raised in defense against a bully.

Camden grinned in what looked like pure satisfaction at the response.

Arabelle cleared her throat. "Are you acquainted with Major Camden, my lord? If not, allow me to make introductions."

Lord Penshaw pivoted on his heel with a twist that wrenched the life from the map under it, earning a gasp of alarm from her father. Their newest guest didn't seem to notice.

"I am acquainted with his reputation, which is quite sufficient, thank you. May I presume he is an old friend of yours?" He was looking at her father for this part, and stalking toward him with a knot in his shoulders that Arabelle could only term *grumpy*.

Father's eyes snapped from the mauled map to Penshaw. Definitely no more welcome in his gaze. "Not at all. We've only just met ten days ago."

Arabelle pressed her lips against a smile. Father spent enough time with men like this to know his statement would make the earl stiffen all the more. An old friendship—family ties that dated back generations, perhaps—would make it forgivable that the black sheep was here in their home. But a *new* acquaintance . . . Well, he'd be thinking that the Denlers ought to have known better.

"That's right." Camden still perched on the edge of the desk, the bowl in his hands. But he sent his gaze to her with a ridiculously fake expression of affection that even a pompous earl could surely see straight through. "We met at the Staffords', and I was instantly captivated. Isn't that right, darling?"

She very nearly rolled her eyes. "Captivated may be a bit too strong a word. Intrigued, perhaps." With the thought of using her to force a marriage. She added a smile as sweet as rationed sugar. "Unless you mean with my father's adventures—I grant you were instantly captivated by those."

"Not what I mean at all." He winked at her. Pairing it, of course, with one of those knee-melting smiles of his.

She kept insisting to Sue and Eliza that they had no effect on her and that he didn't bestow them all that often anyway. She kept insisting he was only fulfilling a request of her father's by walking her home each evening after their mutual shifts ended. She kept insisting that she wasn't so foolish that she thought there was anything more to it than that.

But if he kept this up, he'd find himself with an Arabelle-shaped puddle he'd have to sop up off the floor, and he'd have no one to blame for it but himself.

"The Staffords." Penshaw stood now before his allotted chair and sniffed. Actually sniffed, as if Camden's proximity offended his olfactory senses.

Camden's gaze lost a bit of its sparkle. "That's right. The duke and I served together."

"And he lived to tell the tale?"

Arabelle had been about to sit again, but instead *her* chin came up. "That is quite enough, Lord Penshaw. If you cannot be civil to our guest, I have no compunction about showing you to the door." That particular tone of voice daily convinced men in agony to hold still for her ministrations. And it had the desired effect now too.

Penshaw wilted a bit and sent an utter failure of a conciliatory smile her way. "I beg your pardon, Miss Denler."

Her only response was to sit.

He followed suit, taking it as forgiveness rather than probation. "Actually," he said, making himself perfectly comfortable in the chair, "I am very glad you're in tonight with your father. I'm hosting a bit of a house party in three weeks' time, you see, and I would be honored if the two of you could join me. We could do with your stories, Denler—a few have made their way to me, and they sound properly exciting. And your beauty, Miss Denler, would make the weekend bright."

He *must* be joking. He didn't sound like it, but he *must* be. How could he honestly think praising her nonexistent beauty would come off as anything but ridiculous?

The bell echoed upward again from the front door.

Penshaw sent her a hopeful smile.

A widower. With an estate in the West Midlands. Not, she was beginning to suspect, with a deep interest in archaeology.

She cut a quick glance over to Camden, who was watching her with a distinct "I told you so" glint to his gaze.

Fiddlesticks. Penshaw must have thought nothing of the fact that he was older than her father. What did that matter, after all, if one needed an influx of sterling and perhaps an heir?

Her father made polite inquiries as to when and where this house party was to be hosted, but Arabelle paid no heed to the answers. She wasn't going.

Camden slid off the desk and inched his way across the floor, careful to lift the map edges and walk *beneath* them rather than on top. Penshaw was detailing which train to take from London when the major reached her chair. He leaned onto the back, bending enough to put his face rather close to her ear.

"Want me to kiss you? That would scare him off for good, I think."

He joked about it so easily. She kept her gaze on Father and the earl but tilted her head a bit. "That sounds just the thing. Though you'll have to make it convincing—make him think you're passionately in love with me, so much so that my poor neglected heart will be helpless to resist." She moved her gaze to him and gave her lashes a few exaggerated bats. "How good an actor are you, *darling*? Can you convince the stodgy old gent that you love an ugly girl?"

A cloud stormed across his eyes. "Don't insult yourself, Ara. I don't take kindly to it when people insult my friends."

That made a little *ping* echo through her. "What happened to *'I'm not interested in making friends'*?"

"Well, if you don't want me for a guard dog, *friend* is your only other option. And I'll not suffer you insulting yourself."

She rolled her eyes. "I choose to believe that the truth is no insult. It is simply fact, over which there is no point in getting emotional."

"But it *isn't* fact."

She blew out a breath. "I'm not fishing for compliments—or defense against insults. I—"

"If we're talking facts, let's get them straight." He was leaning close enough that his breath moved a few of the flyaway pieces of hair at her temple, making them tickle her face.

Parks appeared in the doorway again. "A Mr. Ashton to see you, Mr. Denler, Miss Denler."

"Ashton?" Father frowned.

So did Penshaw.

Camden chuckled in her ear. "Looks like we have another one. I think I've met this chap—wouldn't be a bad choice for you. He seems set on dying of the gout, and I daresay he'll manage it before the year's out. You wouldn't be strapped to him for long."

"Phillip!" She may have done a better job at making him remorseful if her rebuke hadn't turned to a laugh halfway through. She'd met Mr. Ashton before as well.

"There now, see? No one with a single dimple in her left cheek can be called ugly—it's far too charming."

She met his gaze, solely so that he could see the exasperation in hers. "Do shut up, won't you?"

He didn't look so inclined. "But I was about to wax poetic about your eyes."

"Spare me, I beg of you." Another breath of a laugh slipped out. "All right, truce. I won't call myself ugly, and you can relent from pointing out my every not-ugly feature. Let us agree on *plain*."

"Counter offer: understated."

She held his gaze for a long moment. This was the same thing she'd seen him do with his family. All bluster and bad temper one moment, but the first to enfold his sister in a hug or defend his brother if someone even hinted at wrongdoing on his part.

She could do worse for a friend. Much worse.

She held out a hand. "Agreed. Understated. Let's shake on it and let it drop."

He took her hand, flicked a quick glance across the room, and lifted it to his lips rather than shaking.

Just for show. For Penshaw's sake. Still, it sent out a flood of heat from the point of contact, surging up her arm. So utterly predictable—the overlooked, *understated* girl going to mush when a handsome man paid her a few scraps of attention.

She managed to keep her bones from liquefying, though. It helped that Father woefully declared that the maps had better be put away, which gave her a task to distract her from Camden. They had the majority neatly folded by the time Ashton joined them. Though when the blasted bell rang for a third time as she was handing over the stack to her father, she huffed out a breath.

A counterpoint to Camden's laugh.

She gave him a stealthy jab in the side with her elbow—since they were apparently friends and all—and excused herself from the room after the barest of greetings to the limping newcomer.

"Oh, but you aren't leaving us so soon, my dear Miss Denler!" Ashton exclaimed, sweat gleaming on his jowls.

She offered a tight smile. "I shall be back directly, I assure you." Once she'd determined why, exactly, every eligible gentleman in England—or, fine, a representation of them—chose the exact same time to renew their acquaintance. She bustled from the room.

Parks, lips twitching, was mounting the stairs again. "You aren't leaving, are you, miss? You've another visitor. Mr. Llewellyn."

"Fiddlesticks." Another one, as she'd assumed when the bell had rung. "Deliver him to my father. He can handle him." Or Camden could.

She turned into her sitting room a floor down, where the *Evening Standard* sat awaiting her on her desk. A few rustling pages and she was at the society section. More specifically, the marriage announcements. And yes, there it was, as she had suspected it would be. *Edmund Braxton Weds Cassandra Camden.*

The words about the nuptials were few, but a mere mention was all anyone would need. Everyone who knew them would know what that meant for Arabelle.

"Blast it." She braced her hands on the desk and leaned there, staring down at the announcement. It was bound to come out sooner or later, she supposed. But she'd been selfishly hoping for later. Much later. Perhaps hand in hand with the birth announcement for their child.

"Not to say I told you so, but . . ."

Funny how his voice could melt away the irritation. Not that she'd let *him* know that. "Oh, shut up, Camden." She turned her head to find him leaning into the doorway, surveying her private sitting room with interest. "On your way out for your night shift?"

"Soon." His gaze still swept her shelves though, and he seemed in no hurry to depart.

"You look far too intrigued. Shall I launch into a lecture on my color choices and decorating scheme?"

"Mm." He pushed off and sauntered over to the glass-encased shelf on which she'd stowed the prizes of her personal collection. Medical tomes and a few rare devices. The early, rigid stethoscope. The plague mask. The Saracen surgical tools dating from the 1600s. "You know, Ara, some people might call this macabre."

She smiled. "They are the tools of my profession. No different from the model hot air balloons and airplanes you likely have."

He sent her a bemused look. "Aren't you a VAD?"

It's what most people assumed—plenty of gently bred young ladies had found their calling in the hospitals during the war, but most entered it through the Voluntary Aid Detachment, where they had to work their way up from maid to someone to be trusted with actual caregiving. She shook her head. "I'm a trained nurse. I completed my education just before war was declared."

Confusion still clouded his face. "But . . . *why*? You obviously aren't in need of a profession."

"For monetary reasons, no." She straightened and moved over to the bookcase too. "But I needed *purpose*. And there was no telling when my father would be home or for how long. I needed something to do. Something that would help me give back." Something to assuage the endless guilt over her mother's death.

If she'd just *known*. If she'd had a basic understanding of medicine and health, she could have prevented it. Kept her mother alive. If she'd realized that dehydration was as much a risk as the illness itself, she could have forced fluids down her mother's throat. Saved her, maybe. Maybe.

His brow was still creased. "Why not just marry Brax then and start your family? That was your ultimate goal, wasn't it?"

He was determined to probe, wasn't he? She sighed. "My aunt didn't pass away—leaving me her fortune—until May of '14. Before that, I was simply a gentleman's daughter. No one special." No one for a man to ever look twice at. "Brax didn't propose until July, and then when war was declared . . ."

"Idiot."

"At least he was up-front, honest about his—"

"I was talking about *you*." He leaned close, so close that she could see the spark of temper in his blue eyes. "You should never have agreed. You deserve better and oughtn't to have settled for less. And now you have a horde of money-grubbers we have to fight off."

"*I* have to fight them off. You are under no obligation, as we've discussed before."

He folded his arms, tight creases of defiance. "Woof."

Her laughter defused any ire she may have felt. Not that she'd felt all that much anyway. "Fine." Lifting her chin, she arched her brows, too, for a bit of added challenge. "You want to help? You can accept the invitation I happen to know the Nottinghams sent you for their dinner party on Saturday."

His snarl was quick. "It was a pity invitation. Only issued because of the Staffords. Nottingham isn't all that fond of me."

Their personalities certainly clashed. Still. "I want to go, but Father already has plans. I would appreciate an escort."

The snarl faded to a mere curl to his lip, and from there into a sigh. "All joking aside, you're probably right that this is a bad idea. Being seen with me in a social setting can only harm you. I'm a curse."

"That's quite enough." She raised a finger and poked it into his chest. "I won't have you talking so about my friend."

It earned her a crooked smile.

12

De Wilde stared, mouth agape, at the tin Camden had dropped with a *thunk* onto her desk. She'd only sent him a curious glance at first and lifted a hand to pry off the lid. But then, when she caught a whiff of the aromatic beans inside, the shock had kicked in. "You . . . how did you . . . ? This smells divine."

Camden unbuttoned his overcoat and shrugged out of it. "It's rather addictive stuff. I wouldn't blame you if you decided to keep it instead of giving it to your brother." He'd forgotten to ask Den about it until he served him some again last night, but a mere query had his host rushing down to prepare a tin for the De Wildes.

Margot, eyes closed, leaned over the tin and sniffed. "How much was it? Both an arm *and* a leg, or will one or the other do?"

He chuckled and slung his coat on an open peg. "Well, Denler didn't charge me for it, but if you're so willing to pay"—he quirked a brow pointedly at her left ring finger—"that lovely diamond ought to do the trick."

"Oh!" She held up her hand, her cheeks flushing. "Drake's in town."

"So I presumed, unless he either posted a ring to you or you've gone and accepted someone *else's* proposal." As if any other man had ever managed to get so much as a smile from her.

But she positively beamed at the thought of Elton. "He's coming by for lunch. Did you want to join us?"

Were it not for the gem sparkling on her finger, he might have. Elton was one of the few friends he still had, and no one else the world over could help him put things in perspective quite so adeptly.

But they'd be bristling with wedding plans and newly engaged bliss. "Amusing as I'm sure it would be to watch you two staring moon-eyed at each other—"

"I do not *ever* stare moon-eyed." She looked like she might strike him for the mere suggestion.

Camden bit back a smile and pulled out his chair. "Enjoy your lunch with your fiancé, De Wilde. Tell him I said hello, and if he's in London long enough, to find me for a game of chess. And the coffee is free."

She pushed the lid back on the tin and hugged it to her stomach. "Lukas will be beyond thrilled. You're a good friend, Camden."

He grunted. "Not my goal." A useless statement, he knew. Made mostly for the benefit of the other cryptographers shuffling in.

The other gents all gave him their usual scowls of greeting. Part of him whispered that maybe it was time to soften. To stop glaring and snapping at them all the time and try to become one of them. *Really* one of them.

His stomach clenched at the thought. He *wasn't* one of them. He was a pilot, not a cryptographer. A squadron leader with no squadron.

He pulled out his pencil, paper, and codebook and fetched a telegram from the pneumatic tube. It was better for everyone if there was no one else to mourn when the past caught up with him. Bad enough that his family would suffer. Stafford would probably try to defend him, and that wouldn't go well for the duke. And now there were the Denlers. Elton and De Wilde.

No, that was quite enough sorrow to have on his conscience.

He settled at his desk, trying not to think too much of his

newest friends. Maybe, knowing him so little, they wouldn't mourn too much if Mrs. Lewis had her way quickly. That was his best hope. He knew he'd miss *them* already—Den and Ara had a strange way of drawing him in—but they had each other. They didn't really need him. His job in their life was to help keep the wolves at bay, nothing more.

He spread out the roll of paper, anchored it down with the codebook and blank paper, and drew forward the half-filled sheet he'd used for his notes last week.

Mexico. He'd jotted it down, not as he translated it into plain text from one of Mason's communiqués, but as it rattled around in his mind afterward.

Now it all but blazed at him. Mexico. Denler. A connection so obvious he couldn't believe he hadn't made it before. He shot up from his chair and strode into the hallway, aimed at the director's office.

The door stood open, the lights off within—sure proof that Hall wasn't there. He spun for the nearest secretary. Lady Hambro, the one in charge of all the others.

She was already regarding him with that steely, no-nonsense look of hers. "If you're charging down here in search of Admiral Hall, Major, you'll just have to wait. He won't be in until later. Meetings all morning with the First Sea Lord and then likely a press conference."

Camden muttered a curse—not that it ever made Lady Hambro so much as blink. From what he'd heard of her, she could match him word for word and teach him a few new ones.

"Shall I take a message for him?" she asked.

"No. I'll find him later. Thank you." He tacked the last part on more from years of habit than thought, but *that* made her brows hike upward again. Since he'd come here, old habit had been eclipsed by new surliness.

He spun away before she could ask what had got into him. Before he'd be forced to ask himself the same and admit it probably had something to do with a quick-witted nurse who never hesitated to call him on it when his manners slipped.

Blast it all. Less than two weeks in her company, and she was already rubbing off on him. Another two, and he'd probably be humming hymns and talking about the grace of God.

A thought that, for some bizarre reason, made him want to smile more than snarl. What *had* got into him?

The day dragged along, every set of footsteps in the corridor drawing his gaze up only to be met with some figure other than the admiral striding by. Distraction made him slower than usual at his tasks, so he opted to work through lunch.

Drake Elton, clad in the navy uniform he only ever wore when in England, stepped inside just as everyone else was gathering their belongings and slipping out. De Wilde, naturally, didn't even look up from her work. She probably had a sentence or two remaining, and even her fiancé wouldn't be able to steal her attention from it until she was finished.

Elton didn't seem to mind. He dropped a hand onto her shoulder as he walked past but otherwise directed his smile at Camden. "Did you hear that congratulations are in order?"

Camden couldn't quite hold back a smile and so took care to skew it into a smirk instead. "I saw, anyway. Are you sure you want to be saddled with that one for the rest of your life? She's vicious. A chap can't even compliment her without being threatened."

"Speak for yourself." He leaned down and murmured something to her in Spanish. Given the *bonita* Cam caught, it was obviously a compliment.

The corners of De Wilde's lips pulled up, even though she waved him away. "Go and bother Camden for a minute, Eighteen. I have nine words left."

With a chuckle, Elton came to lean against Camden's desk. "So. I've been thinking of that favor you owe me."

Camden barked a laugh. "Other way round, there, mate."

"Not true." Elton raised a finger. "You flourish in danger, and I provided you with some. Ergo, you are in my debt."

Camden snorted and pretended to turn back to his work. He *had* felt more alive while chasing German agents through the city with Elton than any other time in the last three months. Not to mention that Elton had pulled strings to get him into an airplane again when he'd thought those days were over.

And they *were* over. Unless his old friend had need to fly back to the Continent again and Hall was willing to call in a few favors to achieve it. "What do you want this time, Elton? A left hook? I still owe you one of those."

"Ha." Elton narrowed his eyes. "I still need to work the details out with the admiral on when exactly I can have some extended time back here in England, but we're hoping for a spring wedding. May, perhaps."

"And you want me to fly you across the Channel? Steal me a plane again, and I'm your man."

Elton gave him an unblinking look. "I want you to stand up with me. I haven't that many friends left here. I'd be honored if you would."

Camden's fingers went tight around the pencil. He glanced up, even though he shouldn't have. His eyes would tell his old friend more than he wanted them to. "Don't know where I'll be in May, Drake." Or *if* he'd be. Three months from now . . . well, three in the other direction, and this nightmare had only just begun. Another three seemed an eternity.

Elton didn't flinch. Didn't look away. Just pointed downward. "You'll be right here." Little did he know he was pointing directly at the desk drawer, where a half dozen letters from Mrs. Lewis now resided. Unopened.

With a clatter of pencil on desk, Camden leaned back in his chair. "You don't know that."

"I know that Hall's on your side, and that's enough to move mountains."

"Even he—"

"Just agree, Phillip."

He growled. "You're a blighted bully, do you know that?"

"*I'm* the bully?" Elton laughed. "You greeted me for the first time in years with a fist to my shot-up gut!"

"I told you," he enunciated with exaggerated clarity, "that I didn't know you'd been shot. If I had, I would have socked you in the nose instead. Maybe a second break would have straightened out the knot from the first."

Elton laughed again and straightened. "I'm sure Red will stand up with me too. And Margot's brother, of course. With you as a third, I think I'm set."

"I didn't agree."

De Wilde appeared beside Drake, the tin of coffee in her hands. "Speaking of Lukas, look what Camden found for me—to give to him for his birthday."

Drake glanced at the coffee beans and then sent him a pointed look. "We're hoping for mid-May. We'll make sure you have the details."

Blast that blighted coffee. A nail in his coffin. He glared at De Wilde. "Now look what you've done."

She could smirk every bit as well as he could. "It was your own soft heart that did it."

"Watch yourself, De Wilde. I'm not above taking revenge on a woman."

She called his bluff with a roll of her eyes and tucked her hand into the crook of Elton's arm. "I'm terrified. And just for that, I'm going to tell Drake all about the nurse you've been escorting home every night."

She'd seen them? Blighted nosy woman. Lucky for him she was the antithesis of a gossip or everyone in the OB would be wondering aloud about it.

Drake's eyes sparked with interest. "Really? A nurse? From what hospital?"

"Yours. Charing Cross." De Wilde tilted her head. "I suppose it's likely you met her while you were convalescing. What's her name, Camden?"

He folded his arms over his chest. "Stop it, both of you. It isn't like that."

"No? Well, that's even more curious. I've never known Phillip

Camden to spend any time with a girl when it wasn't 'like that.'" Drake waggled his eyebrows. "Curious indeed. What would make him escort a young woman home nightly if he had no romantic interest in her?"

"An excellent question, as usual." De Wilde pursed her lips. "It began as soon as he got back from Portsmouth. I do wonder if there's a connection—and I saw in the paper that your sister was recently wed. Is that why you went home? Is this nurse a friend of your sister's, perhaps?"

They'd never let up. Margot De Wilde couldn't stand a puzzle without a solution, and Drake Elton thought it his life's mission to pry information out of people with clever questions. Quite the pair. He gusted out a sigh and held his hands up in surrender. "All right, fine. Her name is Arabelle Denler, and we met at the Staffords' right before I went home for a few days. Her father and I hit it off, and we've been planning an expedition to South America when the war is over. Since I've been going that way after my shift anyway, I agreed to see her safely home. Satisfied?" They ought to be. It had enough of the truth in it to be convincing.

De Wilde looked appeased. But Elton was frowning. "Arabelle Denler? But she really was one of my nurses. One of the best. The one with the lonely dimple, right?"

Another woman may have taken issue with her fiancé having noted another girl's dimple. It didn't seem to occur to Margot.

Camden grunted.

Drake knew him well enough to know it meant *yes*. He turned to his intended. "Definitely not 'like that,' then. I can't think of a girl less likely for him to be involved with romantically."

And why did Cam's defenses spring up like an overeager machine gunner? "What exactly is that supposed to mean?"

Drake breathed a laugh. "Well, for starters, she's obviously a woman of deep faith—she prayed over us all each day. You, my friend, deny its validity."

Camden glowered. The denials had begun mostly as a way of annoying Jeremy. He hadn't *meant* them. Not until everything fell apart, anyway. But surely Drake Elton, of all people, knew that all his acerbic comments on the subject were more bluff than belief. Or lack of belief. Or . . .

Since when would a statement like that even bother him? Blast, but there was something wrong with him.

Drake took Margot by the arm and turned her halfway toward the door. "Not to mention the fact that you favor girls of a certain . . . look, let's say."

Was he calling Camden shallow or Arabelle unsightly? Either way, he rose to his feet, ready to take issue with it.

"But mostly," Drake went on, taking a few steps away, "you're unsuited because she's a perfectly nice girl and you're an utter bear."

Cam took a step forward and then thought better of it—largely because of the playful grin on his friend's face. He was *trying* to rile him, and by rising to the bait, he was probably proving some point or another in Elton's mind.

Tugging his jacket back down, Camden retreated to his chair.

Drake laughed his way out of the room. "I'll find you later, Cam. You still owe me a rematch in chess."

"I'll be at the Denlers' until around eight."

"Good—glad to know you're not brooding alone in your flat every night!"

With *that* echoing down the corridor after him, Camden let them go with only a mild grumble under his breath. The last thing he would admit was that it was indeed a wonderful change to be spending his spare time with people who didn't judge him, didn't really expect anything of him, who simply accepted him into their company with easy jokes and abundant smiles.

He didn't deserve the acceptance. Certainly not the lack of judgment. But he needed it. It was a balm on the burnt edges of his soul.

With the room now quiet, he settled back in to work. It was all the usual bunch of information. Movements of the German fleet, U-boat targets, weather reports. They'd be able to use precious little of it—they always had to be careful not to tip their hand and let the enemy know they were intercepting their every signal. So before they could ever put any of the information to use, they had to first devise a cover story for how they came by it.

But only the really important items were given such treatment. None of what he was currently working on, probably, though he couldn't be a good judge of that, as he had such a small sliver of it before him.

Mexico. His gaze flitted over the word again midafternoon, when the hive was once again buzzing. He checked the clock when the crick in his neck grew unbearable, scowling when he saw it was nearly time to go and fetch Arabelle, and Hall still hadn't come in.

Maybe he wouldn't today. Or would wait until this evening, after the day shift's crowd had eased.

Then, at five minutes until the hour, the unmistakable sound of Blinker Hall's voice barking out a command to someone echoed down the hallway.

Camden stood. He didn't generally see the wisdom in interrupting a shouting admiral, but there were occasions for everything. And since this may well improve the man's mood . . .

He needn't have worried anyway. By the time Hall charged into his office, whatever underling he'd been upbraiding had peeled off. Camden glanced over for a secretary, but none were currently stationed outside his office.

And Hall wasn't taking his usual seat behind his desk either. He stood riffling through a filing cabinet. Coat and hat still on.

Camden rapped a knuckle on the doorframe.

Hall didn't so much as glance up until he pulled whatever file he was looking for from the cabinet. Then he spun fully around, brows arched. "Major Camden. What can I do for you?"

"I think it might be the other way round, sir." He drew in a breath and straightened his posture. He'd never had a moment's hesitation going to his superiors in the RFC with an idea. But that was his world. This most assuredly wasn't.

Hall tapped a finger to the file. "Go on. Concerning what?"

"Mason, in Mexico." If it were Stafford before him, or the general in charge of Northolt, he'd not feel so out of his element. He cleared his throat. "Forgive me if I'm out of bounds, sir—I know solving his problems isn't my business."

Hall let loose a quick laugh, staccato and low. "Every problem is the business of anyone who can help with it." He drew his pocket watch out, clicked his tongue, and motioned with the folder. "Your shift is finished, is it not? Walk with me and tell me your idea along the way."

"Yes, sir." They moved into the flood of people in the corridor. Camden paused at Room 40 to grab his coat and cap, then fell in beside the admiral again.

It wasn't until they were out in the biting wind that Hall signaled him to begin. "Well, sir, I've recently made an acquaintance who may be of some help. Lawrence Denler—do you know of him?"

Hall's brow creased. "The name sounds familiar. A military man?"

"No. An explorer."

"Ah. Yes, I think I read an article he wrote some years back." Hall nodded. "Searching for the City of Gold, wasn't he?"

"He was, yes. In Mexico."

"Mexico." Hall aimed not for the car still idling a few feet away, but around the building. "I believe I see where you're going with this."

"He has countless connections there, Admiral. Natives who speak the language, and many of them former law enforcement from the previous regime. Guides and scouts. Those skilled at, let us say, procuring difficult-to-find items."

"The very sort Mason would require." Hall paused at the corner and scanned the streets ahead of them. "You think Mr. Denler will be willing to share some of his resources?"

"I cannot think why not—especially with Mason, given the man's former career as a novelist. Den has all his books in his library."

"That does sound—just a moment, if you please." He held up the arm with the folder and shouted, "Mr. Pearce! Could I impose upon you for a quick errand?"

The admiral took off toward the figure in a brown hat and wool coat twenty yards away. Camden didn't know Pearce all that well, though he saw him frequently about the OB—the chap was some sort of family or another with De Wilde, though Camden wasn't exactly sure how. He was always running errands, but not the typical sort, it seemed. And atypical meant secretive around here, so Camden didn't follow his superior. Hall probably didn't want him eavesdropping.

"Phillip Camden! Is that you?"

The voice, feminine and vaguely familiar, drew his gaze to the right, to where a statuesque blonde was striding his way with a brilliant smile on her lips and a hand up, waving to him.

"Dee Mettler." A smile of greeting settled on his lips, even as his chest squeezed tight. Talk about the past catching him up. Though it wasn't *her* fault that she'd been part of the group right before The Incident. He held out a hand for her gloved fingers to settle into. "Still as lovely as ever."

She laughed and squeezed his fingers as he raised hers to his lips for a polite kiss. "And you are still a flatterer, I see."

Not so much lately. Charming pretty girls wasn't exactly high on his list of priorities in recent months. But he grinned as he released her fingers. "How have you been?" He didn't know what else to ask her. Hers wasn't exactly a profession that lent itself to polite conversation on a street corner, and his time since last they met hadn't exactly been all rosebuds and serenades.

She adjusted the brim of her hat. "Well enough, thank you. Though the pub has been lonely without you and your men nearby. Were you all reassigned?" Her gaze flitted to the building behind him, and a pretty little frown played over her face. "Is this not a navy building?"

How was it possible that she didn't know what had happened? Even if she'd not read any of the papers—and he wasn't sure her reading level of English, to be honest—she'd have heard, wouldn't she? In the pub?

Camden cleared his throat and glanced at the OB too. "I've been reassigned, yes."

"So that is what has kept you from me." She gave him a playful pout and a flutter of her lashes, then a coy grin. "Well, luck has brought us together again, at least. We should have tea. Talk about . . . old times."

The grin emerged by rote, but there was no quickening of his pulse. No knot of attraction in his stomach like had cinched tight there when first he saw her six months ago.

And why was that? Just because he'd already tasted those lips, had those arms around him? No. Because of his squad and her inadvertent ties to that last, fatal argument? Maybe.

Or was it . . . something else entirely? When he blinked, he saw a set of hazel eyes snapping with laughter.

He blinked again to clear his mind. What had she said? Tea. Talking about old times. He chuckled and darted a look toward Hall, who was coming back. And probably making all sorts of assumptions—most of them accurate—about why Camden would be chatting on the street with a too-pretty blonde who wore flirtation like he did his uniform. "Tea, perhaps. But I daresay talking about old times wouldn't be appropriate in a teahouse."

She giggled in that way girls like her had perfected eons ago. The way meant to sound both innocent and sultry. To make a man want to both laugh with her and stop her from laughing.

That did nothing for him just now either. Maybe it was Hall's nearing presence.

She must have noted the direction in which he looked. No one could ever accuse Dee of not being observant. She laid her fingers on his wrist and squeezed. "Lyons in Piccadilly? Name the day and time."

"Em." His first thought was to put her off. Walk away. Get back to business with Hall, fetch Ara, and forget all about running into Dee. But her fingers pressed, and he heard himself saying, "I have Tuesday next off. Two o'clock?"

"Perfect. So good to see you again, Cam."

He couldn't force the obvious words past his lips before she was scurrying away. So he said nothing. Just watched her go, watched Hall approaching with a frown, and wondered why he could taste the guilt in the back of his throat. He'd not hurt her. He'd not hurt anyone with his brief dalliance with her. She was a burlesque dancer who, like most burlesque dancers, hand-selected a few paramours from her admirers to keep her in style in return for her favors. Not a decent young woman whose reputation he'd besmirched.

"Who was that?" Hall slid to a halt at Cam's side, eyes on the retreating form. "She looks familiar."

"Does she?" Odd. He was pretty good at reading people, and Hall did *not* strike him as the sort to foster an acquaintance with Dee's sort. He'd met Mata Hari, for heaven's sake, and called her a *"fat hag completely devoid of charms."* The blokes in Room 40 were still telling stories about that one. "Her name is Dee—short for something, though I don't recall what. Mettler. She's Swiss. Has been . . . working here."

Hall's eyes didn't brighten as information clicked into place. They went still behind his knowing blinks. "Diellza. That's it—and no, she hasn't been. Not lately. You are no doubt unaware, as it was about the same time as your own fall from grace, but Miss Mettler was expelled from the country some three months ago."

"What? Why?" Even as he asked, he knew the answer—there was only one reason the Director of the Intelligence Division would know a dancer's name and immigration status.

Hall arched a brow. "On suspicion of espionage."

Only one answer, but still it stole his breath. "She . . . kept company with the officers. In the RFC, I mean." Had she been trying to get information out of them? He scoured his mind for anything she'd asked, though honestly, he couldn't remember anything in particular. Her questions hadn't been his concern—

and people were *always* asking them questions they couldn't answer in honesty.

Hall blinked at where she'd disappeared in the crowd. "She shouldn't have been let back into England." The gaze shifted to Camden. "Are you bored, Major?"

"I beg your pardon, sir?"

A hint of a smile touching his lips, he motioned Camden onward again. His hands were empty, meaning the folder must have been for Pearce. "If you wouldn't mind a bit of mild fieldwork, I'd like to know what she's doing here. And how she got in. Have you a way to get in touch with her?"

"Ah. Yes. And I can do that." *Action*. Only drinking tea and trying to pry information out of someone suspected of prying information, but still. It was action.

"Good. Now. This Mr. Denler. I'd like to speak with him. Let's set up a meeting, shall we?"

Desk work just got a bit more interesting. "Absolutely, sir."

13

Diellza shut her bedroom door with the softest of clicks and then slid to the floor, letting her breath quaver as it had been wanting to do for the last hour. She'd talked with plenty of officers before, but never one as high ranking as the fellow Camden had exited the Admiralty building alongside. She didn't know who the admiral was, and she certainly had no reason to think he knew who *she* was, but even so. She'd very nearly turned and fled.

Nearly. But she'd clutched the pendant and reminded herself of why it was worth the risk.

And worth it, it had been. Her eyes slid shut, and she sucked in a long breath. He'd been surprised to see her. Not quite sure of what to make of her sudden appearance in the heart of London, to be sure. And not exactly *thrilled* that she was there. But that was likely just because of the proximity of the admiral. There'd been no anger in his eyes. No hatred or bitterness. No suspicion.

She had her in. Pressing a hand to her stomach to settle the nerves, she peeled her eyes open again. Her trunk met her gaze. A smile toyed with her lips. She'd meet him on Tuesday with wide eyes and quivering lips. Claim she'd just heard about his misfortune. Encourage him to pour out the story to her.

Thanks to the newspapers, she had names of people who considered him an enemy. But she needed to know *which* names. Which names to pursue. Which strings to tug.

And then, as Alwin had instructed, she had to make certain that when the curtain closed on Camden's act, it was with a flourish loud enough to get the attention of absolutely everyone.

She had her primary target: the First Lord of the Admiralty. But if she did her job well, she'd be able to put more than one magic bullet to use. And with each additional one she fired, she was sure to gain that much more respect and acclaim in Alwin's eyes.

A tap on the door made her jerk away from the wood and push to her feet. Realizing she'd yet to take off her gloves or hat or coat, she tossed the first two aside and then opened the door while unbuttoning the last. A smile ready for whichever fellow boarder was knocking.

"Hello." Faith, who lived just above her, grinned and held out the electric curler she'd borrowed. "Thanks again for letting me use it."

"You are very welcome. Anytime."

One never knew when one might need a friend.

16 February

"I'm so glad you could join us." Rowena Nottingham pulled Arabelle into a quick hug, whispering in her ear, "And thank you for your advice."

Ara chuckled. "I hope it helps." She pulled back with a grin. Frankly, it had been a relief to realize that the duchess's wan cheeks and shadowed eyes were indicative of a happy ailment instead of a more concerning one. "Though I admit this is hardly my area of expertise these days." Nursing wounded soldiers certainly didn't give her any experience with expectant mothers.

Rowena smiled and darted a glance over at her husband, who was bidding farewell to Camden a few paces away. She touched a hand to her abdomen, still flat under her silk evening gown. "Perhaps this one will be a son for him."

"And if not, you'll have an excuse to try for another." Ara winked and clasped her friend's hand, gave it a squeeze. The Nottinghams already had two daughters, both the sweetest little things with their mother's eyes and their father's charm. But the fact that the duke had no heir meant he was playing it safe during the war—safer than Stafford, at any rate. He too wore a uniform, but his work was safely behind a desk. He didn't seem to bristle at that quite so much as a certain *other* office-bound officer who'd been a bit moody these last three days. Well. Moodi*er*.

Funny how accustomed she'd grown to him and his moods in two short weeks.

Camden took a step away from the duke and lifted his brows. "Ready, Ara?"

She nodded and was soon tucking her gloved hand into the crook of his arm. They'd already said their farewells to the Staffords and the Caytons and the other couples still within. It was only nine, but she'd promised Father they wouldn't be late. He'd been eager to share a new plan with Camden and rather annoyed that dinner plans would steal his favorite new friend away for the evening.

Father had been dodging her questions about what he and his maps of Mexico had been up to for the last thirty hours, yet he seemed eager to chat about it with Camden. What were they plotting?

She narrowed her eyes at Camden as he led her out into the night, pulling his hat down over his brow as they exited. He'd donned evening wear instead of his uniform for the occasion, much as he had for that first dinner at the Staffords'. And for some reason, the sight of him in a top hat made a grin twitch onto her lips. Even so, her amusement wasn't going to deter her questions. "Are you ready to come clean?"

"What?" He jerked as if she'd zapped him with an electrical current.

Arabelle shook her head. "What is the matter with you? You've been acting oddly since Thursday."

He faced forward, to where her Standard idled at the curb, the Nottingham chauffeur having pulled it round for her. "You've not known me all that long, Ara. Who's to say this isn't normal?"

It was true. Yet struck her as false. "Has your stomach been ailing you? Perhaps you have a rash."

"Ara."

"No need to be shy with me about it, even if it's in an unmentionable place, you know." Yes, she prodded solely because she knew it would goad him. She leaned close. "I've seen my fair share of trench—"

"Stop." He laughed. And winced. And shook his head. "Sometimes your conversation is decidedly unladylike."

She tucked away a smile and nodded her thanks to the chauffeur when he opened the passenger door for her. Camden had insisted on driving here—an affront to his pride to be ferried about by a girl, no doubt—and would clearly insist on the same now.

She waited until he'd settled behind the wheel and had pulled out onto the dark street before delivering her next calculated prod. "I find it curious that your sudden increased surliness coincides almost exactly with my father's suddenly going mum about his research."

Camden grunted.

She was beginning to learn how to translate his grunts. This one, she was fairly certain, was reticent acknowledgment. Ara tapped a fingertip to her lip. "Some may wonder if you two had a falling-out over something. But that doesn't hold up, given that, if anything, you've been spending *more* time at my home these last two days. And I'm all but certain I saw my father walking below the hospital Thursday. Not that he stopped in to see me— he was aiming for you, though, perhaps . . ."

"I don't know what you're on about, darling. I . . ." He let off the gas, brow creasing, and stuck his head out the side. "Do you hear that?"

"Hear what?" But the mere question made her heart slam against her rib cage. All the more so when he pulled over and killed the engine. "*What?*"

But she could hear it then. Engines. From above. *Oh Father, Lord my God, help us.* "Gothas?"

"Not certain. Could be, or Giants." He opened the door and got out, head craned back, not even noticing when the top hat fell to the street.

She slid across the seat and climbed out behind him.

"Come on, lads. Where are you?" His eyes scanned the heavens, finally spotting a shadow to the east. One that seemed to grow larger with each passing second, until it became wings and body and buzzing engine.

She didn't mean to latch onto his arm, but she couldn't seem to stop her fingers from trying to weave their way into the fabric of his coat. "Maybe it's ours. A patrol."

But Camden was shaking his head. "It would be RFC if it were, and that's not one of our planes." He spat out a curse as the plane was silhouetted against the moon. She could hardly blame him for it just now. "Giant."

"Where are ours?"

He just shook his head, his jaw ticking.

Her stomach went tight. She knew that the waters were patrolled by the navy's air division, the RNAS. Over land, the RFC took over. If a German plane—no doubt one of many at the start—had reached the heart of London, it likely meant that some of their own had been shot down.

"Get in. I'll take you home and then—"

"Don't be an idiot, Camden. If they succeed in—" Before she could even finish her sentence, a massive *boom* cut her off. And then, to the west, a flicker of flame slashed the darkness. A bomb had indeed found its mark, and not all that far away. A mile at the most.

Her hand dropped from his arm. Her nerves steadied. A bomb. A fire. It meant injured people, panicked people. "Let's go. They're going to need our help."

Camden just stood there though. "Are you mad? I'm taking you *home*, not to—"

"Shut up and stop wasting time." She slid back into the car—but shut the door behind her and gripped the wheel herself. "Get in or stay here, but I'm going. In five . . . four . . . three . . ."

He cursed again and tore around the bonnet to all but leap in on the passenger's side. She didn't even wait for him to close the door fully before she was off, following the beacon of the flames slapping at the sky and setting the horizon aglow above the familiar buildings of London.

"Your father will have my head for this."

She ignored him, trying to pull up before her mind's eye a map of the city. Possible targets. "Where do you think they struck? Victoria Station?"

He mumbled something she couldn't quite catch over the growl of the Standard's engine as she barreled at full speed down the empty street. "May have been what they were aiming for, but it looks as though they missed. That's more to the south. I can't think of anything this direction they would have been targeting specifically."

Neither could she. But as the flames and screams and sirens drew nearer, she feared she knew what they *had* hit. "No. No, no, no."

"What?" Camden, to his credit, didn't growl as she careened around a corner. He just held on.

The heat hit as soon as she turned onto Chelsea Bridge Road. Waves of it, crashing outward like a tide. Breaking over the car, threatening to drown her.

Camden gave her yet another taste of his too-colorful vocabulary. "Can't approach from this side. Take that alley, get us around the back. Doesn't look like that other wing is on fire." He coughed when a billow of smoke rolled through his window. "What is this place? It's enormous."

"Royal Hospital." She turned into the alley, where the sickly orange light of the fire was blocked by hulking shadows.

"Servicemen? Maybe it *was* their target, then, though that would be a low blow, even for the huns."

She shook her head. "No. Not here. It's pensioners." The old, the infirm veterans from previous wars. Surely not the target—it would give the Germans no strategic advantage to take out Royal Hospital, not like one of the train stations or even Charing Cross Hospital would.

But the damage . . . that took her breath away. She'd visited Royal Hospital before and knew that far too many of its residents were, on the best of days, largely immobile. But now, with their home ablaze? It must be chaos.

She pulled the car along the curb at the rear of the building and leapt out before Camden could so much as breathe a warning to wait.

Sirens whined through the night. Fire crackled and roared and snapped its teeth. People shouted and screamed. Arabelle took a moment to recall the layout of the building, to note where people were rushing out of the doors, to try to guess where the injured would be.

Camden appeared at her side, and she turned to him. "I've a first aid box in the boot. Will you fetch it?"

He lifted his brows. "Travel prepared, do you?"

"Well, one never knows what might happen when one is out for a drive." Another time, she may have joked about being kidnapped by a grumpy pilot, for instance, but she hadn't time for teasing now. Spotting a knot of people that seemed to include a few injured, she ran that direction.

Camden caught up with her when she was but a few steps away.

A soot-stained man stepped into their path, hands up. "Please, miss, stay back. Parts of the building are unstable."

Arabelle lifted her chin. "We're here to help. Where are we most needed?"

The man opened his mouth, refusal clearly poised on his tongue. Then his eyes darted to Camden and down to the box in his hands. "Are you a doctor, then?"

"No. But she's a nurse from Charing Cross." He touched a hand to her back. "Trained at the Nightingale School. And I'm strong, with a decided lack of a self-preservation instinct and happy to scramble over wreckage. Put us to work." How, even now, could he both put himself down and be amusing?

The man turned with a sigh. "We're taking the injured over there." He pointed to a swarm a good distance away, crowding the street. And followed his own finger toward them, as if forgetting already that Ara and Cam were there.

Camden pressed her kit into her hand. "Go on, I'll join you there later. I'll see if I can find a way to dirty this ridiculous suit of clothes first."

She caught his hand, squeezed it. "Be careful, Phillip."

"Why?" He shot her a crooked grin.

"Why?" She sent him a narrow-eyed glare. "Because if you're injured, I'll have to try to save *you*, and then I won't be helping the rest. Don't be selfish."

"Better way to go than before a firing squad, isn't it? I can see the headlines now: BLACK HEART DIES SAVING PENSIONERS FROM BOMB SITE."

After a quick search of his eyes, she released his fingers, satisfied that he didn't actually have any desire to die a hero tonight. Which freed her to obey the tugging inside, the one pulling her toward those in need.

Ara pulled off her white satin gloves as she ran, stuffing them into her coat pockets. She had work to do.

14

It might have been an hour. It could have been two. Much like when he'd been flying over enemy lines in France, dodging Fokkers and Gothas and clearing the way for their observers to take aerial photographs of the enemy's position, Camden couldn't be bothered with things like seconds and minutes.

There was only the objective. The obstacles in his way. The means of taking out the one to achieve the other. In that case, manning a gun, sending the enemy pilots to the ground in a blaze, keeping his own lads alive another day. In this case, clearing rubble, scrambling over chunks of brick and block and stone and wood, seeking the feeble cries for help.

The fire brigade had arrived at some point in the infinite expanse of dust and heat and shouts, and soon there was more smoke than blaze.

"Help." It wasn't a cry so much as a mew. Weak. Tired.

Camden followed it, sliding down a slab of crumbling something that had once been wall or floor or ceiling and was now a henge around this would-be burial mound. "I'm coming. Hold tight."

"Help."

He followed the trembling voice past a pipe gushing icy water. Squeezed himself through an opening between two piles of rubble and lifted an arm to shield his face from the sudden blast of heat. Fire still ate away at the hospital somewhere in here. He couldn't see it, but he could hear it chewing on the walls. Feel it pulsing, radiating.

"Where are you?" he called, searching the darkness with eyes that ought to have adjusted to it by now. But this dark was too befouled with choking smoke. He hooked his elbow—tuxedo jacket long since gone and white shirt turned black—over his nose and coughed.

"Here."

Close. "Keep talking. We need to hurry."

"Here. Here."

He felt metal—cold from water. Broken tile—hot from fire. And there, the soft padding of a mattress. A tangle of blankets. And a bony leg. "There you are."

"Can't . . . walk."

Camden felt around the bed. "You're pinned?"

"Paralyzed. In the . . . Crimean."

At least he didn't have to lever a ceiling beam from across him. "All right. Have you use of your arms?"

In answer, a hand found his shoulder.

"Good." He slid an arm under the man's knees, another under his back. The old chap was naught but a skeleton wrapped in skin, weighing no more than smoke. "Hold on, sir. Let's get out of here, shall we?"

They'd been able to evacuate many of the injured through the undamaged sections of hallways and corridors. In and out through the doors. But when Camden turned toward where the door to the corridor ought to be, the heat increased. Fire.

"We'll have to go out the way I've come in." He pivoted, seeking the lighter darkness of the night where it shouldn't be visible, through the wreckage that had once been an outer wall. "Ever do any mountain climbing, sir?"

The bloke in his arms wheezed. "Michael. I'm called Michael."

"Well, Michael, we're going to be scaling a bit of a cliff face here shortly." He edged a foot to the left, close to where he must have entered this room. "Up for it?"

"No." A paper-thin cough. "Just leave me."

"Rubbish." There, the hole he'd squeezed in through. "I don't leave men behind."

But the screams of his squad suddenly filled his ears. The cough of the engines. His nose filled with the bite of fuel and spark, smoke choking him.

No. He blinked, shook his head, and eased the old bloke up the wall or floor or ceiling. Camden scrambled beside him, then past him, and pulled the fellow up until they reached the ledge.

How far had it been from top of wall to semisolid ground? Not far. Five feet, perhaps. He maneuvered Michael to the edge and then eased himself over it, careful to keep a hand on the fellow's arm. His feet hit something firm. "All right. Your turn. Lean my way however much you're able." If he pulled on him, that rough edge would likely take a few bites from his back.

With a weak cry, the man strained his way, fingers grappling up Camden's arms like hooks.

"Perfect." He pulled the chap off the cliff's edge, back into his arms.

A rumble. A crack. Not from their little wall-mountain but from beyond, in the room where they'd just been.

The old man's fingers dug into Camden's shoulder. "Fire. Coming."

"We won't be here to become its snack." He could see better now with the aid of moonlight. Hear more than the teeth of flames and the agonized scream of its wood and plaster victims. But there were people, not far off. He headed for them at as quick a pace as the debris littering the ground allowed. Not quite running. Not quite walking.

There, a chap in a fireman's hat, waving arms and running toward them. Camden came faster, not sure what lit that frantic motion in the fireman but knowing it must not be good. "Hurry!" the chap called.

He hurried. Stumbled as he cleared the edge of what had once been an exterior wall, not objecting when the fireman all but yanked the old bloke from his arms. Something bit the knee Camden had to put down to keep from sprawling face first into the street full of debris. But then he was up again, chasing after the fireman and Michael.

He heard someone shout something. Something about canisters. He heard—no, felt—the rumble. And he looked back just in time to see it.

Fire. Not red-orange tongues, but a ball of it. Bursting, tumbling over itself, flying outward.

Fire. Chomping its teeth over them, eating through the fuel tanks, rolling outward, upward, downward until it caught De Were's wing. Miller's tail. Greyson's belly.

"No! Lewis!" He lurched, jerked, fingers convulsing around the stick—not there. He had to pull up. Bank. Circle around. *Quickly*, shouted every instinct, every nerve ending. *Slowly*, shouted every minute of training and experience. Too quick, and his plane would stall too. The engines, greedy for air, would choke and sputter. The smoke would suffocate them. He would plunge, along with that fireball, into the Channel.

He should have. He should have jerked the stick back. Let the stall take him. Joined the others. Taken his chances with the fire and the water and the smoke and the shouts.

"Phillip. *Phillip!*"

Sunlight. Sunlight had blinded him, pale in comparison to the fire that had scorched his eyes. Where had it gone? There was darkness now. Black and billowing and hard. Hot and then cold. He was shaking, his hands seeking the space in front of him for the stick.

"Phillip!"

There'd been the pounding of feet as he'd brought his Camel to a bouncing halt on the runway. Male shouts, deep and accusing. Rough hands.

Feet pounded, but they were softer. And the figure that materialized from the darkness, though tall as the mechanic who had reached him first, was lithe and willowy. The face—the face. No accusation there, no fury. Fear, but not for her own life.

And then hands. Not gripping him by the uniform and pulling him forcibly from his Sopwith, but gentle. Seeking their way over his face, through his hair, retreating when he winced.

Her eyes. He needed her eyes. The hazel depths of them. The brilliant light of them. He sought them, found them, and anchored them there, right before him, with fingers knotted in her hair.

Hers anchored him too. "Now, what did I tell you about not getting injured?" She held his gaze, held it as tightly as her hands did the sides of his head. Right there. Right before him. "Look at me. I'm here."

"Ara." He couldn't blink. If he blinked, she'd go and they'd come back. Those bright eyes would disappear and the hate-filled ones would loom again. The fire would fist again. The screams would lash him again. "Lewis." *No.* No, he couldn't say it. Couldn't think it.

The hands moved, fingers combing through his hair and then returning to their position, palms on his temples. "You're bleeding."

Not possible. He'd already bled out. Everything red and pulsing and alive long since gone. He hadn't a heart anymore, just a slab of rock. Black and hard and lifeless.

"Phillip, we—"

"Don't let go." His fingers obeyed the command he meant for her, tightening, locking into her hair. It probably hurt her. He didn't want to hurt her. The last thing in the world he wanted to do was hurt her. *Let go. Let go.*

The command he should have obeyed that day. Just let go of the stick. Let the fire and the smoke and gravity have their way. Send him plunging into the Channel with his men.

He plunged now, into the black. The depths. His fingers loosened—*don't bring her down with you*—then tightened again—*don't let her go.* "Ara."

"I'm here."

Shadows and shouts. Flashes and whispers. Rumbles. Bumps. Something white-hot pierced him behind the eyes, and then he was vaguely aware of arms. Hers, on the one side—familiar and steady, stronger than she should have been. But another, on the other side. Someone a bit taller than her, who smelled of soap and sandalwood. Then lights—an onslaught of them that sent him reeling backward again.

The sun, blinding and accusatory. Glaring down on him while the waters devoured the flaming wrecks. Fire, red and orange and scorching.

Then the night of the cell. Dark as smoke. Cold as death. Something throbbed at the back of his head, but it couldn't be pain, couldn't be blood. He had none left. None. They'd taken it all, every last shred of it, down with them.

Miller. Greyson. Montagu. De Were. Lewis. *Lewis.* Blast him to Hades and back. Cam had failed him. Failed all of them. Tugged them all blithely into a life they didn't know how to live with. A life that led them all to their deaths.

"They're not here." Her voice, soft as a prayer, tugged him away from the cell. "But I am. Wake up, Phillip. Please. Talk to me."

He blinked once, saw her blurry form silhouetted against a smattering of lamplight. Even that was too much. He let his eyelids fall again. Back to the cell, where he belonged.

"Is he coming to?"

"I hope so. The gash isn't all that bad, but head injuries can be strange."

"What happened to him?"

"He fell back when the gas canisters blew, knocked his head on the remains of a wall."

She couldn't be talking about *him*—he didn't recall any of that. Just Lewis, the look in his eye as he pulled back too quickly on his stick. That terrible sound as his engine stalled. The crash into Montagu's Camel.

The fire. Always the fire.

"Phillip." Hands, cool and gentle and mingling the scents of antiseptic soap with smoke. They stroked his face, calling to him as surely as her voice did.

He gritted his teeth and told his eyes to open again. To stay that way. To banish that edge of fear from her tone. It required a bit of blinking to turn the blur of her into *her*.

Dark hair, tumbling down—his fault?—and secured in what looked like a precarious braid, having nothing tying it off. The sparkling bauble she'd had in her hair for the dinner party still nestled there, its glimmer coated in black grime. Brows, too thick with soot, drawn together in a frown over the hazel eyes.

That's where his gaze latched. She had the most beautiful eyes. "Ara."

"Thank God." Those eyes shuttered for a moment, two, then opened to him again, her fingers tracing the line of his cheekbone. "Have I ever mentioned how much I hate head wounds? Capricious things. You gave me a fright."

He could see beyond her, and it made *his* brows knit. A bed was beneath him, papered walls across from him. "Not a hospital." Why had he expected it to be? The antiseptic soap smell, he supposed.

She shook her head and straightened. "The hospitals will all be overcrowded tonight, with the influx of the gents from the Royal. I thought it best to tend you at home."

Home. Not his, that was for certain. His walls were merely painted plaster, no paisleys and whatnot papered on. "Michael?"

She frowned again for a moment. Then she brightened. "Oh, you mean the fellow you'd rescued last. He's well. Uninjured but for a few scrapes. The fireman had him well away when those canisters went."

She was still wearing her evening dress—ruined. Streaked with black, torn in places. Her face bore smudges at the edges, down her neck.

He was fairly certain he'd never seen a more beautiful sight in all his life. She hadn't the right to look so beautiful when she wasn't even pretty and was covered with ash and soot to boot.

How did she manage it? It was the eyes. Somehow pure and good and yet so blasted *knowing*. How could she know so much and still be so good? Life didn't work that way.

Then there was Ara. Hands that tended the wounded day in and day out, eyes that had seen the ugliest results of this blasted war, and still that *light* in them.

He pushed himself up. Elbows, then hands. There were pillows behind him, the solid wood of an ornate headboard behind that. And a room in front that tilted and whirled.

"Stop! What are you doing? You may well have a concussion; you need to be still!"

"I'm fine." Mostly. Except that her hands fell to his shoulders to push him back down, and he was suddenly quite aware that her skin rested directly on his. He glanced down, frowning. Scrapes, bandages, but no shirt. "Well now, that's not fair. You've got my clothes off me and I don't even remember it. We had fun, I hope."

He was angling for a flash of dimple, but all he got was a roll of her eyes. "Don't act the scoundrel, Cam."

"But I'm so good at it."

"Mm. Well, it was Father who got your shirt off, so you'll have to ask *him* if any fun was had." At the face he made, the dimple winked at him. Then vanished into her sigh. "You're a mess. What were you doing, crawling over every jagged edge you could find?"

"That more or less sums it up."

She muttered something and stood up, returning a moment later with a tube of what must be ointment and clean white bandages. "Once you've stopped bleeding all over everything, Father brought a nightshirt for you. We've dispatched Parks to your flat to get you a proper change of clothes." She squeezed white cream from the tube onto her finger.

He hissed when she dabbed the stuff onto his stomach. "How's he getting in? Breaking a window?"

"Your keys were in your trouser pocket."

"Searching my pockets too?" It came out high and tight, given that he was holding his breath against another swipe of her finger

167

over his broken skin. When that one didn't sting so blighted much, he let the air out. Tacked a smile on. "Did you at least do that searching, or was it your father again?"

Instead of answering him with anything but an exasperated look, she set the ointment down on the bedside table and, still sitting there beside him, her hip to his sheet-covered one, picked up something else. Then his hand. Put metal to palm. "This was in your pocket too."

His fingers closed around the brass wings, each groove familiar. His hands were scraped up, but he squeezed the pin tight until it made his palm burn. His eyes slid closed.

"The names you kept repeating. Lewis and Montagu and . . . Liller?"

"Miller. Greyson. De Were." They marched off his tongue like a litany. Tasted like punishment. How many times had he shouted those names? In jest, in command, in simple greeting?

But no more. Now they were just a list. A list of the people dead because of him. Because he'd thought he could fight and threaten his way out of that morass as he had countless times before. Because he'd thought Lewis would see reason. Thought if he just pushed the bloke hard enough . . .

"Your squadron." Her palm over his knuckles, her fingers encasing his. Warm and steady and smooth.

His nostrils flared. "I don't want to talk about it."

"No. But I think you should." Warm. Steady. Soap-scented . . . and still smoke-scented, too, because she'd been there in the thick of it. The one who'd insisted they go, insisted on helping.

He opened his eyes so he could look into hers. Golden. Specks of green, specks of brown. All light. He craved it. Wanted to pull her closer until that light had a hope of reaching him, edging out the black.

But that wasn't the way the world worked. All he'd do was darken her. "No. Not with you. It'll just ruin you, as it did them. Not everyone was suited for the life I'd chosen. I was a fool to ignore that."

Her hand had worked its way, somehow, under his. Palm to palm, the wings between them. Her fingers coiled around him, his around hers. "A pilot's life?"

"A gentleman's." His lips curled around the word, and his eyes slid closed. "Jeremy was right. He was always right. That life . . . it came at a cost. A cost I didn't see. One my men paid."

"I don't understand." Her words were soft, softer than the stinging balm.

He squeezed his eyes against the truth. "Every pilot was made an officer. And every officer had . . . invitations. Just fun, I thought. House parties and dinners and . . ." Trysts. Batting eyelashes. Games and wagers. *Fun.*

"Not the sort of life to which those who came from humbler backgrounds would be accustomed," she finished for him.

She understood. Because somehow she saw everything. And still it didn't dim her eyes.

"I ruined them. Good men. Good men who had been happy with their lives before I showed them something else."

"And then . . . they were distracted that day?"

Distracted? No. Focused. Too focused. But he couldn't put words to that. He could only shake his head and force his eyes open again.

"You were saying their names. Something about fire. The Channel."

His fingers tightened. Too tight, probably, but she didn't complain.

His gaze fell, shifted. Paisley wallpaper. Wooden floors. Turkish rug.

"Does it happen often? Flashbacks to that day?"

"No." How could he flash back to it when it never left him? Not for a second. He focused his gaze on their hands. His were clean now, too, though they surely hadn't been before.

"It was probably the fire, then, that brought it back. We're not allowed to use the term *shell shock* anymore, but—"

"I'm not a coward." He shot it out like ordnance, slicing his eyes over to hers and then dropping them in contrition again at that steady light in her gaze. "Half the men claiming shell shock—it was just an excuse. When war was too much for their delicate sensibilities—"

"I'm not calling you a coward—the opposite. You proved yourself a hero tonight. But don't speak ill of the others either. I treated many of those men. Perhaps some were wallowing in their weakness, but others . . ." Her fingers squeezed. "There's a reality there. A trauma. You saw something horrible that day."

He hadn't just seen it. He'd smelled it, heard it, felt it, tasted it. *"You'll either be a hero or a villain, Phil. Try to pick the right one, will you?"*

"I'm no hero."

"Michael might disagree. As would the dozens of other pensioners you helped rescue tonight."

"That's not heroism, that's just . . . *doing*, because it needed done."

Her laugh was sunlight—not the glaring, fireball kind. The soft, spring kind that dappled the leaves and inspired the birds to sing. "What do you think heroism is but doing what needs done when the situation tries to prevent it?"

He shook his head. "They didn't deserve to go out like that. The fire . . ." The pensioners, he meant.

Only he didn't. He meant *them*. The litany.

"I know."

He had a feeling she did. He sat forward, not really sure why except that he was mildly aware of a stinging on his back—another scrape? But when his elevation changed, the room tilted, and when he tried to move to compensate . . .

Her arm slid around him, steadying him, her fingers splayed against his back. His head sagged onto her shoulder, his face nestled in the crook of her neck. He ought to be embarrassed—so weak he couldn't even sit up without falling over her—but he couldn't be. Because she smelled of soap and smoke and just the faintest hint of lilac that she must have dabbed on beforehand.

His insides quaked and liquefied until it seemed the whole

world was an ocean. The Channel, its waters swaying and un-dulating and threatening to swallow him.

He was sinking, and he needed more of an anchor than those five splayed fingers against his shoulder blade. He pulled his hand from hers, abandoning the wings to her, and slid his arm around her waist. There. Better. More solid. More warmth. More steadiness. He breathed in soap. Breathed out smoke. Willed it all to steady.

Maybe, if he could stay right here forever, anchored to her, he'd weather it. Maybe he'd plant his feet on solid ground again. Maybe he could even soar once more in the clouds. If he could just stay here, with her pulse a steady cadence under his ear. Her heart could be his. Beat for him. Fill his veins with something other than darkness.

Her voice came in a whisper, sliding over him, like the hand that rubbed a circle of calm onto his back. Like the fingers she lifted to soothe back his hair over the bandage wrapped about his head, as she'd done at the bomb site. The words themselves made no sense—words like *Father* and *Lord* and *peace* and *please*—but the tone was a song. Clouds skittering before a sunset. Touched by gold. Cool as balm.

He listened through the entire hymn. And then heard his voice whisper, though he couldn't quite fathom he actually said the words, "Sing 'Hide Not Thou Thy Face from Us.'"

She did, without even a breath of laughter that he—the black-hearted scoundrel—would request such a song.

And cast not off thy servant in thy displeasure.

The words dug their way down. Deep, and then deeper. To the place he'd sworn was shut away for good. God hadn't been the one to cast him off—that's what Jeremy would say. Camden had done the casting, the straying. Happily, with no regrets. Because he didn't believe in regrets.

A lie as complete as the ones he'd told his men as he tipped more gin into their glasses and nudged them toward the cluster of smiling dancers who seemed eager to lend some "comfort" to a few of England's heroes. *There's no harm*, he'd said.

How wrong he'd been.

He didn't know how long he sat there, draped around Ara, but his neck was starting to ache by the time her words petered out to a hum. He knew the tune of this new song, maybe. Something that brought to mind school chapels and the cathedral in Portsmouth and Jeremy bellowing in the bath while Gil covered his ears as they walked by in the corridor outside the water closet.

Then a voice came from a few feet away, deep and amused. "Need I go and fetch a shotgun, American style?"

He didn't budge. Couldn't convince himself to pull away from her. If Den meant to make him marry her, they'd have to perform the ceremony right here.

Her lips pressed to his hair. Her hand came to a rest against his back. And he could feel her head turn, toward her father. "Is Parks back yet?"

"Just, yes. Are you awake, Cam, or have you passed out there on my lovely pillow of a daughter?"

"I'm not entirely certain," he said into her neck.

She chuckled. "Regardless of his state of consciousness, I believe the bleeding has stopped, if we wanted to get him into the nightshirt."

"Capital."

Was it? Camden may have disagreed, if he'd had the chance. But she was urging him up, and the light from the lamp assaulted his eyes, and the movement made his head swim again. The next thing he knew, Den was pulling white cotton over his head and Ara was guiding his arms through the sleeves like he was two years old. And then he was against the pillows once more—not the lovely, warm, Ara-shaped one, but the downy squares that felt none too soft against the aching back of his head.

His hands spread against the counterpane in objection. "Ara." His head hadn't quite stopped spinning this time when it stilled. Or perhaps it was just that someone was beating a drum inside it. A jungle-worthy *thump* for every beat of his pulse. No, he hadn't a pulse. It must be to every beat of hers.

Her fingers touched his brow. Adjusted something—presumably the bandage that wrapped round his aching skull—and then pried his eyes open. He winced and pulled away.

"Don't be a bad patient. I'm just checking your pupil dilation."

He held still, though he scowled. "I liked you better as a pillow."

There, the dimple flashed. "Yes, well, your pillow needs to get cleaned up." She turned to her father. "We'll take shifts with him."

"I don't need—"

"Hush." She stilled his objection and returned the wings to him, placing them under his hand. Her gaze was still on her father. "He can sleep, but we'll have to wake him every few hours to check his alertness. I don't think coma is a real danger in this case, but head wounds are so very unpredictable. If at any point he becomes unresponsive, we'll have to get him to hospital."

Den gave her a salute. "Aye, aye, Nurse Ara. Let me go and fetch my book, and I'll take first shift."

Camden ought to insist he didn't need to be watched. That he wouldn't be able to sleep anyway, with these dratted Amazonian drums banging about in his head. But when Den disappeared and Ara looked at him again, the arguments died on his tongue.

His fingers traced the brass wings. Hooked them. Held them. They were him, these wings. What he was—a pilot, one of England's "reckless fellows," as they had been dubbed. But not just that. He was the pin that ripped and tore at the Corps. He was the clasp that wouldn't work right. He was the blight on them. Not just replaceable, but disposable.

He turned his wrist, opening his fingers so that the badge rested in his palm. Useless. Soon to tarnish. Destructive.

Her fingers plucked up the metal, and for a moment his throat closed with something so foreign he could scarcely find a name for it. Something that made him think *maybe not*. Maybe she saw what he didn't. Maybe, in her hands . . .

She set the pin softly, carefully onto the end table.

It had been hope. But he only knew its name when it died, snuffed out like a candle. That was the way it should be. The way it *must* be. If she held on to him, if he clung to her, he'd pull her down with him. They'd drown together.

She deserved better.

"I'll check on you soon." She cupped his cheek in her palm and pressed a kiss to his forehead.

"You treat all your patients this well?"

She laughed—softly, carefully, like a pin on the table—and her dimple winked at him.

Before he could think better of it, he caught her head with a hand, pulled it back down, and pressed his lips there, to the dimple. And said the only thing he could think to say. "I'm sorry."

She pulled away enough to show him her frown. "Phillip Camden doesn't apologize."

"Not for what I do." He let his hand fall away. It felt heavy. Heavy as a headache.

"Then why?"

He let her gaze hold his in its embrace of gold. Let her see, if she cared to look, all the sharp and bent and broken pieces inside. "For being Phillip Camden."

"Don't be sorry for that." Her fingers tangled with his for a moment, even though her body was angling away. "I rather like Phillip Camden."

Well. That made one of them.

15

For a long moment, Arabelle could only stare. Perhaps it was the fact that she'd only managed about three hours of sleep, but the image before her simply made no sense. The white bandage around his head was the only piece that fit what she'd expected.

Otherwise . . . she was either losing her mind, dreaming, or Phillip Camden was the most frustrating man in the history of the world. "What do you think you're doing?"

What he *should* have been doing was sleeping. Perhaps asking for some breakfast or a cup of tea or even some of Father's coffee. Certainly demanding aspirin for what must be a splitting headache. But *not* sitting in the chair against the wall, tying his shoes of all things. Dressed in his uniform rather than her father's nightshirt.

He didn't look up at her. Probably because moving his head so quickly would make it pound. Which is why he ought to have been in bed still. Instead he said, like an idiot, "Putting my shoes on."

She planted her hands on her hips. She was dressed for church and had only meant to stop in long enough to tell him she was going and would be back shortly, ask him if he needed anything. "*Why* are you putting your shoes on? You have not been released from Denler Hospital yet, Major."

Shoes tied, he straightened—slowly—and even pushed himself to his feet. He offered a grin, but it was tight around the edges. "I'm afraid you haven't the authority to keep me here, Nurse. Not unless the admiral has given his leave. I have a shift today."

She could only blink at him and wait for the words to form. They didn't. Not until he actually took a step away from the chair, reaching for his hat. "Stop! That will hit right where the wound is." She charged forward and snatched the thing from his hand. "And it's *Sunday*."

If not for the pain shadowing his eyes, he might have looked amused. "I'm aware. Hence why I'm going to work. I always work Sundays—that one two weeks ago was the exception, not the rule."

That made no sense at all. "You work in an office now, don't you? Why is there a Sunday shift at all?"

"Because the war doesn't stop just because some people want to go to church." He debated the hat, took it from her, and tucked it under his arm. "And since I don't anyway, it made sense that I take the Sunday shift with the other so-dubbed heathen. Dilly the atheist and—"

"Well, that's convenient for you, isn't it? A handy excuse for *why* you don't go to church."

"Not that I need one."

It must be the exhaustion that had her eyes burning. Why else would she get so unreasonably upset at what she already knew? The fact that he'd requested a hymn last night meant nothing more than that he had fond memories of it. He'd made it no secret that he had no use for the trappings of religion. And with some people, she was perfectly willing to grant that they could have a sincere faith without those trappings.

But Camden didn't have *that* either. And it yawned in him, a greedy black monster. Couldn't he see it? "How long do you think you can neglect your soul, Cam, before it shrivels?"

He'd been reaching for the items on the side table—his keys, his brass wings—but paused. Shot her a look. "Haven't you heard? I don't have a soul."

"Rubbish." And oh, how she wished he'd stop parroting all those ridiculous accusations lobbed at him by journalists seeking to sensationalize his dastardly deeds. "I might as well claim that I have no body."

He breathed a laugh—wincing a bit, but that didn't stop him from sweeping a rakish look down her figure. "One fault with that argument." With two big steps, he stood before her, close enough that she had to tilt her head back to see the two inches up into his eyes. Close enough that she could feel his heat. Close enough that her breath hitched. His blue eyes burned. "I can *see* your body."

A few years ago, the way he said it would have made her blush. But she'd spent too much time around men whose manners were hindered and sometimes altogether removed by medication. She lifted her chin. Looked him square in the too-blue eyes. "And I can see your soul."

For a moment he made no reaction. Then a smile seeped out the corners of his lips and lit the depths of his eyes. "I think I believe you."

"You should. Just as you should trust my insight as a woman of medicine." She lifted a finger and drilled it softly into his chest, right above his heart. "You're a strong, fit fellow. You obviously understand the value of exercising your body. Because if you neglect it, your muscles will weaken. Use them not at all and they atrophy. What do you think happens to your soul when you neglect *it*?"

He eased back half a step, something dark and hurting pulsing in his eyes. "My brother lectures me?"

She shook her head and dropped her hand. "I worry for you, Cam. I've worried for you before I even knew you. When I watched you walk by day after day and saw the anger and emptiness in you."

She expected him to brush her off. Turn away. Instead, he gave her a crooked smile. "And I bet you've been praying for me, haven't you? Before you even knew me."

"Of course I have."

He shook his head and scooped up the bits of metal from the

table, shoved them into his pocket, and then met her eyes again. His looked a bit less shadowed. Perhaps some of the pain was easing as he moved.

And move he did, shifting back to that space too close to her. The hand not anchoring his hat lifted, rested against her right cheek. In the next second, his lips touched her left cheek. "Thank you." Then he was stepping past her, toward and out the bedroom door. "I'll stop by after my shift so you can check my pupils and fuss over my bandages and whatnot. All right?"

Perhaps by then her pulse would have returned to normal. Assuming her heart could handle two such should-be-innocent kisses within twelve hours of each other and didn't explode. "If your headache worsens, tell your superior what happened and let him send you home."

His answer was to stride into the corridor.

She followed. "Promise me, Phillip, or I will pay you an office call to check on you after lunch."

That at least made his pace hitch for a beat. "You're as bad as my mother, do you know that?"

Having seen how much he adored his mother, she wasn't going to let *that* comparison deter her. "And I daresay she'd thank me for my care."

"No doubt. All right, darling, I promise. If it gets worse, I'll plead ill and injured and leave early."

Figuring that was the best she was going to get out of him, she said no more. Though she *did* follow him down the stairs to make sure he gained the entryway without mishap. If he could manage those, with the turns and altitude changes, she was fairly confident he could manage the flat, short walk. Even so, "I can drive you, if you like."

He yanked open the door—where was Parks?—and shot her a half-amused, half-annoyed look. "I don't like. The last time you drove me somewhere, I ended up crawling through a burning building, if you recall."

Well, his sense of humor was certainly intact. He must not be feeling *too* poorly. She folded her arms over her chest, gave him her best stern-nurse look, and managed not to smile until he'd closed the front door again.

She let out a whoosh of a sigh. The Lord was pursuing him. Calling him. She knew it, could see it in those flickering shadows in his eyes. She'd known it even before she met him. And now her prayers for him would have to redouble. And try not to get confused by anything she might wish of him beyond that.

With a shake of her head, she turned back to the stairs. She had to grab her hat and gloves, then she would be ready to leave too. Father had already declared himself too exhausted to join her this morning, and given that he'd taken a double shift at Camden's bedside, she tended to believe him.

Besides. When she stepped out into the brisk winter air ten minutes later, the solitude felt rather delicious, giving her a few minutes as she walked to church to process the last unbelievable twelve hours. The bombing. The street-side triage. The slap-dash infirmary she and a few other nurses had set up in the house of a kind neighbor to tend those who were injured. While most of the hospital had been undamaged and would likely be open again soon, smoke had been billowing throughout the whole thing, and they hadn't been certain whether the brigade would get the fire out before it spread. Evacuation of every patient and staff member had been necessary.

Not quickly enough for some. The bomb had taken out the entire North East wing, and though Arabelle hadn't heard an exact count of how many had been killed, she knew that the Captain of Invalids and his family had been among the number. The nurses had been distraught when they realized that the Ludlows hadn't emerged and their quarters had taken a direct hit.

Always so much death, and only so much she could do to stave it off. Hands burrowed deep in her pockets, Arabelle turned the corner and set her gaze on the familiar steeple.

◈ ◈ ◈

"Do you need a lift home?" Brook, little Ambrose on her hip, was frowning at Arabelle as they made their way down the aisle after the service. "You look absolutely done in."

She felt it too. But a blast of wind blustered its way in through the open doors and made her perk up a bit. "Thanks, but I'll be fine. A little walk will wake me enough to take my lunch first." She'd not risen in time for breakfast, and she'd regret it if she skipped another meal.

"Are you certain?" Ella gave her arm a quick squeeze. Young Addie had a hold of Ella's other hand, little James attached to hers in turn. "You had quite a night, it seems."

Her brows knotted. She'd not had time to tell them about her adventures after leaving the Nottingham home last night. But it didn't sound as though Ella was referring to the dinner party. How would they have realized she'd followed the fire to the Royal Hospital, though? Someone could have seen her pull out in that direction rather than toward home, she supposed.

"Miss Denler, I'm so glad I caught you. Have you a moment?"

She spun at the voice, her spine instantly straightening. She recognized it immediately. Every nurse and VAD at Charing Cross ought to, as it belonged to the hospital matron. "Mrs. Jameson—yes, absolutely." She sent a quick smile to her friends. "Excuse me, please."

With their murmurs of good-bye following her, Ara stepped out of the receiving line with the matron. They bypassed the vicar and congregants shaking his hand and squeezed through the door into the February air. Not until they'd gone down the steps did Mrs. Jameson turn toward her again.

She was a kind woman, strength etched into her every feature. Her hair, silver threaded with a few remaining strands of brown, was always pulled back in a chignon at the nape of her neck, and her eyes were always ready to praise, offer encouragement, or deliver a challenge—whichever was needed.

Now she linked her arm through Arabelle's and offered a warm smile. "When I heard about the terrible bombing last night, I rushed directly over. I've a good friend who works there. She said you arrived within minutes of the attack and that you were invaluable."

"Oh." That was why her superior had found her at church? Mrs. Jameson didn't attend here, so far as Arabelle had ever seen. "Well. I saw the plane fly over, and then the blast. I could hardly return calmly to my home and go to bed when I knew people would be in need of help. I am only glad I could be of service."

"Which is your usual way. It has not gone unnoticed." Outside the wrought-iron gates of the church, Mrs. Jameson paused and turned to look up into Arabelle's face. "You are aware, I'm certain, that Nurse Wilcox lost three of her sons in the first year of the war?"

Though she couldn't think what one had to do with the other, Arabelle nodded.

Mrs. Jameson's eyes went sad. "She just received word yesterday that her last living son has been injured—though not fatally, praise be to the Lord."

"Oh no!" Arabelle's hand flew to her lips. She'd seen Nurse Wilcox's devastation when telegram after telegram had shattered her world three years ago, but she could only imagine the fear when another terrible yellow slip appeared in the hand of an army messenger. "What happened?"

"Artillery fire. He lost both arm and leg on his left side, I'm afraid." Mrs. Jameson's lips thinned. "Understandably, our dear Maryann has decided that her nursing skills must be given solely to him now. She has resigned, effective tomorrow, when he'll arrive by train from the front."

Though Arabelle had never before thought of Nurse Wilcox as *our dear Maryann*, she was rather inclined to just now. "Can I help in any way? Other than my prayers, which they will certainly have."

"That's why I've sought you out today, and I pray you'll forgive me for intruding upon you at church to discuss business." Mrs. Jameson offered another smile, tired and tight. "We find ourselves in need of another ward matron. You were the first nurse to spring to mind for the position."

"Me?" Arabelle blinked at her, sure she'd misheard. Seniority, that was how these promotions usually worked. The nurse in charge of the entire hospital must be the most experienced, and then she placed those who came nearest her years of service in positions of authority under her. And while Ara was among the more experienced these days, there were at least two women who had been at it longer.

Yet Mrs. Jameson was nodding. Definitively. "I have seen how skilled you are at managing the volunteers and guiding the younger nurses. Frankly, I would have offered you such a position before now, but I couldn't be sure Braxton wouldn't decide to marry you sooner than you'd said and take you away from us. Your first priority has always been, as it should be, your family. But now . . ."

Now that she'd been cast off, Arabelle was more dependable. She had nothing to take her away from her work.

It was true. So why did it make her throat go tight? "Yes. Quite right. And I would be honored to assume the position, ma'am."

"Good." Mrs. Jameson heaved a sigh. "You cannot know the burden that removes from my shoulders. There is but one more thing I wanted to ask." The older woman began moving again—a leisurely pace that aimed them in the direction of Arabelle's townhouse.

"Yes?"

"Forgive me if this sounds like prying, my dear, but . . . what is the nature of your relationship with Major Camden?"

Arabelle's feet may have drawn to a halt if Mrs. Jameson's arm through hers hadn't insisted she keep moving. And given the parishioners—her neighbors, her friends—milling about, she was in favor of propelling herself out of earshot of them anyway. "I beg your pardon, ma'am?"

The matron gave her a look that defied easy classification. A bit of motherly concern. A bit of caution. A bit of apology. "You know as well as I that a nurse's most important possession is not her skill or training—it is her character. And I'm afraid your continual presence by his side does shed a question upon yours."

Arabelle's fingers balled into a fist so tight she could feel her nails even through her gloves. "With all due respect, ma'am, if my character is so feeble that it can be besmirched by walking home with an officer and a gentleman—upon my father's request—then I haven't much of one to begin with, have I?"

The life of a gentleman. Camden had sounded so bitter, so . . . guilty as he'd spat out those words last night. Proving what Arabelle had long known—that being a gentleman by birth certainly did not make one worthy of the name. Indeed, far too often it seemed to make one the opposite, by promising a man insulation from the consequences of sin.

But Camden recognized it, at least now. That spoke of a character far deeper than he'd probably once admitted.

Mrs. Jameson's breath eased out. "Pray, don't grow angry with me, Arabelle. You know I have superiors as well, men who are quick to insist upon a dismissal at the first whiff of inappropriate conduct by any of my staff. We are in delicate situations—you know that."

"I also know, as should anyone who either knows me or even *looks* at me, that there is not, nor would ever be, anything inappropriate between Major Camden and me. It's laughable."

"It isn't. My dear, please don't take offense at this, but . . ." Mrs. Jameson hesitated, tilted her head, and looked into the distance as if willing the words to walk near. "I don't mean to be gauche, but you are a woman of means. Even if a man such as Major Camden may not be quick to show you interest otherwise, that alone . . ."

How many times had Ara said, in a self-deprecating joke, that she had exactly one million two hundred thousand reasons why a man might wish to marry her? Well, less than that now. An even million, after her gift to Brax and Cass.

And yet hearing it stated so clearly by someone she respected, who seemed to respect her as well, made it all too clear that it was no joke. There was, in the eyes of any who cared to look at all, nothing to ever attract a man like Cam to her other than her money.

She forced her fingers to relax. "I am aware of my assets and their limits. But I assure you, Camden isn't after my money. He has, in fact, taken on the role he has in order to protect me from those who are."

The turning of Mrs. Jameson's lips said, *What a clever ploy on his part* and *Surely you're not fool enough to fall for that?* Her tongue said, "Just . . . be cautious, my dear. I have known far too many women who, distraught over a break with one man, fall unwisely into a relationship with—and sometimes," she added in a whisper, "into the arms of—another."

At the mention of his arms, her mind swung back twelve hours, to when his had indeed come around her. When his face had stayed buried in her neck for so long that she felt cold and bereft when finally she urged him away. She could feel again the press of his lips to her cheek.

But that—all of that—had been different. He'd been hurting. Ripped apart by the memories as much as the stone that had cracked his head and scraped his entire torso, the rubble that had punctured his knee. He hadn't been seeking bodily pleasure. He'd been seeking—whether he knew it or not—spiritual balm. Someone, something to chase away the darkness.

In answer to the matron, she shook her head. "I assure you, ma'am, there is no danger of such in this situation. Camden is a friend. More, one I believe has been treated unfairly by the press. He does not deserve to be judged so harshly. And certainly his intentions toward me—or lack of them, as the case may be—are above reproach."

Mrs. Jameson lifted iron-grey brows toward her hat. "You will really argue that he is a good man?"

The word gave her pause. *Good* wasn't what came to mind when she thought of Phillip Camden. Complicated. Deep. Loyal.

Heroic. Those all fit him far better than the overused *good*. She shrugged. "I think—no, I *know*—he would sooner die than harm those he counts as his own. And I do venture to claim that much of a bond. He respects me. Cares for me, in a brotherly way. He would never harm me, nor take advantage." She lifted her brows, too, returning the challenge. "Will you call me naïve?"

"That's just the thing, Ara. I know you're not." The woman sighed and looked forward again. They were nearly to the intersection where Arabelle would have to bear right to reach her townhouse. "Tread carefully—that's all I shall say on the matter. That, and keep in mind that those who hold your career in their hands will not look kindly on anything more than *brotherly* when it comes to that man. And I would hate to see you throw away a promising future over what would only be a passing *tendre*. You could go far, my dear. I can so easily imagine you in my position someday, running an entire hospital."

Could she? Could Arabelle? She'd never even considered it. Her future had so long been determined. Brax. Family.

She'd not yet paused to consider what now lay open to her. The breath she drew in shook a bit. "My father is determined I accompany him to South America after the war." She didn't know why she said it, other than that it had become the new plan.

Mrs. Jameson's eyes went wide and sparkling. "Oh, but that's perfect! A mission hospital! It's just the sort of thing I can imagine you spearheading, my dear."

For a moment, Arabelle caught a shimmer of the vision—jungle foliage, bamboo huts, she and a few other staff in mud-stained white, tending dark-haired children—then it vanished in the next blink like a wisp of smoke. "Oh, I . . ." She came to a halt at the corner. And realized, with exhaustion weighing her down, that she couldn't believe it. Couldn't believe her father would actually take her with him.

Mrs. Jameson turned to face her and clasped Arabelle's hands within her own. "A door has closed for you, Ara. But I pray you see the one our Lord is opening instead. Keep your eyes on that—

don't go lurching through a window that will only deliver you to a hard, cold reality beneath it."

She meant well. Arabelle knew it, even as she wanted to argue more, again, that Phillip Camden was no dangerous window. And that he had no interest in her jumping out of him anyway.

Best to change the subject. "Shall I report at my usual time in the morning?"

Mrs. Jameson gave her fingers a squeeze, then let them go. "Yes, and come directly to my office. Your hours are going to change—there will be more of them, and you may find it best to grant yourself odd shifts, as you will be managing both day and night nurses for your ward. You may want to find times to catch them both, as Nurse Wilcox did. And there is the paper work you'll be responsible for filling out. But we'll cover all those details in the morning. For now, get some rest. You clearly had a long night." She drew away a step and then sent Arabelle a pointed look. "How is the major? His head wound was nothing serious, I trust?"

How had she . . . ? Her friend at the Royal must have seen and reported that as well. And probably that Arabelle had asked a fireman to help load his half-conscious figure into her car, and she'd driven off with him.

Well, she wouldn't be ashamed of helping him. "He gave us a fright, but he seems well enough. My father and our butler proved excellent interim nurses."

She waited to see if her superior would offer any chastisement.

She didn't. She merely hummed something that could have been agreement or general approval of his condition and then gave a nod of farewell. "Tomorrow, then. Cheerio."

Tomorrow. When she'd become the ward matron. Excitement trilled a bit, but it was muted by exhaustion. And by the *other* half of the conversation. Shaking her head against it, she turned for home.

No sooner had she let herself in—where was Parks *now*?—than she heard footsteps coming from the study.

There was her butler, and he greeted her with lifted brows. "Forgive me, miss. The telephone was ringing—it's for you."

She stared at him dumbly for a moment. There had been callers aplenty, both physical and over the phone, in the last few days—the very men Cam was set on protecting her from. Dropping by, calling to invite them to this or that. Usually Parks fielded the nonpersonal ones for them, taking note of any invitations so they could respond at their leisure. "Who is it?"

He stepped out of the doorway and motioned her in. "Mr. Braxton. I assumed you would want to take this one, and as I heard you entering . . ."

"Yes. Thank you." Brax? Why in the world was *he* ringing her up? Tugging off her gloves, she hurried as much as her tired legs would allow into the drawing room, where the candlestick phone had a table to itself against the far wall. She snatched up the receiver from where Parks had set it carefully upon the table, her eyes drifting to the newspaper he'd also positioned there. The *Sunday Pictorial*, with its images taking up all the space that other papers reserved for text. "Brax? What is it?"

"Ara! Thank God. Are you all right? What the devil were you thinking, going to a bomb site?"

What? How had he . . . ? Dread coiling, she picked up the newspaper. Though the top of the front page merely carried the headline of London Bombed with startling photographs of destruction, when she flipped it over, she saw the photograph beneath the fold, with a subheading that knocked her breath away. Black Heart Plays the Hero.

Cam, climbing out of the wreckage with an old fellow in his arms. He certainly *looked* the hero—the sort that would set all the VADs to swooning anew. But what had that to do with her?

There, in the background of the photograph. She was but a grainy shadow behind him, probably not recognizable to those who didn't know her. But Brax did.

"Ara? Are you there?" His voice cracked its way through the static.

She sighed. "I'm here. And I was there because it's my duty, Edmund. I'm a nurse, if you recall."

"And it's mere coincidence that *he* was too?"

She gripped the phone until she feared she'd crack it. "Are you upset that I was there, or that your brother-in-law was as well?"

Crackling, noisy silence. Then, "I just wanted to be sure you're all right."

Bonny of him to be concerned for her well-being *now*. She squeezed her eyes shut. "I'm fine, I promise you. How's Cass?"

Another beat. "She's doing well. She spent a week at Middlegrove acquainting herself but then returned to Portsmouth. I've been granted family quarters, so . . ."

So he'd put his family in it. "Good. I'm glad the two of you can be together."

"Ara . . ." Was it the connection that was bad, or just the conversation? "Look, I . . . I also called to thank you. As I should have done days ago, but I've not had the chance. I know it was you, though. It had to have been. No one else would send so generous a gift."

This was exactly the conversation she'd wanted to avoid—though she had supposed that he'd figure it out, despite the fact that she'd given the money anonymously. Even had she thought to tell her trustee to wait to send it until the announcement, still he would have assumed.

Even so, she wasn't about to admit to any large gift over a party phone line. "I don't know what you're speaking about, Brax."

His laugh popped its way over the miles. "Right. Well, listen. We know, Cass and I, that we owe you everything. Everything. So if ever you need anything, anything at all . . . We're your friends, she and I. Remember that. Never hesitate to ask if there's anything either of us can do."

Her lips tugged up a bit. She wouldn't mind seeing Cass again, visiting with her when emotions weren't so high. And for that matter, she didn't exactly dislike Brax, even now—though she had to think she'd feel a bit awkward in his presence for the rest of time. Maybe someday she'd pay a visit to the area. See them together, happy and complete.

Oh, how she prayed they remained that way. That the war didn't snatch him away, that life treated them well. That they could hold tight to each other when it didn't.

"You could name me godmother to a child or two. I wouldn't object at having a reason to send lavish gifts on occasion." Auntie Ara. The only role she'd ever play now.

He laughed again. "We would be honored. Well, I'd better ring off. But remember, Ara. We're here."

"I know. Thank you." She sank to a seat on the chair beside the table, said her farewells, hung up the receiver, and then picked up the *Pictorial* again.

This was how Cam *ought* to appear in the papers. Saving the day. She read the article on the second page, a bit surprised, given the photograph, that they made only passing mention of his presence there.

Exhaustion making every limb heavy, Ara leaned onto the arm of the chair, its polished wood barely softened by brocade-covered padding, and rested her head on her hand.

Maybe this would convince a few people that he wasn't a villain. Wasn't a scoundrel. Wasn't to be feared.

Maybe, somehow, last night could prove a stride forward for him.

16

Not good. This was not good. Diellza left the newspaper where it sat on the table and dashed back up to her room rather than out the door. She had to finish those letters *now*. She'd only written two of the five, but she had a feeling her timetable had just shifted.

Press like that could change things. Too many things. If Camden began to be viewed as a hero, then a court-martial was less likely. The brass really *would* be hesitant to accuse an officer who was a public hero, at least when the evidence against him was circumstantial.

No. What she needed was a renewed call for justice. And someone to come forward with new information.

Whether it was true or not.

The other girls in the house were at church, promising her an empty hallway, at least. She'd said she'd be right behind them, but this was far more important than sitting on a hard pew and trying to convince her landlady that she was pious.

Tugging her key free, she skidded to a halt in front of her door and fitted the iron into it. Twisted, turned the handle, let herself in. Sunlight filtered through the gauze of her curtains, weak and wintry, falling directly on her trunk.

"Yes," she whispered to its secrets. "I know. I'm *working* on it."

She pulled off all the outerwear she'd only just put on two minutes earlier and tossed them on her bed. Relocked her door and scrambled around the tight space to kneel before the trunk.

She should write to Alwin while she was alone in the house too. He'd demanded regular updates on her progress, providing her with an address to which she was to write and making her memorize a simple code to write in. In English, he'd insisted. It would draw less attention than German.

Lifting the lid, Diellza swept her gaze over the contents of the trunk. Her paper and fountain pen were there, in the tray that sat in the top. She took those out and then removed the whole tray. Shoved aside all the bits and baubles that served as a cover and opened the false bottom.

There, nestled in among the pieces of her weapon, were the letters she'd already written. These she pulled out to copy, then replaced the lot.

The floor was cold, but since her room had no desk, it would be her chair anyway. She curled her legs up under her on the rug she'd moved here for this purpose and closed the trunk so she could use its flat top for her table.

Paper—several sheets, so that the bottom one would intercept any too-firm pressure from her pen and keep the words from tracing themselves onto the trunk.

First, the letters to the other widows. She spread out one of the two she'd already written and copied the same words onto her fresh sheet, aside from a new name and direction.

Dear Mrs. Montagu,

Please forgive me for being forward, but I am aware of the terrible tragedy your family has suffered at the hand of Major Camden. I am acquainted with the gentleman in question, if he can rightly be called such, and I believe I may be able to help you if you wish to bring this matter back to the attention of the authorities. . . .

She continued writing with sure, even strokes upon the page. She'd worked for two hours upon the initial letter, going over her English time and again to be sure it was all right. That no one would read it and think right away, *This is from a German speaker*.

The fact that she had an accent probably meant it was good she had to contact them through letters and not in person, much as she would have preferred to travel to their homes and meet them face-to-face.

She was far better at convincing people to do what she wanted in person. That was, after all, how she'd managed to discover where each of these women lived. Two were in London or the outlying areas, the others spread all over England—one even in Canada, which made it highly unlikely that *she* would prove useful.

Not that Diellza intended to leave any stone unturned.

She set each letter aside as she finished it to let the ink dry, then moved on to the next. Her hand was cramped by the time she'd finished, but it was pain that said she'd accomplished something. Satisfied, she folded the letters into the envelopes she'd already addressed.

Then pulled another blank sheet forward. The letter to Alwin. It could have none of what she *wanted* to say to him in it, of course. It had to remain strictly business, sound innocent on the face, and then contain the letters and numbers of the code he'd taught her.

Dear Tim,

I have found a goat for our sister to purchase; the price is a bit steep, but that is to be expected in these times. I am confident it will be of great help to our life here. The lambs will flock to it. . . .

She wrote a bit more, smiling at the hidden meaning even in the English words. She'd found a goat, all right—their scapegoat.

Contact had been made. And if all went according to plan, those lambs would flock to it, not knowing they were coming to their own slaughter.

It took her another half an hour to put a few of the crucial details into the code, scratched in small script into the margins and between lines. When she was finished, she sat by with a sigh.

Two days. Two days until her meeting with Camden. One of many, if she could work her magic on him. From him, she'd find out all she could, all the papers hadn't said. Who his worst enemies were.

Then it would be a simple matter of manipulating the men exactly where she wanted them to go.

She smiled at the envelopes ready to go in tomorrow's post. The men . . . and the vindictive women too.

Camden lifted a hand to scratch at the back of his head, barely remembering in time that he'd regret it if he did. Ara had at least managed a less-obtrusive bandage, and he'd sworn he'd wear his hat in a way that it wouldn't rub at it. Easy, he'd assured her, since it was his day off, after his Monday night shift.

Or it should have been, had Admiral Hall and Lawrence Denler not decided that made it a fine time to schedule another meeting. He could have opted not to attend, he supposed. But when the admiral invited him . . . Well, he wasn't going to turn him down.

Every time he touched his head, though, he didn't think only of Saturday night and the Royal Hospital. He thought too of the successful bombing of St. Pancras Station the following night. He hadn't been there to lend any aid, either on the ground or, as he'd prefer, in the air. More bombers, sneaking past them. More of their own, shot down. And where had he been? Holed up in Room 40, decoding the messages that reported the success and grinding his teeth at his own inability to do anything about it.

He nearly collided with another cryptographer as he rounded a corner, pulling up just in time to avoid a collision. "Ho!"

The man smiled. *Smiled*. Camden couldn't ever recall Montgomery—their "Fighting Padre" as they called him—smiling at him. "How's the head today, Major?"

With any of the others, he may have attributed the sudden friendliness to glee over his injury. But the clergyman had never seemed particularly cruel. Just smart enough to direct his smiles at someone other than *him*.

Camden nodded. "Improving."

"Glad to hear it—I've been praying."

Camden made a show of rolling his eyes. "You and my brother would get on well. And that isn't a compliment."

But Montgomery laughed. Then yawned. "Sorry. My neighbor's new puppies were yipping away all night. Don't suppose you need a cocker spaniel? Or five?"

"Don't offer the innocent pups to *him*. He might feast on them for breakfast." Commander James strode by as he delivered the line, not so much as pausing. But he was grinning. And he *winked*, proving it a joke.

What was with everyone these last few days? Did a crack on the skull really prove him not despicable? Regardless, Camden couldn't let that one slide by. "Only if my rations are cut."

James laughed. As did Montgomery, though it mixed with another yawn. "Well. Back to work, I suppose."

Camden nodded and stepped out of the padre's way, aiming once more for the office at the end of the hall. Denler, the guards below had informed him, had come up just five minutes earlier.

And when he knocked upon the door and obeyed the summons to enter, he found that his friend and the admiral were already fully involved in their conversation, bent together over a map.

Camden closed the door with a quiet click.

Hall blinked up at him. "Good morning, Major. How's your head?"

"Still attached to my shoulders." He slung his hat onto one corner of the empty chair they'd left for him, his overcoat on the other.

Den was, as usual, perched on the desk rather than a chair. It didn't seem to faze him that it was an admiral's desk and not his own. He tapped a map. "He's likely here. Though I don't know how your lad over there will find him if he doesn't mean to be found. And Juan often doesn't want to be found."

DID studied the map, too, leaning onto the opposite end of his desk from where his guest perched. "What do you suggest, then? Can you get in touch with this Juan chap from here? Or is there someone else on the police force that you know?"

"Likely." Denler screwed up his mouth in thought, making the dimple he'd passed down to Arabelle appear. "But I can't be sure; it's been so long since I've been in country. If only Sebastian would answer my telegrams, this would all be a breeze. I hope no ill has befallen him."

"Mason *has* made some inroads." Hall tapped a finger on the desk, his gaze distant with thought. "As well he should have, having been there since summer. Perhaps our only recourse is to let it play out. I do appreciate your willingness to help us, Mr. Denler, but if this Sebastian is unresponsive, I don't see what else we can do."

Denler granted the point with lifted brows. Inclined his head. And, eyes sparking in that way Camden had learned signaled a plan every bit as reckless as any of his, said, "Or . . ."

The admiral's eyes sharpened, and he straightened from his lean. "Or?"

"We can eliminate the distance." Denler popped off the desk and stood to his full height, two inches over Camden and several above Hall. "I've a yacht. I can have a crew together within the fortnight. Be in Mexico before the month is out."

Camden held his breath for a beat, his eyes on his superior, waiting for him to point out the obvious. When he didn't—the man actually folded his arms over his chest and let a thoughtful look cross his face—Cam nearly exploded. "That's idiotic."

Both older men looked over at him. Hall with an expression of amusement. Denler with one of betrayal.

Camden motioned to the map on the desk. "Aren't you forgetting something rather crucial, Den? The reason you've been in England and not Mexico to begin with? Between here and there is a rather large ocean patrolled by U-boats that have declared open warfare on any craft hailing from an Allied port."

"Oh, bah." Denler actually waved that declaration off as if it were nothing more than a mosquito, his face shifting into a smile. "They're not going to target one small yacht heading to the Americas when there are naval ships and supply freighters for their torpedoes. I've only let that deter me as an excuse. I needed some time with my girl, that's all. It would have been a shame if she'd got married and moved off before I'd even had a real chance to know her."

Camden could feel the storm clouds rolling over his own face. "So now that Brax has tossed her over, you're just going to leave?"

"Well, not for *long*." Denler, grinning, turned back to the map. "A few months, I should expect. Six, at the outside. She'll scarcely notice I'm gone, what with all her new responsibilities at Charing Cross. If anything, she'll thank me—I daresay all those annoying callers will by necessity cease without me there as a chaperone for their visits."

"She will *not* thank you." Camden jabbed a finger into the air in Denler's general direction. Maybe it would send a pulse from all this energy coursing through him and zap this mad idea from his mind. This was *not* what he'd had in mind when he recommended Denler to the admiral. He'd thought he'd merely be able to put him in touch with useful contacts in Mexico. Make a few introductions. Send a letter or two. Not *go*. "You are all she has."

"Don't be ridiculous. She has you now too."

The jolt seemed to have reversed, zapping *him* instead. For a moment he could only stare at the man. "What father in his right mind would be content to leave his daughter in *my* care?"

Admiral Hall snorted a laugh. "I wouldn't."

But Denler chuckled as if it were all a joke. "You'd sooner die than see her hurt, and well you know it."

"Not to the point." He lifted a hand to rake through his hair, felt the bandage under his fingers instead, and spat out a curse. "If you leave again, without even a reason that you can tell her, she'll be devastated. She'll think that you, like that idiot Braxton, chose something more alluring over her. That you've abandoned her after all those plans of including her in your life."

There, that seemed to have gotten through to him. A bit. His eyes shifted, lost some of their gleam. He looked to the admiral. "He does have a point, sir. If I say I'm only going off on another of my expeditions, my daughter will be distraught. Couldn't I at least tell her I'm lending aid to the Admiralty? Without any details?"

Hall considered for a moment, his habitual facial twitch indicative of nothing but his ever-moving thoughts. The man seemed capable of processing a hundred different points at once, weighing them all, drawing connections where normal people saw none. "That would be acceptable."

Camden cursed again. "He's here to *consult*. Not to become an agent. Why are you both talking as though this has already been decided?"

"Because it has," the two said in unison.

Camden spun away. "Madness."

"Poppycock. Just a bit of adventure, and doing my bit for king and country to boot. You, of all people, ought to appreciate that, Cam."

Camden shut his eyes against Denler's words. Yes, he understood. In principle. And in relation to himself—he, who had nothing to lose and no one to mourn him if a torpedo sent him to the bottom of the pond. But this was entirely different. "Ara will be furious. And frantic."

"She's a reasonable girl. And an independent one. She'll be fine."

Camden opened his mouth to argue more, but Hall stopped him with a lifted hand and matching brows. "Haven't you an appointment to keep, Major?"

He held his superior's gaze for a long moment, his fingers curling against his leg. He'd voiced his objections. He'd been overruled.

And while part of him wasn't all that opposed to the idea of insubordination, in this case it could land him back in prison—and then he wouldn't be there to make certain Ara weathered this blow.

Jerking his head in a nod, he snatched up his coat and hat again and stormed from the admiral's office.

Paper crinkled in his coat pocket as he jerked his arms into their holes, reminding him that he'd planned to jot down every word Dee Mettler said over their tea as soon as he was on the train home. He'd forgotten a pencil, though, so he detoured into Room 40 to grab one from his desk.

The others didn't even look up at him as he stomped his way in. They were used to his moods by now, which served him well, as he had no desire for any more conversation.

He yanked the drawer open, muttering a few choice words when the stack of folded papers inside it caught on the ledge and resisted his efforts. He pulled a handful of the letters out, fighting the urge to fling the white squares at the wall. Had he been in his flat, he would have.

But not here. This lot was too curious, and he didn't need them all wondering who was writing him threatening notes every day. Instead he shoved them into his pocket, added a pencil to the mix, and slammed the drawer shut again.

The only response that earned him was a quick, frowning glance from Culbreth.

He ignored it and charged back into the corridor, down the stairs, and out the doors. As he strode across the parade grounds, he told himself he wasn't going to look up. Wasn't going to risk catching her eye in a window, knowing that soon her father would be leaving her again. Maybe he wouldn't even go by the hospital.

But he did—habit?—and he couldn't keep himself from slanting a look up at the fourth floor windows either.

She wasn't there. No one was, aside from a serviceman with a white bandage ensconcing his head that put Camden's little ribbon of one to shame. And that was *not* disappointment that pierced him; it was relief.

She wouldn't have time anymore for staring out windows. Frankly, she probably never would have taken the time had it not been at the end of her shift. But that would also be changing now. Her hours would be unpredictable. Not so conveniently aligned to his. Seeing her home wouldn't be a simple matter of waiting here for her to emerge.

For that matter, he could hardly spend every evening at the Denler home with her father gone. Den's absence might keep the obnoxious money-grubbers away, but it would demand the same of him. Which made his mood plummet all the more. Evenings in his flat, with only a book and his own low spirits for company, sounded about as appealing as another head wound.

Blast Denler. Camden wouldn't curse her promotion—she'd earned it, and the light in her eyes when she'd told them of it Sunday over dinner . . . well, his chest had swelled with pride for her. In her. But her father's decision was something else entirely. That took a newly challenging situation and made it impossible. How was he to look after her when he couldn't blamed well spend any time with her without society gasping in horror?

Raindrops inspired him to head for the tube station rather than walking to Piccadilly, despite it being so near. The train was crowded—mostly with women, a few children, and the old. He was one of the few men of serving age, and he knew well it was only his uniform that kept some of those women from sneering at him. Heaven help the civil servant who wasn't in uniform these days—they were generally branded as cowards, even if their positions were vital to the empire. No one could know that at a glance.

A tottering old grandmother shuffled her way on behind him, and Camden looked about for a seat for her. There were none, and he wasn't exactly going to tell the other women they ought to get up.

Though a younger man—looked barely more than a teenager, truth be told—stood and motioned to his seat. "Here you are, ma'am."

The old woman gave him a crinkly smile and shook her head. "No, no, young man. You sit." She gripped a handhold.

The idiot actually sat again with a shrug and shook open a newspaper. Camden rolled his eyes, reached over, grabbed the lad by his courier-uniform's collar, and hauled him up.

"Hey!"

"Hey yourself. You stand. She sits."

"But she said—"

"I don't care what she said. We aren't just gentlemen when ladies give us permission to be." Camden gave the lad a helpful push toward an empty handhold and presented the empty seat with a flourish of his hand.

The old woman pressed her lips against a grin and slid onto the seat, apparently thinking better of arguing again.

Well, that improved his mood a degree or two. He settled in for the short ride with a bit less tension in his shoulders. He still had to determine the best course for Ara. But for now, he'd better shift his focus to Dee—and determining what in the world *her* course was.

17

Diellza watched him striding up the street from her table at the window, letting a smile curl over her lips. He *did* have a presence, that Phillip Camden. One that, depending on his mood, either cleared his path or brought people flocking to him. Which side, though, would he present to her today?

She traced a lazy finger around the rim of her water glass, pushing down the tendrils of nervousness that tried to stretch their way up from her stomach. *Calm. Pleasant. Alluring.* She had to convince him to meet her again, in case she didn't get what she needed this time.

Her finger had the slightest quaver to it. She tucked it into her lap and drew in a deep breath. He was coming in now, holding the door for two exiting ladies. No doubt smiling at them, given the head-ducking, eyelash-batting, and flirtatious smiles she could see on the faces of the women. Another minute and he'd be shown to her table.

For exactly three seconds, she granted her eyes the reprieve of closing. Only three.

How had she got here? Five years ago, had someone told her she'd be a cabaret dancer who entertained men for money on the side, spying in England, and plotting an assassination, she'd have laughed in their face—or slapped them across it. Then Alwin had shown up and . . .

"He'll be your ruin." Friede had frantically whispered those words to her, clasping Diellza's hands in her own and begging her with her endless dark eyes not to do it. Not to sneak out to meet him.

Should she have listened? Had she not gone out that day, not given herself to Alwin . . . No. She couldn't fathom that. Perhaps her life would have been more normal, more predictable, but who wanted a normal, predictable life?

Three seconds, overflowing as they were, were over. She opened her eyes again and set the muscles of her face into the expression she'd perfected in the mirror of her room at Mrs. Humbird's. Pleasure and pain. Apology and desire. She stood as he appeared around the partition—his overcoat and hat already checked—and held a hand out for him as he approached.

"Camden. I am so sorry." The moment his fingers took hers, she leaned forward, up, and pressed her lips to his cheek. "I had no idea what had befallen you and your men—I must have sounded the dunce the other day. I had been visiting my family back in Switzerland, you see . . . I had no idea."

She pulled away, holding his gaze with her misty-eyed one. A few of her summoned tears spilled over. A skill she and Friede had practiced even as children.

His smile looked about as tight and comfortable as an ill-fitting corset, but he presented it nonetheless. He was, after all, a gentleman. An English one. Stiff upper lip, politeness, all that rot. He might eschew it in some situations, but not in one like this.

"No need to apologize," he said. "Not your fault." He moved to the chair she'd been sitting in and held it for her, scooting it in while she sat.

She kept that same expression on her face as he rounded the small table and sat opposite her. "What a horrific time you have had, though. My landlady has a store of old newspapers, and I glanced through them. They have treated you so ill!"

The sympathy didn't seem to make him soften. If anything, he went stiffer. "I'd rather not talk about it, Dee. Why don't you tell me about your trip home? For Christmas?"

Not exactly the direction she wanted to go, but she'd get nowhere by pushing him right away. So she lapsed into the story she'd worked out for him, recounting one of her last Christmases with her family, just with a few updates to make it fit the wartime reality, adding in a few more recent details, like her sister's children and husband.

Something must have slipped across her face, though, when she mentioned Friede and her babies. Camden tilted his head, expression tightening. "What is it? Is everything well with your sister?"

She hadn't meant to venture into that territory—she ought to have just ignored Friede's very existence. Her gaze dropped of its own accord to the cup of tea a serving girl had brought while Diellza had been describing the evergreen tree her father purchased every year. "She . . ." *Lie. Tuck it away. Say your sorrow is over leaving her again.* She swallowed, prepared the masking words. "She died. In childbirth. Just a few weeks ago." *Blast.*

His fingers brushed hers where they rested on the table. "Oh, Dee." That was all he said. *Oh, Dee.* No inane apology, like she'd offered him about his men. No empty sympathy. Just a touch of his fingers, soon gone, and a look in his eyes that said he knew the pain.

He did. He'd lost a brother, if she recalled aright. His elder one. She sniffed, blinked, and marshalled a smile that was more bluster than truth, but which he would surely appreciate. "How is *your* family? You have a younger brother and sister, correct?"

"They are well, both of them." He filled her in on the meaningless details as they ate the bland cakes and biscuits that war had foisted upon them.

Not the information she needed. But she *did* need him to relax with her. Open up. Want to meet with her again.

In fact, she'd better secure that agreement as soon as possible.

Once he'd finished relating a story about his little brother's ridiculous schemes to get Camden into church, she reached across the table and rested her hand on his. She made sure her eyes still glimmered with laughter over this Jeremy who would probably be so very quick to condemn her to eternal damnation. She'd come to detest his sort. "Oh, this has been good for me, Camden. A bit of laughter in these dark times. We should do this again. Make it a standing Tuesday arrangement. Yes?"

He'd changed so in three short months. Then, his eyes would have either gleamed with suggestion, or he'd have laughed and waved her off, told her he'd introduce her to someone else who could make her laugh on Tuesdays. He'd said more or less that to her once before in a way that, somehow, made him seem all the more charming and not like he'd had his fill and was dismissing her.

Now, though, his amusement over his brother faded away and, nothing else rising to replace it, he nodded. "That sounds pleasant. Here? Same time each week?"

"Perfect." She looked at their nearly empty tea tray. Might as well push now. They'd be taking their leave shortly. She let silence clatter for a moment, filled with nothing but other people's spoons and cups and conversations. Then she drew in a warning breath and met his gaze. "Tell me, Cam. Tell me what really happened. With your men."

He didn't wince. Didn't darken. Didn't flinch away. He didn't, frankly, do anything. Just finished chewing the bite he'd slipped into his mouth, took a sip of tea, and then said, "There's nothing to tell," in such an even, rock-solid voice that she knew she'd not be able to chisel away at it.

Not this time.

She relented with a smile. "When you are ready."

He took another sip. "I've done too much of the talking. It's your turn, I think. You never did tell me what brought you to England. Seems a strange time to seek opportunities here, when your own country is neutral and arguably better situated for the war."

The cover story she'd memorized before Alwin sent her here the first time required a self-deprecating laugh and a one-shouldered shrug. "What do you think? I followed a man here. Fell out of love with him but found I rather liked the country, so . . ."

"Even though you missed your sister?"

Another one-shouldered shrug. "I missed her. Loved her. But she . . . was a bit judgmental."

"Ah." His gaze sliced into her. "Well, I'm glad you got to spend Christmas with her and the rest of your family. That they welcomed you home despite any . . . differences of opinion, let's say."

"Yes." She scraped a nail over a chip in her saucer. "It was lovely to see them all again."

"Mm. Well." He checked his watch and offered her a smile. "I suppose I had better get home. I've a mountain of tasks that need my attention yet today. Though it was good to see you again, Dee."

"It was." And would be a relief to get back to her room. Dissect the conversation and see what she might be able to glean from his words or manners that hadn't struck her right now. Thus far, all she'd ascertained for sure was that he wasn't quick to defend himself about the crash and was fond of his siblings. Useless.

He signaled for the check and, after paying, led Diellza back to the front of the tearoom, where they waited for their coats to be returned to them. Now that she had a better feel for how he reacted to certain subjects, she'd plot out a few careful questions for next week. Questions that he would react to whether he verbally answered them or not. Reminisce about his squadron members, perhaps. See which, if any, got more of a response from him than the others. Perhaps bring up the opinions the widows had voiced in the papers and watch him for a stray tic or flinch or tightening of his mouth.

For now she was content to walk back into the cold air with him and bid him farewell. She did so in her usual way, leaning up to press a kiss to his cheek.

Something crinkled in his coat when she pressed against him.

205

Paper. Quite a bit, from the sound it made. Probably nothing. Maybe something. And so she caught his gaze as she lowered back down, held it with a smile so her fingers could slip undetected into his pocket. "It was so good to see you, Cam. To pass an hour with a handsome face."

She slid a rectangle of paper out of his pocket, into hers.

He'd steadied her opposite arm with a hand on her elbow when she'd stretched up, and he gave it a light, friendly squeeze. "Have a good week, Dee. Stay out of trouble."

The same command he'd given her back then—only he'd delivered it before with a smirk and a twinkling eye. Now it seemed almost serious. Now he'd tasted more of trouble than he'd ever wanted to do. It had jaded him.

She gave him a sad smile and stepped back. A silent signal for him to go on his way.

With a pivot of his heel, he did.

She turned the opposite direction, waiting until she'd rounded a corner and was well out of view before she fished the paper back out of her pocket.

And then . . . then her smile wasn't sad at all.

Saturday, 23 February

Ara stepped out into the noonday sun, drawing in a bracing breath. This Saturday morning had dawned beautiful and bright, hinting at warmth if not actually providing it. And her world inside the hospital was just as gleaming.

"Hold the door, Ara!"

She did, smiling as Lily Blackwell slipped out, a camera in her hands. "Taking more photographs of our patients?"

"And the nurses." Lily grinned and then wrinkled her nose at the satchel full of paper work Arabelle was holding. "Far better than what *you* now have to spend your time doing."

Arabelle chuckled. "The fount of it is never-ending, to be sure.

I've come to the conclusion that if I mean to actually get it done without interruption, I'd better do it at home." She waved a hand toward the Strand. "But you know, I even enjoy this part of the new position."

"You make a wonderful matron. I know all the other Darlings are thrilled to be answering to you now."

Her grin refused to be stifled, in part at the VAD's longstand-ing nickname that the nurses had given them—Very Adorable Darlings. And in part just thinking about her new position and how well suited to it she'd found herself to be. "Thank you, Lily."

"Well, take a few minutes to enjoy the sunshine while you're between tasks. I intend to take advantage of it." Lily lifted her camera as evidence, gave Ara a grin, and turned to the direction opposite. "See you on Monday, Ara."

"Have a lovely weekend."

Turning fully toward the Strand, she caught herself looking around for Camden and had to roll her eyes at herself. Her odd hours today wouldn't match his. She knew that. Still, she looked for him. Because since he'd elbowed his way into her life, he'd never not been here to walk her home.

A new first. And not one she particularly enjoyed.

"Don't be a ninny, Ara," she muttered to herself, repositioning her satchel and picking up her pace. "You've only known him three weeks."

It seemed like more. If one counted acquaintance in number of hours spent together rather than days, then she'd known him far longer than any of the others in the ridiculous parade of men haunting their townhouse. Better than she'd known Brax, who had made it a point *not* to be in her company through most of their shared childhood. Brax had never sought her out. Never smiled at her opinions. And he'd certainly never engendered the habit of kissing her on the cheek each time he said farewell, as Camden had taken to doing this last week.

She'd thought he'd stop after those first two times. But no. Every time he took his leave now, he'd lean over and brush his lips across her left cheek. Her palms went damp against the leather of her satchel just thinking about it.

"Aaagghh!"

The cry of pain brought her to a halt and had her pivoting, looking for the source, before her mind had even processed fully what it was. A woman. *That* woman—the one with hair only a shade off a carrot, a wilted hat, and an overcoat that had seen better days. She had a pram's handle clutched in one hand, but the other was stretching toward her ankle. Her face was a mask of sudden pain.

Ara hurried toward her, shifting the strap of her satchel to cross her body so that she could push it to her back, out of the way. She glanced around to see if Lily was still nearby to lend a hand, but her friend was nowhere in sight. No matter. "Are you all right?"

The woman looked up, the pain flashing in her eyes along with something that resembled trepidation. She dropped her ankle and held her arm up, palm out toward Arabelle. "It's nothing. You needn't—" But when she put her foot back to the sidewalk, the pain must have protested loudly enough to silence her words.

"It's all right. Let me help you." Arabelle offered her a gentle smile and noted that for all her hopping about on one foot, her right hand hadn't for a second let go the handle of that pram. "I'm a nurse."

"I gathered." The woman darted a pain-filled look down Arabelle's uniform—the long white kerchief over her hair, the grey dress with white apron, the dark blue cape. "But you needn't worry over me. I just turned my ankle is all."

"Let's see, shall we?" Arabelle indicated the step leading up to a doorway. "Here, sit for a moment."

Having a feeling the woman wouldn't obey of her own volition, Ara slid an arm around her, put a hand on the pram, and guided both mother and wide-eyed but silent baby toward the doorstep.

The mother sat with a whoosh of expelled air, her eyes on the little one.

Arabelle took in the baby too. The dingy white clothes and tiny grey cardigan gave her no indication as to whether it was a boy or girl, but whichever, it was adorable. Round cheeks, bright eyes, and a few wisps of hair the same color as its mother's. She couldn't help but grin and reach in to tickle the little one's tummy. "How precious you are," she crooned. "An absolute darling."

"That's Gigi. Well, Georgiana, but her siblings have called her Gigi."

Ara trailed a finger down Gigi's silken cheek, melting when the girl gave her a toothless grin. "How old is she?"

"Seven months tomorrow."

"So sweet." Arabelle lifted the front wheels of the pram just enough to put it into a position in which it wouldn't roll away and then turned her smile on the mother. "Let's have a look at that ankle, shall we?"

Gigi's mother darted an apprehensive look up and down the street. "Oh, I . . ."

"I'll be discreet, I promise you." She crouched down and reached for the injured foot, bringing it gently to rest against her leg, careful to keep the woman's brown skirt in position. "I'm Ara." Usually she would have introduced herself as Nurse Denler in such a situation, but her patient obviously needed to be put at ease. "What are you called?"

Realizing there was no help for this street-side examination, the woman sighed. "Kath."

"Well, Kath, it's certainly no secret what caused your mishap." Arabelle tapped a finger to the heel of the woman's pump, which dangled from the rest of the shoe by one frayed piece of fabric. "Just let me make certain you've not done anything serious to it."

As she sent her fingers on a gentle, probing exploration of Kath's ankle, she listened for each intake of breath and smothered gasp of pain. "You've other children as well?"

"Six more of them." Kath winced as Ara touched the place just under her ankle. "Gigi's the youngest, obviously. The eldest is Gregory—he's just ten."

"Seven children!" Arabelle wouldn't have pegged this woman as old enough for a child of ten. She didn't look more than twenty herself, but the freckles must have disguised a bit of age. "How blessed you are." Her fingers slid up the woman's leg a few inches, but there was no swelling anywhere but around the ankle, and that was slight.

Kath's lips brushed against a smile, but it was lost to shadows. "I was. Until we lost their father."

"I'm so sorry." It was a tune all too familiar today. So many husbands and fathers, gone. Arabelle lowered Kath's foot carefully back to the ground. "You're right that you've only twisted it. Rest it as much as possible this evening, and I daresay it will be nothing but an occasional twinge by tomorrow. May I help you home, or to the tube station?"

"Oh." The woman darted an anxious glance along the street. "Thank you, but no. I was—I was going to visit my brother at Charing Cross Hospital, so I'm already here."

Arabelle's brows lifted. "Not only here, but you've passed the door." She nodded past where the mother and child had been when her heel had betrayed her.

Kath flushed. "My mind was elsewhere, I suppose."

"Understandable." Ara stood and held out her hands to help Kath do the same. "I'll just see you in—"

"Oh, please. You needn't bother." Kath met her gaze and offered her a sweet smile. "I appreciate your help, Ara, but my ankle is already beginning to feel better. I'll be perfectly fine."

She considered for a moment. The injury really wasn't severe, and at this point, given the flush of her companion's ears, she suspected it was mostly the woman's pride that was stinging. So she relented with a nod and stepped back, grinning down at the precious little baby again. "Take good care of your mama, sweet Gigi." She kissed her finger and trailed it over the babe's head, then nodded a farewell to Kath. "You'll be in my prayers—you and your children." A family of eight, with no father and husband left to support them. They'd have his military pension, assuming it was the war that had taken him, but that would barely be enough to scrape by with so many mouths to feed.

She wanted to ask how they were managing, whether the mother had work . . . but she could tell from the quick scurry of the woman back toward the hospital doors that she wouldn't take kindly to such inquiries from a stranger. Kath bore herself with that stiff sort of pride that had taken a battering but refused to budge.

Arabelle's heart ached as she watched her for a moment. *Is there anything I can do, Lord?*

She waited, but no immediate surge of purpose filled her. Still, she'd pray for this grieved family and if there were a way to help them, or others like them.

"Ara!"

She looked past the door, toward Whitehall, frowning at Camden as he steamed toward her with his usual brisk stride. "What are you doing here?"

He laughed at the greeting. "And a good day to you too, darling." He nodded toward the hospital door. "Who was that?"

She shrugged. "Just someone who'd twisted her ankle. I thought you were working today."

"I am. Lunch break." He refocused his gaze on her even as he took her hand and wove it through his arm. "Thought I'd check and see if you were taking one as well."

"Not exactly. I have mountains of paper work and thought I'd stand a better chance of making progress on it at home." Though even as she said it, her heart was thudding. He had wanted to take his lunch with her?

"Well then." He pointed them toward the Strand with a grin. "We can have lunch there."

She let him pull her onward. She let the warmth of it seep into her bones. She let the thought of sharing an unexpected meal with him send other worries and distractions flying.

She was surely a fool for allowing the smile to affect her as it did. But lecture herself as she might—he'd only befriended her out of guilt, he had no romantic interest in her, she couldn't get involved with him even if he wanted to lest she lose her new position—words could do nothing to stem the flood of joy that swept over her.

She glanced over at him. "Any pain in your head today?"

"No, Nurse." His grin colored his voice. It was good to hear. "How about you? All those new responsibilities are probably giving you a pounding headache."

She grinned too. "I love it. Even the boring bits."

"You make me question your sanity." But he covered her fingers with his free hand.

They chatted about countless topics on the walk home. Her father and his maps and plans, the crowd of gentlemen still clamoring to call each evening, Cass and Brax. Her new position, his latest news from home.

It didn't strike her until they made their final turn that these were the topics they *always* spoke about. And it brought her brows together. "Why do you never talk about your work?"

"Hmm?" He'd shifted to a step behind her as they navigated through the press of people and now drew even with her again. The better to direct a frown at her, no doubt.

She waved a hand in the general direction of Whitehall. "We talk about everything in the world we have in common. We talk about *my* work. Your family. But I know absolutely nothing about the work you do for the Admiralty. Yet it must be something important if you were released from prison for it."

He winced, but she wouldn't apologize. It was part of who he was, part of his story. A part she knew nothing about, aside from what had been in the papers.

All she could be certain of was that the papers were wrong. This man—the one who still carried his brass wings in his pocket every day, the one who relived the death of his men in moments of trauma, the one who defended those he cared about so fiercely— was no villain.

Her hand found its way to its place on his arm again. And he met her gaze with a sigh. "It isn't that I *don't*, Ara. It's that I really *can't*. My work now is . . . of a sensitive nature, let's say."

Intelligence, then? She didn't know what else would come with a hush warning. She buttoned her lips against the next questions that leapt to her tongue. He clearly wouldn't answer them anyway. "All right. I'll leave off pestering you about it, then."

"You're not pestering me." He said it cheerily enough, but there was a heavy note in his voice.

Or perhaps it was her imagination. Perhaps brought on by the fact that she was recalling again seeing her father walking down the street toward Whitehall that week before the bombing. He'd said something that night that made her think he'd seen Camden during the day, that convinced her he'd gone to the Admiralty. She'd not had time to dwell on why. The Royal Hospital fire had been so soon afterward, and then her promotion had chased away those thoughts.

But if he *had* seen Cam, and Cam was working in intelligence . . . ?

It could make sense. Her father had contacts and friends the world over from his travels. Perhaps he'd been called upon to advise on something relating to them.

She let herself into the townhouse—where in the world was Parks *this* time?—and turned to Camden to say she'd just drop her satchel in her sitting room before lunch. But before she could get out more than the first word, Father appeared on the stairs.

"Is that you, Cam? I've just been looking over—oh. Ara, sweetling." He stopped two steps above the landing, folding a map and snapping a gaze between her and Camden. "I didn't expect you home for luncheon."

But he'd been expecting Cam? She lifted her brows but didn't ask for an explanation. He must have offered his insight into something in the Americas. She could think of no other reason for his sudden silence—heaven knew if he'd just invited Cam over to talk more about Atlantis, he wouldn't go mum upon spotting her.

"I was hoping to grab a quiet hour to finish my paper work."

She screwed on a casual smile and took her satchel's strap over her head. "Pretend I'm not here. I'll just have a sandwich while I work."

"Nonsense. You can have your hour *after* you eat, like a civilized person." Camden's lips twitched up as he delivered the command.

As did hers as she unclasped her cape. "Are *you* really lecturing me on acting civilized?"

"I recognize the absurdity. Even so." He took her satchel from her hand, set it aside, and eased her cape off her shoulders. "Don't deny me your company."

Her throat went dry. Or perhaps it was just that her chest went tight with the swelling of her heart. Talk about absurdity. But even knowing it, she couldn't help it. "All right. I'll eat and *then* work."

His eyes sparkled with victory.

Only because his friends were so few these days. He obviously valued those he had. That was all.

She turned away from him before her cheeks forgot that they didn't blush anymore. "Just let me run my things upstairs. I'll be back down in a moment." She grabbed her satchel and the stack of post sitting on the entryway table that had her name on it, then bustled up the stairs, passing her father with an absent smile.

The stack of letters was ridiculously large. More invitations, she suspected, to house parties and dinner parties she had no desire to attend. She flipped through the stack as she walked, dismissing most of them in her mind before even opening them to see what they were. Though there was one from Ella. She shifted that one to the top of the stack, along with a letter from Sarah. Her fingers hesitated over the small envelope behind that one. No return direction, but the script was decidedly feminine. She shifted it to the top as well.

Her sitting room welcomed her with sunlight through the windows, glinting off the antique apparatuses on her shelves.

She set her satchel on her desk, dropped most of the post beside it, and grabbed her letter opener. Curiosity demanded she open this one now. It was too small to be an invitation, but the feminine hand indicated it wasn't just another note from a would-be caller. Yet she didn't recognize the writing, so it likely wasn't a friend of hers.

She slid the opener in, sliced it open, and pulled out the single sheet of small, cheap paper.

Her every muscle went still.

I feel it my Christian duty to warn you. Phillip Camden is dangerous and cruel and will destroy you if you continue keeping company with him. If you are wise, you'll keep your distance from him. I would hate to see you suffer for his sins—for which he will surely pay.

Yours sincerely,
Mrs. Wallace Lewis

What in the world? She read it twice, thrice, four times, and then five. Let each word sink in, each strong sweep of ink, each shaking one. She noted the spot where some had dripped, the stain in the top right corner that looked to be from tea, memorized each line and loop of the signature. *Mrs. Wallace Lewis.*

How *dare* she? Fingers tight around the paper, Arabelle drew in a breath that tasted of fire. This had to be the widow of one of Camden's men—he'd said the name *Lewis* more than any other in his near-delirium the night of the bombing. But what right did Mrs. Lewis have to judge Cam? To say such things about him? To malign and condemn and try to spoil what few friendships he had? How dare she take it upon herself to write to a complete stranger like this?

If she were writing such notes to Arabelle, was she doing the same to everyone else who knew him? His mother? His sister? Other friends? Colleagues? Was she trying to ruin every part of his life—as if the nightmare of the accident hadn't done a fine job of that already?

Was she writing to *him*? If she was, if she was ruining his days with such rot, filling his head with bitterness and condemnation . . .

"Ara?"

She jumped, spun, and saw him lounging into her doorframe, that familiar smile curling his lips and her stomach all at once.

"Coming, or have you already been distracted by your work?"

How long had she been standing here seething at this slip of paper? Too long. She called up a smile, then refolded it and tucked it into her satchel. "Sorry. I'm coming." She strode forward, thinking to pass him by before he got a good look at her face and realized something was wrong.

But no. Instead, she stopped when she was even with him. With him lounging a bit, they were of a height. Making it so very easy to lean over and plant a purposeful kiss on his cheek.

His brows shot up. "I'm never one to complain about a kiss, but what was that for?"

"For being my friend." She patted his cheek, when she would have rather caressed it. Like his sister or mother would do. Like she would do for any of the patients in her care. "Thank you for watching over me."

Grinning, he slid an arm around her waist and guided her out into the corridor. "Woof."

18

Time off was overrated. After a scant four hours of nightmare-ridden sleep, Camden gave up and directed himself toward the OB. Strange he hadn't noticed how empty his home hours were until he'd begun spending so much time with the Denlers. But now his flat seemed hollow, chaotic, and depressing.

How had those two come to mean so much, so quickly? He shook his head and slid through the crowd at the tube station, trying to pull his thoughts away from Ara and Den. Better to focus on work. On the second tea he'd have today with Diellza Mettler. On what Hall had been piecing together about her over the last week.

The sun was at least shining today, hinting at spring as February bowed out, clearing the way for March. Camden left his overcoat unbuttoned as he strode down the familiar streets. Habit had him shooting a glance up at the windows of Charing Cross Hospital as he strode past, but there were no faces peering down at him today.

His stomach gave an odd little twist. He shouldn't miss her so much. Especially given how much he saw her. There was no reason to regret the hours they were apart—that was just ridiculous.

No reason to already dread the weeks her father would be away, making it impossible for him to while away the evenings in her company.

He sidestepped a distracted VAD emerging from the hospital, her nose in a newspaper. Though when he noted the shade of her hair—caught midway between red and gold—he looked again, frowning. She looked . . . familiar. He'd probably seen her with Ara at some point. She was friends, after all, with pretty much every nurse and volunteer in the city of London.

He shook it off and forced his mind forward yet again. Work. Room 40. Diellza. Codes. Something other than Arabelle Denler.

Yesterday, the admiral had handed Cam a file of what they'd put together on Dee thus far. He had an agent or two in Switzerland who had begun digging up whatever they could find on her. Camden had reviewed it all this morning.

Some of it was what he'd expected—she'd been born to a decent family, but something had caused a break. Presumably a man, given what came next. After an ill-advised affair, she ended up in the life she seemed to have embraced so fully. She'd become a cabaret dancer in order to support herself.

What he hadn't known was that one of her paramours—the one she'd been seen with all throughout the war, the one who, in the photograph Hall's agent had sent of the two of them, she looked at with naked love—was a high-ranking German officer. One apparently of interest to Hall.

Nor had he realized that she was one of *the* Mettlers—as in, the family who engineered some of the most in-demand rifles and handguns of their day.

Camden's fingers curled into his palm as he crossed the parade grounds and aimed for the doors. He'd thought her generally harmless. Maybe, at worst, trying to wheedle information out of some British servicemen to send along to her German sweetheart.

But Hall clearly didn't think so. And as Camden had read over the information this morning, he reluctantly agreed with his superior's conclusions. The German officer—Weber—wouldn't have risked sending her back to England just for mundane information, not after she'd already been expelled on suspicion of espionage.

They had something bigger planned. And now it fell to Camden to determine what.

The security guard let him pass with a nod, and he hurried up the stairs and into the hive of the intelligence division. One of the signs declaring No Admittance. Ring Bell. had come off one of the doors and lay haphazardly on the floor, so he stooped down to snatch it up with a smirk. There were no bells on any of the doors. The signs were just the cryptographers' joking way of keeping outsiders from interrupting them.

He fixed the paper back into place and headed for the room that housed his desk, nearly plowing into Denniston, one of the senior codebreakers, as he exited the room.

"Whoa, there." The older man frowned. "Didn't you just come off the night shift, Camden?"

He tried to muster some of his usual snarl but couldn't quite manage it today. He shrugged. "Home seemed rather boring. I trust there's enough work that an extra set of hands will be useful for an hour? I do have an afternoon appointment, but in the meantime . . ."

Denniston smiled. "You're certainly welcome. Go on in."

It took Cam a moment to realize why his throat went tight—then it hit him. *Welcome.* He'd never really expected to find it here. Certainly not after the way he'd antagonized everyone during his first weeks in these rooms.

He nodded and slid into Room 40. Though a few of the occupants looked up, no one else asked him why he'd come in today or seemed to find it odd that he had—perhaps because Margot, who'd also just come off a night shift, was back at her station already too. He could simply hang up his overcoat, fetch a passel of telegrams from the pneumatic tubes, and settle down to work.

The first message he decoded provided nothing out of the

ordinary. But when he pulled forward a new slip of paper, his brows furrowed. It took only a glance to realize that this wasn't in one of the usual German codes. "De Wilde. Take a look at this."

He glanced over, but Margot didn't even glance up. Her lips were silently moving, her pencil flying over her scrap paper.

Camden sighed and waited for her to look back at her main decrypt before saying again, "De Wilde!"

She blinked her way back into the here and now and looked over at him. "What?"

He pushed to his feet and walked the two paces to her desk so he could slide the paper onto it. "Not in one of the German codes. Do you recognize it?" He'd long ago learned, as most of the other gents here had, that she was far faster than the rest of them at identifying what code a message might be in and could save them tons of time spent trying different options.

And indeed, it only took her a moment to scowl with knowledge at the paper. "That can't be right."

"What can't?" He leaned over the desk so he could see the message, too, though no insights jumped out at him.

"That's in one of our codes. But that doesn't make sense—it's not marked with our agents' signal. Hold on a moment." She opened a desk drawer and rooted about inside it, shoving this and that aside before coming up with a paperbound booklet not unlike the one he and Elton had reclaimed from a zeppelin's crash site last autumn, only a different color. And, he noted when she flipped it open, in English. She flipped a few pages, set it beside the paper, and quickly turned a few words into plain text.

It required only four for her to nod. "Definitely this one. It opens with 'To my esteemed colleagues.' Here." She handed paper and codebook over to him. "Go on."

Camden just stared at her for a long moment. It was entirely unlike De Wilde to be so without curiosity. "Aren't you wondering what it is?"

"Show me when you've finished it." She flashed a rather sheepish smile. "I'm working on one of Thoroton's reports from Spain."

In which there was probably a report from or about Drake Elton. That made sense, then. Camden nodded and returned to his desk.

He jotted down the words De Wilde had already provided and then set to work on the rest. Often the decrypts were so routine he didn't pay much attention to what they said after verifying they made grammatical sense. This one, however, was something altogether different. And altogether intriguing.

> *To my esteemed colleagues in Britain. I am able to write to you thanks to your generosity in sharing with my people your system of encoding and decoding. But never did I imagine I would call upon it in this way.*

Camden frowned. The Admiralty was understandably tight-lipped about all their code-based operations. From what he'd heard around the office, France, for instance—England's closest ally in the war—had been summarily denied any help on that front. Only a select few Americans had been brought into the loop of their operations, and they certainly didn't go so far as to hand over any of their codebooks.

Who, then, would have it? The only ones Camden knew of who'd been given any specific instruction were . . . His breath hissed out. The Russians, back at the start of the war. Hadn't Denniston said something about that a month or so ago? An offhanded comment as they'd been discussing the latest news on the Bolshevik Revolution. About how he hoped and prayed it wouldn't come back to harm England now that Russia was out of the war and her people so in tumult.

Camden went back to the message.

> *I pride myself on having been one of my czar's most trusted cryptographers. But in these violent times, I find my life is in grave danger because of that very favor I so carefully sought. I have fled Russia, narrowly escaping with my life.*

I write to offer my skills to you; a similar message has been sent to France. I am willing to work tirelessly and diligently for either of my czar's allies, assuming I will be offered sanctuary and a chance to build a life in your country, as I have been denied the right to do in my own. If you wish to communicate with me, please send a wire to 20 Rue Jacob, Paris, France. Your colleague in the art of cryptography, Zivon Marin.

Camden sat back with a long exhale, staring at the words he'd scrawled out. Definitely not a routine report on weather or fleet movements. He stood with the decrypt in hand, thinking to show it to De Wilde as she'd requested.

But Denniston strode back in, and he was more likely to know what Camden was to do with this. Signaling him with a lift of the paper, he met the other man halfway. "You might want to have a look at this. It's from one of Russia's ousted cryptographers."

"You don't say." Denniston took the sheet of paper from his hands with eager fingers and lifted brows, reading over it quickly. He breathed a staccato laugh. "Could be a boon—I know DID is most anxious over what's going on in Russia, certain the Red Army is going to prove as large a threat as the huns eventually. A chap like this working for us . . ."

Nodding along, Camden slid a hand into his pocket and fingered the brass wings. "Assuming he could be trusted, he could prove a valuable asset moving forward. Do you know the name?"

"No. But DID may, as he's the one who instructed them in how to set up a system mirroring ours." Denniston clapped a hand to Camden's shoulder. "Well done, Major. I'll go show this to the admiral—and I'll be certain to mention that you were the one to crack it."

"I hardly deserve any credit." Cam waved at De Wilde. "All I did was pull it out of the tubes. De Wilde provided the book for the decrypt, and you certainly know more about the value of this chap's offer than I could."

Something shifted in the man's eyes, flashing a bit brighter than before. A bit softer. *Respect.* "Even so, old boy. You saw the value rather than passing it off or putting it in a pile to be addressed when we've spare time."

Humility wasn't Cam's usual mode of operating. But this wasn't his world—the brass under his fingertips reminded him of that. He had no right to claim any success here, not when others worked as diligently and passionately at this art, as the Russian had called it, as Camden did in his cockpit. He shrugged and turned half away, eyes seeking the clock. "Happy to do my bit. But I'd better bow out for the day. I'll leave that in your capable hands."

"I'll take it directly to the admiral. Have a good afternoon, Major."

He nodded but pressed his lips against the return sentiment that sprang to his lips. If he flipped entirely into pleasantness, his colleagues would probably think him up to something.

He said good-bye to De Wilde and made his exit. It was only a ten-minute walk to Piccadilly. Just enough time to clear his head before he faced Diellza again. Try to determine why, exactly, things had begun to shift at the OB.

Was it them? Were they simply becoming immune to his attitude? Or was it him? Was he changing, despite never making a conscious effort to do so?

He shot a glance up the street toward the hospital and chose a different path. If the change was in him, he knew exactly who to blame, blast it. And it was hardly fair. He was the one with the reputation for being a danger to decent young ladies—so how in the world was she the one exerting an influence on *him*?

Mother would get no end of delight from it if she knew. As would Jer. He would just have to make sure neither of them learned how much he enjoyed the time spent with her.

He paused at the intersection to wait for a lorry to trundle by and then crossed, still scowling. It wasn't that Ara didn't deserve credit for brightening his life as she did. It wasn't that he really even minded the softening of his edges.

It was . . . It was that he didn't deserve it. Didn't deserve to be enjoying his evenings with her when his men would never again go home to their wives. He didn't deserve the comfort of her hand on his arm. The joy of pressing his lips to her dimple. The warmth that filled him each time she grinned at him or rolled her eyes at his flirting.

He craved it. But he shouldn't let himself have it.

His nostrils flared with the breath he drew in. He had to stop this, whatever it was. Cut himself off before he began to justify it to himself. Before he started to scheme up ways to make sure she stayed a part of his daily life forever. He couldn't do that to her, couldn't ask her to stand beside him.

How could he? Borrowed time, that was all he had. Not life. Just a postponed death. No blood in his veins, nothing left in his heart but echoes.

He'd join his men; he knew that. In a week or a month or a year. He'd pay for his mistakes. For pushing when he should have listened. For shoving Lewis despite the resignation in his eyes. For denying him his last request. For those words that had blistered his tongue.

"Not if I kill you first."

If he hadn't shouted that . . . Deliberately loud, because he'd wanted Lewis to face the attention of the others. His brothers. His friends. He'd wanted the man to see that there was a world wider than the one inside. He'd pushed, literally and figuratively, because pushing had always worked before.

Your reckoning is coming soon. That was what the latest note from Lewis's widow claimed.

He turned a corner and increased his pace, thinking maybe he could pound some of the thoughts from his head with his feet. But he couldn't. Because his reckoning was already here, his accounts settled. He stood condemned. Judged guilty. Sentenced. Perhaps not by a military court, but by all of England.

By his own conscience.

Footsteps matched his, and a figure came alongside him. Not

224

unusual on a busy street, so he gave the bloke room to go by if he wanted to and clicked his own pace back a notch to give him room.

The other bloke matched him and eased closer. Only then did Camden actually look at him. And when he did, he had to frown. It was that mysterious errand boy of the admiral's. "Pearce, isn't it?"

Pearce didn't so much as glance over at him. Just said, "Do you know you're being followed? Blond woman. The one you were talking to that day over a week ago, when Hall walked out with you."

"What?" He made to look over his shoulder, but Pearce tripped, slammed into him, and then caught him with wide eyes that were not apologetic so much as screaming.

"Don't be an idiot—you don't just *look* when you have a tail. Good grief, some people don't know the first thing about this sort of work." Making a show of brushing off Camden's coat where he'd clutched it to keep him from toppling to the ground, he offered a neutral smile. "I only thought you'd like to know. If you mean to spot her, use the reflection of a store window or turn a corner quickly or something."

Camden pulled away and tugged his jacket and overcoat back into place, scowling. "Who in blazes *are* you, anyway?"

"Your new best friend—or so says Hall. He sent me after you to see if you need me to help in any way on your day's assignment."

The tea? How the devil was someone else supposed to help him with that? "Such as . . . ?"

Pearce put his hands in his pockets, looking entirely casual as he said, "Oh, you know, the usual. Follow someone, take down the address of where they're staying, poke about in their personal belongings while they're out—that sort of thing."

Camden very nearly staggered to a halt but caught himself and kept walking. If Diellza was back there, watching, they had to look normal. Just two blokes having a chat after a run-in. "*That* is what you do for Hall?"

"When necessary. So?"

His fingers found the wings in his pocket again and traced its contours. "How do you mean to follow *her* when she's seen you with me, now?"

Pearce dismissed that with a snort. "Oh, trust me. Girls like that pay no attention to blokes like me. I'll put on a different style hat and a grey overcoat instead of the brown, and she'll look right through me. Assuming she spots me tailing her at all, which I doubt she will. Now, blokes like *you*—bit more difficult to be invisible, what with your face being plastered on the front page of every newspaper for months on end."

Camden couldn't exactly refute that statement. "I suppose that could be helpful. She hasn't told me where she's staying, just set up this time to meet. And if I asked outright, she'd probably think I was trying to invite myself to . . . visit." Something that, a few months ago, wouldn't have bothered him a bit.

Now it made his stomach sour and an image of hazel eyes flash through his mind.

"Best if she thinks you don't have a clue. That way if she notices anything awry—though I'm careful, I promise you that—she wouldn't think you're to blame."

Camden nodded. "Very well. If Hall thinks it's a good idea, then no arguments from me. How will you work it?"

"Well, if this is a weekly appointment—yeah?"

"Yeah."

"Right. That helps. I can follow her home, watch the place for a few days, and find my way in next Tuesday while she's meeting you, when I know she'll be gone for a set amount of time. Unless another opportunity presents itself before that."

Camden nodded again. "All right. Though if she's at a boarding-house, I don't see how you'll manage it."

Pearce laughed. "If I can't, I've sisters who can. Leave that part to me." As they neared the next intersection, he stuck out a hand. "I'll part ways from you here. Lyons in Piccadilly, correct?"

"That's right." He shook Pearce's hand. "Two o'clock. I imagine we'll be leaving by three."

"See you then. Though you won't see me." With a flash of a grin, Pearce peeled off and turned to the left while Camden aimed straight.

Peculiar chap—though the sort he could well imagine DID finding ample use for. Even before he joined Room 40, Camden had heard a few stories about Blinker Hall's unusual—and occasionally ruthless—methods of achieving his goals.

It took all his self-control to keep himself from turning and searching the pedestrians on the street behind him for Diellza's blond head. Why was she following him when she knew well where he was going? Had she been waiting near the OB?

That's where she'd found him the first time. He gripped the brass wings and kept up his pace, not looking back. No, looking ahead. He had to figure out what she was angling for. Why she'd sought him out as she'd clearly done.

Last week she'd tried to get him to talk about The Incident. Why? Could that have something to do with her goals? Or had it just been a bid for him to open up emotionally? To trust her?

Well. He squeezed the pin until it dug into his palm. He'd play along. But trusting her was the last thing he'd do.

19

Will you be able to have that for me by end of day, Ara?" Nurse Jameson stood in front of the desk in Arabelle's new office, a smile on her face that didn't entirely erase the frazzled look in her eyes. "I'm to meet with the board of directors at five this evening."

"Of course, ma'am."

"Nurse Denler!" A panicked Eliza stuck her head into the office, eyes wide. "Corporal Moody is at it again, and we can't hold him down."

Arabelle sighed. "I'll be right there." To her superior, she added a smile. "Perhaps I had better finish up that report elsewhere, if I mean to have it to you by four."

The hospital matron chuckled. "My preference is to plant myself at my favorite teahouse for an hour and get through it with a nice cup of tea and a few treats—such as they are these days."

"That sounds like just the thing. After," she added when Eliza widened her eyes still more, "I help with Corporal Moody." The poor man had suffered severe burns all along his left side and seemed to think that the best remedy was to press his skin—all of it, unhindered by his dressing gown—to the cold windows.

After chiding the drug-addled corporal back into his coverings and his bed, she gathered the files she needed to compile the report for the matron and made a mad dash down the stairs and out the door before anyone else could summon her.

Once on the street, she paused to consider which teahouse she ought to visit. Lyons, perhaps—it was close but not the one the other nurses favored.

Perfect for her needs today. She set off at a brisk clip, using the walk to mentally sift through the paper work she needed to finish. What was impossible at the hospital was quite doable when alone. She'd have everything read before she finished her first cup of tea and the report written shortly thereafter.

Entering Lyons was a bit like coming home. The fragrance of tea and baked goods wafted out to greet her, and the familiar décor was exactly as it had always been. She smiled a greeting to the maître d', eyes already scanning for which table she'd ask for. Preferably one by a window, but tucked behind a plant to provide a bit of privacy. She looked to see if her favorite was by chance available.

And froze. At a table not ten paces away, familiar dark hair caught her eye, along with too-blue eyes and a face handsome enough to make the wind catch its breath. But it wasn't Camden that made her every muscle go stiff. It wasn't even—entirely—the stunning blonde who sat across from him, smiling and trailing the tip of one finger over his hand.

It was the fact that he saw her the very moment she saw him, and she knew all too well the expression that flashed through his eyes. *Guilt.*

Stupid. Stupid, stupid idiot. She spun away, unable to offer the maître d' so much as a wobbling excuse.

"Ara!"

She heard his voice. The scrape of his chair's legs. Just as she heard the incredulous laugh of the woman. "Who is *that*? Do not tell me *she* is your latest paramour—that gangly mouse?"

Arabelle couldn't gain the door fast enough. She reached for it long before her arm—gangly as it was—had a hope of touching the latch. Oh, to be able to block her ears. To keep from hearing his response. To vanish, just *vanish* before reality came crashing down.

But he didn't even answer his companion. Perhaps such a question was too ridiculous to deserve a rebuttal. He just called, "Ara, wait!" and then his footsteps pounded after her.

She burst back onto the street, even as she knew she hadn't a prayer of outrunning him. Why couldn't she have spotted him without his ever knowing it? Why hadn't he been so caught up in the perfect face of that other woman that he failed to note who had come in? Why, *why* couldn't she have just slipped away?

"Ara." But no, there were his fingers, curling around her arm, insisting she stop. And there was the rest of him, jumping in front of her. And there was his face, a mask of regret and apology and all the emotions he swore he was beyond. "That wasn't what it seemed."

It wasn't him having tea with one of the most beautiful young women Arabelle could readily recall seeing? One with perfect golden curls and a profile worthy of a sculptor's chisel? She squeezed her eyes shut for a moment—just one—and drew in a breath. "It doesn't matter what it was." *Calm. Peaceful.* All the emotions she had learned to convey in a hospital ward when they were the furthest thing from what she felt. All the emotions she certainly *wasn't* feeling inside. "I'm sorry I fled—just surprise, I suppose. I'd come for quiet, not expecting to see anyone I know. Work." She patted her satchel.

His eyes were blue arrows, piercing straight through her façade. "It *does* matter. I don't want you thinking—"

"Stop." She couldn't hold his gaze. Hers dropped to the olive-green collar of his uniform. He hadn't paused to grab his overcoat. "You're welcome to have tea with whomever you please. I have never presumed that my *friendship* is the only one you need."

"Don't act so cool with me; I know you better than that." Thunder darkened the edges of his voice. An odd contrast to the gentleness of his fingers as they slid down her arm and tangled with hers. "And don't pay attention to what she said."

"You mean the bit about your *latest* paramour?" She bit her tongue, but too late.

The glance she dared showed lightning in his eyes to match the thunder in his voice. "No, actually. But if that's the part that has you upset—"

"I am not upset." Though it was only the busy street that kept her from shouting the words rather than hissing them.

"Then you do a fine imitation of it." He shifted half a step closer. "Listen to me, darling. That woman in there—she's nothing. I'm only here meeting with her because my superior asked me to, all right?"

"You don't need to explain yourself to me," she said, even as she frowned and shook her head, following that claim with the questions burning inside. "And why in the world would he ask that of you? Do you know her? Was she—?" She snapped her lips closed on that question, at least.

Latest paramour.

Camden's thumb stroked over the side of her hand. "What do you want me to say? Was I once involved with her? Yes, briefly. Is that why the admiral tasked me with finding out what she's doing in England when she shouldn't be here? Yes, that's why. But am I enjoying it? No. I find I've had my fill of her sort. She's just a cabaret dancer, darling. She's nothing."

"Nothing?" Before she could stop them, hot tears scalded her eyes. She backed up, away from him, even though his fingers still trapped hers. "How can you talk of someone that way—as if she isn't someone's daughter, someone's sister? Especially now, with what your own sister has faced?"

Through her blurry vision, his frown looked confused. "What does this have to do with Cass?"

"Are you quite serious?" Her fingers shook in his. "What is the difference between Cass and 'her sort' but for the reaction of her family? Do you think most women *choose* that life? Where would your sister be right now, Phillip, if your mother had turned her out instead of turning to you? If Brax hadn't stepped up? What would she have been forced to do?"

"My sister," he said from between clenched teeth, "is *nothing* like Diellza Mettler."

"Maybe not. But perhaps Diellza Mettler"—the name felt awkward and stiff on her tongue—"would not be like Diellza Mettler had men like you acted as gentlemen around her instead of using her and then tossing her aside like so much rubbish."

In one second, his fingers tightened nearly painfully around hers. And then they loosened, and he let out a breath that hinted at amusement. "You would defend her. A woman who has freely chosen a life of what you deem sin."

The tears, at least, had consented to being blinked away for now. She met his eyes again. "It is no more her sin than the men's who participate in it with her. I will call it what it is—wrong and not what God intended for His children—but I will not stand as her judge." She lifted her chin. "Just as I won't stand as yours. But I will pray. I'll pray you both see how such behavior hurts everyone. Her. You." *Me.*

She didn't speak that last word. She was sure of it.

Yet she could have sworn, by the way his gaze swept over her face, that he heard it. Then he eased away another six inches, and his fingers loosened still more, though they didn't quite slip away from hers. "I already apologized for being who I am."

She shook her head. "I didn't ask you to apologize. Certainly not to me. But this is not who you are. Who you are is a man who will move mountains to protect those he cares about. Maybe you've let yourself think that the very lovely woman in there isn't deserving of such regard. But deep down, you know better. You know right from wrong, Cam. You know the truth. You know how dangerous that life is—you said it yourself, in regards to your men, so you cannot claim to think it different for you. You know that you're not excused from being a true gentleman just because it's not demanded."

His eyes flew up again, and one corner of his mouth pulled up before falling once more. "I recently had a similar conversation with a boy on the train."

"See? You know it, and not even deep down." She squeezed his fingers and then tugged hers free. "Go and have your tea, Cam. I've work to do."

He leaned closer again rather than away, eyes locked on hers. "Tell me, first. Tell me you believe me. About this, now. I can't have you thinking that I'm spending my days willingly seeking out . . ."

"Beautiful women to spend your time with?" She forced a smile and prayed the teasing she tried to inject into it came through. Prayed he couldn't see her thundering pulse in her neck. Because he couldn't be hinting at what it seemed he was—that she was something special, that she had a right to be upset at the thought of him with another woman. "I believe you, in this case. We're friends. You would tell me if you were earnestly interested in a woman, wouldn't you?"

Though she'd thought Brax would grant her that much too.

She couldn't dwell on thoughts of him, though, not when Camden's fingers lifted and brushed across her cheek, making her jump.

"I would," he whispered. "But that isn't a conversation I ever anticipate having with you."

She stepped away—too quickly, probably. To match her breathing. Neither of which would escape him, blast it all. But she wasn't going to have this conversation. Not here, on a public street. Not now, when she couldn't even let herself hope that he meant what it nearly sounded like he did, because to hope in that would mean to resign her new position—perhaps *any* position at Charing Cross. When she *shouldn't* hope it, because while the Lord was clearly tugging on him, Cam was clearly resisting the tug.

Hope, ill-suited or not, didn't stand a chance anyway. Not with reality clawing at her. He didn't *anticipate* it. He wanted her to understand how things stood *now*.

But she knew all too well that a girl like her didn't keep the attention of a man like him—not for long, if at all. Brax hadn't anticipated it either. Hadn't sought it, he'd said. Hadn't meant to fall in love with someone else.

It just happened. It *always* "just happened."

"I'll see you tonight. All right? Ara?"

She nodded and kept her features schooled. "Sorry if I complicated your . . . assignment." The smile she put on now felt despicable on her lips. "Just tell her you're courting me for my money and had to convince me not to toss you to the curb. She'll believe that."

"Arabelle."

Ignoring the chiding in his tone, she spun away, rushing toward the nearest corner without really caring where it would take her, as long as it was out of his sight.

Camden would have abandoned the mission and gone home if it had been a viable choice. But it wasn't, so he stalked back into Lyons and took his seat again, pointedly ignoring the curious looks other patrons sent his way.

A few would probably recognize him. With his luck, there would be another ridiculous article in tomorrow's paper, expounding on what a rake was Black Heart.

Diellza greeted him with a smirk. "Seriously, Camden? *Her?*" Her laugh grated on his every nerve. "I hope she is rich, my love, because she is certainly not—"

"Stop." His tone may have been biting, but at least it was quiet. He topped it with a smile. "I don't really want to talk about her right now."

Because he would *not* say those things about her. Even when she'd told him to, even when Dee had already offered the excuse, even when saying them would smooth the situation and preserve his goals.

He would not. He would not give voice to the thing that would tear her down. That would label her as so much less than she was.

Diellza bit her lip, all flirtation again. "I can hardly blame you for *that*." She looked as though another laugh might slip out at any moment. "I do hope I have not caused you any . . . trouble."

He curled his hands into fists in his lap, tucked well out of sight beneath the tablecloth. "I hope so too." His old grin was hard to call up, even harder to hold in place. "Though you never seemed to mind the possibility before."

She lifted one shoulder in an elegant, somehow suggestive shrug. "If a gentleman cannot remember whether or not he is already committed, then who am I to remind him?"

He nearly flinched. *Gentleman*. His mother had raised him to be one, to be sure. But he'd been all too eager to accept the leniencies that came with it, far more than the expectations. Gentlemen could live a life of pleasure. Gentlemen could get away with treating others poorly. Gentlemen could indulge in whatever *affaires de coeur* they wanted.

He ought to have acted better. Not just, as Ara had pointed out, because treating Dee as he'd done must have hurt *her*, must have told her she was worth less than other women. But because he'd set an example for his squadron. For the pilots who had *not* been born to his class. Who looked wide-eyed upon the world he led them blissfully into.

The world of house parties and wagers and trysts with no consequences.

Until there *were* consequences.

He sucked in a breath. Maybe there were *always* consequences. Maybe he'd just never seen them, not really, until the day it all fell apart.

Until on the street outside, when he'd looked into the eyes of a woman who meant everything and saw the pain and disillusionment in her eyes over what he'd done. What he was.

He'd expected fury—like she'd had for Brax. He'd been afraid she would think he was betraying her. Perhaps even seethe at him over betraying her with a dancer.

She'd surprised him though. It seemed she was always surprising him. How could anyone have a heart so deep? So pure? So good?

"Camden? Are you all right?"

"Fine." He tried to shake away thoughts of Ara. And when he failed, he figured he might as well use them instead. He let his smile go wry. "All right, time for turnabout. You witnessed my troubles today, so tell me of yours to make me feel better. Do you still love him?"

She startled—which was what he'd been hoping for. A moment, just a moment when he could see truth behind the mask she always kept over her features. Not that it lasted long, but it was there. A flash of shock, of pain . . . of longing. Then her blinding, fake smile. "Who? The man I followed to England? No, I—"

"No." He picked up the half of his scone still sitting on his plate. "I mean the one that led you into all this at the start."

Her eyes sparked. "I do not know what you mean."

He angled her a look and motioned with his scone. "Don't be coy. You told me last week of your family, remember? You mentioned your sister didn't approve of your life. You can't tell me you just stumbled from one world to another without help."

Her chin lifted. "I make my own choices."

"Mm-hmm." He chewed the bite of scone he'd taken, measuring her. "We all do. But some we make with others—and some we make *for* others. Come now." He leaned closer, winked. "You can tell me. I won't consider it a slight to my charms to know you're still pining for some Jack or John or Peter back in Stockholm."

"Zürich." She bit it out . . . and then looked as if she wished it back. Though she swiftly smiled. "Stockholm is in Sweden, you *Dummkopf*, not Switzerland."

"My mistake." She still felt ties to her country and city, then.

236

She was not, as she'd originally claimed, simply enamored with England. "Geography was never my best subject."

"And they let you fly missions over France?" She gave him that flirtatious smile again. "It is a wonder you did not end up scouting your own lines instead of the enemy's."

He chuckled but narrowed his eyes at her. "Trying to deflect, are you? Don't want to tell me about Jack-John-Peter?"

She sighed and toyed with the edge of her napkin. Held his gaze for a moment and then dropped hers to her empty teacup. "I was to marry a man named Max. My father had it all arranged. But then . . ." She glanced up, grinned. "Then John-Jack-Peter came along and I . . ." Another shrug. "I fell in love. My father said if I chose him over Max, then he was finished with me. Never guessing, I suppose, that I would do it. But I did."

That matched the information Hall had given him. And made it seem more likely that Alwin Weber was the one who'd been responsible for the break with her family, not just a later par-amour she'd fallen for. Probably. Maybe. He tilted his head. "Do you ever regret it?"

"Not for a moment." A bit too much passion slipped out, though she tried to cover it with a bat of her lashes. "How could I, when it led me here?"

Definitely Weber. Camden deflected the flirtation with a steady look and a soft restatement of his question. "Do you still love him?"

She looked away. "There is something eternal about a first love, do you not think?"

"I wouldn't know. Never fallen prey to that particular plague." He offered a grin to lighten the moment for her.

And to keep her from noticing the way his fingers went tight around his teacup.

◈ ◈ ◈

Arabelle finally convinced her fingers to let go of the satchel she'd been gripping like a lifeline through the entire walk home.

Her nostrils flared as she stared blindly at the familiar items before her. Bag with paper work. Chair. Desk. But just now, they meant nothing. Her eyes slid shut.

What she wouldn't give for a cup of tea and a long chat with Sarah. Someone who would understand the tightness in her chest. The heaviness in her feet. Someone who would know it wasn't just about hopes and fears tied to a too-handsome pilot. Someone who would know, without needing to be told, how much deeper it went.

Something hit the floor above her, drawing Arabelle's gaze upward. Father must be home. Her gaze flicked back to her satchel only for a moment before she pivoted for the door. Paper work could wait a few more minutes. First, she could use a bit of cheering.

Whatever he was doing in his study, he wasn't exactly doing it quietly. She heard another thump as she was on the stairs, and his muttering slithered out of the room long before she stepped into it. It took her a long moment to spot him by the shelf in the corner, crouched down to sift through the cabinet on the bottom half, tossing artifacts aside with a litany of mumbles all to the effect of "No, not it. Not it. Where the devil are you?"

"Do you need help looking for something?"

"Ara!" He jumped, nearly cracking his skull on the cabinet top, and leaped to his feet. He didn't look exactly happy to see her. More . . . panicked, to be honest. He glanced over to his desk.

She did, too, where she could see a variety of papers strewn about. Not that she could read a word on them from here, but the fact that Father immediately began edging that way made her fairly certain they were the same papers he always hid the moment she entered.

Fire swept over her as surely as if a Gotha had just dropped a bomb in her heart. Her chin came up. Her hands fisted. "If you've secrets you don't want to share, all you need to do is say so, you know. I'm not going to pry. It isn't as though I'm not keenly aware that there's plenty of your life of which you don't want me to be a part."

Father's scuttling came to a halt. But his wide eyes contained as much guilt as sorrow at the accusation. "Sweetling. Why would you say such things?"

An incredulous laugh, devoid of all amusement, puffed its way from her lips. "You can really ask that as you're trying to slip over to hide everything on your desk?"

"I'm not *hiding* anything." He took another step. Toward the desk. Not toward her. "Merely attempting to tidy up."

"Don't bother. I'll just leave." To prove it, she pivoted, ready to charge out of the room again.

But her feet wouldn't budge, and it had nothing to do with his half-chiding, half-pleading "Arabelle!"

No, it had far more to do with the breath-stealing realization that even here, in her own home, she wasn't wanted. Wasn't welcome. That even now, all these years later, he still chose his adventures over her, still kept her an arm's length—no, an ocean's width—away.

She spun to face him again, the old ache clawing her to bits. "Why? Why were we not enough? Why did you not want us *with* you? Was it me? Was it Mother?"

Now he moved toward her, but only a step. His hand stretched out but then just stayed there, suspended, still leaving so much space between them. "Of course not. You must know that, Ara. You were always my sweetling. And I loved your mother like nothing else."

"Did you?" Her throat was tight. Hot. Suffocating. Maybe he did—how could he not? She was the sweetest woman Arabelle had ever known, after all. But love certainly hadn't equated a real marriage, one spent together. It hadn't given her mother a life lived side by side with her beloved. She shook her head. "That didn't matter though, did it? You loved nothing, no one more than your blighted adventures. We were just afterthoughts. Never important enough to actually deserve any of your time."

"That is *not*—"

"It *is*!" Her shout echoed through the room, ringing in its shattering present tense. Not *was*. Is. Still true, even now. Her eyes burned. "You are a selfish, thoughtless man! You care about absolutely *nothing* but your own wants."

His nostrils flared. "If that's what you think of me, it's a wonder you even welcomed me home four years ago."

Another dry laugh, crackling like tinder in the fire, scraped its way from her throat. "Oh, but that's the really pathetic thing. I love you. Not just that—I *like* you. I lap up every minute you toss my way like a puppy. All I ever wanted was to be with you. I wanted to hear your every story and be part of your adventures, and you would never grant me that. Never!"

She waved a hand at the desk. "And now here you are. Doing it again, just like when I was fourteen. Telling me all about the next trip, saying I could go with you that time. Making plans. But you never meant it. Because when it comes down to it, you don't want me there."

No one ever did. She was never the one people made decisions *for*. Only *about*.

His eyes flashed. "I *was* going to take you with me. Your aunt wouldn't hear of it, though."

"You were my *father*! You didn't have to listen to your sister!" She sliced a hand through the air, wishing she could cut away the past with the stroke. But it seemed that no matter how many times she thought she'd forgiven him, it was always there. Clinging to her. Tangling her up. "But it doesn't matter, does it? Do what you want. Like you always do."

"Arabelle."

She wasn't looking at him anymore. Couldn't. She faced the corridor, the stairs, anything but the insecurities she couldn't ever shake. "You needn't bother hiding anything from me, Father. I really don't care anymore."

But it wasn't just *don't*. It was *can't*. Because it hurt too much when he chose something else.

Everyone always chose something—or someone—else.

Ignoring his next call, she hurried back down to her sitting room. Snatched up her satchel. Flew all the way down the stairs and out the door. The hospital was the only place she was really wanted. Really needed. So back to the hospital she would go.

20

Diellza stepped over the toddler who made no attempt to move out of her way, sidled around the teetering pile of laundry that completely covered a chair, and tried to keep her smile on her lips and her face completely clear of judgment.

"So sorry for the mess." Mrs. Lewis, her cheeks a bright pink, set a lingering gaze on the laundry. "Had I known you were coming . . ."

"Oh, it is hardly a mess." Which was true enough. There was the pile of clothing, yes, obviously awaiting its turn on the ironing board set up beside the chair. But otherwise, nothing out of place littered any surfaces.

Perhaps in part because there were so few surfaces for anything to litter. The flat was Spartan.

"Our cottage in the country was far nicer." The widow glanced around, sad eyes lighting on each of the prominent features of the room—the window with a cracked pane, the peeling wallpaper, the scarred floorboards under a faded rug. "But we let it go so the children and I could move here, to be closer to Wallace when they stationed him at Northolt."

"You must have been so pleased to be able to see him regularly."

Mrs. Lewis blinked, her gaze falling to the floor and seeming to see something far more than wood grain. "When they sent him home, I'd thought we were past the worst. So many of them died over France—and to read how easily he spoke of it, how they laughed at the danger." She shuddered. "When he sent word about coming home, I thanked God with everything in me. Now . . . now I wish he'd have stayed in France. He may have survived if he had—he'd done so that long. Maybe he'd be alive still."

"Things we can never know." Diellza nearly reached up to tug at the tight collar she'd worn today. She'd grown unaccustomed these last few years to constrictive clothing, opting usually for lower necklines. But *alluring* was not the look she wanted to portray this morning. No, she'd worn her most conservative dress, done her hair in a plain chignon rather than setting it first in waves, and had forgone her rouge altogether.

Mrs. Lewis drew in a deep breath and lifted her chin again. She didn't look nearly as old as she must be. Maybe it was the freckles that made her seem so young. "Forgive me. You didn't come here to listen to me muse about might-have-beens." She held out a hand, indicating the worn but neat sofa. "Please, have a seat. May I fetch you a cup of tea?"

"Oh, no. Thank you." Handbag clutched in front of her, Diellza sat down on the firm cushions and looked again toward the toddler who sat on the floor in the doorway, a few wooden blocks keeping him occupied. "What is your little one called?"

Mrs. Lewis's lips flitted into a smile, and then out of it again, when she glanced at her son. "That's Jeffrey. He woke early from his nap, but he didn't disturb his sisters, at least." She took a seat on the other end of the sofa. "Forgive me, Miss Boschert. In your letter, you said something about helping me. I appreciate your concern, but I'm not certain . . ."

"I cannot do much, it is true." Diellza pressed her lips together and looked deliberately around, then down at her own clothes—not only modest but utilitarian. Ready-made. Not so different in quality from what this widow wore. "I cannot improve your situation. But from what I have read, your concern

243

is not only the circumstances in which your husband's death has left you, correct? You are also concerned with justice for his murderer."

At the word—carefully chosen—Mrs. Lewis flinched. Her face clouded, her eyes went dark with pain, and she turned her head away a few degrees under the guise of tucking back a stray wisp of red-orange hair. "I would do anything—*anything* to see that monster brought to justice. I have been sending a flood of letters to everyone I can think of, demanding they reopen the case, that they bring him to trial. But at this point, I'm beginning to fear they've gone deaf to me. They don't *want* to find more evidence. He's one of their own. A gentleman. They'll be looking for reasons to pardon him, not to convict."

"Perhaps. But they will not be able to do so if, perhaps, you can present them with new evidence."

The woman went still. Utterly still for a beat, two, three. Then she sucked in a breath and met Diellza's gaze with eyes that sparked with green fire. "What new evidence?"

Diellza spread her hands, palms up. "I can help you, I think. I have not come forward before because . . ." She forced a blush and looked away. "I am not proud of how I came by this information. And I was not certain the authorities would listen to me when they heard where I learned of Major Camden's plans. But as I have watched this unfold and saw that article about the dire straits you and the other widows are in because of this . . . well, I cannot keep silent forever."

Eyes sparking like live wires, Mrs. Lewis scooted a few inches closer and cast her voice down into a near whisper. "What information? What plans? Have you proof that that devil did it deliberately?"

Diellza dropped her gaze to her lap, where she'd set her fingers to fiddling with one of the fake pearl buttons on her dress. She'd already worked out the story she would tell—first here, to this grieving widow who would believe anything, and then later, to the proper authorities. This was a sort of test run, really, to work the kinks out of it. "It is still circumstantial, at best. I was certainly not in the air that day to see what really happened. I know only what he said beforehand."

"Black Heart? When? What?" Mrs. Lewis scooted closer still and reached for Diellza's hand. Even the tops of her hands were freckled, and the palms were chapped, callused. Probably from the mountains of laundry—her own, or had she found work doing it for others?

Diellza Mettler would have no trouble looking a woman like this in the eye as she confessed exactly who and what she was. She'd chosen her path, and no one else was going to judge her for it. But she wasn't here as Diellza Mettler. She was here as Friede Boschert. And Friede would be mortified if ever she had to confess that she'd become privy to sensitive information when in a man's bed.

Well, Friede would also be mortified at *lying* about what she'd heard in a man's bed, but that was beside the point. Diellza called up more of a blush and looked away. "I was . . . I am ashamed to say it, ma'am, and I pray you do not judge me for falling prey to base instincts. I had hoped—I had thought—" She squeezed her eyes shut and, needing the right expression on her face, thought of Alwin instead of Camden. How the love had seized her, quickly and completely. How she'd been willing to do anything, lose anything to be with him. "I loved him. I made a mistake, but . . ."

The fingers holding hers tightened. "Are you saying you were . . . involved with Major Camden? Romantically?"

Careful to avoid the woman's gaze, Diellza nodded. She didn't dare to look up, over, into those green eyes. Not only because Friede wouldn't, but because she knew what she'd see there—she could feel the condemnation in each finger. And if she saw it, she might just forget herself and resort to a snarl. Or a smug smile, when she recalled how happy this woman's husband had been to forget, for an evening here and there, that he had a nagging wife and seven whining children at home.

Mrs. Lewis dragged in another long breath. "All right. I know—from what I've read—that he's a charming sort. You are probably one of many decent girls he's ruined."

Her nostrils flared before she could stop them. *Ruined*—a word she despised. But she wouldn't argue, not now. Not with her. "I have not let myself think of such things. I suppose I still hoped, deep inside, that he loved me. That he was no monster. But as I play over and again what he said . . ." She shook her head and glanced over now.

Just in time to see Mrs. Lewis's eyes brighten. "What did he say? Tell me. I beg of you."

Diellza moistened her lips and lifted her face. "He said—the night before it happened—he said he had had enough of pretending they were all his equals. That he meant to teach the upstarts—those not born gentlemen, I mean . . . your husband and one named Miller—that he meant to teach them a lesson. That if they spoke to him again as they had done before, he would send them . . ." She trailed off, looking away again. Waiting, waiting for the woman to lean closer.

She obliged. "Send them what? Or where?"

Oh, she had her. Right where she wanted her. A target so easily hit that Diellza could have taken aim with her eyes closed. Injecting sorrow into her eyes to match her voice, she looked Mrs. Lewis in the eye. "He said he would send them both to the bottom of the Channel."

Wednesday, 6 March

Darkness had slithered its way through the streets hours ago, and with it had come renewed cold and a fine rain that stung like ice. Arabelle ducked her head against it and wished for a hat with a brim rather than her kerchief over her hair. It was later than she'd meant to be getting here—quite a bit—and exhaustion weighted her bones. But she was only two minutes from home. And home meant a fire, a meal, and a steaming cup of tea. Comfortable clothes.

It also meant strained conversation and air thick with tension. She'd avoided her father's study this entire week, since their argument. She'd scarcely spoken to him at all, other than to ask him to pass the salt.

Her heart felt bound up. Tight and heavy. She had to put things right, she knew that, but . . . but every time she opened her mouth to try, the words wouldn't come.

She didn't want to open up again. For once in her life, she wanted *him* to be the responsible one, to be the adult, to take care of *her*.

And instead, he sat silent across the table from her day in and day out, all his words aimed at Camden rather than her.

Cam was likely already here, closed up in Father's study with him. If he didn't find her to walk her home, that's what he'd been doing. Waiting here for her.

No. Not waiting for *her*. Just here with her father. Plotting whatever it was they were plotting. She'd not asked. Not looked. Didn't want to know. Just as she'd not asked anything more about that beautiful blonde.

Fiddlesticks, but her fingers were frozen. It was March—why had the cold not gotten the note and vanished? She couldn't seem to lay hold of the key in her pocket as she hurried up the doorstep. But maybe, for once, Parks would actually be nearby to open it for her.

A girl could dream.

It certainly didn't swing open upon her approach, but that was really too much to ask. He'd be tending to Father and Camden, after all. So she rang the bell before sending her hand on another dive into her pocket. She'd misplaced her gloves, that was the problem. And now the icy tips of her fingers had gone numb.

But she eventually came up with the metal even colder than her hands and fumbled it into the lock, expecting Parks to arrive at any second and save her the trouble.

He didn't. "Blasted cold," she muttered in a cloud of breath as she opened the door and let herself into the entryway.

Her brows immediately drew together. No light was on down here to welcome her—odd indeed. Despite blackout requirements and rationing of gas and electric, Father *always* insisted a light be left on when she arrived home after dark.

"Father?" The cold of her fingers and nose seeped inward, deeper. Latched iron jaws around her heart. "Parks?"

She dropped her satchel to the floor by the table—the only sound to be heard. "Ruth?" She would have added a shout for their cook, but she always left in time to get to her flat before dark. "Is anyone here?"

Someone *had* to be—someone *always* was. What possible reason could there be for them all to be gone? Father, certainly—he could well be at the Explorers Club. But Parks and Ruth both had quarters here.

You're worrying over nothing, Ara. Perhaps Father had given them the evening off to visit their grandmother. Yes, that must be it—he'd done so before. She forced her shoulders to relax as she reached for the light knob.

A golden glow blossomed, pooling around her and stretching up the stairs. She unlatched her cloak, unpinned her kerchief, and left both on the chair beside her. If Father wasn't here, then he'd have left a note telling her where he could be found. They may have been at odds this last week, but surely he'd still do *that*.

There was nothing on the table in the entryway, though. Her gaze went up to the ceiling. She'd stoutly refused to step foot in his study these past seven days, and he'd not been happy about it last night when he'd pointedly invited her in and she'd pointedly refused. It would be just like him to force the issue. To say that if she wanted to know where he was, then she'd blamed well have to get over her pride to find out.

She hesitated a long, long minute. But the echoes of an empty house proved too much.

The jog up the stairs managed to restore some warmth to her limbs, anyway. She rubbed her hands together as she gained the landing that would deliver her to the study. No light came from within, but she remedied that with another twist of a knob.

Her breath caught at what it revealed. "What in the world?" The stacks of maps, the notebooks, the pottery and artifacts—all gone. The only thing still there was the giant globe.

She eased inside, hating the cold that seeped right back into her chest. It looked . . . it looked as it had *then*. Before Father came home. Before he'd taken up residence with her. Before he'd become an actual part of her life. *Empty.*

Or nearly empty. A rectangle of white rested in the center of his desk, on the green blotter. *Sweetling* was scrawled on the face of it.

Arabelle picked it up, but her fingers must still be numb. She couldn't feel the texture of his stationery. Couldn't judge its weight. Her hands shook as she tried to convince the seal to give up its hold.

At last she ripped it open and pulled out the folded sheet inside.

Arabelle, my sweetling,

You have called me selfish. And perhaps you were right. I told myself I was protecting you by leaving you in England when you were a child. I told myself that you were happier here than you'd be with me. Maybe I was wrong. And if so, forgive me. I may not know how to be a good father to you, but I do love you. More than you'll ever know.

I wanted to tell you this in person last night, but when you refused to join me, I thought perhaps it was best this way. Perhaps you'd rather not look at me while I share this news. Perhaps you'll call me a coward for that, but at least you'll not be able to call me selfish. Not this time, anyway.

I've gone to Mexico—but this is no flight of fancy. I've gone to lend much-needed aid to the Admiralty. My connections there could make a real difference in this war. Perhaps then

you can be proud of your old father. If all those selfish ad-
ventures of mine can help to save England, then they were
worthwhile, weren't they?

But know this isn't a long task. I'll be home by the end of
summer, I promise you. It in no way changes our plans for
Brazil after the war. I want nothing more than to take you
with me, sweetling. To show you my world. To make you a
part of it, if you'll permit it. And in the meantime, I've charged
Camden with your care. You'll see to each other, won't you?

There was more, but she couldn't read it. In part because her
hand was shaking too badly, in part because her eyes had blurred,
and in part because a shrieking was coming from the hallway.

She spun around just in time to see Ruth come to a rocking
halt in the doorway, her face mottled and streaked with tears—
and a valise in her hand.

Arabelle frowned. "Ruth?"

Her maid pointed a finger at her. "This is all your fault. I knew
we shouldn't hire on here—I *knew* it! It's always the same, the
other maids told me so. The moment your father gets another
harebrained scheme, off the young men go with him."

Arabelle's fingers tightened around the letter, crinkling the
edges. "What are you . . . Parks? Parks has gone with my father?"

"Gone with him? He all but danced out the door!" Ruth swiped
at her wet cheeks and backed up a step. "I believed you when
you said he wouldn't go anywhere until the war was over. I *be-*
lieved you. But now they're gone, and who's to say if ever they'll
return? He barely got off the battlefields with his life, and now
he'll probably be sunk by a U-boat!"

Oh, heavens. Arabelle squeezed her eyes shut. They were on
the yacht. Out in the Atlantic, where the Germans prowled. "I'm
sorry. Ruth, I didn't know, I didn't—"

"Save your apologies. And consider this my resignation." Ruth's
footsteps punctuated her words.

For a moment, Arabelle just stood there, the angry echoes

clanging about inside against the shards of ice. Then she forced
her eyes open. "Ruth, wait!" She took off after the maid, though
the young woman was moving at a brisk pace. "You needn't resign! I know you're angry and distressed—I am too—but storm-
ing off will do no good. Please."

"No!" Ruth shouted up the stairwell. "I won't serve the family
that stole my brother away. I wouldn't stay if you *begged* me."

Arabelle raced down the stairs after her. Ready to beg. Because if Ruth left, if Parks and Father were both gone, that
meant no one else was here. No one. She'd be alone, completely
alone, as she'd never wanted to be again. No family, no guard-
ian, no staff even to fill the empty rooms. No one, no one at all.
Just like when her mother had died. It would be just Arabelle
and the emptiness and the anger.

He'd left her. Again. It didn't matter that she was a grown
woman, it didn't matter that she knew how to get along without him, it didn't matter that she could hire a new maid, a new
butler—he had *left her*.

Her feet kept her on their course down the stairs, even as
the ice of fear and the fire of panic began to shift, to steam. How
could he? How could he do this again?

She stumbled, grabbed the banister to keep from falling. Choked
on the heaving breath that would *not* turn to a sob. Better anger
than tears.

The doorbell rang, but even as Ara registered it, she heard
the heavy wood slam into the wall and Ruth's voice. The words
themselves didn't quite make sense through the rushing in Arabelle's ears, but the tone certainly didn't sound any friendlier
than it had a moment before.

Not Father, then, having changed his mind and brought Parks
back with him. She dragged in a breath and started down again.
If it were one of those ridiculous callers, she would boot him
directly to the curb.

Four more steps and she was on the last landing, able to see
into the entryway.

Camden. Camden coming in even as Ruth pushed past him, slamming the door shut behind her. He, at least, was still here. He hadn't left her, hadn't run off with her father for adventure. For escape. He was here. . . .

I've charged Camden with your care.

Her knees nearly buckled, but she propelled herself forward instead. Toward him.

I've gone to lend aid to the Admiralty.

The Admiralty. Where Phillip Camden went every day. Where she'd seen her father go. Where they'd been meeting, talking, for *weeks*. Those conversations that had come to an abrupt halt when she came in. The mysterious silences. The meals they'd had here without her.

"Ara?" He was spinning from the door he'd watched slam, his face an etching of concern. "What—"

"You *knew!*" She flew at him, screamed at him, poised to claw at him. "You knew he was leaving—you knew and you said *nothing*. You didn't talk him out of it, you didn't see fit to *tell me*—"

His curse cut her off, though she wasn't sure if the sentiment was aimed at her father or her. Probably her, given the fact that he'd caught her arms and was fighting her for possession of them. She tugged with all her might, got one free, managed to land a screaming hit on his arm, then was caught again.

She pulled, she tugged, she twisted and writhed, but all it seemed to accomplish was a tighter prison. She couldn't see him through the blur over her eyes, she couldn't hear him over the pounding blood in her ears, she couldn't feel him over the raging heat that devoured her.

She jerked again on her wrists, and this time he let her go, but it did no good. She was trapped, a wall behind her and him before her, and she couldn't get leverage enough to get another hit in. She could only pound her fists uselessly against his chest.

"You *knew*." It wasn't a scream this time. It was a whimper, strangled by the tears. "You knew he was leaving."

"Ara. Darling." His arms were around her, his hands moving

up and down her back. "He said he would talk to you last night. He promised me, made *me* promise I wouldn't say anything until he'd had a chance."

She could only shake her head. If only it could force it away, if only she could deny it was happening. If only she could be the twenty-five-year-old woman she was instead of the ten-year-old she currently felt like.

Touching her mother's cheek and realizing it was cold, not fever-hot. That her chest was still. That the house was empty.

Seeing those dreadful words on the telegram, saying her father's base camp hadn't heard from him in over a year.

Hearing the whispers of the vicar and his wife in the other room. *"What are we going to do with her? Who can we find to take her now?"*

No one. No one ever wanted her. Not enough to live for her. Not enough to come home for her. Not enough to stay when there was an opportunity to leave. Not enough to love *her* when they could have someone else.

"Ara."

The tears were hot on her cheeks. Burning her. "He's gone."

"Not for long. He'll be back."

Maybe. For a while. Until he left again. Probably, again, without her. Her fingers splayed out, only to curl up once more, this time into the wool of Camden's overcoat.

The anger trickled away, draining out under the force of her tears. If only she could have clung to it a little longer, held the hurt at bay. Better the anger. Better that than the pain. The yawning emptiness.

She closed her eyes and let her head fall forward, onto his shoulder. Not that she could rest her forehead there, as a shorter girl could—she had to settle for her cheek. And not that she should let herself take any solace from him.

He'd known. He'd not told her. And now, with Father gone, he'd probably fade out of her life too.

"I'm sorry, darling." His hand slid up her back, up her neck, into her hair. "I tried. I know you've no reason to believe me, but I did try. I tried to talk him out of going, and I insisted he couldn't go without telling you."

"Why should he bother? My thoughts on the matter were obviously of no consequence." She tried to relax her fingers and realized only then that the letter was no longer clenched in them. She must have dropped it somewhere.

She hardly cared.

"Ara, look at me." He moved his shoulder, forcing her head up.

She looked at him through her tears. He was close—so close. Closer than he'd been any time other than the night of the bombing, when it had been *his* head on *her* shoulder. His eyes were too blue, deep with concern, his brow in its once-perpetual frown.

What did he expect her to see? Or want to see from her?

His frown furrowed deeper still. "Don't. Don't vanish on me, darling. Don't go empty. That's not what you do. Not you. You pray or sing one of those hymns or say something about God being there when no one else is. Isn't that right? Isn't this where you bring out all the lines about faith filling one up?"

She slid her gaze away. Down, to rest on his chin rather than his eyes. His chin, chiseled as it was, was far softer. Easier. "It will." When she let it. When she could push this aside enough to turn it over to Him.

But she couldn't. Not yet. If she did, she'd fall apart, and she couldn't fall apart any more than she had. Not here, not now. Not with Cam here.

"Then let it. That's my Ara. Rant a bit, rail a bit, pray a lot—that's who you are. This is nothing to change that, is it? It's just a voyage."

"Right. Just another voyage." Her voice sounded flat. Hollow. False.

And Phillip Camden wasn't one to let that slide past him. He angled her face, forcing her eyes back up until their gazes caught, knotted. "Don't," he whispered. "Don't try to placate me. Don't shut me out. I know how this must hurt you."

"Do you?" Her fingers convulsed again around his lapels. "Have you any idea what it feels like to be so utterly alone?"

"I have." Calm. Even. Shadowed. "Try sitting in a military prison for a few days."

She wanted to deny it was the same, to make this *more* . . . but that was the very thing that had first called to her about him, wasn't it? That she saw in his hunched shoulders and angry stride the same thing she'd felt too often in herself.

"I thought I'd forgiven him. I thought I'd let it go, but the pain . . . it's always there. All I ever wanted was to be part of a family, but he . . . ." The tears were clogging her throat again.

Cam's fingers stroked through her hair, from temple to chignon at the nape of her neck. "You *are* family, Ara. He loves you."

She shook her head wildly, barely noticing when the action, combined with his fingers, sent the coil of her hair unfurling down her neck. "No. That isn't good enough. All I want—all I have *ever* wanted—is for him to be here. But he never is. No one is. No one ever wants to stay for long. I'm just not enough, I—"

"Stop." His hands framed her face, anchoring her, refusing to let her look away. His eyes blazed. "Don't believe those lies, Arabelle. Not for a second. You are everything. *Everything*. Everything good, everything bright. Everything worthwhile."

She tried to look away. It seemed the wise thing to do—no, the necessary thing. To escape his gaze before it consumed her, before her knees went weak and made a fool of her. But she couldn't. His eyes held her captive, those blue flames shooting sparks at her that said the impossible.

He eased closer. An inch. Two. The hands still framing her face tilted it up just a bit more. His gaze caressed her face. His intention was clear in the dip of his head.

He was going to kiss her. Phillip Camden was going to kiss her.

So she did the only reasonable thing she could do. She slammed her hands hard into his chest and pushed him away with every last bit of willpower she could summon.

21

Camden staggered back half a step from the force of her shove, his hands losing their place against her cheeks and forced to settle elsewhere. Her waist, though that brought another flash to her eyes.

Not exactly a flash of disdain, though.

"Don't." Her voice shook, strained, made him at once want to pull her close and to run away, to spare her another moment of his company and yet never to leave her again. "There is exactly one reason for you to ever kiss me, Phillip. And it isn't sympathy—"

"I'm unfamiliar with it." He eased a few inches closer again.

"Or pity."

"Never waste my time on it."

Her chin lifted. "Or even affection. I know this may be how you're accustomed to comforting girls, but I'll not have it. I won't."

He winced. She was probably right, a bit—he was used to a physical answer. But she was wrong too. Because he'd never cared enough to comfort a girl other than his mother or sister. He'd never wanted to hold one until all her troubles went away. Not until her.

"There's only one reason." She said it this time in a resigned tone, falling back against the wall. Defeated.

One reason. He knew very well what it was.

Love.

That was the only reason she'd accept for a man like him to kiss her. He took the last half step. Deliberately. Gaze tangled with hers. "I know."

Her breath caught, and she shook her head, but it wasn't in refusal. It was in denial. Disbelief.

He couldn't blame her. All of England knew he didn't have a heart—how could he love? How could he yearn so entirely to be part of her, to protect her, to encourage her, to kiss her until she didn't doubt—*couldn't* doubt for a moment that she was the most beautiful creature ever to live?

But he did. Somehow. Perhaps through her power, her heart, since his own was black and lifeless. He loved her more completely than he'd ever thought possible.

He lifted one hand from her waist to bury it again into the hair at the nape of her neck, hanging now in long, thick waves. He tilted his head. Eased it down, over, closer. Holding her gaze all the while. Shouting silently, over and again, *I know. I know.* He knew what he was doing, what he was asking. And he was doing it anyway, because he couldn't *not*. Couldn't bear another moment of it.

She didn't shove him away this time. Didn't make any other objection. She just drew in a sharp breath, knotted her fingers again around the lapel of his overcoat, and strained forward to meet him.

Her lips were cold at the first brush of his, but they warmed when he lingered there. Soft and hesitant and yet urgent. Or perhaps the urgency was his. Because much as he told himself to be patient and gentle, that single touch of lips wasn't enough. He took seconds, thirds, then gave up and parted her lips, taking her deeper, pulling her closer.

She clung to him, one of her arms finding its way around him while the other stayed pressed to his chest. An anchor, those arms—the only thing that told him that his own needs weren't so loud in his veins that he was just ignoring hers.

And this wasn't *want*. It wasn't just desire, which he'd had plenty of experience with before—too much, his brother would say. *She* would say. Clearly, they were right. Because what he'd always thought was enough, was all there was, faded into nothingness now. *This* was what a kiss should be. This was what a man should feel—should know—when he held a woman in his arms.

That she was the only one in the world who mattered. That making her happy was the only thing that would make *him* happy. That when happiness wasn't even possible in this world of pain and disappointment, sharing the sorrow would make it bearable.

And yet . . . that would be all there was for her, if he asked this of her. Pain. Disappointment. Ruin. He was a dead man already, living on borrowed time.

He eased his mouth from hers, breath ragged, but couldn't convince himself to pull away entirely. It would be the kind thing—but he'd never claimed to be kind. He rested his forehead on hers. "I'm sorry."

Her arms went tighter rather than releasing him. "You say that quite a lot for someone who doesn't apologize."

He stroked his thumb along that place where her jaw met her ear. His lips tingled at the thought of kissing that spot—he'd only have to lean over the smallest bit—but he held himself in check. "Only to you. You're the only one who's ever made me wish I was different."

"Phillip." The way she said his name, the gleam in her eyes that turned hazel to gold, made his throat go dry. But then she shook her head, her eyes sliding closed. "This is absurd. You can't love me."

His every muscle jolted, shocked. That wasn't right. The first utterance of love between them shouldn't have a negative attached to it. He pulled her closer, shook his head a bit against hers. "I know it seems impossible. I know it seems I haven't a heart capable of such. But somehow, Ara—"

"No, you idiot." The hand against his chest slapped at him—

feebly—and *idiot* sounded like an endearment when she said it on that little breath of laughter. "I don't mean *you* aren't capable of loving. I mean it isn't possible that you'd love *me*."

He pulled away enough to better see her eyes. Held her head still with his hand. "You've got it all wrong, darling. It isn't possible that I'd love anyone *but* you."

Another little laugh slipped from her lips and tickled his, begging for a kiss. He obliged it. Though he granted himself only one short taste this time. "Aren't you supposed to say something too? About loving *me*?"

A nobler man wouldn't ask her to give him such words. A humbler man would wonder if she did. But he'd never been those things either, and he knew her well enough to know she'd never melt against him like this if it weren't true.

Her hand somehow found its way to his neck, into his hair, sweeping his hat off and sending it flying. And oh, her eyes shone like gold in a fire. "I think I've loved you since you closed your umbrella and sat with me in the rain."

His heart—maybe it *was* still there. Because it ached like nothing he'd ever felt before. "Took you that long?" Another laugh begged another kiss from him. "I'm pretty sure I've loved you since . . ."

Her other hand splayed right over the aching, throbbing place in his chest. "Since?"

He grinned. "Since you socked Edmund Braxton in the nose."

Her laugh, soft as a summer rain, made the ache resonate like joy. "You did not."

"You're right. I think it was since I saw you staring at me from the window of the hospital with that challenging tilt to your chin."

It tilted so even now. "I was not *staring*. And now you're just being ridiculous."

Heaven help him. He trailed his nose along her cheek and kissed that challenging jawline. "I am," he murmured, chest so tight he feared it would crush him. "I'm ridiculous to think this is a good idea. And I'm selfish and cruel to say such words to you when it can only end badly. I'll only bring you pain." His hand curled into a fist around her hair, and his eyes slid closed. "I'm a dead man."

Her finger settled on his lips, silencing him. "Don't speak that way. They've let you go, Phillip. They're not going to come back for you now."

He shook his head, not believing that for a moment. They would. Eventually, they would. And even if they didn't . . . He kissed her finger. "I've been dead since that day, Ara. When my men went down. I don't deserve to be alive when they're not. I don't deserve to have you."

"Phillip—"

"And you certainly deserve more. Better than me. Someone without my past. Someone who has a future, whose days aren't numbered. Someone who has a bit of life inside him other than what he has to borrow from you."

Her fingertips soothed over his face, scraping against the shadow of stubble along his jaw, easing onto the smoother skin of his cheek. He watched the thoughts tumble over one another in her eyes. The hope and fear and disappointment and love.

Then *she* leaned over to kiss *him*. Once, with determination. Like that day she'd kissed his cheek. Proving a point. "My love. We're *all* dead. All our days are numbered. That's the beauty of what Christ did for us—dying so that we could finally taste real life. Pouring Himself out so that we could be filled."

Laughter danced its way over his lips. "There you are. *That* is what I expect of you."

Her eyes snapped with resolve more than amusement. "You know it's true. You know you need Him."

Blast, but he could drown in those eyes. "I need *you*."

She shook her head. "Don't put that responsibility on me. I'll fail you—people cannot help but fail. Not to mention . . ." She narrowed those eternal eyes at him. "How exactly can you claim you care nothing for matters of faith if they're part of what you stand here claiming to love about me?"

He narrowed his eyes right back. "Blast, but you sound like Jeremy. You really ought to have fallen in love with *him*."

Her lips twitched. "Well, ring him up. Perhaps his offer of becoming Mrs. Vicar is still—"

He cut her off with a growl that mixed with her laughter, pinning her again against the wall, feasting again on her lips until his own thundering pulse told him he had better ease up or he'd earn another shove from her.

It was the hardest six inches he ever moved. But he was rewarded with the sight of her eyes gone hazy and warm. His throat was tight as a tourniquet when he tried to swallow. "I guess maybe I do know it's true—about all the faith nonsense. But knowing it, Ara . . . it doesn't make it any easier to reconcile what I've been taught with the world I've seen, the life I've lived."

A hint of a smile touched her lips. "The reconciliation has already been accomplished. All you need to do is accept it."

As if it were so easy. "Will you only love me if I say the right words about this?"

Her fingers found his cheek again. "There are no conditions on my love. Besides." She smiled. "You'll not be able to run from Him much longer. I know it."

Part of him thought maybe she was right. And part of him wanted to run all the faster to avoid it. He wasn't ready to look his sins fully in the face. So he distracted himself with another kiss. And then pulled away with a long breath. "I had better leave. I can't be trusted with a young lady without a chaperone, you know."

A riot of thoughts rampaged through her eyes. Doubt, confusion . . . dread. Her arms tightened around him. "But . . . he's gone. There's no one else. How—when can you, then . . . ?"

His concern exactly, and one Den had done absolutely nothing to address. "We'll find a way. I can still see you home. We can share meals in public." It wasn't enough, not nearly. Not when they were accustomed to long, lazy evenings of shared company.

The breath she drew in shook. "Can't you stay just a bit longer now, though? I'm not—I'm not quite ready to be alone."

When she was soft and pliant in his arms, weakened with uncertainty and her father's latest abandonment, desperate for someone to prove she was worthwhile? Perhaps if he didn't love her so entirely, he'd welcome the opportunity to be that kind of villain. To pit his desire against her convictions.

But that was the quickest way to lose this gift he didn't deserve to have to begin with. He shook his head and put another six inches between them. "I have a better idea—why don't you go and pack a bag and we'll both leave?"

That just made her brows knot. "And go where?"

"You can stay with Brook for the night—until we find you new domestics. You know she won't mind." He nudged her toward the stairs. "Go, darling. I'll give her a ring. And we'll hire you new help tomorrow so the place won't be empty."

She relented with a nod and started up the stairs—though she climbed only three before pausing and turning back to him with a smile that tied his stomach into knots. "Are you going to kiss me again before we go?"

She was lucky he didn't charge up those stairs and kiss her again now. But five minutes away from her would hopefully convince the heat in his blood to cool a few vital degrees. "Darling, I intend to kiss you every chance I get."

She hurried up the stairs, leaving Camden to shake his head at himself. Or at her. Her foolishness in actually loving him. His at asking her to. In a life comprised mainly of reckless decisions, it was, without question, the most reckless thing he'd done.

When he turned from the stairs, his eyes caught on a slip of crumpled white. He snatched it up, sighing when straightening it out revealed Den's script. The letter he'd written to Ara.

He had no intentions of reading it, but his own name grabbed his eye.

I've charged Camden with your care. He shook his head—how

she'd known, he supposed, that he'd been aware of Den's plan. *You'll see to each other, won't you?*

> *I fear I've jaded you too much for you to seek a marriage for reasons other than security and convenience, as you would have had with Brax. I'm sorry for that. And I pray you'll see that love is worth the risk. Even when it leads to heartache, it's worth it. Give Camden a chance to prove himself a more dependable man than I, sweetling. Though I would appreciate if you held off on the wedding until I can get home again.*

Camden lowered the paper. "Ara?" he called up the stairs.

Her voice floated down a moment later, faint and distant—she was probably at the floor that housed her bedroom by now. "Yes?"

"Did you finish reading this letter from your father?"

"Not yet—I only got so far as his implication that you knew. Slide it into my satchel for me, won't you?"

His eyes sought and found the familiar leather bag slumped against the entryway table. "All right." He fingered its edge, not moving.

Wedding. The natural aim when one loved a woman. But not something he'd ever had any interest in attending, especially as a groom. So why did no panic light in his chest at the thought now?

Well, that wasn't quite true. There was panic—but not at the thought of marrying Arabelle. At the thought of marrying her only to be torn away from her. Or worse, being taken back into custody before he *could* marry her. Or the very worst, asking her only to be refused. She might love him without condition, but that didn't mean his reluctance in matters of faith wouldn't keep her from binding herself to him.

He strode over to the satchel. Unclasped and opened it, trying to decide where among the clutter of paper work he ought to put this so that she could find it. After a moment of staring, he decided on the small front pouch. He had to refold the letter to fit it in, but it looked as though it wasn't the first letter to find its home there.

He shifted the bag so he could slip it in with the other folded sheet. But then his eye caught on the script on that one.

Familiar script. *Too* familiar. Muttering a curse, he pulled it out, just to verify those looping letters were the ones he saw far too often.

As if his eyes wouldn't know it anywhere.

He didn't open it. Didn't have to. He just stood there, staring at it, steaming, until he heard her step on the stair again. And then he spun, wielding it like a sword. "Were you going to tell me about this?"

Her eyes snapped to the letter, held there a moment, obviously trying to place what it was. Then she continued toward him, a small valise in hand. No apology on her face. "No."

"*No?*" He shook his head. "Why not? What did she say? Did she threaten you?"

She looked—blast it all—*amused*. "No, because I saw no reason to worry you over a silly letter that contained no threat. Though I believe she thinks she's warning me away from you for my own good." Her brows lifted. "I take it she's been writing to you too. Were *you* going to tell *me* about *that*?"

He ground his teeth together.

She sidled up to him. "I thought not." Far too at ease, she raised her free hand and rested it on his cheek. Then she leaned over and rested her lips on his.

His anger melted, a pool of useless wax at his feet. He kissed her back, soundly, then muttered, "I still don't like it."

"My kiss?"

A snort of laughter slipped out, and he tugged her flush against him. "Yes, that's it. You'll have to practice more. As often as possible."

The grin he expected. The flicker of uncertainty in her eyes he could have cursed himself for. "Ara." He took her chin in his hands and held her gaze. "I was only joking."

"I know." And clearly she did, as she was the one who started the joke. But knowledge never held the uncertainty at bay, did it? How well he knew that. She sighed, her gaze dropping from his eyes to his nose. "I'm sorry. My own insecurities, nothing more."

Her insecurities combined, no doubt, with his past. With seeing him last week with Diellza. With wondering if he was comparing her to others. Blast his former self—why hadn't he listened to all that wisdom that had sounded like rot when Jeremy and Mother spouted it?

He gave her his warmest smile. "Insecurities I am very much looking forward to banishing. Because for the record, darling . . ." He stepped away to grab her cloak, sweeping his gaze down the length of her when space permitted it. "There isn't a single thing about you I don't like."

She arched a brow, but the unease had retreated a bit from her eyes. "My gangliness?"

"Not gangly, darling—willowy." He winked and moved closer to drape her cape over her shoulders. "And I quite like your height. Easier to reach your lips whenever I crave them."

Her cheeks actually went a bit pink—the first blush he'd ever seen from her. "My plainness?"

"We've already covered that one. Understated. Barely—the more I look at you, the more I find to capture my gaze. Though I was right about the dimple." He kissed it again now, as he'd let himself make a habit of doing. "I adore that dimple."

She pressed her valise into his chest and bent down for her satchel, cheeks still flushed. "All right. That's enough convincing for one night. Did you ring up Brook?"

"Not yet."

"I'll do that. And then we'll go."

He held tight to the valise, but his smirk faded as she walked away. He didn't know how long it might take to convince her that she was everything. What if he didn't have time enough before the past caught him up?

For the first time in years, he considered breaking his silence with God and saying a prayer. For her sake. Heaven knew *he* didn't deserve any mercy.

But Ara . . . she deserved everything.

22

Camden's clock was chiming eight by the time he let himself into his flat and aimed directly for his telephone. He'd deposited Ara with Brook and come straight home, knowing he needed to make this call before it got any later. His mother would be panicked if the telephone rang too late.

He gave the operator the exchange and waited for it to connect, for the line to ring, for someone to answer. It took forever, but at last the dignified voice of their longtime butler answered. "Good evening, Foxwood House."

Camden puffed out his relief. "Watt. It's Phillip—is my mother in?"

"Yes, Master Phillip. One moment, please."

Too antsy to sit, he paced as far as the cord would allow—all of two steps in either direction.

At last, his mother's voice came crackling over the line. "Philly? What's wrong?"

He sighed, hating that was her first assumption. "Nothing. Well, plenty, but nothing new. Exactly." He scrubbed a hand over his face. "Look, I . . . do you remember when you said some ages ago that I could have Grandmother's ring if ever I needed it—the diamond and sapphire one?"

Silence crackled so long he feared the call had been lost. "Mum?"

"I remember." Her voice came through as clear as it ever did. Which meant he could easily make out the note in it that he could only label as dread. "Why are you asking?"

He planted his feet, staring at the candlestick of the phone as if he could see her through it. "Why do you think?"

Her sigh blustered across the miles. "For *whom* are you asking, I suppose I ought to say. Have you got someone in trouble?"

"No! Why do you just assume—" He cut himself off with a growl, aimed more at himself—and partly at Cass and Braxton—than at her. "Nothing like that. I promise you."

"I didn't mean to assume anything." She cleared her throat, and he could well imagine her shutting her eyes for a moment, drawing in a deep breath. "My apologies. I'm only surprised. So far as you've seen fit to tell me, there's not been anyone special in your life."

"Yes, well, there is."

Another beat. Then, "I see. And may I ask who this is to whom you mean to give my mother's ring? Or should I assume I wouldn't know her by name even were you to tell me?"

"You'd know it." He was tempted to leave it at that, just to poke her back a bit for her dread and assumptions. But as she had every reason for them, he relented and added, "Ara. Arabelle, I mean. Denler."

"Really!" Now the ice vanished from her voice, replaced by a laugh. "Oh, Phillip, you can't know what a relief that is to me. A good Christian girl! From a reputable family, no less! I—wait." And just like that, her joy tumbled back to dread. "You care for her, don't you? This isn't . . . ?"

"Mother." He'd been many things in his life, but never a money-grubber. "Give me an ounce of credit, won't you? You met her. Do you think after all that recently transpired she'd give me so much as a consideration if I didn't love her?"

"You love her." Now, if he wasn't mistaken, tears were clogging her throat. Though maybe it was only the static. "Of course you can have the ring. In fact, I'll deliver it myself. Oh—my calendar is rather full these next several days. But I can come up next week. Will that do? And perhaps I could stay awhile. Get to know her better."

Perfect. Finally able to relax, he melted into the hard wooden chair by the telephone. "That will do nicely. You can stay with her—her father's just left on a trip, and she could use the company." And what better chaperone could there be than his own mother? "As a matter of fact . . ." He reached for the pencil and paper he kept on the small table. "Does Cass have a telephone? I have a favor to ask of her as well."

"Cass?" Mother sniffed and chuckled, presumably at her own happy tears. "They've just had one installed, yes. I can give you their exchange. But what do you need to ask of her?"

He grinned and readied to write down the number. "I need her to exercise a bit of her new authority, that's all. As mistress of Middlegrove."

He might not be able to spend as much time now at Ara's house. But he would sure as blazes make certain she wasn't alone.

Arabelle stood on Agar Street, staring at the familiar sign outside the hospital demanding quiet for the wounded. For a moment, the breeze—more temperate today than wintry—might as well have been a bucket of ice water.

In the last twelve hours, she'd basically resigned her position here, and she'd not even paused to consider it. By kissing Camden, by admitting her love for him, she'd broken the terms on which she'd been promoted. The one place she felt welcome, needed, and she'd thrown it all away.

She'd be sacked. As soon as they found out, they'd let her go and make an example of her. And what was she to do? Try to hide it? That was hardly honest.

But then, their threats were hardly fair. Not that they expected impeccable morality from their nurses—she agreed with their standards. But that they would judge him so cruelly, on nothing but hearsay and slander. He was not what the papers had made him out to be. If only he would defend himself, if only he would try to clear his name, then . . .

No. She let her breath out and forced her feet into action again. She couldn't ask that of him for her sake. Not when she knew the pain it would bring him.

Whatever actually happened that day, it still tormented him. It feasted on his spirit, on his peace. And he *felt* guilty. He wasn't, she was sure of that. He had *not* deliberately killed his men. But they'd still died while he lived, and he couldn't yet accept that the guilt of that didn't deserve punishment.

Father God . . . She pulled open the door and entered to the familiar sounds and smells of Charing Cross. *Father, please help him see that this is not his guilt to bear. Not for my sake, but for his own.*

She didn't *want* to give up her position here, not yet. But she knew what it felt like to have someone always choose other pursuits above her. She couldn't do that to Cam. She was certain that wasn't what God would want of her—right?

Or was that wishful thinking? Her own heart trying to convince her mind that there was wisdom in something utterly foolish? Her father was in favor—words she could scarcely believe when she finished reading his letter last night, tucked safely into her borrowed room at Brook's house. But was that an indication of her heavenly Father's will?

She started up the stairs, pressing her lips together. So little experience she had with romance. It had seemed no great thing to promise forever to Brax, when he had no real faith to speak of. But then, they knew they'd lead separate lives anyway. This . . . this whatever-this-was with Cam was entirely different. Involved. A future with him would look nothing like one with Brax.

But a few kisses didn't equal a promise of forever, did they?

Even when they accompanied words of love. She had no way of knowing if Camden even *wanted* a future with her.

She shook her head, forcing such thoughts aside as best she could. Though as soon as she managed that, more concerns flooded her. When was she to find the time to hire new domestics? This, she supposed, was what a housekeeper was for. Perhaps they should have replaced Mrs. Stadler when she retired three years ago. At the time, it really hadn't seemed necessary, but . . .

As she neared her office, familiar red-gold hair caught her eye, bringing a much-needed halt to other thoughts. "Lily! Good morning. Are you waiting for me?"

Lily smiled, clutching something to her chest. "I am. I have something for you."

A corner of Ara's mouth tugged up. "Not more paper work, I hope."

Her friend laughed and followed her into the office. "No. Just a small gift. Let's call it a belated congratulations on your advancement." She offered the paper-wrapped rectangle to Arabelle.

Warmth filled her chest, pushing out some of the questions. "How sweet of you." Since Lily stood there, her lip between her teeth, clearly waiting to see Arabelle's reaction to whatever her gift was, Ara obliged. She unwrapped the paper, revealing first the back of what was clearly a picture frame.

When she turned it around, her breath caught. She and Camden, arm in arm, looking at each other in profile and smiling. Their faces glowing with affection. She traced a finger along the edge of the frame, brows knotting. "When did you . . . ?" It was London in the background, yes, but not the London she'd seen of late. This London had trees in bloom and clear skies and no black-out curtains or lamps. But she hadn't even *known* Cam last spring, and no blossoms had touched the trees yet this year.

Lily chuckled. "Do you recall that day when I followed you out with my camera? I'd just come back around to fetch something I'd forgot, and I saw you two walking away. But Agar Street didn't make the loveliest backdrop, so I took the liberty of putting you somewhere more appealing."

Arabelle blinked at the beautiful photograph. "I know such alteration can be done. But, Lily, this looks seamless. It looks *real*." She looked up again and smiled. "Thank you so much."

Lily returned her smile and motioned to the office—still bare of any personal touches. "I thought you could use a bit of decoration in here."

"That I could." Ara laughed . . . even as her fingers tightened around the frame. She couldn't leave this here. It would serve as a sign that said, *Sack me!*

But . . . no. Perhaps it was the perfect statement. More, perhaps this was, at least in part, the Lord's answer to her questions as she came in. She set the frame on her desk, angling it so that she'd be able to see it whenever she looked up. "There. Again, Lily, thank you."

"My pleasure. Again, Ara—congratulations. I can't think of a better nurse for the position. Now, I'd better get to work before the ward matron comes after me." With a wink at the joke, she hurried out.

Arabelle hung up her coat, let her eyes linger for a moment more on the beautiful photograph, and followed her VAD's example.

Another nurse nearly bowled her over the moment she stepped into the hall, looking frazzled. "Oh, Nurse Denler! Thank heavens. Mrs. Jameson is out with a nasty cold, and there's a train of new patients due in any minute. Here." She shoved a pile of folders into Arabelle's arms. "I need to see if those cots are made up yet."

Arabelle chuckled her agreement. And tried not to feel *too* relieved that her superior wasn't there to see that photograph quite yet.

The morning was nearly stretching into afternoon when Susan appeared at her side in the ward. "You've a visitor, Ara. I showed her to your office."

At the mention of *visitor*, her pulse hammered. But at *her*, it eased back down to normal. She handed Susan the tray of lunch she'd been about to deliver and smiled. "Thank you, Sue."

Through the open door of her office she could see the visitor as she approached. A woman, on the short side, dressed in a sensible suit of dark blue, auburn hair pinned in a neat coil beneath her outdated hat.

Arabelle squealed and rushed inside. "Sarah!"

Her best friend turned with a wide grin, arms outstretched. "Ara!"

They embraced, laughing, their words tumbling over each other—how it had been too long, how they'd not expected a visit for months after the one that never happened, how proud Sarah was of Arabelle's new position.

When she pulled away and waved her friend into a chair, Arabelle's smile was so big she feared it would strain her cheeks. "But what are you doing here? And why didn't you tell me you'd be coming to London? I'd have met your train!"

Sarah, green eyes twinkling, sat with a smirk. "Well, it was the strangest thing. There I was last night, finishing up my work for the day, when I'm informed that my new mistress is on the telephone, asking for me."

"Cass?" Arabelle pulled a second chair near to Sarah's.

Sarah lifted her brows. "If that's what you call the new Mrs. Braxton, though *I* would never dare. I thought perhaps she'd be telling me of another upcoming visit—but no. Instead, she ordered me to London."

Ara frowned. "Ordered you here? Why? Are they coming to Town?" But that hardly made sense. The Braxtons had a house here, but it had its own staff.

"It seems," Sarah said, leaning close, "that Mrs. Braxton's brother had just rung her up, asking for her to dispatch me here so that I could keep a certain someone company for a week and hire her a new staff while she's busy running a hospital ward."

For a second Ara could only stare. Cam—Cam had done this.

He'd left her with Brook last night and then must have rushed home to call his sister. To arrange for Sarah to come. To ease her loneliness and solve her employee problems in one fell swoop.

Tears stung her eyes, necessitating a few rapid blinks to banish them back to where they belonged. "And you came."

"A week of paid holiday while I spend time with my dearest friend? Why wouldn't I come?" Laughing, Sarah reached over, plucked Arabelle's hand from the arm of her chair, and gave it a firm squeeze. "I took the first train this morning. And I imagined all number of explanations for *why* Mrs. Braxton's brother had arranged all this. Can you slip out for lunch, do you think? I'm dying to know why Black Heart himself has done this."

Ara glanced at the watch she kept pinned to her bodice. Ten minutes until noon. "I can certainly slip out." She looked back up, having a feeling that something more than appreciation glowed in her eyes. "And I assure you, Phillip Camden's heart is far from black."

23

Camden threaded his fingers through his hair as he stared at the evidence stacked up on Admiral Hall's desk. Evidence that Ara had been right in more ways than she'd known—a man was a fool to assume a woman was nothing more than the image she portrayed.

Whoever Hall had tasked with finding information on Diellza Mettler in Switzerland had done a bang-up job. Newspaper articles, school photographs, even transcribed conversations with her old neighbors. And a few newer ones.

Sometimes it was a bit terrifying, the information Hall could so easily get his hands on. Made him rather glad he was on the admiral's good side.

Camden let out a breath and pulled one particular newspaper article closer. Clipped to it was a typed translation, with a headline that read "Mettler Daughter Wins Tournament." *Mettler*. She wasn't just the gun manufacturer's daughter; she was an expert marksman. A girl who had dazzled her father's colleagues with her expertise in his weapons as a child and had begun winning competitions at the ripe age of eight. She could, the article reported, field-strip and reassemble a pistol in two minutes, a rifle in three. She could hit a bull's-eye at a hundred yards with her favorite handgun. When armed with a rifle, they declared her "unstoppable. A sniper to rival any trained by the military."

And there was the visual proof, if the words hadn't been enough. A photograph of a younger Diellza, standing proudly with a curious-looking rifle in hand—a bit smaller than most, as if it had been scaled to fit her. It probably had been. She beamed from under the proud, protective arm of an older man who was clearly her father.

"From what my man in-country could glean," Hall said, sifting through a few other pieces of paper, "she had always made a great effort to be her father's darling, especially after her mother passed away. The younger sister, Friede, never seemed to take as much interest in marksmanship, but Mr. Mettler encouraged Diellza in her talent. You'll find there an entire article on her weapon of choice—a semi-automatic carbine that has interchanging barrels and stocks to make it either pistol or rifle. A bit like the Mannlicher 1903. Her father made it specifically for her."

"To startling effect." Camden flipped to another article declaring yet another competition win for "Eagle Eye Mettler." "I imagine it was excellent publicity for Mettler's operations."

"Indeed. At least until she was seventeen. That's when all articles stop."

Camden sifted through the remainder of the stack Hall had handed him, verifying the truth of that. The last newspaper clipping wasn't like the others, though. It was an engagement announcement. He frowned. "She's married?"

"No." Hall punctuated the word with a scoffing laugh. "Engaged very briefly. According to the neighbors, everything went sour for the Mettlers that summer. Most didn't know exactly what had happened—aside from the obvious deduction that a man had been involved. Just that Diellza had vanished, her father refused to so much as mention her name, and soon it was Friede engaged to this Max Boschert instead of Diellza."

Camden reached for another photograph, the one Hall had shown him before. The one where Dee was smiling with clear affection at a blond man with nearly delicate features, but for the scar running from temple to ear. Alwin Weber. One of Germany's top intelligence officers—a position it seemed he'd gained not only from skill but thanks to a family with political connections going back generations. Alwin Weber was a key player in the High Command. "When Weber entered the scene."

"Exactly. From the information I've gathered about his movements in recent years, he travels several times a year into Switzerland, beginning that very summer, when he was sent to inspect the offerings of a few gun manufacturers."

Camden quirked a brow. "Mettler among them, obviously."

"Indeed—though Diellza's father has no love of the huns, it seems. Even then, before the war broke out, he refused to sell to them. Tensions were already high. But his dislike of them could have played a role in his disapproval of Weber."

A knock on the door interrupted Hall's musings, shortly followed by his command to enter. "Ah, Mr. Pearce. Excellent timing. We were just discussing our Swiss friend. What have you found?"

Camden turned and saw Pearce closing the door behind him again. He had a satchel in hand and a serious look on his face that made Camden's gut tighten.

With a nod of greeting to Camden, Pearce withdrew a file from his bag and handed it to Hall, then took a seat in the chair beside Cam's. "You're not going to like it, sir."

Camden scooted closer. "You slipped in on Tuesday?" While he'd sat through a third excruciating tea with Dee, his mind had wanted to dwell instead on the last-minute plans Den was making for his trip—and on how to elicit that promise from him that he'd talk to Ara that evening. Not that the promise had mattered.

Pearce shrugged. "Sunday actually proved the better time— the entire boardinghouse was empty during church hours. Mrs. Humbird's rules, apparently. Though we were still piecing a few things together these last few days too."

"Did you find any communications between her and Weber?" Hall asked even as he flipped the file open.

"I may have done." Pearce flashed a grin. "That wasn't the name on what I found, but it seems likely. The half-written letter in the secret compartment of her trunk certainly struck me as suspicious. Or rather, struck Rosie as such—I certainly don't read German. It was a good job she came with me."

Camden had no idea who this Rosie was, but Hall seemed to. He actually looked up to spare Pearce a smile. "And how is Mrs. Holstein? V reports that she's made you an uncle yet again." All right, so a sister, clearly. One who didn't mind breaking and entering along with her brother.

"She did, at that. A little sister for Will, whom they've named Tamsyn. Pete's over the moon."

"Naturally."

Squelching the urge to snap his fingers to get them back to business, Camden settled for peering over at the next bundle that Pearce pulled from his bag. More photographs.

"Rosie copied the letters, of course, and we took photographs of everything else we found." Pearce leaned forward to spread them out onto the desk. "I dropped them off at the darkroom directly afterward, and Miss Blackwell just provided me with these prints."

Camden frowned. "Who's Miss Blackwell?"

Pearce lifted a brow. "Haven't you met her? She's the admiral's photography ace."

"She doesn't often come up here." Hall came around to their side of the desk to inspect the line of photographs with them. "Her mother disapproves of her lending us aid, but I've yet to find anyone more talented at altering photographs. A skill I daresay she didn't use on these."

"I suspect she didn't have to." Pearce tapped one that seemed to be peering into a box. A box at the bottom of which were unmistakable pieces of metal and wood.

Camden sucked a hissing breath through his teeth. A gun. No, *her* gun. "It would seem Weber sent her here for more than information gathering."

"Indeed. But who is her target?" Hall straightened again, his rapid blinks seeming to increase in time with his thoughts. "Someone in the Admiralty, perhaps. You must have a connection to whomever it is, Camden, or she wouldn't have sought you out."

"Or the RFC. Most of her conversation is about them. Trying to get me to talk about my squadron, my superiors."

Hall tapped a finger to his chin. "She'll be targeting decision-makers, I should think. With the way the war has been going for us, they'll be looking for a way to turn the tide. Rally the German troops. Give them a second wind."

Pearce cleared his throat and nodded toward the paper still in Hall's hand. "Correct me if I'm wrong, sir, but that letter Rosie translated—assuming we were reading the imagery correctly— seems to indicate more than one target."

"Bold of her," Hall muttered. He looked at the transcription again, brows furrowing. "How would she mean to do that? She'd have to be very confident in her ability to escape after the first one. Or . . ."

"Or get multiple targets in one place." Camden leaned back in his chair. That would make the most sense. And yet . . . how did *he* factor into that? Especially at this point in time—he knew very few people who filled the bill Hall described. He didn't keep company with decision-makers.

"Quite possibly." Hall's eyes skimmed the page he held, and he let out a long breath. "We'll have our boys analyze all you've found. There may yet be a clue as to her targets in all of this. Have you tracked her movements?"

Pearce pulled out another sheet of paper. "The girls have taken turns. They've mapped out everywhere she's gone in the last week."

A smile curled the corners of Hall's mouth. "Your family is most efficient, Mr. Pearce. V certainly did well to recruit you all." He flicked his gaze toward Camden. "We'll combine it with the transcripts you've provided of your conversations with her."

An effort that suddenly seemed paltry, compared to what

Pearce and "the girls" had accomplished. "I don't think I've helped all that much."

But Hall laughed. "You've done all I've asked of you, Major, and then some. But spying on Weber's spy is hardly your sole purpose." He inclined his head toward the door. "In fact, I believe a few more decrypts have come in that you could be most useful for. The boys have made precious little sense of them until someone suggested that perhaps they were aeronautic in nature. Could you lend them your eye?"

"Yes, sir." He stood, knowing a dismissal when he heard one. Though he'd not so much as turned toward the door when another knock sounded upon it.

Denniston poked his head in as soon as Hall gave him permission. And his eyes were positively gleaming. "He's here, sir. The Russian—Marin."

Hall dropped the papers to his desk and straightened. "Already?"

Denniston barked a laugh. "He said he was invited to arrive at ten o'clock, and so here he is, on the dot."

"I said any time *after* ten." Hall sounded more amused than put out. He put a hand on Pearce's shoulder. "Very good. I had better get our newcomer settled personally."

Camden fell in behind Hall and Denniston, making use of the wake they made to get to Room 40.

The corridor was far more crowded than it should have been this time of day, cryptographers and secretaries alike meandering about as if trying to look busy, when clearly they all just wanted a peek at the newest arrival. A path cleared before the admiral, though, eventually revealing the object of their curiosity.

The Russian. He sat stock-still in a chair outside the open door to Room 40, hands folded neatly in his lap. Within them he held a pair of black gloves—the removal of which had revealed, on his right hand, a ruby ring that was nearly gaudy in its ornateness. His overcoat was long, black, and showed at the neck a crisp white shirt collar and impeccable tie. On his head was still positioned a fur-brimmed hat, more suitable for the deep Russian winter than London's current near-spring.

But then, he'd likely fled a deep Russian winter.

Camden slipped to the side, toward Room 40, though the door was blocked by his colleagues. What in the world was so interesting about this man?

He suspected he had his answer when he realized, twenty seconds after he'd spotted him, that the man hadn't moved an inch. He wasn't looking at the milling crowd, wasn't studying his surroundings. He just sat there, gazing straight ahead. His face—long, thin, clean-shaven—was set in a neutral mask, dark eyes muted behind a pair of spectacles.

Camden frowned. The way the chap sat so motionless, posture perfect, put him in mind of an older man. But when he looked at the face, he realized it was unlined. Almost youthful. This Marin fellow couldn't yet be thirty.

Hall had stopped directly before him. "Zivon Marin, I presume?"

Marin shot to his feet and executed a precise bow. "At your service. Are you Admiral Hall?" A slight Russian accent filled out the vowels and made the Ls roll.

"I am." Hall held out a hand. "How do you do?"

Resuming his straight-spine position, Marin shook the admiral's hand. "Very well now. Thank you. I am ready to begin work."

Hall breathed a laugh. "I appreciate your eagerness. But let's chat first, shall we?" He motioned toward the end of the corridor where his office was located.

Camden edged back a little more, wedging himself between Culbreth and Montgomery. "How long was he sitting there without moving?" he mumbled to whomever wanted to answer.

The padre's lips twitched. "Four minutes and twenty seconds by my count."

"Four minutes and thirty-one." Margot's voice came from inside the room, where Camden would be willing to wager she still sat at her desk, working even as she noted everything going on in the corridor. "Valuable time you all are wasting."

"She's just sore that she'll no longer be our only non-British recruit," Montgomery said in a stage whisper, loudly enough to carry in to Margot.

Given that she was still the only female and younger than most of them by nearly a decade, Camden had his doubts that she really minded the loss of that particular badge.

"On the contrary. I think a Russian perspective could prove invaluable. I just fail to see why every single person in this building had to rush to see him, as if he were an animal at a zoo."

Camden glanced to where the admiral was now leading their new recruit away. The crowd began to loosen, figures drifting back to their respective rooms.

"And how many people have you met who have managed to escape from the Bolsheviks?" Montgomery shook his head. "I know *I* would like to hear his story." A yawn interrupted his final word.

Camden smiled. "Puppies still keeping you up?"

"They've settled—only a couple are left, I believe. The fault goes to an interesting book this time." Montgomery rubbed at his neck and angled himself toward the door across the hall, where he had a desk.

Camden touched a hand to his arm to still him, the idea already fully formed in his mind. "They're old enough to leave their mother? The puppies, I mean. And still for sale?"

Montgomery lifted his brows. "I believe so. Why—interested?"

Another smile took possession of Camden's mouth before he could think to rein it in. "I believe I am."

24

What a bizarre twenty-four hours it had been. Arabelle slid the last of her paper work into her satchel and looked at the watch pinned to her bodice. Six o'clock. The scents of dinner had worked their way up to her sitting room, and she was looking forward to sharing the meal with Sarah. And, if the note he'd sent round before she left the hospital could be trusted, Cam.

Her palms went damp at the thought. Which was ridiculous. She'd been having dinner with him nearly every night for almost five weeks. This one would be no different.

Except that every other night, her father had been there. And never before had she tried to sit across from Camden at the table after he'd kissed her. Told her he loved her.

She'd whispered a bit about it to Sarah over lunch, and the look on her friend's face had made her stomach churn. Sparkles of hope and joy, yes. But shadows of caution. Of fear. Though she hadn't said a single negative thing, Arabelle knew exactly what Sarah was thinking.

That Phillip Camden was just a cad of the highest talent, taking advantage of Ara's distress so that he could relieve her of a bit of her money. Or of more than a bit, if he could convince her to marry him. That he didn't really love her. Not *really*.

Answering fear had sprouted in Ara's chest. Not because she thought for even a moment that he was so base. But because when she wasn't looking into his eyes, her doubts were so much louder than her confidence. How could he love her? How could he *choose* her? Choose to be with her, not as a friend but as a . . . a . . . what? She didn't even know what to call him now. A beau? A *boyfriend*, as some of the girls were now calling their men? She couldn't imagine applying that word to him.

She had no experience with this. Brax had just gone from being her friend's brother to her fiancé, no courtship to confuse her along the way.

"Ara?" Sarah stepped into the doorway, smiling and smoothing her apron. "I've reviewed the candidates the agency recommended and sent back my request for interviews on Monday. I'll conduct those while you're at the hospital. Do you want me to set up a second interview for you with my final picks?"

How tempting it was to say no, to leave it all in Sarah's capable hands. But Sarah wouldn't be here long, and it was Arabelle the new staff would have to answer to. She had better establish that from the start. "That sounds wise." She pushed herself up and told the acrobats still performing in her stomach to take a flying leap somewhere else.

"Are you certain this Major Camden is coming?" Sarah fell in beside her as Arabelle exited the room and turned toward the stairs, checking her own watch with a frown. "I thought you said he usually walked you home, that your shifts were over at the same time."

"He does. But his note said he had an errand to run." And she'd left earlier than usual, given Sarah's arrival. "I imagine he'll be here any moment, though."

Sarah pressed one dubious lip to the other and, again, said nothing.

Arabelle sighed. "I appreciate you letting him join us, Sarah. I'm eager for you to meet him."

"Mm-hmm." Sarah lifted her chin, looking every inch the prim housekeeper. "I'm rather eager to make his acquaintance myself."

Ara reached over, linked their arms together, and leaned close. "How I've missed you." There were so few people in her life who ever bothered to worry for her. She knew Father really did love her—and she'd taken the time when she got home to write a long letter to him assuring him that she knew that. But he never *worried* about her. He assumed she was capable of taking care of herself because she'd done it for so long. Because she'd *had* to do it.

But sometimes it was so very nice to have someone else take care of *her*.

Sarah bumped their shoulders together. "Not half as much as I've missed you. I was so disappointed when you wrote to me of breaking off the engagement. I admit to some horror at the thought of a different Mrs. Braxton that I'd have to answer to."

"Oh, but Cass is a sweetheart!"

"She is." Sarah grinned. "I'm thoroughly convinced of it *now*, if I hadn't been before. But still. She isn't *you*."

No, she certainly wasn't. She was younger and prettier and more effervescent and . . . and Ara was glad Brax had met her and fallen in love with her. Glad, because that was how *she* had met and fallen in love with Cam. Who actually loved *her*. As Brax never had. She didn't know what the future held, where God might lead, but just being loved . . . Father was right. It was worth it.

They reached the main floor, and Sarah pulled her arm free. "I'll start bringing dinner out. You just go on in and wait for me."

Ara nodded, though she had made it only a step toward the dining room when the doorbell sounded, so she did an about-face and called out, "I'll get it," so Sarah didn't come rushing back out. It would be Camden anyway, she assumed.

She checked through the peephole first and then pulled open the door for him with a smile. The acrobats had returned, but they were focused more on her heart now, and their flips and twirls didn't make her uneasy so much as eager.

He pushed his way in, a grin on his lips and an enormous box in his arms that made her blink in surprise.

285

"What in the world?" She had to back up, pulling the door wide so he could fit through it, then shut it again behind him. "What have you brought?"

"Well, darling, I've been giving it some thought. And since *I* can't keep playing guard dog quite as much as I'd like now that your father's gone, I thought I'd better find myself a replacement."

The box—it *moved*. She blinked at it, certain she'd imagined it, and then looked at Cam, who was crouched down next to it. "You . . . what? A replacement?"

He lifted the lid, and a brown head popped up with a yip. "That's right. A vicious guard dog."

Vicious? She had to laugh at the puppy that tried to leap from the box—all curly-haired ears and lolling tongue and gorgeous dark eyes that lit upon her with seeming joy. "Aren't you lovely?" Crouching down, she let the pup sniff her hand and then pet its silky head.

"Careful now. She's an attack dog in training. Sure to protect you from every money-grubbing gent that comes your way."

Arabelle laughed again and scooped up the puppy. "Right. She looks terrifying—about as terrifying as a chocolate drop."

"Don't let the curly ears fool you. I've already begun her training. See?" He chuckled when the dog tried to clamber its way up her to lick her chin. "She'll lick you to death."

Arabelle couldn't wipe the grin from her face as she tried to control the squirming bundle of cocker spaniel. And what a beautiful one—chocolate brown, long-haired . . . exactly the kind of dog she'd once dreamed of having. She'd never had a pet of her own before, though Aunt Hettie had kept a pug.

"You're a little darling," she told the dog. Then she moved her grin to Cam as he stood again. "And you're a *big* darling."

He'd done this. For her. All of it. He'd arranged for Sarah to come, he'd bought her a puppy—and, from the looks of the box, all the supplies she needed to care for one—he'd taken her to Brook's last night. All to make sure she wasn't alone.

He stroked a hand over the puppy's head, but his eyes were fastened on hers. "I think you should call her Killer. Maybe Banshee."

The puppy's wet nose snuffed its way down her neck, making her shriek in laughter again. "No, I think she's a Caddie. Short for Cadbury."

Camden released an exaggerated sigh. "You are *not* naming your attack dog after chocolate."

"She likes it. Don't you, Caddie?"

Caddie yipped her agreement.

"What is going on out—oh!" Sarah's exclamation was cut off with a gasp. "Who's this little dear?"

Sarah, unlike Arabelle, had *always* had a pet of her own, which was largely how Ara was acquainted with dogs. "She's called Caddie. Isn't she precious?"

"She's beautiful!" Rushing forward, Sarah gave the pup a tickle under her chin. Then glanced at Cam.

"Oh! And this is Major Camden." Arabelle grinned up at him. "Cam, Sarah."

He nodded, looking almost—nearly—bashful. Something she'd never seen on him before. "How do you do?"

Sarah's lips pursed their way into a knowing smile, and she reached down for the box. "Very well, thank you. Though I didn't mean to interrupt. I'll just take all this to the kitchen for now."

"I'll carry it—it's a bit awkward." Camden plucked it up before Sarah could and offered them both a smile, topping it with a wink for Ara before he strode off.

Sarah watched him go and then pivoted back to face Ara with wide eyes. "The pictures in the papers don't do him justice."

Arabelle chuckled and, when Caddie gave a forceful squirm, set the pup down. "I told you."

"Yes. You did." She gripped Arabelle's hand when she straightened again. "And the way he was looking at you when I came out . . ." Her fingers squeezed.

"He brought me a puppy." She flicked her glance from her

best friend to the little spaniel sniffing around her feet. "Not to mention *you*."

"All right. I'll stop fretting. Or I'll *try* to stop fretting. Clearly he adores you, which means he's got sense. Though even so, Ara—he's in quite a spot of trouble. And I hate to think of you inviting heartache."

"I'm not. But I . . . I love him."

Sarah leaned over for a quick hug and then bent down to the puppy. "I think I'd better take Caddie into the back garden while you thank him for her. And then dinner."

"Thank you, Sarah." She smiled at her, and then at Cam when he swung back out, empty-armed.

Not for long. She hurried forward and threw herself into them as she'd dreamed for far too long of doing. "You're the best."

"I'm not, but who am I to disillusion you?" He chuckled into her ear and held her tight. "You like her? I had a moment's hesitation on the tube, when it belatedly occurred to me that perhaps you didn't *want* a dog."

"She's perfect. And I love that you thought of this." She pulled her head away enough to look into his eyes and lifted a hand to trace down his cheek. Heavens, but he was handsome. That strong jaw. The chiseled lips.

The eyes gleaming perpetually with mischief. "You know, if you want to thank me properly . . ." His gaze flashed down to her mouth.

A tingle washed over her at the very thought. Though it was nothing compared to the warmth that overtook her when she leaned over those few inches and pressed her lips to his. It still felt so odd, so unfamiliar, so . . . unexpected. But so brilliant at the same time. So deliciously warm and right, pulling her in, making her sink deeper until she wasn't sure if she was still standing on her own power or if he was holding her up.

After a long moment, she pulled away, dragging air into her lungs. Sarah would be back soon with Caddie. And . . . things needed done. Probably. Though she couldn't think what.

That smug smile on his lips didn't help clear her mind any. He took one more kiss and then released her. "My mother's coming to visit in a few days. Arriving Wednesday, I believe."

"Mm." Fiddlesticks, her head was an absolute fogbank now. She pressed him back another step, suspecting she was grinning like an idiot. Though so was he, so what did it matter? "Your mother. Good. I'll enjoy spending more time with her."

"Good." Amusement twitched his grin. "Because I told her she could stay here with you, as I haven't a spare room. I suppose I should have asked first though, shouldn't I?"

Laughter tickled her throat again. "Such thoughts don't ever seem to occur to you."

He lifted a shoulder in a shrug. "When I see the best way forward, it seems more expedient to act first and bother with permission later." His eyes darkened. "I suppose some would say that's how I end up in the scrapes I do."

But it was also how he ended up here—her friend. Her love.

She brushed her fingertips over his lips, still warm from their kiss, snagging his gaze again. And she smiled. "I like how you chase what you know is right. And your family is welcome in my home anytime. Anytime at all. You know that."

He kissed her fingers. "I don't deserve you. Luckily," he added, grinning, "I never let that stop me."

A happy puppy bark signaled that Caddie and Sarah had reentered the house, which inspired Ara to ease away another half step. Though she made no objection when Camden caught her hand in his and wove their fingers together.

She couldn't help but smile. "Luckily indeed."

Monday, 11 March

Diellza hesitated only a second before raising her fist and rapping her knuckles against the door. She knew well Faith was still in, and that she had to leave soon. She could only hope that her upstairs neighbor's preoccupation with getting to the office for the day would mean she wouldn't pause to ask too many questions.

When Faith swung the door open, Diellza already had her smile in place. Friendly, warm, and just a little bashful. "Sorry to bother you," she said, edging her way into the room. Its layout was identical to her own, but Faith had clearly lived here for a while. Every surface was strewn with belongings that declared their owner's identity.

The luxury of someone with nothing to hide.

"Friede! Come in. Can I help you with something?"

"Yes, I . . ." Blast, this went against every image she'd portrayed to the girl. But there was no help for it. Her money was running low after that last necessary purchase, and she had to do what needed to be done. Alwin's telegram, delivered yesterday, had been a single word in response to her last letter detailing her plan. A plan complicated enough that she'd had to write it down first in German and then translate it carefully into the English he insisted she send through the post, just to be sure she got it all right.

Proceed, he'd said.

She'd contacted Kath Lewis immediately. Their plan was a go, and the timing couldn't be better. Everything was lining up perfectly.

Soon it would all be over. But it had to start now, with this.

She sucked in a quick breath and held out the blue dress she'd carried up. "I was hoping we could make a trade."

Faith's eyebrows flew up even as her gaze dropped down to the dress in Diellza's hand. "A trade? Oh, Frie, I have nothing to trade you for that!"

"Yes. You have, actually." She pasted on her smile and shook the dress out. She'd seen Faith admiring it, and the blue would match her eyes. "I need a grey skirt and a simple blouse." The dresses she'd brought with her had been understated . . . she thought. But when she surveyed them all this morning, she realized they wouldn't do for today's activities. They wouldn't do at all. She didn't need to look like a normal, middle-class girl just now. She needed to look like a poor one barely scraping by.

Faith's brows knit. "But . . . why? I mean, you can borrow anything you like—you know that. But . . ."

Diellza lowered her hand again. How much to say? She flushed, and found it easy to do just now. "I am applying for a position today. And I do not want to come across as . . ."

Notable. Recognizable. Like herself.

This, today, would be the biggest risk of the entire operation. When she walked with Mrs. Lewis into that den of military men, she would be putting herself willingly into the hands of her enemy. If they recognized her, if they realized who she was, that she'd already been ejected from the country on suspicion of espionage, she would be arrested. Simple deportation probably wouldn't happen on a second offense. She could be executed. Like Mata Hari in France.

Faith's features softened all the way into a smile. "I understand. Some employers—female ones especially, hmm?—don't appreciate it when their employees are prettier than they are." She gave a cheeky grin. "Not that this is something *I* encounter personally, but I've seen it. Here. Take your pick."

Diellza followed Faith to her armoire and sent a practiced eye over the options within. She chose ones that she hadn't seen Faith wear all that often, and that hadn't fit her quite right when she did. She wouldn't miss those, and Diellza didn't want her changing her mind or asking for them back in the next few days. She pulled them out, her brows lifted in question.

Faith met her silent inquiry with a smile. "Certainly, if those are the ones you want."

"They will do perfectly. Thank you, my friend. Here." She refolded the blue and slid it into the drawer in exchange. "Wear that on the next warm day and your Corporal Baker won't be able to take his eyes off you."

Mentioning the name of the man whose attention Faith had been trying to secure did exactly what she meant it to do—made

Faith grin and also reminded her that she needed to leave in the next few minutes. A perfect excuse for Diellza to say another thank-you and a quick farewell.

Back in the safety of her own room a minute later, she made quick work of changing into the serviceable clothes. They were big enough to hide her figure and boring enough that no one should look twice at her. Until she wanted them to.

From her trunk she extracted the wig that had taken far too much of her stash of money—but she'd needed a good one, one that looked natural. This one was exactly what she'd been looking for: medium brown, curly, very different from her straight blond, but still a shade that complemented her skin tone.

She stashed it in her bag and hurried outside, not daring to put it on here. No, she would do that at Kath Lewis's crowded little flat.

Her nerves hummed with energy as she made her way to the Lewis residence for the fourth time. *Purpose*—that was what it was. Today would finally be a day of action. Not just of preparation but of *doing*.

Proceed. She saw the word again in her mind's eye as she took a seat on the tube. Black ink against yellow paper. A world of meaning in those seven little letters. Confidence. Trust. Approval.

She gripped her bag tight against her middle and let her mind float ahead. Not just to this afternoon, not to next week or next month. To next *year*, when this would all be behind them. When she would be with Alwin. In Germany, at the cottage he'd promised her. She'd plant flowers and learn to bake and make such a cozy home for him that he'd want to spend all his time there. With her.

Her fingers dug into the bag. According to the plan they'd set out before she came here, he would have men in place to help her escape England after she'd completed her mission. She would tell him the day, and he would send his men in. They'd get her to safety. He'd promised it.

But he'd promised help last time, too, and no one had ever stepped forward. What if . . . ?

No. She wouldn't think about it. She wouldn't doubt him. He wouldn't leave her to fend for herself, not if she succeeded in the assassination he so needed. Even so, she'd have her own plan of escape. It was, after all, her life on the line.

Her stop approached, and Diellza stood, along with the others debarking, and made her way back out into the mild spring rain. A few minutes later, she was knocking on the Lewis door, ready to get this next step in the plan under way. A somber-faced Kath opened it and ushered her in with "I found someone to watch the little ones, finally. She should be here any minute."

"Good. I need a few minutes to put my wig on anyway." Not waiting for permission, she made her way to the lavatory and put the small, foggy mirror to use. She took her time with the wig, needing it to look seamless—and to be secure. Then she withdrew the little pot of brown eye paint she'd purchased the other day at a cosmetics counter, colored to match her new hair, and carefully applied it to her brows, thickening them a bit too.

There. She didn't bother with any other cosmetics—no rouge to heighten the color in her cheeks or lips, for certain. The last thing she wanted to do on their first stop was grab attention. But she would put a bit on before they ventured to the more important appointment later in the day. She didn't want the general Mrs. Lewis had demanded to see to recognize her, but she also didn't want him to disbelieve the tale she was going to tell him, or to take one look at her and decide that Phillip Camden would never have wasted his time with her, much less told her his secrets.

Satisfied with the results, Diellza exited the lavatory again to the sound of a new voice in the hallway. She stood back while Kath answered the newcomer's question and then gave a few additional instructions on naptime and what she'd left for the children for lunch. Precious little, that.

Soon, they'd said farewell to the little ones and were making their way to Westminster, though they'd not even gotten to the tube station before the look on Mrs. Lewis's face demanded a bit of attention. Diellza sighed. "Do not tell me you are having second thoughts."

The woman's eyes flashed to her, then back to the street. "About finally giving Camden the justice he deserves? No. But . . . I hate to involve *her*."

Diellza gripped the handle of her umbrella until it hurt. "You said you wanted to hurt him—to hurt him as he hurt you. Nothing will hurt him more than this."

He'd tried to hide it that day in the teahouse, but she'd seen. For whatever unfathomable reason, Camden was in love with the ugly heiress. Which worked well enough for her. She'd known only her first name—Ara—but Kath had supplied the rest. Arabelle Denler, one of the single richest women in England. She'd even known her address already.

It had been a simple matter to badger the Denlers' cook for household news. The dowdy old woman probably hadn't thought it was anything suspicious—Kath did a fine job of looking like a pathetic widow desperate for work, and all she'd asked about was the possibility of a position.

Their timing, it seemed, had been perfect. A stroke of luck that would have had Vater mumbling about the hand of God.

Maybe He was up there. And if so, He must surely be on Alwin's side. Maybe even God couldn't resist his charms.

Kath was nodding, gripping her own umbrella like it was a lifeline. "I know. And I *do* want to hurt him. But . . . she's kind. I thought my game was up when she caught me following her from Charing Cross, but she took care of me."

"Then she ought not to have been stupid enough to get involved with the likes of *him*." Perhaps she spat it out a bit too harshly.

But maybe not, because Kath's spine straightened, her shoulders edged back, and she nodded. "You're right. In the long run, this is a favor to her."

Assuming Diellza didn't actually have to make good on the

threat they'd be making, certainly. "There now. No more doubts. We stick to the plan."

"But . . ."

Diellza barely reined in her growl.

Kath's brow puckered. "But what if I don't make it through this first round of interviews? Even using my maiden name, as you told me to do, if she realizes who I really am . . ."

"Then the next step will be a bit more difficult, that is all. But still quite doable. No. More. Doubts."

Kath bobbed her head in agreement, but she still didn't look entirely convinced.

That was all right. A bit of uncertainty looked endearing on her youthful face. She would get the second interview; Diellza was certain of it. *She* wouldn't—she didn't want to, couldn't risk Arabelle Denler recognizing her as the woman from the teahouse. She was only applying at all because a tour of the house was promised to all applicants who arrived at ten o'clock, and Diellza wanted to be sure Cam would have no unforeseen means of escape when they sprang their trap. She couldn't be certain that he wouldn't decide that this Arabelle woman was a reason to fight, to flee, to preserve his life. She must learn all the exits of the house so they could ensure the authorities could cover them all.

Kath, if all went according to plan, would make it through this first round of interviews. And when she then sat down across from Miss Denler this evening and *she* was recognized as the unfortunate mother of seven whose ankle the nurse had inspected . . .

This time tomorrow, Kath would be in her employ. Which meant she'd be there to let them in. To lock any doors they wanted locked. To feed Major Phillip Camden to the lions.

Diellza smiled into the rain.

25

"He's still just sitting there, reading the newspaper."

Camden looked up at the stage whisper, having a feeling his frown matched the one on De Wilde's face when she did the same. They didn't need to ask who "he" was.

All morning, the whispers had been flying about the Russian now in their midst. He'd been assigned a desk in the room across the hall from their own, and he had reported to it at exactly nine o'clock. He'd hung up his coat, taken off his hat, sat . . . and pulled out a newspaper.

No one had said anything to him. No comments about getting to work and not wasting the day, as they certainly would have said to anyone else. Even Commander James, when he'd come by to see what all the fuss was about, had only shrugged and disappeared again.

Camden hadn't been particularly surprised by all the curious whispers of the secretaries. But this latest whispered observation had come from Adcock, a cryptographer.

"He's moving!" Adcock slipped more fully into Room 40, hiding behind the wall. Or so it seemed to Camden.

Culbreth slid to his feet, mumbling, "Unless he's performing a Cossack dance, I don't see why that's deserving of an announcement."

Such a hush fell that Camden was able to hear Zivon Marin say, in the other room, "Something to decode, if you please."

Cam had no idea to whom the man was speaking, but it earned a snort from Adcock at the wall. And a derisive look on his face that Camden had thought the fellow willing to give only to *him*.

"What does he think, that we're here to serve him?" Adcock shook his head, even as a flustered-looking secretary from the other room dashed in, her eyes seeking and finding the place where the pneumatic tubes came to a halt by the door. For the most part, the secretaries weren't expected to wait on the cryptographers—simply await the decrypts, type them up, and send them on to Commander James.

Camden leaned back in his chair. "If I were to guess, I'd say that's how it was done in Russia."

Culbreth had just joined Adcock at the door, and they both turned to look at him, their brows lifted. "Are you—Major Phillip Camden—Black Heart—*defending* him?"

At the look on Adcock's face, Camden could hardly resist a grin. "Not that I mind if someone else takes on the role of untrusted newcomer, but it stands to reason that until someone tells him how *we* do things, he'll just do them the way he's always done them. I mean, this bloke's been in the game since the start of the war too. Just in a different country."

The others looked to be considering his point. And their shrugs and softening faces seemed to indicate that they bought his argument.

But Camden was stuck on his own *we*. Even a month ago, that's not what he would have said. He would have said *how you do things*. Even a month ago, these colleagues would have called him on it.

Now, Culbreth nodded. "I daresay you're right, Cam."

Cam. No one here had ever once called him Cam.

It was such casual comradery that he didn't know what to do with it. So he leaned forward and picked up the pen he'd let fall to his desk. "Though if seeing him act so bothers you, you

297

could always put him in a storage closet. I happen to know that the one at the end of the corridor works quite well for an office."

They laughed, all of them. And Adcock said, "No, old boy, we only employ that with *snarling* newcomers."

"Ah. My mistake."

Culbreth, satisfied with whatever view he'd had, moved back to his desk. "You know, Camden, you may still have had us going if you hadn't rushed into that burning building to save those pensioners. Hard to call such a chap a villain, though."

He refocused his gaze on the stack of intercepts they'd asked him to look over. "Well, had I realized at the time I'd be compromising my carefully constructed image . . ."

"Right." Adcock had drifted farther into the room, too, given the playful punch he landed on Cam's shoulder. "I'm sure you'd have left them all to die. And we still would have figured you out, when you actually proved *useful*." He motioned to the stack of decrypts that they suspected might reference aeronautics.

"Twelve."

They all looked at Margot, who hadn't so much as glanced up again from her work. She must have felt their stares, though, as she clarified, "Twelve times I tried to tell you all he was only hiding behind a mask of surliness."

Before the gents could respond to her point, the secretary spun on them, eyes wide and fists full of telegrams. "How do I know which to give to him?"

Adcock chuckled. "It doesn't much matter. They all need doing. Although . . ." At that particular twinkle in his eye, Camden pushed to his feet.

"Oh no," he said. "I know that look—and it resulted in you giving me the wrong codebook for the telegram you assigned." He elbowed Adcock aside and motioned the young woman back toward the stack of incoming messages. He pulled out a few that would be fairly straightforward, from the looks of them. Even though Marin claimed to be an old hand at it, there would surely be a bit of a challenge doing it all in English. "Here. Take him these."

"Thanks." She looked half relieved and half skittish, backing quickly away with a glance up at him to tell him *why*. Apparently not *everyone* in the OB had come to see through his snarl.

He shook his head and returned to his seat.

The morning marched on, quickly when he considered the amount of work still to be done, and slowly when he counted the hours until he'd be able to fetch Ara from the hospital and see her home. He wouldn't dine with her again tonight—she would want some time with her friend, after all, and he wasn't entirely certain whether a housekeeper that was one's own age was *really* a proper chaperone or not.

He'd be doing enough damage to her reputation if he convinced her to marry him. He certainly didn't need to ruin it beforehand.

Blast it all. He finished off another decrypt and let the injustice of it burn for a minute. Loving him shouldn't be so dangerous to her. How was that fair? A year ago, had they met, he'd have been a perfectly acceptable match.

A year ago, had they met, he probably wouldn't have looked twice at her. His hand went still over the basket for the secretary, handwritten plain text message still in his fingers. A year ago, she probably wouldn't have looked twice at *him*. He'd have come off to her as nothing more than what he'd been at the time—a reckless, selfish, superficial cad.

At the clearing of a throat behind him, he put the paper in the basket and turned to find De Wilde standing there with one of her own, her brows lifted. "Having second thoughts on your translation?" Her gaze darted to the paper he must have looked reluctant to part with.

He sighed. "No. On my life."

Now her brows knit. "Your nurse friend?"

"No." He flashed a smile, though it fell quickly away. "I mean the life before . . . The Incident."

She snorted and put her own paper in the basket. "Good. From what I'm given to understand, you *ought* to have second thoughts on that part."

"Mm. No doubt. Still, it's a rather unsettling thought that if I hadn't watched my men die and been accused of orchestrating it myself, I never would have known her." And why in the world was he just blurting it out in the middle of the OB?

De Wilde seemed to be having the same question. She blinked, a sideways smile sliding onto half her mouth. "If you're going to start tittering about it, I'm going to excuse myself. I haven't time for romantic nonsense."

He echoed her snort and stepped aside, glancing up at the clock on the wall. Lunchtime. He would have slipped over to Charing Cross if he didn't know that Ara would be working through lunch so she could get out this afternoon at her old time and be home to conduct interviews. "Says the girl soon to marry."

"A ring on my finger did not turn me into an idiot."

He was pretty sure nothing could possibly turn Margot De Wilde into an idiot. Although, that did beg a question. "What exactly are you going to do when you marry and children come along? I can't imagine you giving all this up."

"Who said I would?" She strode back to her desk. "God will give us what children He wants us to have—but Drake doesn't expect me to forsake all other dreams. We'll work through the challenges as they come, but, God willing, I will be attending university after the war."

Camden fetched his coat and hat. He might not want to disturb Ara, but a lunchtime walk sounded like just the thing. "I suppose you've both families nearby to help with the children."

She huffed out a breath. "*Why* are we talking about children? You're as bad as the secretaries."

"My apologies." Though he grinned, because it was the first time he'd ever heard her talking about the feminine subjects that those dreaded secretaries chattered about so often.

He stepped into the corridor—and came face-to-face with someone stepping out at the same moment from the door across the hall. A Russian someone, who came to a quick halt and sent a gaze down Camden.

"Hello." Cam jutted out a hand. "Major Phillip Camden. Glad you arrived safely."

Marin took his hand and gave it a firm shake. "Zivon Marin. I thank you." He narrowed his eyes. "Your uniform is not like the others. You are major, you say? Army?"

Camden nodded. "Royal Flying Corps. I'm here on . . . special dispensation, let's call it."

"Ah." Marin motioned to the corridor. "You are going this way? May I walk with you?"

"Of course." Camden adjusted the collar on his overcoat and continued toward the stairs. He was casting around in his head for a nice, friendly question to ask—not the sort he'd specialized in lately—but Marin beat him to the punch.

"Royal Flying Corps. I just was reading about them. And the Royal Naval Air Service. It seems that in a few weeks they will be one unit, yes? A combined Royal Air Force."

A pang echoed through Camden. There'd been talk of combining the two since before The Incident, to eliminate some of the pointless competition between the two services and the need for arbitrary boundaries—the RNAS patrolled the waters over the Channel, for instance, halting at the coast, where the RFC took over. Camden had deliberately *not* kept up on the progress of the merger. It hurt too much. Raised too many questions.

What would they do with *him* when his entire branch of service dissolved? Would this uniform he still wore be the one they kept, or would the pilots all don the naval blues? He plunged a hand into his pocket to feel for the wings.

Maybe . . . maybe Hall would somehow arrange for him to become navy, like the rest of the cryptographers. Maybe this would be one of his last weeks in olive green.

He couldn't decide if it felt like losing himself or finding himself.

He cleared his throat of the tightness before he dared to answer. "Right. Did they give a date for it?"

"First number of April."

Camden blinked at the wording, but he nodded. Three weeks. Whatever the answer to his own questions, he'd know it soon.

Ara, cheeks still warm from the good-bye kiss Camden had given her after walking her home, unclasped her cape and tried to convince her lips to stop grinning. A complete failure, that attempt, but she did *try*. She didn't want to look like a ninny when she went in to interview the candidates Sarah had chosen for her.

There were three of them, Sarah had said over lunch. Her face had gone a bit sardonic as she added that eliminating half the applicants had been a breeze, as she was fairly certain they'd only shown up because of the promised tour of the house.

Arabelle could hardly blame them for their curiosity. The first time Aunt Hettie had pointed out their new home to her, Ara had been dumbstruck and burning with curiosity too. It seemed absolutely certain to her that a house this grand must have some delicious secrets to it. Hidden chambers, perhaps. A tunnel leading under the street to the palace. Mirrors with magic enough to sweep her away to another realm. *Something*.

They'd probably been disappointed, as she had been, to realize it was just a house like any other.

Caddie must have heard her entrance, as she came running from the back hall, a bark of greeting making Arabelle laugh. She bent down to scratch the pup's ears, grinning when she rolled onto her back and wiggled for a belly rub too.

"Ara?" Sarah followed her voice into the entryway, a clipboard in hand and business on her face, though it nearly cracked into a smile at the squirming dog. "There you are. I've our three candidates sipping tea in the kitchen and have set up a little interviewing spot in your sitting room upstairs. I thought you'd be most comfortable there, rather than in Hettie's rooms down here."

How well her friend knew her. Arabelle smiled and straightened again so she could hook her cape onto the coatrack. "Are you quite certain I can't lure you away from Middlegrove?"

"Were my entire family not there . . ." Sarah handed over the clipboard. "The one on top is, in my opinion, the best candidate. She's young—only eighteen—a second daughter who had much responsibility in her own home and was employed by the same household for whom her mother worked until they closed up and left London a few months ago. And she loves dogs," she added with a smile for the puppy.

Ara flashed a grin and skimmed the application. "Helen Smithfield."

"Seems a solid, even-tempered sort. Wants to help care for her family, but she hasn't any attachments at present that would take her away in the foreseeable future. The second candidate, Kathleen Reed . . ." Sarah frowned and let out a breath. "She has seven children she's trying to support on a war widow's pension. I put her on the list because she quite clearly needs the position, and I know how you like to help people who genuinely need it. But seven children . . ." Sarah shook her head. "I daresay she wouldn't be the most dependable employee with so many little ones at home. This is, I believe, the first position she's applied for since her husband's death."

Poor woman. A widow, with seven children! She couldn't imagine. Though her brows knotted. What had her name been?

"The third is Bess Chambers. A bit gruff and no-nonsense for your tastes, I think, but she has twenty years' experience. If you don't wish to hire another housekeeper, she could be a good compromise, as she has experience both running a house and cleaning it."

Arabelle nodded and cast a look in the general direction of the kitchen—not that she could see the room from out here. "Give me a few minutes to get settled upstairs, and then send the first one up, if you would." She patted a hand against her leg. "Come on, Caddie. Come with me."

The puppy followed along, climbing up the many stairs so awkwardly that Arabelle eventually gave in with a laugh and carried her the rest of the way. Once in her sitting room, she deposited both dog and satchel. She smiled to find a teapot awaiting her on her desk. Leave it to Sarah to see she had a cup too. She'd just gotten her belongings stowed away, her tea poured, and a blank sheet of paper drawn out, in case she wanted to take notes, when the first applicant knocked on the door. Ara looked up with a smile for the young woman, who introduced herself as Helen as she dipped a curtsy.

She was, as Sarah had promised, a lovely girl. Bright and positive, and certainly full of the energy a house of this size required. She'd be grateful to take up residence here, she said, and was agreeable to every single term Arabelle named. Not a thing to object to. As she bobbed another curtsy upon taking her leave, Ara figured Sarah was probably right about her top pick.

But then the second woman entered—and that niggle in the back of Arabelle's mind turned to a full bell ringing. She stood, hand outstretched, darting a gaze toward the patch of sunlight in front of the window to make sure Caddie was still curled up there. "Good afternoon, Mrs. . . . ?"

"Reed." The woman sucked in a breath as their gazes and fingers met.

"Kath." Arabelle squeezed her hand, smiling. "How is your ankle? We met outside Charing Cross—"

"Yes, I recall." A blush stained Mrs. Reed's cheeks. "Not that I realized it when I applied, of course, but now that I see you . . . It's mended. Was right as rain by the next day, as you promised."

Seven children. And Ara had been right to assume it was the war that had taken her husband. She motioned her into the chair Sarah had positioned near the desk and took her own. She glanced down at her paper, where she'd jotted the questions she'd asked Helen Smithfield. She'd ask the same of Kath Reed.

But she wasn't sure she really needed to. A burden had settled on her heart the moment she saw her. She'd wanted to help this woman weeks ago. She'd prayed there on the street about how she could—and now here she was.

Kath's answers to the first questions were about what she'd

expected—she'd never been a domestic before, but she had ample experience keeping her own house. She was motivated. She came with plenty of character references. Though when Arabelle mentioned taking up residence here, Kath's face fell.

Arabelle lifted her brows. "Is that a problem?"

For a moment, Kath's mouth moved with no sound emerging. Then she cleared her throat. "I'm afraid I can't, Miss Denler. I realize many domestics leave their children in a family member's care while they work, but I've no family in London. I've found a neighbor who will watch the little ones during the day, but I can't be gone from them all night too. I'm sorry."

"Oh, I didn't mean you should come without your children." Ara said it before she could really give much thought to what she was promising with those words. Promises she knew well Sarah wouldn't exactly approve of. But the thought brought nothing but a surge of giddiness to her own chest. "I adore children and have always wanted a large family under my roof. You could bring them with you—we've four rooms for staff, none of which are currently occupied. Would that be enough for the eight of you?"

Red lashes blinked at her. "Are you . . . I mean . . . you can't want that, Miss Denler."

Arabelle held her gaze, wondering at her own determination. This woman before her certainly didn't seem eager. Not like Helen. She seemed, if anything, resigned. Determined, but certainly not excited by the thought of the position, nor by the accommodations.

She could practically hear Sarah in her head, whispering that if Kath felt no enthusiasm, Ara certainly shouldn't. She gripped her pen. "I wouldn't have brought it up if I weren't agreeable to it. And I am specifically looking for live-in help. So if I were to hire you, that would be a requirement. Room and board for you and your children would be provided."

Sarah mumbled in her head again about room and board for *one* being far different than for *eight*.

Kath Reed fiddled with her skirt, not quite meeting Arabelle's eye. It must be a terrible affront to her pride, having to apply for a position like this when she'd once had a house of her own. "I . . . I suppose that would be doable. And is quite generous of you. Though . . ." A glance up, a brush of gazes, and back down her eyes went. "I've already paid my current flat through next week, and I'll not be able to get it back from my landlord. So if—if you were to offer, I mean—if I could wait until then to move, I'd just as soon have the time to pack up. I could begin right away, though, working during the days."

"All right." Arabelle made a note. With Sarah here, and then Mrs. Camden set to arrive in a few more days, that wouldn't be so bad. She looked back up with a smile. "Have you a telephone where I can ring you up with my decision, or should I send a note round?"

"I haven't a telephone, no." Kath stood, nervously tucking a stray wisp of red behind her ear. "I thank you for your time, Miss Denler. Your housekeeper has my direction." Her gaze swung over to the window and snagged there.

Arabelle glanced that way too. There was a fair view of the palace from this room, and of the street below, though Father's study had the best prospect. Even so, Ara could understand why it would grab her guest's attention. She'd spent countless hours over the years looking out at Buckingham Palace.

Kath shook herself and made a quick exit with a muttered thanks.

Arabelle let out a long breath. She wanted to help. And yet had a feeling this choice wouldn't be the easy path. Still—the best paths were never the easy ones.

She turned over a fresh sheet of paper and prepared to meet the final candidate . . . even as she mentally composed the note she'd send round to Kathleen Reed tomorrow.

26

Diellza froze, her hand still reaching for her bedroom door—the door cracked open when it should have been closed and locked. Her pulse was already galloping simply because it was Wednesday. Wednesday, the thirteenth of March. The day that would see all her plans put into motion. The day that began the fulfillment of her every dream.

But the gallop turned to a hammer that made a headache break upon her skull. Because her door was cracked open. Which meant that something was wrong, though everything had seemed to be going right. The officers they'd met with on Monday had heard them out. They'd believed their story—even if the looks they'd given Diellza had been more condemning than sympathetic. They had even accepted their advice on when and where to move.

Kath had been hired and had worked her first day as the ugly Miss Denler's domestic yesterday. She would be in position today when the Military Police came marching down the street. All had been going according to plan. So what had gone wrong?

A shuffling sound came from within her room, along with a hum that at once made Diellza's shoulders relax and her frustration bubble up. She pushed the door open, and the look she sent to Faith—who was fiddling with her pots of cosmetics—was far from the warm one she usually gave her. "What are you doing in here?" Then, when the girl spun, she forced herself to add something to maintain her trust, splaying a hand on her chest. "You scared me to death!"

"Oh, I'm sorry!" Faith rushed forward, cheeks nearly as pink as Kath Lewis's had gone when she'd recounted how Miss Denler had looked at her with one of the things she hated most: pity. "The door was unlocked, and you'd said you needed that brooch back this afternoon, so I was just putting it away."

Diellza glanced at the brooch, now right where it had been before she lent it to Faith—amid her cosmetics—then back at the door. She'd locked it that morning, hadn't she? She *always* locked it. It was habit. Rote. Survival.

Perhaps she'd been so distracted with thoughts of the Military Police that she'd forgotten?

Or perhaps Faith wasn't quite the innocent she seemed. Diellza forced a smile. "It is all right. My pulse will settle back to normal eventually." Though probably not today. How could it? This evening was the most important one since she'd stepped foot back on English soil. Everything hinged upon it. Everything.

Faith offered a sheepish smile. "Sorry to have frightened you." She stepped past Diellza, into the doorway. "Are you coming down to dinner? Shall I wait?"

"No. Thank you." Another forced smile. "I am meeting a friend."

Faith nodded and slipped down the corridor without another word—probably as startled by Diellza's interruption as *she* had been by the girl's presence.

Diellza curled her fingers into her palm, savoring the bite of nails on flesh as a distraction from the unease in her chest. After closing the door behind her, she sent her gaze over the room, looking for anything out of place.

There. The latch on her trunk. She always kept them fully closed, but one was lifted, the wire caught in place but the lever attached to it raised rather than lowered. Dread curling through her stomach, she eased over to it, half expecting someone to jump out from under her bed and arrest her.

Foolishness. The room was empty. Now. But it hadn't been, clearly. Someone had been in here today. Faith? Or someone else, someone who had left it unlocked so that Faith *could* come in?

She flipped up the second latch, lowered both hooks over the knobs, and lifted the lid of the trunk.

At first glance, all was exactly as she'd left it. The tray still rested on the top with her extra scarves and shawls and a pair of stockings that had snagged last week. Everything in exactly the places she'd put them, including the toe of the stocking tucked between the tray and the side of the trunk—which she'd done deliberately. A trick she'd learned back when it was just Friede she was trying to detect snooping. Only her diary she was hiding.

She removed the tray, the items under it, and finally the false bottom.

Her breath fisted in her chest. Again, everything was exactly as she'd left it.

Everything except that little slip of white resting like a snake atop the barrel of her pistol. Paper, with typed text upon it.

Tut, tut, Diellza. You know better.

A German curse spilled from her lips. She pulled out the weapon's action, checking it for obvious tampering. Everything looked right, and even her ammunition was still there. She'd have to check it all more carefully later, but she hadn't time for that now. She had to get out of here. She didn't know who had been in here, but if they knew her real name . . .

Alwin would kill her if she ruined this for him. What was she to do? Tell him she'd been compromised? Admit defeat and run?

No. No, it could still be salvaged, surely. Once the wheels were set in motion, there was nothing anyone could do to stop it other than physically stop *her*. So all she had to do was stay a step ahead. Safe. Out of the reach of whoever had discovered her.

She tossed a few items into her small valise, mostly to cover the weapon, still in pieces, that she tucked into the bottom, along with all the accessories and ammunition. The rifle barrel *just* fit. She'd chosen the valise specifically because she knew it would. She'd left the wig at the Lewis home anyway, so she needn't worry with that. Just the necessities. Anything she'd need between now and whenever Phillip Camden would first appear in court.

Satisfied, she slid back out into the hallway and locked the door behind her, saying a mental farewell to everything else in that room. She never meant to step foot in it again.

"Is everything all right, Friede?"

She barely kept from jumping at Mrs. Humbird's voice, but she managed it. Managed even to fasten a smile to her lips as she turned and saw her landlady standing at the landing, concern on her face. "Why would it not be, ma'am?"

The woman glanced down the stairs. "Faith seemed a bit embarrassed. She hasn't overstepped, has she? I know she has been so grateful for all your attention." Then her gaze settled on Diellza's bag, and she frowned. "Are you going somewhere?"

"Oh. Just overnight." She patted the case and kept her smile in place. "A friend of mine has landed a new position as a domestic and is expected to take up residence there. I offered to stay with her children tonight until she could find a more permanent solution for them."

Mrs. Humbird relaxed at the partial lie. "How very kind of you."

"It is little enough to help." She started for the stairs at a sedate pace. As if she had nothing to hide. As if she even relished a few more minutes in the older woman's company. "I am lucky to have made such a good friend in my time here." Lucky to have found such a willing conspirator, anyway.

Mrs. Humbird patted her arm. "I'm glad you have. Friends make all the difference, don't they?"

They could, sometimes. They could be useful. It was why she'd befriended Faith—but that may have proven a huge mistake. The girl seemed innocent, so bright and fresh and unassuming. But was it all just an act, like the one Diellza put on? Was there even a corporal she was trying to impress, or had it all been a ruse to get close to Diellza? Perhaps she'd been watched since the moment she stepped foot back in England. Perhaps it had all been part of someone else's plan.

"You won't be here for breakfast tomorrow, I assume? Do let me know if you'll still be away in the evening, or if you'd like your dinner waited."

Always so accommodating, Mrs. Humbird was. But was that also just part of the plan? Perhaps she was the one who had seen through her. Perhaps she'd even tasked Faith with investigating her.

"How kind of you, ma'am. I certainly will." Careful to keep her smile bright, Diellza checked the hat she hadn't even had a chance to take off, tightened the belt of the lightweight coat she'd been wearing all day, and made for the front door.

No one waited to pounce on her when she stepped outside. No authorities, no police, not like that time months ago. No one to put her under arrest and bring her in for questioning. No one to force her onto a boat back across the Channel—or worse, which was what they promised would happen if she returned.

She gripped her valise and hurried down the street toward the nearest tube station. Let them do what they would. The worst possible punishment was being away from Alwin anyway . . . and that was a consequence he would enact himself if she failed him.

Well, she wouldn't. That was all. She'd succeed. And she'd start tonight.

Camden gave the enormous globe a spin, hiding behind it so his mother and Ara didn't see his grin. The tour of Ara's house had ended here, on the topmost floor, where her father's absence was so keenly felt. Already Cam missed spending so many hours in this room, with its rich woods and endless theories, and her father had only been gone a week. Even with no maps carpeting the floor, adventure seemed to saturate the paneling.

Caddie obviously agreed. The pup must not have seen this room yet, because she was sniffing every single nook and cranny, occasionally punctuating her discoveries with a happy yip. She'd already raced over to Ara half a dozen times, tail wagging, as if to say, "Come and see this!" but then taking off again to chase down another scent before Ara could even lean down to pet her silken ears.

"And what is *this*?" Mother had stationed herself at the shelves and was leaning over now to inspect a turquoise-covered head. Or mask, perhaps? Camden had never gotten the story on that particular artifact to know exactly what it was.

Ara bent over to study it as well. "I . . . have no idea," she admitted on a laugh. "Though it doesn't exactly have a welcoming look on its face, does it?"

Mother laughed too. "Rather fierce. Look at all those teeth. What are they made of, do you think?"

"Good question. It doesn't look like ivory. But it's so white. Perhaps some sort of shell?"

Camden slid around the desk, jamming his hands in his pockets. Mother had whispered to him on the ride here that she'd brought the ring, but they hadn't exactly dug it out on the train. And Ara, Caddie on her heels, had met them at the door when they arrived here and immediately taken his mother on a tour while the new ginger-haired maid was given the task of unpacking his mother's belongings in a spare bedroom.

Though his fingers itched to get ahold of the ring, to examine it and imagine it on Ara's finger, he wasn't about to interrupt the women. Mother would probably get it out tonight when she retired and slip it to him tomorrow.

Soon enough, he supposed. Even though it wasn't. Once he'd made up his mind to ask Ara to be his wife, he'd wanted it already done. He'd etch it in stone if he could. Bind her to him forever, before she could change her mind and realize what a bad decision it was.

A short bark at his feet drew his gaze down. Grinning, he scooped up the puppy for a scratch, laughing when she strained up to lick his chin. "Have you been keeping our girl company? Hmm?"

The lolling tongue and sparkling eyes were answer enough, he supposed. One couldn't be lonely when one had a curly-eared puppy. It just wasn't possible. Caddie leaned against him for a beat and then squirmed to be put down again and raced over to Ara.

His lips twitched as he watched Ara, so long and lean and confident, crouch down to pet her puppy. She'd argue with him if ever he mentioned what a bad decision loving him was. And he'd let her, because he was at the core a selfish man. And he couldn't imagine going back to life without her.

The ladies moved a few steps to another artifact on display, and Camden drifted over to the window. He loved the view from up here of Buckingham Palace.

A flash of red caught his eye, dragging his gaze down from rooflines to the street again. Even before his brain had really registered exactly what it was, his stomach had knotted.

He knew that shade of red. The red covers on the peaked caps of . . . A curse slipped out.

"Phillip! Watch your mouth!"

His mother's chastisement barely registered. He gripped the window frame with one hand, the other curling around the brass wings in his pocket. Red caps.

Ara was at his side in half a moment, warm and tall and stalwart, even though the world was about to come crashing down. "What is it?"

He dug his fingers into the wood, not letting himself look over at her. He couldn't. Not with those red caps marching this way. "Military Police." The words were a breath. A curse in themselves.

She sucked in air, held it. Expelled it in that way that said she was trying not to panic. "I'm sure it's nothing. Soldiers come by here all the time—"

"No." How could he explain what every nerve ending knew? What the weight that settled over him foretold? For months he'd been waiting for this. Waiting, every moment, for justice to catch him up. He knew it when he saw it marching in unison down the street. "They're coming for me."

"What are you on about? Why would the Military Police search you out *here*?" Mother, all cool reason as always, had joined them, too, on Ara's other side. But the hand she lifted to the sash trembled, and her cheek looked pale in the evening light.

"That's a good question." Why wouldn't they have come for him at the OB? Or waited at his flat? Why *here*?

But even as he asked it, he knew. Knew that *they* knew, somehow. One way to guarantee he wouldn't fight was to put Ara and Mother in the crossfire. But the fact that they knew that meant that someone had been watching him. All this time, or just recently?

Mrs. Lewis—she'd never let it rest, not for a minute. And she'd obviously known Ara was part of his life, given the letter she'd received. She must have been following him, seen him come here.

Blast it all—he'd done this. He ought to have listened to good sense when he first determined to protect her. He ought to have realized that he could never achieve it himself, that he'd bring more trouble to her door than he could possibly keep away. Why had he thought he could mitigate it? Why had he thought it worth the risk?

Because he'd known, from the moment he met her gaze in that hospital window, that she was someone special. Someone he wanted to know. Someone he *needed* to know.

Ara spun around. "I'll tell Kathleen to bar the door, or say no one's at home. We'll—"

"No." He caught her by the arm. He'd already brought this

much upon her. He wouldn't let it get any worse. "No, do that and you'll land yourself and Mother in trouble along with me. You don't want to be arrested for interfering, Ara. Trust me."

Her face went hard. Determined. Loyal. To *him*, who deserved it so little. "I'm not just going to stand by and let them take you again! You've done nothing wrong."

Sweet Ara. How could she say that with such confidence, when she knew nothing about it? He shook his head, squeezed gently on her arm. "But I have. I made a foolish mistake, and I have to pay the consequences of it. I always knew I would."

She lifted her hand so that she was gripping *his* arm in return, her hazel eyes burning gold. "I don't know what happened that day, Phillip. But I know you didn't willfully kill your men, and you will *not* be punished for it as if you did."

Mother squeaked out a protest. Given that her gaze was still out the window, that told him all he needed to know about the direction of the Military Police.

"Maybe I didn't mean for them to die. But it's still my fault." The words, so long held down, trapped under a torrent of regret, bubbled up. "He never would have done it if not for me. If I hadn't led him into that life, if I hadn't told him it was all right, that it didn't matter—" He cut himself off, squeezed his eyes shut. He couldn't bear to look at her. Not when the love in her eyes would go dim at his words, as it must do.

Her other hand settled on his other wrist. His hand was still in his pocket, the wings biting into him, but she tugged on his wrist until it came out. Wrapped her long, beautiful fingers around his. "Who? Who did what?"

"Lewis." The name eked out, a drip of castor oil from a faulty engine. That's all life had been since that day, a faulty engine ready to die. No, since before that day. He just hadn't seen the telltale signs until then. Hadn't realized that he was, as Jer had warned him time after time, already in a spiral, destined to crash and burn. "He couldn't live with himself. With the man he'd become to fit in with us—the gentlemen. The wagers and the . . ." He swallowed, but the truth wouldn't go down again. "The women. He'd been a good man, Ara. A good, God-fearing man, until we got our tenterhooks in him. And he couldn't—"

From downstairs, a bell echoed up. Caddie started barking in earnest. His blood chilled. This wouldn't be another unwanted suitor he could scare off with a few flirtations and sneers.

Her fingers slid around his fist, spread out. Inviting him to open up. Stretch his fingers out opposite hers, palm to palm, from fingers to wrist. To hold on and be held. He obeyed the silent urging before he could think better of it, the wings pressed between them. His eyes drifted back open to latch onto hers.

"What are you saying? That Lewis was the one who did this? That *he* took out the squadron?"

He shook his head, wild and panicked as he'd been that day, watching it unfold. "Not on purpose. He wouldn't have. He only meant—he meant to kill himself. He'd tried to give me a letter beforehand, for his wife. He couldn't risk it being discovered in his quarters, didn't want to send it in the post, lest it be seen by a censor. If they knew it was suicide, his pension would be denied, and with seven kids . . ."

Something flashed in Ara's eyes. "Seven?"

"I tried to stop him. Believe that much. I thought—I thought I could cajole him out of the plan." *"You'll not kill yourself,"* he'd shouted at his friend. *"Not if I kill you first."* A jest, he'd thought. Something ridiculous enough to snap Lewis from his guilt-induced despair. But it hadn't fazed him. So Camden had gone to the rest of the squadron, told them all what Lewis had said. "I should have grounded him that day." It was so easy to see now. "I shouldn't have let him get in an airplane, but I thought . . . I thought it would be safer than leaving him alone. We were all watching out for him. The other men, they knew too. They knew, and they weren't about to let him do something stupid. They flew a tighter formation than they should have. Thinking, I suppose, that he wouldn't try to put himself into a stall if he couldn't do it without risking them."

But he had. He'd pulled up too quickly.

"Phillip. It wasn't your fault."

"It was. I led him to the sins that weighed too heavy on his conscience. I failed him as a leader. I failed them *all*, letting them all take a risk that ended in their deaths." His vision blurred, showing him fire and smoke instead of her perfect face.

The slam of a door shook the walls, the floor, his bones, the world. It was over. What he'd wanted at the start, wanted for months. Now it was here, and he couldn't escape it, now that he wanted nothing *but* to escape it.

He uncurled his fingers from her hand and lifted it, leaving the wings there. Closed her fist around it. Then he looked over her shoulder, to where Mother now stared at them, horror in her eyes. "Give it to her for me."

Mother pressed a hand to her lips. "This isn't your end, Phillip."

The heavy feet racing up the stairs said otherwise. "It is. We all know it is."

"No." The hand Arabelle still had on his upper arm gave him a shake. "Tell them the truth."

"They wouldn't believe it."

"They *must*. We'll find the letter, the one you said he tried to have you deliver. Where is it?"

Poor Ara. He shook his head, his lips curling up, though it was more sorrow than smile. "He put it in his pocket, darling. It's at the bottom of the Channel." He leaned over and let his lips linger on her dimple. Pulled away only when it hurt too much to stay there another second. "Besides, I can't do that to them. You have to know that, sweetling. I cannot destroy that family any more than I've already done."

She gripped his lapels, shook him, her eyes wild. "What about *your* family? What about *us*?"

"You're strong." He encompassed them both with his gaze. The floorboards shook under them as the Military Police neared, and poor little Caddie's barking was nearly frantic. She didn't seem to know whether she ought to race toward the sound or stand guard in front of her mistress. "You're the strongest people I've ever known." They would be fine without him. Better even, perhaps. They wouldn't fall to pieces as Mrs. Lewis had done; they weren't in desperate straits. He crouched down, picked up the puppy, and pressed her into Arabelle's arms. He didn't want her to get under anyone's feet.

"Major Phillip Camden?" It must have been a voice that boomed out from the study doorway. But it sounded like thunder. Like ordnance. Like one airplane crashing into another.

He rested a hand for a single second against her cheek and turned to face his end. "That would be me."

The man's mouth moved; more thunder spilled out. But it was all just noise in Camden's ears. Nonsense. He could only make out the shouts of protest from his mother and Ara.

Not that he needed to hear the man's words to know what he said. The handcuffs shouted louder than even the women. The clang of metal on metal deafened him, encircled him, froze him.

He'd always known they'd come back for him. But he'd never thought it would hurt so much. His shoulders hunched with the agony of it, his gaze dropping to the floor.

Two of the soldiers stood between the women and him, two more took him by the arms, and yet another two led the way downstairs.

What sort of fight had they expected from him, that they sent six armed men to arrest him?

The stairs went on forever and yet ended far too soon at the entryway. The front door still stood open, ushering in the cool breeze, guarded by a seventh red-capped soldier. And a small ginger-haired woman. The maid.

Except she'd taken off her apron and held it in a fist, pure hatred branding her face. "I warned you, didn't I? I told you that you wouldn't get away with it. You're finally going to pay for what you've done to Wallace. To *us*."

She might as well have punched him, as fast as his breath

evacuated his lungs. This woman who didn't look more than twenty—*this* was Lewis's wife? The furious, bereaved widow?

He wanted to tell her he was sorry. That he'd tried to stop him. Tried to save him.

But she wouldn't hear him even if he tried. So instead he fastened his gaze on the world outside the door and was glad of the brisk pace the soldiers holding his arms set. A few seconds and they were past her, out on the doorstep.

More people crowded in the moment they appeared, but these wore no red, authoritative caps. They wore fedoras and bowlers and carried cameras with huge flash-lamps and shouted a cacophony of questions at him that he made no attempt to untangle.

One figure was more still than the rest though. Shorter, and wore a woman's hat instead of a man's. His gaze nearly swept over the brown curls without recognition, but he knew the face too well not to notice it. He stiffened in the hands that held him.

"You." Why? Why had Diellza Mettler taken part in this? How could it possibly play into her goal?

She smiled at him—catty, mocking. "This seems to keep happening to you, Cam."

Something inside him burst. He didn't know what she was up to, but if she was here, if she'd been helping Mrs. Lewis or these men, then it had to be bad—and much bigger than him. He exploded forward, nearly breaking free of the hands holding him. "I know who you are," he growled at her. "Who you *really* are."

"Do you?" She looked more amused than upset by that news, going so far as to saunter a few steps closer. Her hand landed on her hip, where she'd worn the holster in those photographs. She had on a lightweight coat, but he was fairly certain her hand came to rest on something other than her hip under it. "Then you know to take me seriously when I say that if you fight this, they will be the ones to pay." She darted a glance at Arabelle's front door.

All the fury drained out of him as quickly as it had gripped him. Because he knew the truth just as clearly as the gleam in her eyes said she did. They'd found his weakness. They'd exploited it expertly.

They'd won.

27

Arabelle flew down the stairs, ready to race out the door and catch that little liar by her red chignon. The door slamming in her face, pulled shut by one of the soldiers, wouldn't have deterred her for long. Not if familiar hands hadn't taken hold of her arms and pulled her away.

"Ara! Whatever is going on?" Sarah's face filled her vision.

Ara still held Caddie to her chest, a wriggling ball of fur who had run out of patience with her. She put her down, and the dog went scampering off toward the kitchen. Only then was Ara aware of the brass pin still in her hand, where Cam had pressed it.

He'd put it into her hand once before, the night of the bombing. But she'd thought he just wanted her to put it somewhere safe. This time, she understood. This was his heart. This was *him*.

"Ara?"

She looked at Sarah and then toward the stairs, where Mrs. Camden was hurrying down, though at a slower pace than Arabelle had flown.

She looked so pale that Ara's training kicked in, pushing emotion willfully aside and elbowing its way into its usual place at the helm of her body. Her pulse slowed. Her breathing regulated. Actions flooded her brain. She slid the pin into her pocket and hurried over to meet Mrs. Camden.

She had to get her into a chair and make certain she was all right. Get her something warm to drink. Take her pulse, make sure her heart hadn't suffered more than emotionally from seeing her son forcibly removed by armed soldiers. He'd not be quick to forgive if something were to happen to his mother because of this, though it would be himself he'd blame more than Ara. All the more reason to act quickly.

Ara met Sarah's eye. "Would you get some tea for Mrs. Camden?"

Her friend was savvy enough to see the woman's distress with a glance. Holding her questions, despite the fact that Ara hadn't answered them, she nodded and spun away.

Arabelle intercepted Mrs. Camden at the base of the stairs, taking her by the arm and steering her directly into the drawing room she still thought of as Aunt Hettie's.

"We have to stop them." The woman's gaze was latched on the door, though it required craning her head over her shoulder for it to stay there. "We can't let them do this to him again. I'm none too certain he'll survive it. It destroyed him last time—broke him to pieces."

"I don't believe it was prison that broke him so, ma'am—it was the loss of his men." Arabelle tried to urge her into a chair.

Mrs. Camden shook her off, squared her shoulders, and lifted her chin. "You needn't coddle me, Miss Denler. I am no fragile flower that will shrivel away at the first blast of wind."

"I never thought you were." But this was hardly the first blast. Still, her eyes had snapped back into focus, and color was returning to her cheeks as they spoke. Good signs. Arabelle made no attempt to disguise her actions, though, when she reached for the woman's wrist and pressed two fingers to her pulse.

Mrs. Camden huffed out a breath but didn't pull away. "I'm perfectly well."

"And I'll make sure of it, thank you." Her lips settled into the practiced, calming smile she used at the hospital, and her attention went to the blood hammering along in the woman's wrist. Her heart rate was elevated, but that was no surprise. Perfectly consistent with the adrenaline that would have flooded her. Her flesh wasn't clammy, and her respiration was steady. "We're not going to rush out there—it will achieve nothing. We're going to sit, have a cup of tea, and develop a plan."

It would give her time to monitor her guest's health and make sure she was really as resilient as she claimed. And it was a reasonable thing to do in general.

"You think I want *tea* at a time like this?"

Arabelle eased her wrist back down, satisfied on that count. "No. I don't either. But we also don't want to make it worse for him, and charging at the armed soldiers with our fists flying would probably do just that."

Mrs. Camden's lips quirked up the slightest bit. "I nearly kicked that one in the shins upstairs."

Arabelle smiled too. "I'd have kicked the other. But they'd have probably taken it out on Cam."

The sound of footsteps and squeaking wheels signaled that Sarah was wheeling in the tea cart, which she'd no doubt already had ready for after their tour. Though when Arabelle spun to face her, she saw more than a bit of irritation on her friend's face. "I don't know where Kathleen has got to," she said.

Just like that, Arabelle's calm tensed into fury again. "I suspect she's gone. For good, unless she returns to gloat."

"I beg your pardon?" Sarah parked the cart and straightened, frowning.

"I don't think she was entirely honest with us about her name. I think she ought to have called herself Kathleen *Lewis*."

The name didn't mean anything to Sarah, but Mrs. Camden sucked in a fast breath. "Related to the man Phillip was talking about? The one who is responsible for this?"

"His widow." It had clicked partially into place the moment he mentioned the number of children Lewis had left behind. Not that there weren't plenty of families with that many offspring, but the few words she'd heard the wretch snap at him had confirmed it. "I ought to have pieced it together sooner."

She wasn't sure how she could have, but surely there'd been a clue. That day on the street outside the hospital—Mrs. Lewis had probably been following her. Or lying in wait to follow Cam, anyway. And no doubt that wasn't the first time—how else would she have known where to send the letter? She'd likely been keeping an eye on her house for weeks, and so when she realized they were hiring . . . "She only applied so she could be here for this, I daresay. Probably told the Military Police when to come."

After all he'd done to *help* her—to cover up her husband's weakness and keep her and her children from suffering more.

And Ara had played right into her hand. She sank to a seat on the sofa, her own chest tight even if Mrs. Camden's didn't seem to be. "What a fool I am. I brought her here—I offered a home to her children. And all the while, she was plotting against us."

A hand landed on her shoulder. "It is to your credit, Arabelle," Cam's mother said softly. "You saw a stranger in need and tried to help. As you did with my Cass. And, for that matter, with Phillip himself. You couldn't have known who she was."

She shook her head. Maybe she couldn't have known before. But she knew *now*. She looked up, straight into the blue eyes that Cam had inherited. "I love that he wants to protect them. But I can't let him. Not when it will cost him his life."

"On that we agree." Mrs. Camden sat beside her. "But what can we do? We can tell them what he said, but they will think it the biased support of his mother and sweetheart, nothing more."

His sweetheart. Oh, how it ached. So few days she'd had to claim that title. Never yet in public, or to anyone but his mother and Sarah.

But she couldn't let the hurt distract her. She had to focus on what they could do, not on what they couldn't change. "The note."

"The suicide note?" Mrs. Camden frowned and reached for Arabelle's hand. "But Lewis had it with him, Phillip said."

"Yes. Which means it's still there, at the bottom of the Channel." Waving off the cup of tea Sarah held out to her, she sprang to her feet, pacing with thought. "That means it's recoverable. Brax's letters always used to be filled with the miracles of what they'd bring up. Things I never would have thought would survive any time under water—like paper. He's said that it just needs to dry out and is perfectly fine. That's why the Admiralty pays them extra to dive to enemy U-boats in search of anything that might be of use."

Sarah sighed. "But this isn't a U-boat, Ara. It's a plane, with an open cockpit. Who's to say what happened to a single slip of paper?"

Arabelle shook her head and pivoted, aiming for the telephone table in the corner. "No. He would have been wearing a heavy coat that day—it was winter, after all. If he had it with him, he would have put it in an inner pocket. It would have been protected, and he would have been belted into the plane. Brax can dive down, recover it." He owed her a favor, he said.

"Ara." Sarah appeared between her and the phone, brows still knit. "Much as Mr. Braxton may wish to help, I daresay the navy doesn't just let him take the diving equipment out in the Channel whenever he wishes. Besides, wasn't there fire involved? I assume you're talking about the incident for which Major Camden was first arrested?"

Fiddlesticks. She had a point, which sent Ara pivoting back toward Mrs. Camden.

His mother was shaking her head. "No. Well, yes, but not Lewis's plane. I've read the newspaper reports a hundred times, and it was the others who crashed into one another. Lewis stalled and plunged straight into the water."

His plane, his remains, his suicide note ought to be preserved, then. Not burned. Ara nodded. "Come on."

The lady stood, though she wore her question on her brows. "Where are we going?"

"To pay a visit to Whitehall—*I* might not be able to order Brax's superiors to let him dive to the crash site, but I daresay the admiral knows someone who can."

Oh, how she prayed that Camden hadn't antagonized his new superior as much as he'd seemed to do others.

Admiral Hall wasn't a large man—he was slightly built, shorter than Ara by several inches—but his presence filled up the room as he regarded them from his seat behind his desk. His blinking was most likely a tic, but not one that denoted nervousness. Instead, it gave her the impression that he was taking snapshots of them every few seconds that he could go back to later and inspect.

She shifted on her chair. She'd been a bit surprised at how quickly they'd been ushered up here and into Admiral Hall's office after arriving at the Old Building. She'd laid out the story—the Military Police coming to her house, Camden's confession of what had really happened, her certainty that the divers could recover the evidence they needed to clear Cam of the charges against him—but the admiral's face gave nothing away as he heard her out. Did he believe her, or was he simply sitting there, regretting ever going out on a limb for Phillip Camden?

Ara glanced over at Mrs. Camden, who occupied the second chair in front of the desk, and then glanced at Sarah, who had stationed herself against the wall at Arabelle's side. A young woman named De Wilde had taken up position in the corner of the room; Ara had first thought her a secretary, but she wasn't taking any notes. And wasn't that the name of one of Cam's coworkers? Whoever she was, she now stood stock-still. Listening, watching. But reacting not a bit, as if she were more statue than girl.

At last, Admiral Hall moved, leaning forward until his elbows came to a rest on his desk. "Margot, dear? Could you see if Mr. Pearce is still here? I believe he was fetching more photographs from Miss Blackwell."

"Of course." Margot De Wilde sprang into action and was out of the room a few seconds later.

Ara went stiff. *Miss Blackwell?* She would have chalked it up to some other Blackwell, had the name not been said in the same breath as *photographs*. But it couldn't be Lily, could it? What would she be doing here?

Her father worked here, though. Somewhere in this building, though Ara didn't know where. Perhaps she came in with him sometimes? To do something with photographs?

Arabelle hadn't the energy to think any more about that just now.

The admiral cleared his throat and met Ara's gaze. "First, Miss Denler, allow me to apologize."

Not the words she'd expected to tumble from his lips. "I beg your pardon?"

His smile was warm, the kind that insisted he was trustworthy, dependable. "When I sent your father to Mexico, I insisted he be very vague in what he told you. But I do believe Camden was right, that you could have been trusted with the entire story."

He was the one—the very one—who had sent Father away? For a moment, Arabelle could only stare at him. Then she shook herself and straightened her spine. "I could have, yes. But I will assume for now that my father is safe on the *Daphne*, headed for an adventure that he will thoroughly enjoy. At the moment, my concern is Phillip Camden."

"Rightly so. I'm glad you've come by with this information. I had just been informed of his arrest." His eyes flicked to the empty doorway. "But I never did succeed in getting the actual story out of him. That should help matters."

Ara scooted forward on her chair. "Do you think you can arrange for the divers? That the letter will still be legible?"

Hall gave a brisk nod, along with another blink. "We recover papers all the time. I frequently offer prizes to divers who take on risky tasks in their off-hours for me."

"I know."

He lifted a brow. "How would you know?"

"Oh." She waved a hand, glancing over to Sarah. "I was

engaged to a diver in Portsmouth for a while. He told me of a dive to a U-boat he made last year. It was how I knew this was even possible."

His next smile was more amused than warm. "Even so. Most people would have assumed the letter was gone."

"Consider me motivated."

He chuckled and settled his gaze on Mrs. Camden. "I am sorry, ma'am, that you were witness to this. Had I had any foreknowledge of this plan to arrest him again, I assure you I would have taken action. Major Camden has proven himself a quick-minded, loyal young man."

Pride gleamed in her eyes as she said, "I don't need your apologies, Admiral. If this had to happen, I'm glad I was here. That said, I do agree with your assessment. Phillip may have a penchant for trouble, but a more loyal man you'll never find."

Hall nodded and reached for something on his desk. Paper and pen, Arabelle saw. He pulled both to the spot in front of him and uncapped the fountain pen. "We'll do all we can to exonerate him. I am glad to have hope of doing so. But there is more at work here than Camden alone. I'm afraid his arrest is but a means to a far different end."

Ara knew her own frown matched Mrs. Camden's. "What do you mean? What else could there be?"

He underlined something already written on the page and flipped the paper around, sliding it across the desk so they could see it.

It seemed to be a schedule. An itinerary, perhaps. Except that rather than denoting tasks the admiral might have to do, it instead listed things like *8:17—left house on Goldsmith Rd. 8:25—reached Peckham Rye Station. 9:06—reached Lewis residence in Croydon.* It was that one that he'd underlined.

Her mouth went dry. "You were tracking someone." Someone who had gone to Kathleen Lewis's home.

"Indeed. And if any of you can shed more light on the situation, we'll have a better chance of stopping it—*and* of freeing

Camden." He flipped open a brown-papered folder and pulled out a shiny photograph. "Do you know this woman?"

The breath she drew in felt too big, made her chest feel tight. The woman from the teahouse. The beautiful blonde who had laughed at her.

Mrs. Camden shook her head. "I've never seen her."

"I have. With Cam." Ara forced a swallow and looked up into the admiral's eyes. She slid her hand into her pocket so she could find the brass wings. Trace their contours. "He said she was under suspicion. That he *had* to meet with her."

Hall's nod made the brass warm in her fingers. "I'd asked him to pursue the lead, yes."

Sarah had slid closer. "I believe I've seen her too—though her hair was darker. And curly." She met Ara's gaze. "She came for the interview the other day as well—one of the ones who seemed to be there only for the tour."

"Curly brown hair, you say?" They all turned at the new voice. A man strode in and was greeted as Mr. Pearce. He clasped a stack of glossy photographs, which he held out to the admiral. "I believe I've a visual record of that. It's definitely Mettler. I've one here of her wearing the wig and walking with Kathleen Lewis."

"And I didn't employ any creativity on that photograph, I promise you."

Ara spun at the familiar voice. "Lily?"

Her friend's face went blank. Then panicked. And finally settled on a resigned wince. "Don't tell my mother, Ara. She'll have Daddy's head if she realizes I'm working here."

She'd never even *met* Lily's mother. "Of course I won't. Though why—"

"It's a long story." Lily sighed and tightened the belt of her overcoat. She'd apparently been leaving for the day. "But I hope my work can help clear your beau of these charges. Do you need anything else this evening, Admiral?"

Hall looked from the photographs he'd stood up to receive to the young woman in the doorway. "I don't believe so, Miss Black-well. Thank you for staying so long to help with this."

"Well, it will make me late for Mama's dinner party, so my pleasure." She offered a cheeky grin, a little wave, and stepped back into the corridor. "If you need anything else, you know where to find me."

When she vacated the doorway, Margot De Wilde filled it again, sliding back over to her place in the corner. Arabelle turned back to the two men now bent over the desk, examining the pictures together. She had no compunction about leaning forward for a glimpse as well.

She saw mostly what she expected, given the conversation. A shot of Kath walking down the street with the same woman in the other photo, only this time the blonde was brunette. Definitely the same face, though. "Who did you say she was?"

"Diellza Mettler," the admiral replied. "A Swiss native who is working for a German officer." He flipped through the rest of the photographs. "You left the message for her as I instructed, Pearce?"

"Yes, sir." Mr. Pearce's voice was filled with laughter. "And it shook her, as you thought it would. Everything vital has been removed from her rented room, and she's staying with Mrs. Lewis tonight, I believe."

"Perfect." Admiral Hall turned to Sarah. "When she was in Miss Denler's home—I trust she was supervised?"

Sarah nodded. "I led the tour and made sure no one lagged behind or was inspired to take a souvenir, and then the cook watched over them while I was conducting interviews."

Hall nodded. "I daresay she was just getting the lay of the place, if it's where they wanted to stage the arrest. Though you would probably not be overreacting much by having your locks changed, Miss Denler."

Arabelle nodded, though her attention was more on the array of photographs. Particularly on one of what looked like an empty trunk . . . with a padded bottom with very particularly shaped indentations. "What is that? Did she have a—a gun in there?"

"She did." The laughter was gone now from Pearce's tone. "And it would seem she's an expert at using it."

A chill skittered down her spine. "Why? Why has she gone after Cam? How could this possibly be part of a bigger plan?"

"Because . . ." Hall sat again, leaned back again, and steepled his fingers. "With his arrest, they've effectively pitted the army against the navy. I pulled quite a few strings to get him released to my custody—strings now lashing back. In the last hour I've had no fewer than five calls from angry generals and politicians. All of whom have sworn that they'll be at his arraignment, which will happen with all possible speed."

Ara's gaze again dropped to that empty silhouette of a gun. "That's a lot of high-ranking men."

"All in one place." Pearce sat on the edge of the desk and mimicked a pistol with his fingers. "Fish in a barrel, as the saying goes."

This wasn't about Cam at all, then. He was just a pawn in a plot to . . . to . . . "This woman is an assassin?" But that couldn't be, could it? It was too farfetched. Too diabolical.

"This woman is an expert marksman, daughter of a gun manufacturer, in love with a coldhearted snake of a hun." Hall tossed another photograph toward her from the file. Ara picked it up, her heart aching at the image it showed. Diellza Mettler, but in this one her smile was genuine. More than genuine—it was filled with pure adoration as she gazed into the face of a handsome man. "She isn't an assassin *yet*, so far as we know. But that is clearly what she's been sent here to become—and she's not the first woman the Germans have sent to England with such a task. Thus far, we've managed to foil them all."

Mrs. Camden had scooted forward on her chair as well. "She must be stopped—but stopping her won't save my son from the firing squad. We do need that note from the deceased Lewis for that, Admiral."

"And we'll have it. I'll dispatch instructions immediately, authorizing the divers to seek out the wreckage and promising a prize to whoever finds the letter. But I'm afraid I must focus also on the reverse of that, Mrs. Camden." When Hall leveled that particular gaze on them, Arabelle had the distinct feeling that he could put aside this face of friendliness in a blink and be every bit as coldhearted as the German snake Miss Mettler was in love with. "Saving your son from the firing squad won't save the lives of every admiral, general, and politician who steps into Mettler's line of fire."

"Can't you just warn them?" the ever-practical Sarah asked with a wave of her hand. "Tell them to stay away from the arraignment?"

Hall blinked. "If each one of them were to believe me and not suspect I was simply trying to manipulate them into not being there while I pulled some stunt to sway the outcome in favor of my man . . . But they won't."

"What do we do, then? You, but also us?" Ara motioned first to the three of them—Hall, Pearce, De Wilde. Then to herself and Sarah and Mrs. Camden.

The admiral's smile was all warmth again. "First, my dear, you pay a visit to the major in prison tomorrow. I daresay he wouldn't tell me anything more now than he ever has, but he's clearly opened up to you. Get him to tell you anything else that pertains either to the accident, the Lewises, or Mettler. One never knows when the smallest detail may prove relevant—like all those details this former fiancé of yours shared about his dives."

She nodded. "I can do that." She'd have to take the day off work, but she would. Gladly.

Hall's gaze had moved to Sarah. "I suggest you hire whoever else had been a final candidate—perhaps several of them. Keep Miss Denler's house filled with people at all times. I don't imagine she's their target, but a crowd will help guarantee safety."

"Consider it done, sir." She looked to Arabelle. "Perhaps Helen Smithfield's big family would be willing to come with her for a few days. Failing that, I can send for some staff from Middlegrove. I daresay the new mistress would approve it."

"You can be certain she will," Mrs. Camden said with a decisive nod.

"You, Mrs. Camden." Here Hall paused, his face softening. "Try not to worry. We have the best people working to save him." Now he turned in his chair to take in Margot De Wilde. "Have you cracked the code they were using? Mettler and this hun of hers?"

"Child's play." She smirked. For all of two seconds. "Though there was no key in her belongings, only that partial letter—probably by his instruction. We can't use the code without tipping our hand, sir."

Hall looked straight ahead for a moment, the tic in his jaw keeping time with the one in his eyes. After a moment, he shook his head. "It's a risk, but I think it will be mitigated by the outcome. If our message to him succeeds, he won't have the chance to tell his superiors that we've intercepted their communications."

De Wilde folded her arms across her chest. "And if it doesn't?"

"Then it will be because he'll think Mettler has been compromised—he'll simply assume she broke under interrogation and told us their code." Hall stood, shuffling the photographs and papers back into a stack. "Pearce—"

"Keeping eyes on Mettler and Lewis round the clock, sir, as ordered. Anything else?"

"I daresay that's enough." Hall straightened, gaze sweeping the room again. "This isn't a stumbling block—it's a stepping-stone. Treat it as such."

Arabelle's gaze drifted over to Cam's mother and tangled there with hers. Brave words from the admiral, determined words.

But they wouldn't have come so easily if the one *he* loved were the bait in a deadly game of cat and mouse.

28

THURSDAY, 14 MARCH

Light flowed into the prison cell from the single window high overhead, but it might as well have been midnight on a new moon. Camden sat on the floor, his back to the cold stone wall, surrounded by darkness. Darkness of his own making. A past without redemption. A present without hope. A future too short to see.

How many times had he wished for this? Wished they would just arrest him again and get it over with? Wished that the death that yawned before him would just snap him up and end his misery? How many times had he lashed out at everyone trying to help him, claiming they ought to just let him die?

Now here he sat, staring the end in the face.

And he didn't want to die.

Not now. Not when he had Ara, who for some reason loved him. A mother who was proud of him. A sister with a baby on the way. A brother who needed to know how right he'd been . . . about far too much. Not now, when he'd finally found his place in Room 40. When he had a friend who wanted him to be a groomsman in May.

For the first time in months, he'd begun to feel alive. Genuinely alive, not just borrowing Ara's heart or Hall's will. And now this.

He traced a finger along the floor. Was it the same cell he'd been in before? He didn't know—it had all been a blur. A hateful, empty, cavernous blur of pain and disbelief. He'd failed them. Failed to save Lewis, and so failed to save them all.

He'd failed them even before that. Failed to show them that the life of an officer and gentleman was more than reckless decisions and whatever fleeting pleasures they could grasp hold of for an evening. Lewis—he'd already had what mattered. A wife, children, a life he loved. And Camden and the others had pushed and prodded and teased and cajoled until he'd thrown it all away.

That day, when the man had stood before him, broken, Cam hadn't understood. Hadn't understood how something as trivial as an affair could possibly make him willing to end his life.

But that hadn't been it alone. It had been everything. They'd slowly, over months and years, chipped away at the foundation of who he'd once been. They'd left him a shell of the former Wallace Lewis—and then, when that shell cracked, there was nothing left inside to keep him together. Nothing to give him hope. He could only see his failures, only see the trust he'd broken, the betrayal he'd taken part in.

Camden scrubbed a hand over his closed eyes, still seeing that broken gaze before him. He knew, now, how Lewis had felt to have failed so completely the only ones who mattered. He knew it. And he wished he could go back and change things. Everything. But especially those final moments on the ground. He'd take the letter. But more, he'd take his friend by the shoulders. He wouldn't shout. He'd talk. He'd ask. He'd listen.

Maybe he could have saved Lewis for at least one more day—and so saved the rest of them forever.

Why? Why hadn't it happened that way? Why *this*?

A clang, a clatter, and the shuffle of feet. "Ten minutes, miss. No more—I'll come back for you then."

"Thank you, Corporal."

His eyes flew open, and he clambered onto his knees, gripping the iron bars and using them to pull himself to his feet.

"Ara?" No. No, she couldn't be here. Not *here*. "What are you doing here?" The words fell like ice against the stones, shattering and crackling.

Her hands covered his on the bars, her face lighting up the darkness. "What do you *think* I'm doing here? Are you all right?"

She'd come. Here. To prison, to see him. It made his heart warm. For one second—then the fear came crashing down. "No. No, you can't be here, darling. Go home. Take care of my mother—you didn't bring her, did you?" His eyes sought out the dim stretch between the cells, but no one else had come in with her.

"No. Phillip, look at me."

He obeyed, his eyes latching onto hers. It might be the last time he really saw her. She couldn't come back. And it would be a quick journey to the firing squad from here—they'd made sure he knew that.

She gripped his fingers and pressed as close as the bars would allow. "We're going to get you out of this. I've spoken with Admiral Hall, and he's convinced this is all just part of that Mettler woman's plot. It won't defeat us. It *won't*. You did not kill your men, and you'll not pay the price for doing so."

Her fingers felt so warm against his. Proving yet again that she was warmth and life and all things beautiful, while he was cold and death and danger. She should never have loved him, even if he couldn't help but love her.

He had to convince her to call Hall off, to stop. He had to, or he knew well Diellza would see to it that Ara took a bullet. Even if Hall's men closed in on her, even if they stopped her from taking out whichever brass she'd targeted, she wouldn't go down without a fight.

"Don't." The command came out in a strange voice, hard and cold. He pulled his fingers free of hers. "Don't try to interfere with justice."

She gripped the bars where his fingers had been, and he longed to put them back. But he mustn't. If he couldn't convince her to do what needed doing with sheer logic, then he'd be forced to resort to snarling. And he'd never have a chance of forcing her away if first he clung to her.

She was shaking her head, eyes glinting in the window's measly light. "It isn't *justice*. You're not guilty!"

Of the exact crime they accused him of, no. But he was guilty. So very guilty he could scarcely hold his shoulders up. "I am. Of more than you know."

"Yes, I'm sure you are." At the no-nonsense tone, his eyes again met hers. She wore her nurse's face, placid but determined. Never shaken. Never judging. "You've lived a reckless, foolish life for a lot of years. I know that—and you certainly still need to settle that with the Almighty. But *this*, Cam—this isn't about those other things weighing on you. This is about Diellza Mettler and Kath Lewis and what happened with your squadron. Nothing else."

Breathing a laugh as dry as last autumn's leaves, he spun away. "Plenty to be guilty of there too. You yourself pointed that out, the day you met her. I used her and cast her aside, introduced her to the others. Maybe I hurt her, I don't know. Maybe that's why she's targeted me. Or maybe I was just convenient."

"What others?"

"What?" He didn't turn around, couldn't. If he faced her fully, his traitorous hands would reach for her through those bars again. But he turned his head enough that he could see her.

She was gripping the bars like she could rip them straight from the floor. "To whom did you introduce her? The men in your squadron?"

"What does that have to do with—"

"Everything! Or nothing, I don't know. Just answer me."

Blast, but when her eyes sparked like that . . . He eased another step away, even as he turned a bit more to better see her. "The men in my squadron, yes. Though I don't see what—"

"Lewis? Did Lewis know her? Did he . . . ? You said he'd been unfaithful, and that it ate at him. Was she . . . ?"

God in heaven . . . It felt more like a prayer than anything he'd uttered in years, but he didn't know how to follow it up. Could he beg the Lord to steer her away from what suddenly came into focus in his mind?

He forced himself to stand still. To lift his chin. To give nothing away. Had Lewis been involved with Dee? He'd not thought anything of it at the time, hadn't wondered what that laughter in the pub might have led to. But it was quite possible. Likely, even. And if so, if someone were to tell his widow . . . That would certainly sway Kathleen Lewis away from Diellza's side—not that it mattered at this point.

Then he sucked in a breath as another thought struck him. If Lewis *had* been involved with her . . . if the whole reason she'd been deported before was because they suspected her of trying to wheedle information out of officers . . .

Maybe it wasn't only guilt over betraying his marriage vows that had broken Lewis. Maybe it was guilt over betraying his country too.

Ara recognized the possibility—he could see it in the way she straightened, pulled away from the bars a bit.

That brought him a step closer. "No." He was replying to her thoughts, not to her question, but with a bit of luck she wouldn't realize that and would just read truth in his face. "Leave the Lewis family alone, Arabelle. They've suffered enough." And if more attention turned to Dee, if they backed her into a corner, she'd come out shooting.

Her nostrils flared. "Your dying will not bring him back. A lie winning out will not help them heal."

"Well, having their husband and father's morality and loyalty called into question certainly wouldn't help matters either!"

"It doesn't have to be made public for it to clear your name!" She looked ready to pound a fist to the bars. "We can protect their family and still fight for ours."

Ours. It echoed through the cell, in his head, to his heart. How he wanted her to be a part of his. Wanted to create a new one with her. Wanted to become hers.

He gritted his teeth and told himself that this was the only way. The only way to convince her to let it drop. The only way to save her life. "There isn't an *ours*." He hated himself as he said it. Hated himself more than he ever had.

She went still and silent.

He couldn't look at her. If he did, she'd see how the words chipped away at him far more than at her. So he sauntered over to the cot and lowered himself to a seat on it. "There never was. I'm not your family, Ara. This was a fun lark, but obviously it's over now, which is just as well."

He expected silence. A quickly drawn breath. That war that always seemed to be waged within her in hard moments between anger and pain. He expected those insecurities he'd wanted to banish to take hold. *Needed* them to.

He jumped when she slapped at the bars. "Do you honestly expect me to believe that? To believe that's anything other than you trying to protect me? *You* may be an idiot, Phillip, but I am *not*."

Blast it all. He surged to his feet, stormed back over to her. "Stay away! If you love me, you'll do that. Because otherwise, she's going to kill you. And I can't have that on my head, Ara. I *can't*. I can't die knowing you've paid that price!"

She backed up a step, eyes flashing lightning. "That isn't your decision to make." She spun. "Guard!"

He growled as the guard came and led her away, unable to find any words to convey the pain. The fear. The torment.

A shiver coursed through him and somehow shook him to his core. He slid to the ground again and hunched over, but all heat had fled along with her. Darkness swallowed him up again from the inside out, taking with it everything light lent. Heat. Sight. Color.

He'd thought before that he'd lost it all. That he had nothing left to live for.

He'd been so very wrong.

Now he wanted so desperately to cling to it, but his hands snatched at emptiness. He wanted to live. He wanted to fight. But if he did, he'd take others out with him, and he couldn't do that. He couldn't be responsible for the deaths of more people he loved.

It is appointed unto men once to die . . .

The words surfaced like icebergs in his mind. Like storm clouds marring a tranquil sky, promising a ruin to the flight.

Once to die. All these months he'd sworn he was already dead. But here he sat, with blood still coursing in his veins and new pain proving he still lived. New death, *true* death looming.

"I don't want to die." He had to say it out loud, a breath in the darkness, just to counteract all the times he'd claimed the opposite. "God . . ." Was He there? Watching? Or had He abandoned him long ago to his own foolishness?

It is appointed unto men once to die, but after this the judgment.

He shuddered as the end of the verse surfaced, lightning in the clouds. He'd had to memorize it as a lad. He could picture his own smaller hand practicing the words in script, scrawling out *Hebrews 9* beneath it. The dreaded Mr. Norton pacing the rows of students' desks. Correcting an *m* here, the height of a *t* there.

But it wasn't Mr. Norton's voice saying the words in his mind. It wasn't his own. He heard them in Jeremy's voice. Spoken quietly, with complete conviction. Jeremy, looking in his eyes and declaring, *After this, brother, the judgment.*

Cam pulled his knees up, rested his arms on them, and let his head fall onto his arms. He'd pretended for so long that there was no such thing as sin. But Ara had been right. He'd always known. He'd been taught the same as Jeremy. He'd copied out the same Scriptures. Their parents had raised him with the same certainty. He could deny what was inconvenient, but he couldn't escape it, not fully. Deep down . . . deep down, where there was only darkness and ice, he knew. He knew there was a God, and he knew he came up far short of His expectations.

After this the judgment.

A firing squad wasn't enough to punish him for all he'd done wrong. That would require eternity.

Jeremy's voice whispered in his head again. *Don't forget the next verse, brother,* he said. *"And as it is appointed unto men once to die, but after this the judgment: So Christ was once offered to bear the sins of many; and unto them that look for him shall he appear the second time without sin unto salvation."*

Without sin . . . He couldn't even imagine it. Every pleasure he'd claimed hurt no one. Every selfish act that eroded his soul. He could see them now, and they were hideous blotches on his life.

What had Ara said? *"You've lived a reckless, foolish life . . ."*

How right she was. He'd cared only for himself. And so, he'd lost himself. Lost his chance at a life that would lead to true happiness, that would make a difference for good, that would give to others.

She knew that secret. She gave so freely. Out of her plenty, yes—but not just that. She gave of her heart, of her soul. She gave in her loneliness and she gave in her friendships and she gave in her hurt and her pain.

We are troubled on every side, yet not distressed; we are perplexed, but not in despair.

That verse was Ara. Was Jeremy. Was his mother. It was Elton and De Wilde. They all had what he'd eschewed.

Persecuted, but not forsaken.

This wasn't persecution. This was deserved—and so, he couldn't blame God for keeping His distance.

Cast down, but not destroyed.

He *was* destroyed. Utterly, totally destroyed. He'd gambled at life and lost all that mattered, and now he faced the consequences. Destruction, judgment . . . it wasn't just punishment for sin. It was seeing what he could have been without it and knowing it was forever out of reach.

There was no hope for him. The best he could wish for now was to spare the rest of them any more violence. Spare *them* death, they who actually knew how to live.

"You'll either be a hero or a villain, Phil. Try to pick the right

one, will you?" Gil now, in his ears. Taunting. Disappointed. Because Camden had always chosen the wrong one, always. Chosen it by choosing himself above others. That, as he suspected his brother had always known, was what made a villain rather than a hero.

But there's hope. Jeremy's voice was but a whisper through that clamoring din of self-loathing. *There's always hope.*

Stupid, optimistic Jeremy. There *wasn't* hope. Not now.

Don't forget the next verse. Jeremy, always pushing for more. *You know* how *we are cast down but not destroyed. You know it.*

Did he? His breath grew warm in the hollow he'd made for himself, and his mind went back. Back to that schoolroom he so hated. Back to the copywork he tried to get out of. Back to Mr. Norton, who drilled the Scriptures into them in a monotonous voice that had always said *he* didn't much value the words. But he'd made sure they knew them.

Second Corinthians. Chapter four, wasn't it? His breath came faster. *Always bearing about in the body the dying of the Lord Jesus, that the life also of Jesus might be made manifest in our body.*

His breath failed him. He'd carried death around with him these many months. He'd held it close and given himself over to it. But not like that. The death he'd borne had not ended in victory. It hadn't carried in it the seed of life.

So then death worketh in us, but life in you.

Death and life. Both shimmered before him. Death, yes— imminent, unavoidable death. But he didn't want it to be an empty death. He wanted it to be the other kind—the kind burgeoning with new beginnings. He wanted it to be the death that led to life.

"God . . . I want to live." The words were eaten up by the hollow, soaked into the coarse fabric of his trousers. They were true . . . but not quite right. "No. I want . . . I want *life*." Life instead of death. Life *beyond* death. Life *despite* death. Life for them . . . but they already had it. Life for *him*, so that he could finally be free of this weight, of the death always pulling him down.

And he knew. He knew from whence it came. He knew, as Mr. Norton and Jeremy and their parents and Ara had made sure of, he knew the name that could call it forth. With a shuddering cry that tore him in half, he whispered it. "Jesus."

29

I diot man." Arabelle paced from one end of the drawing room to the other, too much frustration and anger and fear bubbling about inside to allow her to sit. She wasn't sure how Mrs. Camden could manage it. How her hands weren't shaking with nerves and pain as she wielded her crochet hook in Aunt Hettie's favorite chair. "Trying to make himself out to be the villain. Taking the blame to protect the innocents. That's what landed him in this mess to begin with."

Mrs. Camden smiled. "Only because he loves you, my dear."

It didn't do much to mollify her. And how long did it take divers to search a wrecked plane, anyway? She sent a glare toward the silent telephone. According to the note Admiral Hall had sent round this morning, they knew exactly where the wreck was and should have already dispatched a team. According to the telegram Brax had sent before he left Portsmouth first thing today, he meant to be the one to find it. And if Brax was good at anything, it was plumbing the waters' depths.

She'd sent a return note to the admiral with the little she'd gotten from Cam before he decided to play the idiot—including the threat the Mettler woman had either made toward her or that Camden had imagined her making.

A yip drew her gaze down to her feet, where Caddie was wagging her tail and dancing in circles. She seemed to think Arabelle's pacing was a game. It soothed a bit of her frustration, and she leaned down to scoop her up.

The doorbell rang for the twelfth time since she'd gotten home from the prison, which only spurred her to make another pivot, another turn of the room. Sarah had been managing all the comings and goings: new locks installed, new maid hired, new maid's family all agreeing to come and stay for a few days, messengers coming from the Admiralty, messengers *going* to the Admiralty.

And the last one: a telegram from Father letting her know he'd arrived safely in Mexico—one relief to her mind, anyway. Praise the Lord. He'd given her an address where she could send that long letter she'd written to him, and she'd composed a telegram too. Short but to the point. *I forgive you. I love you. Pray for Cam. Trouble has caught up.*

She was a bit surprised when Sarah actually entered the drawing room this time, indicating whoever had rung required Arabelle's attention but carrying nothing in her hands to say it was just a message. "Ara? There's a Nurse Jameson here to see you."

Her feet stilled. The churning of her stomach stilled. The roiling storm clouds of frustration and worry stilled.

Today was one of only three days she'd requested off since the war began. Was the hospital matron coming solely to check in on her? Or . . .

Arabelle swallowed down the *or*. "Show her in, please, Sarah."

At her place in the corner, Mrs. Camden lowered her crocheting. "Do you need privacy, my dear? I can—"

"No, that's all right." Ara fastened a smile to her lips. "I imagine she's only dropping by because we've missed each other for the last week while she was out with a cold."

A few seconds later, her superior's face belied that claim as she strode into the room, eyes fixing directly onto Arabelle and not even sweeping the rest of the chamber to note Mrs. Camden's presence. And her expression—complete stoicism. Not a single emotion to crack the calm surface.

She clutched a newspaper under her arm, which made Arabelle's stomach go tight. She'd not looked at any today. She'd not wanted to.

Mrs. Jameson smacked the paper onto an end table. "I trust you have an explanation for this—and it had better be a good one."

Ara didn't even glance down at the thing. It would have a snapshot of the Military Police forcing Camden from her house, she imagined. Some terrible headline reading that the dastardly Black Heart had finally been apprehended again, as if he'd been on the run and not still serving his country. "I beg your pardon, ma'am—I've not had the chance to read the papers today. For what had I better have an explanation?"

A bit of a flush climbed the matron's neck. "Miss Denler." Her voice came out barely above a whisper, tight and pleading. "Don't be coy with me, I beg you. If you're to get out of this mess, we must act quickly and decisively. You must issue a statement to the press at once, disavowing any connection with that man. You must—"

"I'll do no such thing." Ara's arms went a bit too tight, and Caddie wriggled within them, demanding to be put down, poor thing. She obliged her.

When she rose again, she found incredulity on Mrs. Jameson's face. "Arabelle. Surely he has not beguiled you to the point where you cannot see what this means for you. The most notorious criminal in England was arrested *at your home*. The papers are calling you his paramour. Even if I disbelieve them, the damage to your reputation . . ."

Arabelle lifted her chin. Straightened her spine. Stood as tall as a tower. She'd been afraid to confess the truth to the matron, knowing well what the cost would be.

But just now, there was no room inside for fear—not of her, not of the stuffy men on the hospital board waiting to judge.

Compared to what Camden faced, those judges were nothing. Nothing. "May I assume that the board of directors paid you a visit this morning?"

Mrs. Jameson's flush reddened a bit more. "I assured them it was all a misunderstanding. I explained that your father had asked him to see you safely home each evening. But they are demanding an immediate distancing on your part, a—"

"No." One word. It would seal her fate at the hospital. She knew it would. But never had a word been so easy to speak.

Mrs. Jameson drew back, eyes going wide. "What?"

Arabelle's hands fisted at her sides. "I will not abandon him in his hour of need. Phillip Camden is innocent of the charges against him, ma'am."

"It doesn't matter if he is!" The matron gestured wildly at the newspaper. "You have been *ruined*! And now we've all come under inspection, as our hospital was mentioned as your workplace."

For an eternal moment, she just held Mrs. Jameson's gaze. And she saw not only the woman she'd always respected, but all she represented. The work Ara loved. The hospital that had been a second home to her. The calling that had filled not just her days but her heart, giving her purpose when she most needed it. Nursing had never just been about doing her bit for the war, as it was for so many of the VADs. It had never been about reputable work.

It had been about helping people. Doing for them what she'd been unable to do for her mother. Making lives better in what ways she could, ministering to hurting souls and injured bodies as the hands of Christ.

She drew in a breath, slowly and thoughtfully. No rash decisions, no anger clouding her vision now, trying to protect her from the pain. She let it pierce. Let it hurt. Let it settle. "Then give me but a moment, and I'll pen my letter of resignation."

In the corner, Mrs. Camden's hand pressed to her chest, but if she made any noise, it was covered by Mrs. Jameson's gasp.

"Arabelle, that is not what I've come for! I pled for an hour on your behalf and got the board members to agree to give you a second chance. All you must do is speak to the press. Disavow any allegiance to him."

Arabelle was shaking her head long before her superior finished. "I cannot do that, ma'am. I appreciate your ardent support of me, and I'm sorry you went out on a limb only to have me now sever it. But I cannot—I *will* not—speak against him. Even had I not fallen in love with him, which I freely admit I've done, he would still be one of my dearest friends. He is one of the best men I know." At Mrs. Jameson's look of disbelief, a bit of a smile bloomed on her mouth. "He hides it from one's first glance, I grant you. But it's true."

"You don't know what you're saying. You've not thought this through." Mrs. Jameson closed the distance between them and gripped Arabelle's hands. "I know how you love the work. It's what made you an excellent nurse and now an excellent leader. You could run the hospital someday, Arabelle, as I've said before. You have a bright future ahead of you—you cannot toss it away for a man who will be dead before the month is out."

Arabelle's throat closed off, denying her air. Her vision swam. But she shook her head, swallowed down the panic, and dragged oxygen back into her lungs. "He will *not* be executed. He is innocent, and we will have proof of it soon."

Mrs. Jameson shook her head, too, far more roughly. "You can't know he's innocent. And even if he is, you cannot know it will change anything. The outcry against him is too loud. This has become a political issue as much as anything, with the working class accusing the authorities of turning a blind eye to him because of his station."

An arrow of fear shafted through her. Was it possible that she was right? That even the truth wouldn't set him free? That public opinion could prevail against justice? The arrow lodged right there, in the center of her heart, threatening to split it in two.

She closed her eyes for a moment. Cried out silently to God.

No assurance flooded her, no promise of his safety. No certainty that right would prevail. And yet . . . and yet. Peace wisped around the fear, filling the hole it had made. Arabelle opened her eyes again. "I can't know what will happen. But I can trust. I can trust my God will deliver him. And even if He chooses not to, still I will not bow to injustice. If Camden dies, he will die knowing he's loved."

"Oh!"

At Mrs. Camden's soft cry, Mrs. Jameson whipped around. The lady had put down her crocheting and was wiping at her eyes with her handkerchief. "Forgive me," she murmured. "You cannot know how I have prayed he would find someone like you, dear Arabelle."

Arabelle touched a hand to Mrs. Jameson's arm. "Allow me to introduce Mrs. Camden. The major's mother."

She had the grace to drop her gaze. She shifted away a few inches. "Forgive me, ma'am. I didn't know you were there."

Mrs. Camden blinked a few times, somehow settling a gaze of unyielding confidence on the other woman. "Would you have said anything differently had you known?"

The matron drew in a sharp breath. Let it out. "No. My concern is Arabelle."

"As it should be. In which case, there is nothing to forgive." Mrs. Camden put aside the yarn in her lap, stood, and strode toward them. A moment later, she had linked her arm through Arabelle's. "She is a remarkable young woman, deserving of your loyalty. I will be honored to call her my daughter."

Arabelle leaned in, letting her arm rest against Mrs. Camden's.

Mrs. Jameson sighed. "Arabelle . . . is there nothing I can say to sway you?"

"Nothing."

"Then . . . I will deliver your resignation to the hospital board." Her tone was tight, sad, final.

It would indeed be final. There would be no going back, she

knew, even if they prevailed. But Arabelle refused to be sad about it. She wouldn't count it as loss, just as opportunity for God to show her something new.

Not a stumbling block, as the admiral had said. She uncapped a fountain pen and pulled a sheet of paper from the tablet beside the phone. A stepping-stone.

◈ ◈ ◈

Friday, 15 March

The squealing of the door jerked Camden awake. He rolled up into a sitting position, eyes blinking furiously against the light. It took him a long moment to process the sight before him. The naval uniform, the clerical collar.

To his mind, it could only mean one person—Jeremy. Jeremy, whose voice had been so clear in his head yesterday. Jeremy, with whom he so craved a conversation. Jeremy, who had surely not procured another leave so close on the heels of his last one.

No, not Jeremy. A final blink to clear the cobwebs of sleep from his mind, and Camden saw the truth of that. Not Jeremy, but rather Montgomery stood in his cell, a bundle of books and papers under his arm and a chipper smile on his lips.

"Afternoon, Major. Did you have a nice nap?"

Afternoon? He rubbed at his eyes. Daylight had been streaming in again by the time he finally dropped off to sleep, so perhaps that shouldn't be a surprise. "Montgomery. What are you doing here?" Blast, but that sounded rude—a habit he would no doubt have a time of breaking.

His colleague only chuckled and helped himself to a seat on the opposite end of the bare little cot. "My duties, of course, as your chaplain. Even Black Heart isn't to be denied the chance to receive spiritual counsel, you know. Not that you've ever shown any interest in such matters before."

It wasn't Jeremy—but it could have been, the way Montgomery smiled into the face of impending doom. Camden breathed

ROSEANNA M. WHITE

a laugh. "Well, I suppose it's as they say. There are no atheists in the trenches."

Montgomery set the stack of books and papers onto the cot. "Imminent death hasn't made you turn to prayer in the past, has it?"

"No." And it wasn't just the thought of death—something he'd flirted with since the first moment he sat in a cockpit—that had made him turn to it now. "I suppose it was more life that has made me reevaluate. Realizing how high the cost has been for the decisions I've made. And how despite it, the Lord has placed me constantly in the path of His most devout followers."

Silence swallowed them for a second. Then Montgomery let loose a bark of laughter. "Do you mean to tell me you really *have* had a spiritual epiphany? Here I thought that was just my excuse for getting in!"

"For . . . what?" Perhaps his brain was still sleep-addled. Camden frowned. "You mean you haven't come to advise me on how to save my soul?"

Montgomery slapped a hand to his back. "From what I hear, you already *know* how it's done—I've met your mother and your sweetheart. We spoke for a few minutes about your younger brother, too, who sounds like a capital chap."

"He is." When had Montgomery met Mother and Ara? It must have been before she came here—she'd mentioned Hall. She must have gone to Whitehall. "Listen, you have to convince them to—"

"So knowing the facts of salvation," Montgomery continued, as if he hadn't even heard Camden's beginnings of a plea, "all that's left is acceptance."

Camden's shoulders sagged, then straightened again. Jeremy's voice in his head last night had kept whispering the same thing over and over again, keeping him awake. He had to trust. Not just trust the Lord to forgive him—challenging enough—but trust Him too with the ones who really mattered. Trust Him with Ara. Trust Him with Mother. It had proven quite a wrestling match.

351

Peace had come, but only when he'd finally answered invisible Jeremy's question—*Can you accept His will, however it may play out here on earth?*—with a *yes.*

To Montgomery he gave a nod. "I know. And I have done so. I was awake all night pondering and praying and . . . Montaigne, I know, questioned the truth of a faith inspired only by pressing danger. But I pray God does not. It was no rash decision on my part." Desperate, perhaps, but he'd been desperate for months—he just hadn't been willing to admit it.

Montgomery only studied him for a long moment. At last he smiled. "I think the Lord has been stirring your heart for quite some time, Major. I'm glad to see you've finally surrendered."

Surrendered. The perfect word. "Not a moment too soon, I should say. Would that I had been less hardheaded so I could have seen the truth long ago."

"Perhaps you should instead praise Him for using the cruelest of circumstances to achieve the brightest of miracles." He clapped his hands together. "A conversation we can continue later. But for now, work."

Camden glanced again at the papers and books. Codebooks? Were those . . . decrypts? "You have to be joking."

"You haven't anything more pressing to do just now, have you?" Montgomery slid the stack closer to Camden. "We've had a few more come in that seem to be aeronautical, if you'd take a look at them."

Cam blinked at the stack. Then blinked at the man. He *must* be joking. "Shouldn't you be seeking out someone *else* who can help you with such information? I can recommend a few chaps, if you like, from the RFC. Or RAF soon, I suppose."

Montgomery just leaned back, easy as you please. "Why should we do that? We've still got you, haven't we? Besides, we've finally grown accustomed to you—no interest in training someone else, thank you."

"But—"

"Now, don't think it's any better to waste your time in here feeling sorry for yourself. You might as well be productive, and I've got your guards to agree. Eke all the use out of you we can, and all that."

He'd gotten special permission for him to keep all this in here? Camden's brow knotted. "But I—"

"I *am* sorry I haven't more time right now. I'd love nothing more than to continue the conversation on spiritual matters, but I'm afraid DID only gave me time enough to deliver this and report back. I'd better be off." He stood, as if the admiral sending him here to deliver a stack of work made any sense at all. "There's some for you to decode as well, if you would. Do that bit first, Hall says, and peruse the rest at your leisure."

"My *leisure*?"

"Well." Montgomery grinned and moved toward the iron bars. "Before your arraignment on Monday would be nice." He tapped upon the bars. "Guard!"

Monday? It was so soon? Camden's fingers dug into the cot. They'd not even meant to tell him, probably just haul him out without a word, deposit him in front of the authorities, and . . . He shook his head. "Keep Ara and my mother away. Will you do that for me, Montgomery? It's the only thing I ask."

The guard hurried toward them, keys jangling.

Montgomery looked over his shoulder at Camden. "Just do the work, Major."

No promise? Not even to try? Camden watched him leave, wanting to sputter, to shout, to demand he do this. But he didn't.

Long after silence had descended again, Camden sat just where he'd been left, dumbfounded.

His gaze fell to the stack of papers. Heat searing his neck, he grabbed them up, flipping through it all until he found the single encrypted sheet—only a few words upon it. Surely something anyone else in Room 40 could have done without trouble. The codebook provided didn't look familiar—definitely not one of the confiscated German examples. What, then? He opened it up to find a pencil tucked inside.

Working faster than he'd probably ever done before, he sought out each word and letter.

It didn't take him long. The message was only five words. And sent a shock of panic up his spine.

Keep your head down, Major.

Blast it all. What in the world was Hall up to?

30

MONDAY, 18 MARCH

T hough Arabelle had been all but running down the corridor with Mrs. Camden, she froze as she neared Admiral Hall's door. *Letter recovered and delivered.* That was the beautiful message that had arrived at her door with the sunrise this Monday morning. *Come at 9:00.*

Too close for her comfort—the arraignment was at one o'clock. She and Mrs. Camden had spent most of the weekend in prayer. Sometimes alone, sometimes together, sometimes with the friends who stopped by to offer their support—Brook and Rowena and Ella, Eliza and Susan and Lily. Even Nurse Jameson had come again to hold her hand and pray with them.

Ara knew she looked exactly how she felt—exhausted and frazzled. But that wasn't what brought her to a sudden stop, nor was the closed door to the admiral's office.

It was the woman standing just outside it, staring at her with open-mouthed horror.

Arabelle well knew the feeling. Kath Lewis was the last person she'd expected to meet here when she answered Hall's summons. Seeing her now, obviously also summoned by the admiral, Ara didn't quite know what to think. What to feel.

The rage was gone, the fury of the other night long since faded into pain. She could understand why this woman so tirelessly sought what she thought was justice for her husband. She could understand that depth of love. That desperation for something to be put to rights, even if it couldn't restore life to the way it ought to be.

Ara could understand it because she was fairly certain she'd have done the same thing. Well, perhaps not exactly the same. But something similar. Hadn't she demanded the admiral send divers into the Channel, risking their own lives to try to save Camden's? Hadn't she been willing to deny this woman peace in order to spare the man *she* loved? Was it so different?

Even so, she couldn't bring herself to take another step forward. Not until the door swung open and Admiral Hall stepped into the threshold, his gaze taking in first Mrs. Lewis and then Arabelle and Mrs. Camden in consecutive blinks. "Excellent, we're all here. Do come in, ladies. We haven't much time to lose."

Rather than obey, Kath Lewis gripped her handbag and kept staring at Arabelle. "I don't know why I've been summoned, Admiral, but—"

"You'll find out in a moment, Mrs. Lewis. Please come in." His tone added an unsaid *now*.

Mrs. Lewis pivoted and stalked into the office behind him. After exchanging a look, Arabelle and Mrs. Camden followed. Three chairs were set up before his desk, two to one side, the other a bit farther away. Mrs. Lewis chose the single one, which was no doubt what the admiral had anticipated. She sat, but she certainly didn't relax. Her shoulders looked as rigid—and as fragile—as porcelain.

A fissure formed in Ara's heart as she watched the woman grip that handbag even tighter. Just as she'd gripped the handle of the pram with little Gigi inside it. Clinging to whatever she could in the hollow life she'd fallen into. Her husband was gone.

But if that piece of paper resting on a board on Hall's desk said what Camden had been sure it did, then it was worse than that. Lewis wasn't just *gone*—he'd taken his own life, taken his closest friends out with him. Because he'd betrayed this strong, fragile woman. Betrayed, possibly, his entire country.

Arabelle sank into the chair closest to her and hunted for the admiral's gaze. *Don't*, she shouted silently, praying he could decode the message in her eyes. *Don't destroy her any more than she is. Don't tell her what you don't have to. Leave her with her memories.*

Hall only blinked at her and moved to his own chair. He sat, posture perfect, and rested his hands on either side of the board. The paper smoothed against it still looked wet, but Arabelle could see the loops and lines of ink upon it. Legible, if blurred. "I thank you ladies for joining me with so little notice. What I have here will be of interest to you all."

Arabelle glanced over at Camden's mother, who had folded her hands into her lap. She was the epitome of a calm, collected lady on the outside, but Ara knew how anxious she must be.

Kath Lewis straightened her stiff spine a bit more. "With all due respect, sir, I don't see what—"

"What I have here, ma'am, is a letter recovered from your husband's . . . airplane." He blinked, glancing quickly at Arabelle and then back to the widow.

It hadn't just been in his airplane—it had been in his jacket. But though the paper had been preserved, his body no doubt hadn't been. Bless him for not using a word like *corpse* around this woman.

Even so, Kath blanched. "His airplane? But—how—I was told it was unrecoverable, that his body . . ."

"Yes." Admiral Hall offered her a sad fragment of a smile. "We'd assumed, madam, that all the wreckage had burned and hadn't had the time before now to investigate it more thoroughly. Upon doing so, however, we realized that your husband's plane was intact under the water." His expression softened. "His body has been recovered for you, at long last. Along with this letter we must discuss."

Kath's chest heaved. "What letter could you have recovered—and why were you searching the wreckage? For his body? For me?"

"That. And for proof of what really happened that day." He touched the edges of the board. "Proof that it was not Phillip Camden responsible for the tragedy in the air. Proof that—I'm very sorry to say this, Mrs. Lewis. There is no easy way to break such news."

No. Arabelle squeezed her eyes shut, wishing for Kath's sake that there was some other truth. Some other way both to save Cam and not shatter her world any further.

"What news?"

Hall sighed. "War does strange things to a man's mind sometimes, ma'am. I have seen it ravage even the strongest. Your husband . . . he was not in a good frame of mind at the time. This letter . . . it was to you. It was an apology and . . . a farewell."

For a long moment, Kath just stared at him. Then she shook her head.

Hall reached to the side, to a folded sheet of paper, and handed it across the desk. "We've copied it out for you—this original is a bit fragile yet and must remain in military custody. I am sorry for that, as I know you would value seeing his last words in his own hand. But this was the best I could do."

Kath's hand shook as she reached out for the paper. "What . . . what is it? How could he be saying farewell?"

The admiral sighed. "I'm so sorry, Mrs. Lewis. Your husband lays out in this letter a plan to purposefully stall his plane. So that it would look like an accident and you and your children would not bear the penalty for his actions. But he meant to end his life."

No. Arabelle could feel Kath's heart breaking, new fractures opening overtop the ones barely stitched together. She found herself scooting her chair closer, reaching out over that distance, and covering Kath's other hand—the one still on her handbag—with her own.

She was so small. Her hands delicate in size, but chapped. Arabelle covered the knuckles, the fingers, entirely with her own.

By some miracle, the woman didn't pull away, though she shook her head wildly. "No. No, he wouldn't. Wallace would never have done such a thing. Why would he have?"

"As I said." The admiral offered a consoling half smile that surely didn't console. "War can wreak terrible havoc on a man's spirit. In this particular case, it was made worse by something else he . . . feared he had done."

Oh, Father, please. Please inspire him to soften the blow. Arabelle curled her fingers tight around Kath's.

The admiral darted another glance at Ara but then refocused on Mrs. Lewis. "It seems he'd given information to someone he shouldn't have. Quite unwittingly, I'm sure. Information of a sensitive nature, which I've had to censor out of that letter for you, as it deals with military matters."

Kath flipped open the page and glanced down.

Sure enough, even from where she sat, Arabelle could see large swaths of black lines, where sentences and one whole paragraph had been blotted out.

"Unfortunately, this someone he'd been talking to was a German agent. He didn't know this at first, of course. But clearly he'd begun to suspect, and the thought that he had made such a mistake—well, it seems to have eaten at him."

Kath's eyes slid shut. "It would have. But how could he have been so foolish? Who was this man he was talking to?"

At that, the admiral cleared his throat. "From what we've pieced together, he'd likely been in his cups at the pub one night and said too much. Foolish, yes, but as I said—unwitting. The person in question, however, is not a man. It's a woman whom you know as Friede Boschert—though her real name is Diellza Mettler."

"What?" Kath's eyes flew open again, horror tugging her forward, to the edge of her chair. "No!" Her fingers let go the handbag and gripped Ara's fiercely. Did she even realize it?

"I'm afraid so." By way of proof, Hall handed her the same photograph he'd shown Arabelle the other day, of Diellza gazing with adoration at the blond man. Then one of said blond man in a German officer's uniform.

Kath's head sagged. "No. What have I . . . what did *he* . . . ?" She gripped Ara's hand so hard it hurt. Then, seeming to realize it, she loosened her hold a bit, jerked her head up, and looked over at her. "But what of the major?"

"Your husband tried to give Cam this letter to give to you," Arabelle whispered.

"But if he knew—if this is all true . . ." Her eyes darted from Ara to Hall. "Why did he never say anything? Why did the major never offer this version of events?"

"To protect you and your children." The admiral moved the board and wet letter aside and then folded his hands on his desk. "I'm terribly sorry, madam—but no doubt you're aware that pensions are not often paid for those who have taken their life willingly. Major Camden would apparently rather die himself than be responsible for any more misfortune befalling your family. He feels his failure to dissuade Lewis from his intentions most keenly, as well as the actions that led to the deaths of the rest of the squadron."

It sounded almost ridiculous when said so baldly. How could he have let himself be named a villain just to keep the word from being applied to a friend? How could he possibly be willing to stand before a firing squad rather than let a hurtful truth come out? What was a pension compared to a life?

And yet it was so very *Camden*. Especially the reeling, guilt-ridden Camden she'd first met. The one who couldn't bear that he had lived when his brothers had died. When he felt he should have stopped it.

How could she help but love such a man?

Perhaps Kath Lewis wanted to deny it all, to accuse them of fabricating the whole thing to save Cam. But she stared again at the letter. And perhaps she saw her husband's voice in the words, despite its being typed rather than in his hand. Because she sniffed, and she bowed her head, and the fingers still holding Arabelle's shook.

And then she said, "What can I do? What can I do to help put this to rights?"

Admiral Hall smiled. "You can start by sending Miss Mettler out on an errand . . . and then by letting us in to where she's stored her belongings in your flat."

Kath didn't ask for any explanation of what they planned, as Arabelle would have done—and as she intended to do at the first opportunity. She just nodded and released Ara's fingers after a squeeze that felt of gratitude. "Is there anything else? Or may I go? I need . . . I need to let all this settle in my mind."

"I understand. A few of my people are going to see you home. They'll knock a few minutes after Miss Mettler leaves."

She nodded again and stood, her handbag dangling now from one wrist, the letter refolded and clasped in the opposite hand. She looked down at Arabelle. "I'm sorry. I thought . . ."

Though she'd liked to have stood, she didn't want to tower over Kath. "I know. I would have too."

Kath's lips trembled. "He was a good man, my Wallace. He loved us so. I can't fathom what he must have feared would happen, if he thought this his only option."

"I don't know. Though I'm certain he meant to spare you pain, not give you more." He'd not chosen a good way of doing that—but surely it was his intention.

Kath looked as though she was about to say more, but then she bit her lip, blinking furiously against the moisture that flooded her eyes. Without another word, she rushed for the door.

Arabelle waited for it to close before letting out her pent-up breath and looking to the admiral. "I wish there'd been a version of the truth that wouldn't have hurt her."

Hall sighed and spun the board around. "I provided the best version I could, Miss Denler. It wasn't military secrets I left out."

She leaned closer, her eyes seeking out the paragraph that

had been censored from the copy—the fourth one. The one that began with, *I'm so sorry I did this to you, Kath. She wasn't the first, and that kills me.*

Swallowing, Arabelle pulled back, looking up, away from the words. Her eyes had no need to invade that confession. "Thank you. That was kind of you, Admiral."

"I take no joy in inflicting pain on innocents." He turned the board around again. "And now, if you'll excuse me, ladies—yours aren't the only eyes that need to see this."

"By all means." Mrs. Camden sprang from her seat. "Don't let us keep you."

"Thank you. If you'll repair to the reception area on the floor beneath us, you'll find that the Braxtons delivered this to me personally and are awaiting you." He offered a smile, quickly gone. "And, ladies, if I cannot talk you out of being present at the arraignment, do allow me to make one suggestion."

Arabelle paused in her turn toward the door, a rush of unexpected joy filling her at the thought of seeing Cass and Brax again.

Admiral Hall had stood along with them and tugged his jacket down into place. "Arrive early, and stay inside the building until the dust has settled."

She didn't dare ask what *dust* he meant.

Diellza tucked herself into an alleyway and flipped through the stack of telegrams, her frown deepening with each one. They were all from Alwin, which would have been heady had it not been alarming. Why was he sending so many? All at once? And they'd all been delivered to Mrs. Humbird's, though she'd sent him a quick note that she was leaving there. Had he not gotten that one?

It was lucky that Kath had suggested that her eldest son accompany Diellza to the boardinghouse to check for any mail or messages. She'd waited out on the sidewalk and sent the lad in, who had offered the believable story that his mother still needed "Friede's" help. Bless Kath—had she not thought to do so, all these telegrams would just be sitting there still, waiting for her.

She flipped back to the start of them. *You are right. Very many. Well done. Sending help.*

Right? What had she been right about? Her last message to him had simply said that she'd managed to create an event that would pull in multiple targets—she'd estimated no fewer than four from the list of secondary targets he'd given her, other than the First Lord of the Admiralty. It wasn't a question of right or wrong or anything to agree with. But what else could he possibly mean?

And she'd not asked for help—though, granted, it was a lot of targets to try to take out at once and still manage a quick escape. The shooting she could do . . . but with each second spent taking aim, the chances of being caught increased. She *could* do it—but having an accomplice would be better. She'd considered trying to find a way to pull Kath into this part of her plan, but that seemed risky. She was in it to bring down Camden, not the military itself. Had Alwin simply reasoned that out as well?

Had she read this one independently, she would have then questioned whether he'd *actually* send someone. He certainly hadn't before.

But the next notes answered the question. *Coming myself.* Then, *Due in tomorrow morning.* And finally, *Train late. Rendezvous at location. Follow plan.*

She checked the dates, the times, and muttered a German curse. Alwin was already in England, if these were true. How could he risk that? *Why* would he risk it? She, as he'd pointed out, wasn't so important a threat that anyone would be watching for her. She was nothing, nobody. But *he*—Alwin Weber—was an altogether different matter. He was important, a high-ranking officer in German intelligence. He couldn't afford to be compromised.

Was it a trap? But that made no sense. If it were someone trying to lure her into something, why just say they'd meet her at the location? Why not insist she go somewhere and then arrest her?

No, these telegrams must be from him. So why? Why was he coming? Did he not trust her to carry out the job?

He did, though, or he wouldn't have sent her in alone to begin with.

Or perhaps . . . She looked up, her breath quickening. Could it be that he missed her? Wanted to be with her? Still, it seemed illogical, especially considering that if all went well, she'd be back in Switzerland soon.

But maybe he wanted to be *sure* it went well, be sure she escaped.

With energy flooding her veins, she shoved the stack of telegrams into her bag and hurried back onto the sidewalk. She hadn't much time now, but that was all right. She had everything timed down to the minute.

First, the stop at the Lewis flat. She found it empty but for the neighbor watching the youngest children, who were napping. Perfect. She slid into the room she'd been sharing with two of the girls, pulled her valise from under the bed, and carefully removed the weapon. The stock and action she put into her handbag—the barrel she secured in her umbrella, which would remain closed. She added the two magazines she'd prepared to her bag and hurried out again.

Next, the tube ride to Whitehall, during which she sat as if she were just another bored working woman. No one looked twice at her, just as she'd planned. A five-minute walk to the building where the military held their trials. But she didn't turn toward it. She turned toward the building across the street, which she'd already scoped out. She made her way inside, pretending to be one of the many secretaries bustling about.

One man looked at her askance, but she hurried onward. She'd already snuck her way into this building twice before, in order to know where she needed to go and how best to escape. And also so that people might recognize her vaguely as a face they'd seen there before—and hence one they should overlook.

The room she'd selected was nothing but a storage closet at

this point, though too large to have been intended as one, she'd guess. But all that mattered to her was that it had a window that pointed the right direction.

After locking the door behind her—with the key sitting boldly on top of a filing cabinet—she went over to the window and forced it up. Cool spring air met her.

Now for patience. Unless all the officials who were coming happened to arrive together, she'd probably have to wait until the end of the arraignment, when they all exited. She had to get them all within seconds of one another.

A challenge. But not an impossible one. She'd trained for this. All those tournaments, with their random targets bouncing up. She'd hit them all every time. No matter where they came from or how quickly they were raised and lowered.

She could do this. She *would* do this. They were just targets. Her ticket to happiness. To a future.

To Alwin.

31

Keep your head down, Major.

Camden wasn't entirely sure whether the command was literal—should he just lower his head?—or metaphorical—was he supposed to avoid undue attention?—but he was doing his best to obey both meanings.

Though if Hall had meant the latter, that was a bit hard to achieve at his own arraignment. He blinked as he stepped out of the lorry, not so much because of the sun as because of the reporters' flash-lamps. But he lowered his head. And he prayed, with every footfall, that Mother and Ara weren't here. That they were tucked safely away in Ara's townhouse, far from whatever ruckus the admiral had planned.

The sun was warm, the air cool—a perfect spring day that he breathed in with the knowledge that it could well be the last taste he'd ever have of sunshine. He'd likely make it outside twice more—once for the trial itself, once before the firing squad. But who was to say the day would be as fine? Or that he'd be capable of noticing?

He'd soak in every detail today, though. The cooing of the pigeons ever-present on the streets. The way the wind whistled a bit as it wound among the white-faced buildings. The shouts of the reporters, demanding he look up and answer their questions.

He noted the chafing of the cuffs that circled his wrists. The tug of fabric against skin. The glint of sunlight on brass, coming from up ahead.

With all the military men in attendance, it was a veritable sea of olive green and dark blue lining his path. He glanced up, fully expecting the glint to be off a button or a medal or an epaulette.

No. Wings. The sun had caught brass wings and set them ablaze. His eyes latched onto them, registering in a fraction of a second that the wings weren't on a pilot who'd come out to spit on him as he passed. Though the figure was as tall as most any of them. Slimmer, though. More graceful, more feminine. More perfect.

"Ara." His muscles jerked involuntarily, trying to push him toward her. Why hadn't they stopped her from coming? Why was she standing there just inside the doorway, looking breathtaking in a pale dress criss-crossed with yellow, with his wings pinned to her bodice?

"Easy, Major." The guard's hand held firm against his twitch, pulling him back. "No sudden movements. Slow steps. And keep your head down."

What? He tore his gaze off Ara so he could put it on the guard. He'd never seen this one before, had he? Certainly not in the prison, and he wasn't one of the Military Police who had come to arrest him. And yet he looked vaguely familiar. Vaguely. Almost like . . . almost like one of the guards always standing at the entrance to the OB.

His breath hissed out. What in the world was Hall doing? He wasn't going to try to stage an escape, was he? That would be idiocy. And as Hall was no idiot, Cam couldn't think it that. What, then?

Another car pulled up, spilling brass from its doors—the kind he'd expected to see a minute ago. The general in charge of Northolt. Admiral Hall. Another admiral whose name he didn't know. And there, in a second car . . . was that Wemyss? What the devil was the First Sea Lord doing here? And behind him, the First Lord of the Admiralty.

His toe caught a cobble, and he may have tripped were it not for the guard holding him up. The reporters swarmed closer, not looking terribly restrained by the line of bobbies holding them back.

"Major, are you sorry for what you've done?"

"Have you anything to say to the widows of the men in your squadron?"

"What will you plead?"

The guard pulled him a few steps away from them. "Head *down*," he muttered under his breath.

Maybe it was the rebel in him, but the reminder had him looking up at the reporters as he and the guard shuffled by. Most were faces he'd seen far too often in months past. Dogging his steps, jumping out to take his photograph at odd moments. Shouting provoking questions at him just so they could capture a snarl on their film.

His gaze swept over the sea of them—the bloke from the *Evening Standard* who had a double chin. The chap from the *Observer* who always wore that bowler with the frayed brim. The fellow from the *Daily Telegraph* whose nose dwarfed his face. One he didn't recognize—a blond man, with a scar running down the right side of his face.

Camden dropped his gaze, breath fisting in his chest. Blond man. Almost too pretty, but for the scar. He hadn't been shouting like the rest, just holding up his camera and watching.

Not watching Camden. Watching the brass filing out of the cars.

Blast. He turned to the guard. "Weber. He's here."

The guard didn't so much as blink out of turn.

A droning caught his attention before he could reiterate the warning. A familiar low thrum that grew increasingly higher and louder. Airplanes. He stopped, heart racing, even as his ears told him they were Sopwith engines he heard, not Gothas or Giants. Friendly. A patrol over London, nothing more.

Though the patrols didn't usually fly directly over Westminster as these seemed to be doing.

The others had finally noticed the sound, too, a few seconds after he had. All heads craned up.

Keep your head down, Major.

"All the way down." The guard tugged, pushed, sent him sprawling.

On his way to the ground, Camden's gaze met Arabelle's, and he prayed with every ounce of untested faith inside him that she could hear the warning too. *Get down!*

Diellza had them in her sights—all of them. Victory was singing through her veins as it always had whenever she stood on a range, her favorite weapon in hand and targets before her. A few squeezes of her trigger. That's all it would take, and she'd win. The trophy would be hers.

Favor would be hers. Vater's then. Alwin's now. He was somewhere nearby, ready to help.

Engine noise invaded her concentration, pulling her gaze, for one second, up. *Up?* It took her a moment to realize it was a squadron of airplanes flying overhead. Come, perhaps, to taunt Camden.

She hurriedly refocused, smiling when she saw everyone else had looked up too. The reporters, the onlookers, the guards. The admirals and generals and lords. All frozen in place, watching the planes.

Frozen. Waiting. Sitting ducks.

She took aim at her primary target first—the First Lord of the Admiralty. Squeezed the trigger.

Nothing. She squeezed again, but with the same result.

Spitting out a curse, she pulled the gun back to check for a jam—though Vater's guns misfired so rarely, and she'd gone over this one just this morning in the lavatory. It couldn't have—

Crack!

She jumped away from the open window, coughing against the particles of stone raining down. Plastering her back to the wall, she examined the gun more closely and swore. The hammer hadn't fully fallen, which could only mean one thing: the seer was out of adjustment. It hadn't been this morning, but it was now. Rendered useless.

Another crack, another crumble of stone.

Bullets. Not coming from this worthless piece of metal in her hands, but aiming at her window. Someone knew she was there.

She could fix the gun. She just needed a few minutes. A few tools, which she had in her bag. She turned her head just enough to see out. Given where the bullets had struck, the other gunman must be in the building across the street. A few minutes, that was all.

Then she saw a blond head emerge from the mass of reporters when a hat tumbled away. Saw the familiar movements she'd memorized, studied, loved.

Saw her future tumble down. She didn't *have* a few minutes—not with Alwin in the other sniper's line of fire.

Arabelle shoved Mrs. Camden aside none too gently at the first crack of a gun from somewhere up above her. To the right, away from the door, behind the protective stones and plaster. She ought to follow her over—she knew she ought.

But her eyes had gone straight to Camden, where he'd fallen first to his knees, then sprawled onto his stomach when he couldn't catch himself with his bound hands. He'd been shouting at her with those blue eyes of his. She'd heard him. But she couldn't obey, not when she saw blood spurting from his face where it collided with the cobblestones.

Her eyes and ears couldn't make sense of the chaos erupting before her. Dimly, she heard a woman screaming out "No!" from somewhere to the right. At first, she thought it Kath. But the figure that came tearing from the building across the street was no ginger-haired widow.

One of the reporters whipped around, spat out a word Arabelle had never heard, and then pivoted back the way he'd been facing before. He was vaguely familiar, handsome but for the scar.

She sucked in a breath. The man from the photograph. And the woman—Mettler.

She wanted to scream a warning, but before she could give the command to her mouth, she saw the man pull out a gun and point it toward the cluster of officials. What had his name been? Her mind, so used to storing names and pulling them out again, must have had it ready. It tumbled from her mouth in place of the warning. "Weber!"

He hitched, looking her way. Buying all the soldiers and guards a moment to react, she prayed.

Three shots sounded almost at the same moment, coming from above, to the left, straight ahead. Only vaguely did she note the navy men holding the guns. Mostly she saw Weber, red blooming on his shoulder and chest and from the side of his head.

And his eyes. She saw his eyes, flashing with hatred and life. Three bullets had struck him, sent him staggering, but he'd not fallen.

The crowd of reporters had broken up like a cloud in the wind, scattering. The crowd of military men had surged, blocking the line of sight between him and the admirals and generals. Weber spun, gun still up, obviously seeking another target.

His eyes landed on her. She'd run a few feet outside, toward Camden, and now couldn't dive for cover, not in time.

"Ara!" She heard Cam's cry, desperate and pleading. Filled with all the love she'd never thought she'd hear directed at her. Certainly not from him. She saw him move. Lunge.

Fly.

He collided with Weber, knocking the man to the ground as the bullets had failed to do. The gun clattered to the street, quickly scooped up by a man in uniform.

"Phillip!" Ara rushed forward, already digging her handkerchief from her pocket—the closest thing she had just now to a bandage.

A guard had pulled him off by the time she reached them; another had leveled a gun at Weber. None of which mattered in the slightest, except that it meant she could throw her arms around Cam. She gave him a fierce hug and then pulled away enough to press the handkerchief to the abrasion on his chin.

Eyes gleaming a million promises, he looped his cuffed arms over her head and tugged her close again. "You were supposed to stay away. Stay safe. I told you, I couldn't die knowing you'd come to harm."

"Idiot man." She rested her free hand on his chest and looked deeply into those eyes she so loved. "It isn't enough to die trying to keep me safe. I need you to *live* for me."

His eyes slid shut, and he rested his forehead against hers. "If God and the king will allow it, I'd like nothing better, darling."

Diellza hurled herself at him. Alwin, beautiful Alwin, sprawled on the ground. All other figures were but a blur. All other noise garbled nonsense. She could hear only the gurgle in his breathing, the rattling in his chest as she strained toward it. Feel only the distance between them. Shrinking, shrinking.

Staying.

"No!" The scream ripped from her throat as the first had done as she'd emerged from that building and seen him, exposed, in the middle of the fray. What had he been doing there, so close to it all? How did he mean to escape? She flailed at whatever morass held her away from him.

"It is all right. Let her go."

The words made no sense. But the mire released her, and she fell onto Alwin's chest, eliciting a groan from him that sounded like agony and death and defeat.

She pulled her weight off him. His chest was red. So was hers, from him. "Alwin. My beloved." Her words tumbled out in German, whispers tripping their way from her lips to his. "Hold on, my love. Hold on. Don't leave me."

His eyes, hazy, wandered to hers. "Dee."

Other hands joined hers on his chest. Feminine hands, knowing hands, that sought the wound and pressed against it, trying to hold the life in.

She couldn't focus on that, not with his eyes fixed on hers. "Why did you come? Why?" Diellza gripped his coat—the same one he'd been wearing when last she'd seen him in Zürich, the one whose collar she'd smoothed down as she kissed him good-bye. "I could have handled it. You shouldn't have come, you should have stayed safe."

The haze clouded. "You said . . . needed . . . me."

She hadn't. She'd thought it a million times, but never once had she said it, not in words either spoken or written. Even so. "And you came?"

"Of course." His eyes fluttered closed. Back open.

"Hold on," the other woman said, English clashing against their German. The Denler woman. Why was she trying to save him? Pressing cloth to the wounds as if she hadn't played a part in him being shot to begin with? "Don't try to talk."

Diellza shook her head, tearing her gaze off the nurse and putting it back where it belonged. Back on him. He'd come. He'd thought she'd asked, and he'd come. Her hands framed his face. "I love you." More words she'd never spoken. Had to speak.

His swallow sounded sticky. "Love . . . you."

Something hot and tight heaved its way up, through her chest and into her throat. Every hope she'd ever held. Every dream she'd ever fostered. They blossomed to life in that moment, like marcasite flowers struggling against agate winter.

A shudder convulsed him. Winter fought back against the bloom. Diellza's hands fell from his face to his shoulders.

He loved her. Why was that not enough to hold the tears at bay?

Or was it the reason for them? Because the haze was gone from his eyes. The light was gone. All was gone.

The nurse sighed and sagged, head bowed. "I'm sorry."

Diellza squeezed her eyes shut and sobbed against him.

32

Camden batted away Ara's hand, which was reaching, for the thirtieth time in the last two minutes, for the bandage on his chin. "Will you stop fussing?"

"It isn't likely, no." She adjusted something, smiling at him all the while. "Stop scowling, darling. You're supposed to be *happy*."

"I *am* happy." How could he not be? Here he sat in Ara's house, free.

The charges had been dropped. More, the admiral had given him that blinking look of his and said, "I've run out of use for you as a villain, Major. Time to make you into the hero, if you don't mind." Then he'd turned to the clamoring reporters and given an interview not only laying the full blame for The Incident on the German agent they'd watched die—to whom he gave a false name and had forbidden any photographs to be taken—but claiming that Camden had been left to seemingly take the fall these months solely as a means of drawing the enemy out.

Not strictly *true*, of course. But none of them saw any purpose in quibbling with the admiral over details. Especially since, after seeing the information he was capable of discovering and utilizing, Cam was no longer quite certain what *was* true.

What he knew for certain was that freedom had never tasted so sweet. But he'd been hoping for—counting on—a quiet evening.

Just him and Arabelle and his mother, who had promised to disappear for a few minutes with Sarah. Instead, it seemed that everyone they knew had for some reason decided to gather here. Ara had to have invited them—all his colleagues from the OB, Brook and Justin Stafford, and the squadron of pilots under Stafford's leadership who had helped save the day. Even Cass and Brax were here.

Not that he wasn't glad to see his sister and the brother-in-law who had just saved his life with the dive that had recovered that letter. But Grandmother's ring was burning a hole in his pocket, where he'd slipped it after Mother had pressed it into his hands thirty minutes ago. *Why* had all these people descended upon them? Couldn't they have given them an hour or two, at least, beforehand? He'd scarcely had time to confess to Ara the prayers he'd prayed after she'd left him in prison before the masses had descended this evening.

Ara was still examining his bandage and making a clucking sound with her tongue. He rolled his eyes and plucked the sleeping puppy from the cushion beside him and deposited her in Ara's lap to give her something else to focus on. Then held one of her hands for good measure.

She darted a glance at the crowd of people but didn't pull her hand free. No, she smiled one of those smiles that made the dimple flash to life in her cheek. Made him want to lean over, crowd be hanged, and kiss her until she agreed to be his forever.

But he couldn't bring himself to actually argue with the presence of all these people. All these people who took risks for *him*. He stared out at the lot of them, not quite able to wrap his mind around it. Then looked back to Ara. He'd remember that scene for the rest of his life, he was sure. Looking up and seeing her standing there, between him and judgment, his wings flashing on her dress. Declaring her devotion better than words could ever do.

He stood abruptly, tugging her hand. "Come on."

His tone must have sounded as urgent as he felt. She frowned and slid Caddie onto the cushion again, looking worried. "What is it? Your chin? I told you that you needed to let me—"

"And you were right, of course." As if he could even feel his chin just now, with the ring in his pocket. He tugged her toward the drawing room door, muttering an "Excuse us for just a moment, will you?" to Brook, who happened to be nearest to the exit.

Distracted as he was, he didn't miss the knowing smirk the duchess sent them. And didn't mind it in the slightest. He pulled Ara toward the stairs. There was only one room in this house he could imagine doing this in, and it wasn't a drawing room filled with their friends.

"Where are we going? I need my medical kit, and it's—"

"My chin's fine, darling. But what *I* need"—namely, a breath of privacy—"is up here in your father's study."

"All right." She drew each syllable out into three, making the agreement a question.

He just sent her a smile that no doubt had her thinking what he needed was a kiss—not entirely untrue. Her cheeks flushed just a bit, and the dimple winked at him. "All right," she said again, at normal speed. "We oughtn't to be gone for long, though."

He said no more as they climbed the stairs, his mind doing somersaults as he tried to find the words to use upstairs. How did a cad like him go about asking a girl like her to shackle herself to him forever? He could start, of course, by assuring her again that something really had changed in him in that prison cell. The prayers he'd cried, the surrender . . . he'd never be the same. Having his life returned to him had made the decision more real, not less.

Life. Not death. Victory, not defeat. Something only the Lord could have granted him.

Jeremy would never let him live this one down—and Cam would enjoy every obnoxious *I told you so.*

He glanced at Ara on the last flight and saw that her thoughts didn't look quite so happy. A crease had marred her brow. He came to a halt at the top of the stairs. He certainly wasn't going to propose with her upset about something. "What's wrong, darling?"

"Nothing." She met his gaze, sighed, and offered a sheepish smile. "I was just thinking of poor Kath Lewis. Do you really think they'll take away the pension?"

He sighed too. There were cases, of course, where suicide didn't result in the loss of a pension. But there were far more where they did—and especially, he suspected, when the suicide resulted in other deaths. The army didn't look kindly on such things.

His exhale was all the answer she needed. Her gaze went distant for a moment, thoughts flying through her eyes.

He knew that look. Adored that look. "Let me guess—you're going to offer her a position again."

But she shook her head, contemplation still winging. "I think she isn't really happy here in London. She mentioned that their family is in the country—they only moved here to be closer to Northolt, but she hasn't the funds now to move the children home. I could cover that easily, though, if she'll let me. No, I'll just give it anonymously so she can't say no." She folded her arms over her chest, not seeming to notice that one of her hands was still woven with his. With the opposite, she tapped a finger to her lips. "The pension can't have been that much either. I'll speak with my trustee tomorrow and—"

His chuckle interrupted her, and he leaned over, pressed his lips to hers.

She looked almost startled when he pulled away, though he couldn't think why. "What was that for?"

He grinned and tugged her toward the study again. "For being you. Generous beyond reason." Only a heart like hers, so giving, would have given *him* a chance, after all.

He brought her to a halt in the middle of the study, where the globes and artifacts and shelves all spoke of her father. Of adventure. Of the countless evenings they'd spent here, debating and laughing and falling in love. He fished into his pocket for the ring.

He ought to get down on one knee, he supposed. But he rather liked looking her in the eye, so near his own. He liked pulling her close instead of clasping her hands in his. So he did, and let his lips linger on her dimple, smiling at the way her breath caught.

"Ara?"

"Hmm?" Her fingers feathered through his hair. Of her right hand—he still held her left captive.

He lifted it now, enough to slide Grandmother's ring onto her fourth finger. Never taking his eyes off her face, so he could see the way her eyes went wide. "It would be a risk. An adventure. Probably foolish, but if you'll have me . . . I can think of nothing more rewarding in this life than traveling it with you."

"Phillip." She glanced down at the ring but didn't seem to really see the jewels and white gold. She couldn't have in that split second before her eyes lifted again to his. And then she grinned, pure mischief. "I don't know. You'll have to see if you can get past my guard dog."

"Woof." He chuckled, pulled her flush against him, and kissed her soundly. When he pulled away a moment later, he couldn't stop grinning. "Was that an answer?"

She lifted her brows, joy gleaming in her eyes. "Did you ask a question?"

Blast, but he loved her. He brushed a lock of midnight hair from her cheek, chuckling. "Fine. Force me to be traditional, if you must. Will you marry me?"

She linked her arms around his neck. "I will. You know I will."

All the answer he needed—the details they could decide upon as they came. He sealed it with a kiss, lingered there for a long moment. Then, when a clock chimed a new hour from somewhere below, he pulled away with a groan. "I suppose we'd better get back to everyone."

"Mm." She was grinning, examining the ring now. "I suppose."

"Or better still," said a voice from the doorway, making them both start. Hall stood there, Stafford close behind, neither looking particularly shocked or surprised to find Ara in his arms. The admiral lifted a brow. "We'll simply come to *you*. Do excuse the interruption, Major, but you're required to settle an argument between me and this infuriating friend of yours."

Stafford grinned. "I've been given permission to offer you your position back, Cam. There's a squadron at Northolt waiting for you in the new Royal Air Force."

"And *I*," Hall said with a pointed look over his shoulder at the duke, "have been trying to tell him that you're one of us now."

One of them. Not something he'd really expected to be, and yet the entire OB, it seemed, had been in on today's plot. Margot, sending false messages to Alwin Weber over the last few days, detailing an elaborate plan that required his aid on the ground. One with a prize so alluring he couldn't refuse. Pearce, tampering with Diellza's weapon while she was away from the Lewis flat. Miss Blackwell from the darkroom had even prepared some falsified photographs to leak back to Germany, making it look like Weber and Diellza had gone down on a small pleasure craft that a U-boat had sunk that morning.

And yet . . . the skies. Open to him again. Forgiveness, finally attained—from God, from man.

Ara went stiff, though she tried to relax again in the next moment. When he glanced down at her, he found her gaze focused on his chin rather than his eyes. "It's what you love," she whispered, tracing a finger over the woven wings on his uniform.

It was. But it wasn't *all* he loved. And he would never forget the panic in her eyes when she'd realized her father had left again, sailed out into danger. She'd never tell him not to do it, but would she hate it every time he took to the skies in this war?

Before, it hadn't mattered if he died on a mission. Before, he hadn't had anything to live for. Now he did.

She moved her hand to the brass wings still pinned to her bodice, her intention clear. But he reached up, stilled her fingers. Gave them a squeeze.

Then he angled a smirk up at Stafford. "Thanks, Your Grace. But I'm not sure the Admiralty could run without me. They need a good pilot in their midst."

He had no doubt that he'd fly again . . . but for now, the Lord had planted him exactly where he needed to be.

Author's Note

Crafting a story that combines history with imagination is always a fun challenge—but one that I like to explain, so that everyone knows where fact and fiction meet in my books. In this one, I explored some facets of the Great War that I hadn't previously looked into and also combined some historical figures to create characters that fit my needs.

With a pilot as a hero, I needed to do some research into the "reckless fellows" who made up the Royal Flying Corps. I had no idea when I first came up with Phillip Camden that the life expectancy of an RFC flyer was only four months! The fact that he survived his tenure on the front lines was nearly miraculous . . . hence why I created the "reward" of being stationed in London after a few years in France.

The character of Diellza is actually a combination of two historical women who played similar roles. The most famous is Mata Hari, a cabaret dancer who used her wiles for the Central Powers. Though historians today debate whether she was *really* a spy (or at least how effective she was as one), Admiral Hall certainly thought so. He detained her in England, warned her to cease all such activities, and deported her. Soon after, she was arrested in France and executed for espionage. But it was another femme fatale that inspired me to give Diellza her mission. A German-born actress, Beatrice von Brunner, failed in an assassination attempt in England early in the war and then turned her attention to Charles "the Bold" Thoroton, head of intelligence in the Mediterranean later in the war. My character combines bits of these two women with, of course, my own imagination and purposes.

The bombing of Royal Hospital really did take place on February 16, 1918, though Victoria Station had been the aim of the raid. The following day, St. Pancras train station was targeted and hit. With a nurse for a heroine, I couldn't resist featuring this bombing, especially since it happened so near her home.

The combining of the Royal Flying Corps and the Royal Naval Air Service into a single unit—the Royal Air Force—was finalized in April of 1918 and finally managed to eliminate some of the problems both services had been having. Namely, they were competing for resources and had to draw arbitrary boundaries to keep from getting in each other's way. By combining the two forces under one head, all research and development, money, and training would be streamlined.

What I most loved learning about the RFC, though, was how it truly pioneered the way for equalizing its members. Up until then, officers were *only* gentlemen—those born into the aristocracy. But because of that high mortality rate of pilots, they couldn't stay so picky for long. All pilots had to be officers, but no longer did they have to be born to the gentle class. This, however, had some unforeseen consequences. The lifestyles of gentlemen were far different from what a common man would have known, and many didn't know what to make of the affluent life they were introduced to. I highlighted this in Lewis.

It's a sad truth that a high number of soldiers committed suicide during the Great War—and equally sad that a high percentage of their widows were denied their pensions. This was eventually addressed and often rectified . . . but not always. Special thanks to Jim at Small Town, Great War, a webpage he runs about the town of Hucknall, who graciously worked through this question with me. I was thrilled to find someone who not only could answer my questions but also went so far as to take photographs of WWI register books in his library to verify that the withholding of pensions was plausible.

And finally, a quick note on the Russian cryptographer. I hope you were intrigued by him, as he'll be our hero in *A Portrait of Loyalty*, along with Hall's photography ace Lily Blackwell. Zivon Marin is a fictionalized version of a real man, Ernst Fetterlein, who fled the Bolshevik Revolution and came to England specifically to join Room 40, as he'd been one of the czar's codebreakers. The real historical figure provided me with much inspiration, and I look forward to taking bits and pieces of his story and weaving them into Marin's in the final installment of THE CODEBREAKERS.

Discussion Questions

1. Though Arabelle was wealthy, she'd lived through a childhood of abandonment. What do you think of how she used her past pains to minister to people? Were you surprised by her decisions and reactions? How have your past hurts influenced the way you reach out to others?

2. What did you think of Ara's relationship with her father? Of his mission? How would you have reacted to his presence and his absence if you were in her shoes?

3. Though he hides behind a gruff exterior, Camden has a soft and loyal heart. What did you think of the Camden family dynamics? Who in the Camden family are you most like?

4. Were you surprised by what happened in Portsmouth? Did it play out the way you expected? What did you think of Cam's decision to watch out for Arabelle when they were back in London, and of her reaction to that?

5. Diellza is based on a combination of several historical femmes fatales. What did you think of her? Did anything

about her surprise you? What did you think of the ending with Alwin?

6. Camden has to learn over the course of the book that he is guilty of plenty, but not for surviving when his squadron did not. Have you or a loved one ever experienced survivor's guilt? How can one move beyond it?

6. Were you surprised by how The Incident had actually transpired? What did you think of Kath Lewis's view of Camden? What did you make of Camden's decisions regarding her?

7. We see both Camden and Ara make career decisions because of their love for each other. Did you agree with their choices? Would you have done the same in either case?

8. Of all the characters, main and secondary, who was your favorite and why? Your least favorite? If you've read the LADIES OF THE MANOR series, did you enjoy seeing glimpses of Brook, Rowena, and Ella again?

10. Looking ahead, what do you think the future will have in store for the Denlers and Camdens?

Roseanna M. White is a bestselling, Christy Award–nominated author who has long claimed that words are the air she breathes. When not writing fiction, she's homeschooling her two kids, designing book covers, editing, and pretending her house will clean itself. Roseanna is the author of a slew of historical novels that span several continents and thousands of years. Spies and war and mayhem always seem to find their way into her books . . . to offset her real life, which is blessedly ordinary. You can learn more about her and her stories at www.roseannamwhite.com.

Sign Up for Roseanna's Newsletter!

Keep up to date with Roseanna's news on book releases and events by signing up for her email list at roseannamwhite.com.

More from Roseanna M. White

In the midst of the Great War, Margot De Wilde spends her days deciphering intercepted messages. But after a sudden loss, her world is turned upside down. Lieutenant Drake Elton returns wounded from the field, followed by a destructive enemy. Immediately smitten with Margot, how can Drake convince a girl who lives entirely in her mind that sometimes life's answers lie in the heart?

The Number of Love, THE CODEBREAKERS #1

◊ BETHANYHOUSE

 Stay up to date on your favorite books and authors with our free e-newsletters. Sign up today at bethanyhouse.com.

 facebook.com/bethanyhousepublishers   @bethanyhousefiction

 Free exclusive resources for your book group! bethanyhouse.com/anopenbook
anopenbook

You May Also Like . . .

When her grandfather's health begins to decline, Havyn is determined to keep her family together. But everyone has secrets—including John, the hired stranger who recently arrived on their farm. To help out, Havyn starts singing at a local roadhouse, but dangerous eyes grow jealous as she and John grow closer. Will they realize the peril before it is too late?

Forever Hidden by Tracie Peterson and Kimberley Woodhouse
THE TREASURES OF NOME #1
traciepeterson.com; kimberleywoodhouse.com

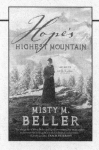

On her way to deliver vaccines to a mining town in the Montana Territory, Ingrid Chastain never anticipated a terrible accident would leave her alone and badly injured in the wilderness. When rescue comes in the form of a mysterious mountain man, she's hesitant to trust him, but the journey ahead will change their lives more than they could have known.

Hope's Highest Mountain by Misty M. Beller
HEARTS OF MONTANA #1
mistymbeller.com

Gray Delacroix has dedicated his life to building a successful global spice empire, but it has come at a cost. Tasked with gaining access to the private Delacroix plant collection, Smithsonian botanist Annabelle Larkin unwittingly steps into a web of dangerous political intrigue and will be forced to choose between her heart and her loyalty to her country.

The Spice King by Elizabeth Camden
HOPE AND GLORY #1
elizabethcamden.com

⬧ BETHANYHOUSE